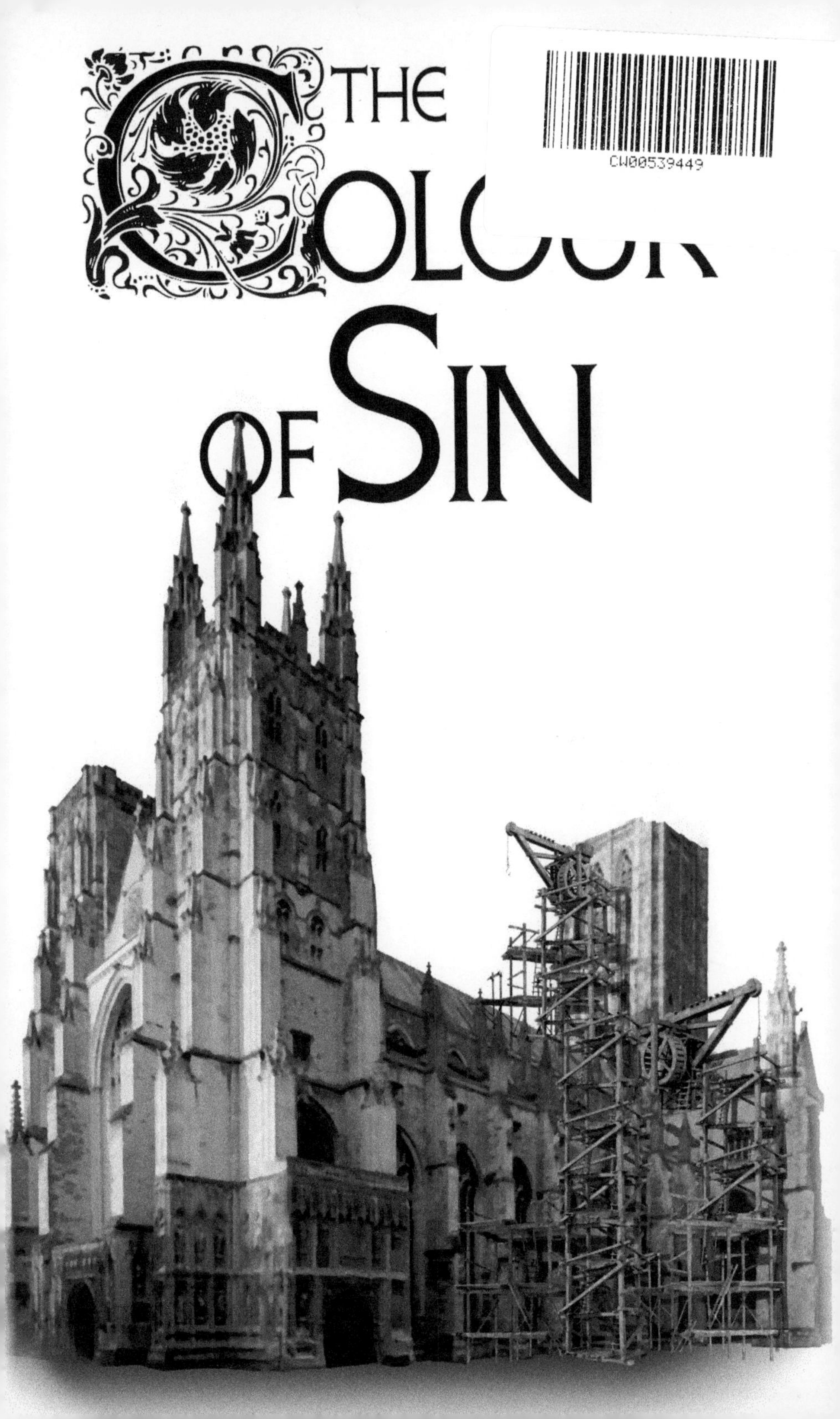
THE
COLOUR
OF SIN
CW00539449

The Colour of Sin

A Sebastian Foxley Medieval Mystery
Book 12

ISBN-13: 978-84-125953-8-3

M

MadeGlobal Publishing

For more information on MadeGlobal Publishing, visit our website
www.madeglobal.com

Dedicated to all the enthusiastic amateur historians
who re-enact our history each weekend, bringing fun,
excitement and knowledge to the wider public.

Toni.

Visit Sebastian Foxley's web page to discover more about his life and times?

www.SebastianFoxley.com

Prologue

THE CHAMBER is dark, lit only by two flickering torches set in sconces at either end, which do but serve to make the shadows deeper and more impenetrable. The place stinks of human sweat, wet wool and fur, made worse by the latrine beyond the door, jutting out over the river. Snores, coughs, farts and grunts are the music of this place as the pilgrims sleep cheek by jowl, stranger beside stranger, all seeking God's grace for some reason or other. Whatever the colour of their sin, no doubt they hope for St Thomas Becket's intercession with God and will be on their knees before his be-jewelled shrine in the cathedral in the morning. There, they will beg forgiveness such that they shall number among the souls destined for heavenly bliss come Judgement Day.

But the intruder has other plans. For some, forgiveness will be too late. Some will never kiss the Blessed Martyr's tomb.

Yet he now faces an unforeseen problem, though a little more thought beforehand would have made it seem most likely. In the spluttering, wavering torchlight, the pilgrims rest upon their straw pallets, crammed together in the gloom. And there are corners and recesses as dark as Satan's heart where recognising a sleeper swathed in his rough blanket proves impossible.

He must find them.

It must be done this night if he values his own life, his own immortal soul.

Averting his eyes from the torches, they grow accustomed to the darkness. Dagger in hand, he moves amongst the sleepers, pausing and holding his breath whenever one stirs. He is searching for two heads of tousled curls of a reddish hue but, the night being chill, most yet wear their caps and hoods which hide their hair. Two freckled faces so alike… but freckles are invisible without the light of day. His task seems hopeless now.

There have been chances. The first went so badly amiss. He should have done it two days since, when confusion reigned at the ford. Or yesterday upon the road through the woods. No time now to regret the hours his courage failed him or matters went awry.

Then, beside the cold stone of a Norman column, he sees two sharing a pallet, close as only lovers should lie. And the faces seem each the mirror of the other, though their hair is hidden by woollen caps pulled down over the ears for warmth. He is certain he has discovered his quarry. He must be swift with his blade, cutting them both before either can cry out.

Stealthily, cat-silent, he draws nigh and folds back a hand's breadth of their shared blanket, revealing naked throats awaiting his knife. In their ignorance, they have made it easy for him. He leans over them: the master's avenging angel, steel glinting in the torchlight.

Chapter 1

Thursday, the nineteenth day of October in the year of Our Lord Jesu Christ 1480 The Foxley House in Paternoster Row, London

'You're quiet, Seb… too quiet. What are you thinking about?'

'What? Oh, aye. My mind was far distant.' I dragged my thoughts back to the present. My goodwife and I were in the parlour, side by side upon the settle. The first fire of the year burned low in the hearth as the eve had turned chill. The little ones were abed; the household fallen quiet and this was the hour we enjoyed together afore retiring. We sat without candles, yet the fading firelight was sufficient for me to see her dear features, at once so familiar but still a wonder to me. I should never tire of those hazel eyes, the perfection of her brow, those sweetest lips.

'Where were you then?' Rose smiled and passed me my cup of ale.

'Somewhere you know and I do not. In truth, I was considering Canterbury.'

'Canterbury? Why ever would you think of that place now?'

'Forwhy folk make pilgrimages there. When Jude was sore injured at the start of this year and seemed like to die, I swore to the Lord Christ that if He should spare my brother's life, I would make a pilgrimage. And Canterbury be most suitable, being the shrine of Thomas Becket, London's own saint and martyr.' I sipped my ale, noting a stain upon my hose come from who knows where. Brushing at it did naught to remedy it.

'Pilgrimage? But why now, husband?'

'Forwhy the year grows late and winter will be upon us all too swiftly. Now be a good time and I spoke with Old Symkyn this morn who understands such lore: he says the fair weather will hold for a week or two yet with a chance of wind and showers upon occasion. Rarely is he mistaken about such matters.'

'But there is no leisure for a pilgrimage. It's impossible, Seb, when there's so much to do here at home.' Rose threw up her hands, dismissing my outrageous idea. 'You can't afford the time away when the shop's busy and orders are rolling in. And what of your new commission to paint the Lord Mayor's wife as a companion portrait to his own? And Stephen says he is nigh ready to knock the doorway through from our house to next door. You can't be gone when that happens: you'll need to oversee that momentous task.'

'In truth,' I said upon a sigh, ''Tis an additional reason why I thought we should go now. The house and workshop will be unlivable, what with the dirt, dust and noise, and the shop will have to close for a week at least. Besides, what knowledge do I possess concerning the breaking of walls and what Stephen calls 'making good' thereafter? I thought we might make the most of this opportunity…'

'We? What, all of us?'

'Nay, Rose. Only we two and the children and Gawain. I wondered…'

'What of the others? We can't just abandon them.'

'I have thought much on that score.' I sipped my ale. 'Kate could spend the time at her father's house; Hugh can return to Master Collop's workshop. He be but on loan to us and has until Christmastide afore his apprenticeship there ends. Ralf could bide with his beloved Joanie for a few days.'

'And what of Adam and the lads and Nessie? And now Meg. Where can they go? Meg has barely settled in here and now you would have her sent elsewhere? That's hardly fair to her, Seb.'

'Rose, pilgrimage is not intended to be easy and convenient.

By its very nature, it has to be difficult, elsewise where be the purpose of it?'

'But it sounds to me as though this will be a penance for everyone else more than us.'

'Then, mayhap, they will also earn some remittance of time to be spent in Purgatory and all our souls will benefit.'

'Even Meg's? You know her opinion on such matters.'

Rose spoke with a growing affection for the lass who had lately come into our household. An unwilling, much maligned and mistreated novice nun, I was in the process of purchasing her freedom from St Helen's Priory in Bishopsgate: a place she should ne'er have been sent to. A prison in all but name for her and her sister. Her sister had died five months since: a tragedy Thaddeus and I were called upon to solve. It had proved a sorry tale indeed. But one more payment to the Bishop of London at Christmastide would see Margaret a free woman. In the meantime, she bided with us, rebuilding her life, repaying me by construing my accounts so well and aiding Rose in the legion chores necessary to run this house.

'Aye, I know of Margaret's grave doubts upon that score but...'

'Do not call her so. You know full well she hates to be addressed as Margaret.'

'I beg her pardon: Meg. But if old Father Thomas and young Father Christian cannot convince her that God is good and harkens to our prayers, then I be hardly qualified to do so. Nor am I any more likely to succeed.' I sighed, recalling long summer evenings spent in that fruitless task. The lass believed Our Lord Jesu had abandoned her and her sister when they were greatly in need and, in return, she had abandoned Him. We all feared for her soul. Father Thomas at our parish church of St Michael le Querne had spoken with Meg at length, to no avail. Father Christian, the new priest at St Mary Magdalen Church in Old Fish Street, who was become a good friend, had tried to rekindle her beliefs but she remained deaf to every kind of persuasion.

'Oh, Seb, I hoped she would consider that you were sent

to her in answer to her prayers, to save her from the priory.' Rose had, likewise, done her best with our sorrowful guest. We all had – except my brother Jude, of course, whose belief in Almighty God seemed ever to be dependent upon whether it was convenient at that moment or not, rather than a matter of faith and constancy.

I extricated my feet from beneath Gawain's considerable weight as he lay sprawled across my shoes, my toes cramped and tingling. My dog was an asset in cold weather, lying thus, warding off icy draughts, but was growing fat of late. A long walk to Canterbury would do him good, the idle colley. He twitched as he slept on, dreaming of chasing coneys or squirrels most like.

'Except that Margaret – Meg – insists she ne'er prayed for aid,' I said, 'Forwhy she expected none was possible; that God would ignore her and her sister's plight, as had been the case throughout their young lives, all the while their father misused them.'

'Then *you* were a miracle, Seb, sent unasked for. That's what I've told her more than once. But what of her and Nessie whilst we're journeying through Kent? And Adam and his lads? It will take eight days at the least, walking with the children and then the time we stay in Canterbury… ten days or more we should be away from home, I suspect. If we go…'

'Longer if we visit your family, Rose? Should you wish to. That be what I wondered upon just now.'

'My family? After my father threw me out! He was hardly better than Meg's father, though it was that hateful apprentice who raped me. My father treated me as if I got with child on purpose to offend him… and then my little Edward… innocent of all… poor sweeting…' She dabbed her eyes with her apron hem. 'Why would I want to see them ever again?'

'Mayhap to forgive them? To show them you are happy and prospering despite all that went amiss so long since.'

'They could be dead for all I know.'

'Do you not wish to find out?'

'No. I don't believe I do.'

'Think on it, Rose, for this may be your one and only chance. Your mother gave you coin as you departed and told you to come to London to seek your fortune. Or so you once told me.'

'Aye. Tuppence she gave me but she did naught to save me from the 'prentice, nor did she try to talk to my father, to make him see sense and let me stay. I was a good glover even then; my stitchery so small and neat. I would've been an asset to his business.'

'Could your mother have prevented what came to pass or persuaded your father to allow you to remain?'

'Probably not. He was a stubborn pig and, in truth, I never told her what the 'prentice did. I never told anyone until it was too late and then my father said it was my own fault for leading the lad astray. But I didn't. I hated his fat, pimply face, his ugly hands.'

'But think on this, my dear one: if none of that had occurred, if your mother had not given you what little coin she could spare and instructed you to come here to the city and were it not for the vicissitudes you suffered at the Pewter Pot Tavern, we would never have met and I would not have found my soul-mate. I trust you do not regret that? For certain, I praise the day I first saw you.'

'As do I.' Rose moved closer and embraced me.

'I recall it was not the most auspicious nor proper meeting. My first sight was of your backside – fully clad, of course – as you searched for something 'neath the bed. A most comely shaped backside it was, I admit, but, as a married man at the time, I averted my eyes.' I laughed at the memory and so did she.

She slapped my hand in playful wise.

'I don't believe you, Seb Foxley. I was naught but a common whore and I wager you looked your fill.'

'Maybe I did, though you were no whore, sweeting, but a lass forced to pay her way by whatever means. And, what if I did look, in which case I must have done a penance for it after, I be sure.'

'Knowing you, that's for certain.' She ran soft fingers across my hand as though to undo the slap and looked at me from 'neath lowered lids. 'Now finish your ale whilst I cover the fire, then come to bed but you must promise to forego any thoughts of penance.' She left the settle and knelt to tend the fire. 'Come now, husband,' she said, brushing ash from her apron. 'I'm not in patient humour this eve.'

I required no second telling. I cared not a jot about finishing my ale and followed her to the stair. If she hoped to divert me from contemplating pilgrimage, she succeeded, for a while at least.

Friday, the twentieth day of October

As we sat at the board in the kitchen, breaking our fast after attending Low Mass at St Michael's, I informed the others of my intentions to make the pilgrimage to Canterbury. Rose rolled her eyes and silently shook her head, realising her measures to persuade me otherwise had failed utterly, despite their being right pleasurable last eve. Afore any could object, I explained my reasoning, that the shop would be closed and the house barely habitable whilst the building work attained its conclusion and the two properties were knocked into one.

'So no work for a week or more? Is that wise?' Adam looked doubtful even as he set about the platter of smoked eel and white bread set before him. He and his stepsons – I knew not how else to call them – came from the house in Friday Street each morn to join us in time for breakfast. 'I can't afford the loss of wage, not with the lads eating enough for an army these days. Simon eats more than I do.'

If true, that was quite an achievement, I thought, watching my cousin at meat in his usual purposeful and resolute manner, wasting not a solitary morsel and holding forth his dish for a second helping. The increasing strain at his doublet lacings and a new notch upon his belt bore testimony to his expanding girth.

And then in likewise, just as his sometime-stepfather had done, Simon did the same. It was a gladsome thing to see the lad copying Adam as closely as a good scribe copies an exemplar. He could do worse than follow my kinsman. Theirs would ever be a complicated relationship: Adam had wed Mercy Hutchinson in good faith, believing her widowed and taking her orphaned sons – Simon, Nicholas and Edmund – as his own. Then her husband returned, rising from the dead, as it seemed, a most unwelcome Lazarus. Within days, it had ended right badly for poor Mercy back in the summer, leaving her lads motherless and then fatherless when her murderous husband was hanged.

Now the Hutchinson lads had no one but Adam who, God be thanked, loved them, despite all the heartbreak he suffered at losing Mercy – or mayhap because of it. He had lately petitioned Lord Mayor Bartholomew James to be recognised as the lads' guardian since they had no other known relatives. And we all prayed that there was no obscure relation lurking somewhere who might, of a sudden, come forth to own them, causing distress and trauma over again. I thought it unlikely forwhy the lads possessed no inheritance worth the trouble of claiming and were, in themselves, a costly burden until they should earn a livelihood. Simon was aged thirteen years and destined to become my apprentice next year, if matters fell out as they should. But troublesome Nick was four and Mundy not much older than our Julia. 'Twould be years afore they might repay Adam with a wage.

'Eat that in haste, Simon, else you'll be late to school,' Adam scolded. 'Nick, cease playing with that eel and making a mess. You're an evil influence on little Mundy, so mind your manners at table.'

Nicholas stuck out his tongue at Adam, with the predictable consequence of my cousin leaning across the board, spilling ale cups in order to deliver a hefty swipe across the child's ear.

Nick gave a deafening howl but it was of short duration afore he returned to flicking bits of eel skin, which he refused to eat, at his younger brother.

'I would have you desist from such punishments whilst we eat,' I whispered to Adam reprovingly.

'He needs to learn and, if not now, then when? A beating an hour hence will serve no good.'

I sighed, knowing Adam was correct but disliking to see such hurtful measures which I be uncertain have any great effect.

'As to your working whilst the workshop be closed,' I reverted to our earlier matter, 'If you desire to fill the time, take whatever you need home with you to Friday Street and work there, away from the dirt and chaos that will ensue here. Be sure I shall pay you as usual, whether you work or not. I intend that as part of the arrangement.'

'What of food?'

'All of you may have to make do with cookshop fare as this kitchen wall will be knocked through, so no fire for cooking nor hot water for washing but that would be the case whether Rose and I were here or not.'

'I shall speak with Pen Hepton,' Rose said. 'Likely, she'll let Meg and Nessie have hot water in exchange for a little aid with her new babe.' She referred to her dear friend Peronelle Wenham-Hepton, a silkwoman who lived by the Eleanor Cross. By God's grace, having been so fearful all along, she had been safe delivered of a daughter last month.

Meg spoke up then:

'Nessie and I could stay at Friday Street, could we not? Then we can use Adam's kitchen and cook for us all. I'm sure we could sleep there also. There is room enough, isn't there, Seb? Adam?'

Forthright as ever was Margaret but Adam looked doubtful.

'What say you, cousin?' I asked.

'Mm, I suppose so. But what of your reputations… two unwed lassies living with me?'

'Pah! I don't give a jot about that.' Meg dismissed his concern with a flick of her hand. 'Who cares what others think of us? I'm a disgraced nun in most folks' opinions anyway. Besides, Nessie will be my chaperone and I'll be hers… if you think we need one,' she added laughingly. 'Were you proposing to ravish the pair of us, Adam?'

I had ne'er seen my cousin's cheek burn so vivid a hue as Adam's did at her words.

'School, Simon. I'll not have you late to lessons,' Adam said. 'I'll see you to Paul's Gate now.'

I smiled to myself. Simon required seeing to the gate across Paternoster Row no more than I did. Meg had embarrassed my cousin utterly. He even left a last spoonful of his meal uneaten.

'What of me, Master Seb?' Kate, my apprentice, spoke up. 'Shall I work with Master Adam at his place?'

'Aye, with Meg and Nessie there, I be sure of the propriety of that, lass,' I said, 'But mayhap you should go to your father's house to sleep and to spend Sundays. In truth, I thought you might take pleasure in a few days spent with your father. You have little enough time together these days.'

Kate did not leap with delight at my suggestion and I could hazard I knew the reason why:

'Mayhap your father will permit Hugh to visit you at Walbrook since he be your intended – well, nigh as good as.'

Now it was Hugh Gardyner who was discomfited, even as he turned aside, attempting to conceal his flamed complexion by addressing Rose:

''Twas a fine dish, Mistress Rose. I greatly enjoyed the eel. I thank you.'

'Hugh, you will return to Master Collop's workshop just for this short while. I be certain he will be glad of your skills this coming week forwhy I hear he has a prestigious new commission from the Grocers' Company for a sizeable tome: an illuminated register of members past and present. The perfect opportunity for your exquisite capitals to be displayed, lad. I know you will be a credit to both our workshops.' I then turned to the elderly man sat silent at the corner of the board. 'And you, Ralf. Have you any preference as to what I might arrange on your behalf?'

'You'll have no problem with me, good master,' Ralf said, grinning and showing his toothless gums. 'I'll work at Friday Street with Adam of a daytime and bide with my Joanie of a night. Couldn't be better.'

Thus it was settled: the Foxley workshop would be temporarily displaced to Friday Street whilst our home and shop were rebuilt and made good under Stephen Appleyard's skilled and careful eye. We must spend this day and tomorrow trundling all necessary stuff to Adam's house and shifting whatever of our belongings remained here out of danger of falling rubble as the walls of the kitchen, parlour and shop were knocked through into the new construction next door.

In truth, I did not want to be here to observe the destruction of much of our home. I knew it required repairs after the soot- and water-damage resulting from the fire next door in May last. Soon, all would be made new and we would have more spacious premises for the expanding business and our enlarged family. Who could say? Mayhap Rose would give me more children in time, God willing. But, even so, I felt somewhat sorrowful that our cosy home would be unrecognisable upon our return from pilgrimage.

In the meantime, I made preparation for the journey, there and back, to Canterbury. I sent word to Dick Langton – he who was Dame Ellen's son – that we might pay him and his family a visit as we pass through Deptford, down river, on our way across Kent. I had not seen him since we were joint executors of his mother's will and not only were we friends but I be godfather to his daughter, Janey. A visit was in order, therefore, and I penned a letter, sending it by a carter on his way to Eltham, to deliver building supplies to the King's Palace there. We heard the king was having a new Great Hall built. It seemed rebuilding was a common thing these days, amongst high and low.

Saturday, the twenty-first day of October

Upon Saturday afternoon, when most businesses were closed, I went to the Thatchers' house across the street from Peronelle's in Cheapside. Some weeks previously, I had observed Mistress Thatcher pulling a little handcart in which lay both her toddling, Annie, and her purchases made at market. I asked her concerning it forwhy it appeared a useful invention. She said her man, Harry, made it long since for bringing in firewood but, having sprained her wrist, she made use of it to carry her little lass and the heavy worts and meats, rather than lug them in her arms. We had agreed then that, since her wrist was now quite recovered, I might borrow it for our journey. There was room enough for Dickon and Julia to ride within, to sleep if they became wearied or to relieve our arms of carrying them. Our spare clothing would provide a bed in the bottom of the cart with a waxen leather cover over all, if it should rain. Well content with my fine idea, I took the cart home, where Rose viewed it with delight.

My next task was not one I relished. If I speak in honest wise, I had been delaying it for a long while, ever since I first determined to make this pilgrimage in fact, as opposed to merely contemplating it as a future duty to be performed, a vow to be accomplished whenever that might be. Now I must tell my brother Jude of it.

Jude Foxley's place at Amen Corner by Ave Maria Alley

The door was open, so I pushed it wide and was greeted by a smell that was somewhat familiar but not quite – ink.

'Mind that!' Jude yelled at me as I stepped about a small cask standing on the floor just within the door. 'Printing ink, cost me a bloody fortune. Different from the stuff you use. Don't ask me why.' My brother bent to lift the cask out of the way.

It was about three hand spans high and as big round as a man's thigh. Awkward but not heavy, I would have thought, yet seeing Jude attempting to pick it up with his injured knee unable to bend, I hastened to aid him.

'Get away, you clod. I don't need you sticking your bloody nose in.'

'Forgive me. I only meant…'

'Why are you here, anyway?' Jude managed to get hold of the odoriferous cask and put it in a corner under the stair for safety. 'Come to spy on me, have you? Can't bear the thought that I can manage perfectly well without you?' He eased himself onto a stool and winced as he lifted his leg into a more comfortable position. 'Or have you come to wreck my press? As you see, it's assembled at last and ready to print. I'll have you out of business by Christmas, little brother, and there's naught you can do to stop me.'

Jude had been attempting to set up a printing press to rival Master Caxton's at Westminster all summer. It took months to assemble the devilish device, imported from Flanders at great cost. For one thing, my brother had no idea how the mighty timbers fitted together and it was a task for two and sometimes three men to lift the heavy oak beams. But his obstinacy prevailed and, by the end of August, the contraption was all of a piece, for the most part put together by his drinking and gambling cronies from the Sunne in Splendour tavern down the street. The Lord knew how, forwhy they were drunk more often than they were sober. Yet here it stood: huge and unwieldy, a testament to Jude's unflagging determination to ruin my business and that of every other stationer in London.

'A courtesy call is all. I came to tell you I shall be out of London for ten days… a fortnight at most.'

'And you think I care? Two weeks without seeing your miserable carcass will be a pleasure. When are you leaving? I'll have a celebration?'

'Monday morn, as early as Rose and the little ones be ready.'

'You're all going? Why? Whose lives are you planning to overset now? Who's earned such a punishment? Whoever they are, they have my commiserations.' Jude leaned from his stool and shifted a pile of discarded clothing – a woman's but that meant naught since his friend John Rykener oftimes dressed in gown and kirtle – to retrieve an ale jug. Liquid sloshed within but as he could not find a cup to hand, my brother drank straight from the jug only to spit it out, cursing. 'Christ Jesu suffering! How long has that stood there? Tastes like piss.'

'Mayhap it is. One of your tavern fellows could have used the jug as a piss-pot.'

Jude pulled a face, worked up spit and spat again before wiping his mouth upon his sleeve.

'So… I suppose I have to ask it: where are you going? Must be important for you to abandon your precious bloody workshop.'

'We are making a pilgrimage to Canterbury?'

'What? Why would you waste the time and money? Pilgrimage is about as much bloody use as the bishop's bollocks.'

'I told you why when you lay so sore injured…'

'Don't remind me of that, you wretch. I spend every hour trying to forget it. Not that my bloody leg will allow me. Talking of which: don't stand there like a useless turd. Find the ale jug. It's around somewhere. And a cup so I can wet my lips like a Christian and not have to drink from the jug like a bloody barbarian.'

I did as bidden, discovering a jug and a half-dozen unwashed cups in the chaotic horror that had once served a good woman as her kitchen. I did not observe too closely forwhy, on previous visits, I had discovered the heel of a loaf, blue with mould and, worse yet, the remains of a meal crawling with little white worms. I chose the cleanest-looking cup and returned to my brother. I made no noise and thus caught sight of him attempting to flex his knee, his features betraying the agony he ever tried to hide. I rattled the cup against the jug, giving him due warning of my approach, such that he might compose himself.

'You're not joining me?' he asked, seeing I brought but one cup.

'Nay. There be little ale in the jug.' I did not add that I preferred my cup washed, not full of days-old dust.

'Please yourself.' He shrugged and then poured a generous measure, drinking it down in a few gulps afore replenishing the cup.

'As I was saying… I intend this pilgrimage to Canterbury, to St Thomas Becket's shrine, to honour my pledge made to Our Lord Jesu, St Mary and to the martyred archbishop if only your life would be spared. I wept and prayed for you, Jude. I truly did. And now I must do as I vowed.'

'You shouldn't have bloody bothered. You think I'm glad my life was spared when I'm left a cripple, in pain every hour? I'd be better off dead. I saved your worthless life that day and have paid the devil's own bloody price for it ever since.'

'I know,' I said quietly, feeling my throat constrict and my eyes prick. 'That is why I must go. If I pray at Becket's shrine with such fervour, mayhap he will grant another miracle and restore your knee… relieve your pain. And I shall bring home holy water to bathe it. I know not what else I may do to make amends unto you, brother. If there were any means by which I might undo that dreadful mishap, I would, as God be my witness, but I cannot. A pilgrimage be all that I can think to do for you now.'

Jude said naught but sipped his ale.

'Whatever your thoughts on my making this pilgrimage, will you at least wish me 'Godspeed'?'

'Bloody waste of time,' he muttered, then spoke up: 'Aye, I suppose so. Godspeed, little brother.' Was that a hint of a smile twitching at the corners of his mouth?

I could not recall the last time I had seen him smile. Was this a first tentative step towards mending our relationship? If it was, this pilgrimage had already caused another miracle to come to pass. I smiled in return.

'How's work progressing on your house?' he asked, having never enquired afore. 'Every time I pass it on my way to the tavern, it looks more like a heap of rubble.'

''Tis coming on apace now. Stephen be about to knock the two houses into one. And since it will be uninhabitable for a week or more, now is a good time for us to make this journey. The rest of the household will bide with Adam in Friday Street for the while.'

'So who will see to it that your abandoned place doesn't fall to bloody looters whilst you're gone?'

'Looters?' I had not foreseen this possibility. 'Stephen and Jack and the labourers will be there of a daytime.'

'And at night? Have you asked the Ward Watch to give eye to it?'

'You think I should?'

'Better to be safe than bloody sorry.'

'Aye, you be correct. I shall have a word with them this eve: promise them a couple of marks if I return to find all be well. And Thaddeus Turner will be dining with us tomorrow, so I may ask him to remind the Marching Watch also.'

'Do you trust the buggers?'

'Do I have a choice? I trust Thaddeus implicitly but he too has doubts upon occasion regarding the watchmen.'

'You could promise me and Rykener and our company – idle sots all – a reward for our time and trouble and we'll keep watch on it from the tavern. Your house can be seen from the window there. I see all your comings and goings, little brother. You can't hide your secrets from me.' He grinned. 'What of that new wench who lives with you now. That's a dainty sweetmeat and straight from the cloister, too, so I hear, which adds spice to the dish. I might have a taste myself.'

'You will do no such thing, Jude. Margaret has suffered naught but ill-treatment and deserves the utmost respect. You will leave her be.'

'You always spoil my fun. Serve you right if it bloody pours with rain all the way to Canterbury.'

I nodded but inwardly I was smiling. This was my brother Jude as of old.

'Will you join us for dinner tomorrow? Rose be preparing quite a feast to say farewell to her old kitchen. You will be most welcome, as you ever be.'

'I suppose that bloody kinsman of yours will be there?'

'Aye. *Our* kinsman Adam shares all our meals, as do his lads.' For reasons I had never quite fathomed, Jude detested Adam. Refused even to say his name.

'In which case, I'll likely eat at the Sunne.'

'The invitation stands, if you change your mind. And I be grateful for your warning about looters. I bid you farewell now… if I do not see you again afore we leave. God's blessings be upon you, Jude.'

'You sound like a bloody priest. Father Sebastian of Paternoster Row, the God-Botherer-in-Chief of London. Now get out. I have work to do, folk to see, business to conduct. And I must puzzle out this bloody contraption if it's the last thing I do.' He levered himself from his seat and limped over to the printing press. 'Damned, accursed devil's device,' I heard him mutter, thumping the platen with his fist, but he turned as I reached the door and was grinning.

We parted, laughing.

Chapter 2

Sunday, the twenty-second day of October
The Foxley House

'TWAS OUR last dinner in our home as we had known it these five years past and, therefore, a poignant repast. We invited all our friends to share the baked pigeons in a coffin with lovage sauce, roasted buntings on skewers with blackberries, turnips in butter and ginger and, to end, a norange and nutmeg syllabub with pokerounce – this last a receipt Rose and I had tasted at a feast given by the Duke of Gloucester at Crosby Place. The little triangles of toasted bread, topped with honey and sprinkled with spices and chopped hazelnuts, had become the household's favoured treat, although little Dickon ever succeeded in getting the honeyed mixture in his hair, up his arms and down his front – anywhere but in his mouth, it seemed.

Young Nick was as bad but I suspected he made the mess on purpose, such was his way, intending to annoy Adam and make more washing for the women. Julia, ever the neat little lady, though the youngest of all, created the least chaos of crumbs and stickiness. It mattered not: we all enjoyed the most excellent dinner. Rose, Margaret – I beg her pardon: Meg – Kate and Nessie had excelled themselves in the old kitchen this one last time to ensure we should ne'er forget this meal.

When the dishes and cloth were cleared, Rose and the other women, including Peronelle with her new daughter swaddled close, retired with the children to the garden to make the most of the autumnal sunshine. We menfolk adjourned to the parlour to chat over our ale. Simon hovered, uncertain of his place, neither a man yet more than a child. Adam solved his stepson's difficulty.

'Come, lad, bring your ale,' he chivvied, nudging Simon along the passageway to the parlour. 'You're too old to play ring-o'-rosy with the babes.'

The lad grinned, pleased to be counted among the men.

The parlour was quite crowded but it delighted me to have so many together, in particular that Jude had joined us as he had not for some months now. Ralf, Father Thomas and Old Symkyn, the beggar from Paul's gate whence he had lately been restored to his place, no longer forced by the pernickety dean to sit at Cheapside Cross, spoke amicably together, laughing at some jest by the hearth. I had kindled the fire earlier to ease their ancient bones.

Adam and Bennett Hepton – Peronelle's wealthy fishmonger husband – had set up the chess board betwixt them and were teaching Simon the rudimentary moves of the game.

'No, Simon, you great clod. You'll lose your bishop if you do that,' I heard Adam say. 'Don't make it easy for Ben; the demon will beat you soon enough anyway.'

Stephen was dozing over his ale cup, which I removed without waking him afore he should spill the contents. But I was intrigued by a surprising twosome: Jude and Jack, heads together on a bench in the corner. Adversaries since the day they met with Jack having suffered countless beatings at my brother's behest for innumerable sins down the years, I wondered at what that ill-conceived pairing was about. The whispering behind hands and furtive glances aside boded no good for someone. I could but pray the victim of their plots was not me or mine.

My friend of longest standing, City Bailiff Thaddeus Turner, and my newest friend, Father Christian, were at ease on the cushioned settle – to be removed when our guests departed to some safer place afore the chimney wall was demolished this week coming – sharing the book I had left there last eve, entitled *A Guide for Pilgrims*.

'You have it all planned then, Seb, every step of the way, to judge from your marginal notations,' Christian said, leafing through the pages.

I sat upon a stool beside him since the pair filled the settle. We had become close since his arrival in London in April last, after he aided poor Mercy Hutchinson's soul in May. We were of an age, although he appeared younger, less careworn than I. In truth, Christian did not look to be the four-and-twenty years required to be ordained a priest. Mind, the women of St Mary Magdalen parish flocked to hear his sermons – or, mayhap, was it to gaze upon his handsome face even as he exhorted them to forego such worldly vanities as good looks.

'I hope so,' I said, 'Although 'tis ne'er possible to prepare for every eventuality.'

Thaddeus stood, finishing his mulled ale and setting his cup on the floor.

'Unfortunately, I can't stay, Seb: a bailiff's duties never end.'

He spoke true, as I well knew. Even on the Lord's Day, crime did not rest.

'I would beg a favour of you, Thaddeus; whilst we be gone and this place stands empty…'

The bailiff held up his hand to silence my request.

'No need to beg. I'll see no harm befalls these walls other than what destruction Stephen will cause to be wrought in the name of improvement. I shall be looking to it in person, rest assured. And thank Rose for the splendid dinner. Best cook in London.' The city bailiff patted his paunch. 'And I should know,' he chuckled. 'But you know you'll miss me as much as I'll miss Rose's dinners. What will you do with no crimes to challenge your skills of observation and deduction, eh?'

'I be contemplating the lack right eagerly. I intend to leave all such wickedness behind for ten days to the great benefit of my soul.'

'Hah! I'll keep my fingers crossed for you then, Seb, for we both know trouble follows you around like a stray cur scenting butchers' scraps.'

'Do not tempt fate, Thaddeus. Our pilgrimage must be pleasing to the Almighty and all the saints. I do not want any evil act to besmirch our efforts.'

'And yet Thomas Becket is only a saint and martyr because he was horribly murdered. Don't forget that your pilgrimage is founded on a heinous crime.'

''Tis true but, leastwise, there was no mystery as to who were the perpetrators, no confusing clues to unravel.'

'Aye, I suppose that's true. Then may God speed your way, my friend.'

After I had bidden Thaddeus farewell at the street door, I returned to the parlour. Father Christian was yet reading my book.

'This pilgrimage will be a fine experience for you: an adventure for your body even as it aids your soul. Do you have a particular reason for making it at this time?'

'I do. My brother, there, be reason enough.' In whispered words, I told Christian my purpose, my intentions, aye, and my hopes.

At length, he nodded wisely.

'I shall pray for your safety upon the road.'

'We shall be grateful for it.'

'How will you manage with a woman and two small children? What of hungry infants who cannot wait until you reach the next inn, soiled tail-clouts and wet smocks? Clearly, you have thought much about the way you must take, where you will rest overnight but what of such matters?'

As with Jude's concern for looters, I had not thought about keeping the toddlings clean, dry and content.

'You know my dearest Rose: a woman both practical and resourceful. She will have considered these things, no doubt.'

'Have you asked her?'

'Well… nay, not as yet,' I admitted, realising my error. 'I have borrowed a hand cart for the children that they may ride if they become too tired.'

'Well, that's something, I suppose.' Christian sounded doubtful. 'But you're departing in the morn: haven't you left it somewhat late to ask Rose what she may need for the journey? In truth, Seb, I think you need more help; another pair of hands to aid you.'

'You do? But it would not be fair to ask Margaret to go on pilgrimage. You know her opinion of such things. Nessie would be more of a hindrance than a help. Kate be my apprentice, not a servant.'

'I was thinking of a man's assistance.'

'With washing clouts and coddling wailing infants?'

Christian shrugged and turned a page, not meeting my eye.

''Tis not a thing unknown. I've done both. I could accompany you to Canterbury, if you allow?'

'You? But you be a man of the cloth. A priest.'

'Aye. Priests go on pilgrimage too, you know.'

'But you have a parish…'

'I also have an experienced deacon who served before I came. He can do so again and the priest from St Augustine's used to come to conduct Mass on Sundays. Likely, I will miss but one Lord's Day and for what better reason than making a pilgrimage? I will arrange it this eve and send word to Bishop Kempe that I require a brief absence.'

'Will he agree?'

'He can hardly refuse me.'

I wondered at this. Why was Christian so eager to come with us? Not for the pleasure of washing babe's nether-clouts, I be certain. And how come he be so sure that the bishop would grant him leave?

'Aye, well, of course you may join us if you wish.' I did not add that anyone could journey to Canterbury for whatever purpose without my permission. 'I shall be singing with Paul's choristers at Vespers later, so you know where to find me. We may make our arrangements then, if you decide to come and the bishop wills it thus.'

'Excellent. I'll find out my stoutest boots and warmest cloak from the coffer I haven't opened since I arrived in London last spring. If I recall, one boot has a broken lace… No matter, that can be remedied first thing in the morn. I shall be at your door by cock-crow, or is that too early?'

'Cock-crow will do well but you may have to wait upon the children breaking their fast for 'tis somewhat like attempting to organise a herd of stray cats and takes a while.'

'Fear not. I'll have them in order in no time,' Christian declared, his eyes bright with merriment.

As with other matters concerning the young cleric, I wondered what he meant. A man of some mystery is he but, I dare say, we would learn much of him upon the road to Canterbury. I could but hope it would be all to the good.

Sunday eve
St Paul's Cathedral

High Mass and Vespers upon the Lord's Day were the offices requiring the choir to give its all. My attendance at choir practice upon Friday eve was ever a chancy thing – much to the precentor's chagrin – and I suffered the customary remonstration from him for missing the most recent rehearsal. Despite this, he knew well that my voice was an asset and I practised in my own time, so his harsh words meant little. My family and, more especially, my journeymen and apprentices knew I sang at my desk, distracting them from their work but not distracting myself. Often, I sang without knowing. It came to me as naturally as breathing.

My voice – an undeserved gift from God, as the precentor said of it – was yet that of a young chorister, unbroken. My speaking voice was of a man grown but, in song, I could attain the highest notes, clear and without undue effort. None knew why it should be thus but it was and I ever thank the Lord Jesu Christ that I be blessed with this joyous means of praising Him.

We stood by the rood screen, just we two, when the office was ended. The precentor wore his formidable scowl, brows drawn so low his eyes could not be seen. Most often, he would stand with his hands tucked into his voluminous sleeves but, instead, his right hand was out, his finger ready to wag at me in gravest displeasure.

'That top note in the third bar of the seventh line of the motet, on the word *caelestis*...' The finger wagged. 'It sounded less than 'heavenly' to my ear, Sebastian,' the precentor complained, as he ever did, no matter how well the choir performed. If the seraphim had sung for him, he would have found some reason to criticise them. 'And you held the note over long.' Wag, wag. 'If you attended practice regularly, you would know how this motet should be sung. It's not good enough, Sebastian, your lack of application. If you fail to attend this Friday coming, when we shall be practising a new piece of my own composition in readiness for the Feast of All Saints and making our final rehearsal for the Feast of Sts Simon and Jude this Saturday...'

'I fear, Brother Precentor, I shall be absent from London for the next ten days or more...'

'What? But you cannot! I forbid it utterly!' he shouted, waving his arms, causing the nearest candle flames to dance wildly. 'What will Bishop Kempe think if the choir lacks for a good clear voice?'

'Then I make my apologies to you and the bishop but Mark Todd can sing my part well enough.'

'Chorister Todd howls like a dog at the full moon. I won't have you letting me down in this manner, Sebastian. Either you're a Paul's chorister or you're not. If you can't attend regularly, I'll dispense with your efforts entirely.'

He flung the threat at me such that I took a step back, catching my heel in my long black cassock and nigh stumbling on the chancel steps. I steadied myself by grasping the head of some long-dead bishop carved into the rood screen.

'I sh-should be right sorrowful if you did so, sir, but I be embarking upon a pilgrimage to Canterbury. For the good of my unworthy soul,' I added, knowing he dare not gainsay me on that point of argument.

'Oh, I see. Why did you not say sooner?' The right hand, with its admonishing digit, disappeared into his left sleeve and I sighed in relief. 'I suppose you must do whatever you feel to be necessary then, regarding your soul,' he continued. 'Will you be returned in time for All Saints' Day on the first of November?'

'I doubt it, sir, but most definitely by Martinmas on the eleventh.'

'And after that, you will attend practice regularly.'

I was unsure if that was a statement of fact or a query.

'I shall do my utmost but family matters and business intervene upon occasion.'

'I want no more excuses, Sebastian. Mend your ways. You hear me? Do I make myself plain?'

'Aye, Brother Precentor, I hear you and you speak plain enough, sir.'

'Well, see that you do or else…'

Mercifully, the precentor's rant was forced to end, my saviour being Father Christian. The two clerics greeted each other in pious wise afore the precentor strode away, scowling worse than ever.

'My thanks for your timely rescue.'

'Did you need rescuing?'

'I dare say you heard what the precentor was saying? How could you not? He hardly berated me in a whisper.'

Christian laughed and held my arm.

'Aye, I heard it all. There was an old fool just like him at Oxford: thought the whole of creation began and ended with solemn plainchant. At least this brother approves of polyphony, which is easier on the ear if sung well. I love the harmonies.'

'None can question Brother Precentor's knowledge of music,

which be why I should hate for him to dismiss me.'

'He won't. His threats are empty ones. Trust me. The bishop won't let him bar you from the choir.'

'Oh? How can you know that?'

'As I said, trust me. Now, as to tomorrow, Bishop Kempe has given me his blessing to accompany you, as I told you he would. So, will you let me join you and Rose?'

'I, er, of course. You be most welcome.' How did a humble parish priest gain audience with the bishop upon a whim?

Christian put his head to one side and frowned somewhat.

'You don't sound too sure, Seb. Why is that?'

''Tis surprising; naught else. I wonder why you would want the encumbrance of a family with small children when you could make the pilgrimage alone, likely in half the time with far less trouble.'

'I enjoy your company. Plain and simple. I like you. You make good conversation, better than anyone else I've met in London. It that not a valid reason?'

'Aye, I suppose it is. Until the morn, then.'

'God keep you in safety this night and bless you and yours, Seb.' Christian administered the benediction as I bowed my head.

I returned home, remaining unconvinced as to why Christian wished to join us on our pilgrimage. There was much mystery surrounding this man.

The Foxley House

Rose and I were folding a few spare items of attire in readiness for our journey – clean netherclouts in the main – then rolling them into a neat bundle to lay in the bottom of the hand-cart as a bed for the children. Above would be a good sheepskin to keep the babes warm with a waxen leather cover overall to ensure children and clothing remained as dry as possible, should it rain. Such were our necessaries. However, a sizable pile of small garments and tailclouts was yet growing upon the coffer at the foot of our bed.

'Do the little ones require so much?' I asked, wondering how it would all fit in the cart without smothering the children. Or was I to be laden like a pack donkey and carry it?

'We dare take no less.' Rose pressed down on a folded mountain of linen, putting all her weight behind it. 'Julia needs a clean tailclout every few hours and Dickon must wear one at night. Suppose I have no chance to wash them or get them dry? We can't have them sitting in their own soil.'

'No. I see your reasoning but we have to carry it, wet or dry.'

Rose was now sitting on the tailclouts, attempting to squash them to such a size so they would go into a small canvas bag little larger than my scrip. I could not see how so much might ever fit inside it.

'And I must then keep the wet ones separate, else none will be dry enough to wear. So this is for the dirty tailclouts…' She waved an empty bag at me. 'And this for washed clouts if I can't put them to dry.'

'Well, 'tis fortunate then that there will be three of us to carry it all.'

'Three?' Somehow, Rose had succeeded in getting all the linen into the first bag and pulled the drawstring close and tight as it would go.

'Aye. Did I not say? Father Christian be coming with us to Canterbury.'

'Oh. Why?'

'I know not, in truth, but he declared himself not only eager but willing to aid us with Dickon and Julia. I could not refuse such an offer.'

'What does a priest know of the care of infants? Baptism is as far as a priest's knowledge goes, isn't it?' Rose frowned, perplexed.

'Maybe he grew up with younger siblings,' I suggested. I ran my fingers through my dark hair and changed the subject:

'Has my hair grown to be all of a length yet?' I asked her. Five months since, half my hair was scorched away as I had fought the fire that damaged our house and reduced the building next door to charred timbers. I admit, *mea culpa,* my glossy dark hair, hanging nigh unto my shoulders, was ever my vanity and having to see it shorn off was devastating to me as watching the flames consume our neighbours' dwelling.

'Aye, almost.' Rose found a comb and wrestled with a tangle where Dickon had given my hair an embrace with egg upon his fingers. 'Another month and a trim should see your hair the same length on either side. Will you then grow it as long as before?' She tossed the comb onto the pile of things to go in the cart – heaven knew how so much would fit. One item more and I feared there would be no room for the babes to ride.

'Mm. What do you think? This length or longer? Which suits me best?'

'Is it not more convenient when it's this shorter length?' Rose asked me, ever practical.

'Aye, I suppose. It does not blow in my eyes on a windy day nor trail through my pottage when I eat but… does it not look at its best when long?'

Rose shrugged.

'I like it either way. Short or long, you're still my handsome Seb.'

None e'er called me 'handsome' but neither had I been termed 'ugly'. My nose was straight enough, and Rose said my grey eyes were 'finer than any man's'. But whether she spoke thus in jest or to please me, who can say? Or did her undoubted love for me make her blind to the very ordinariness of my features? For certain, I was not good-looking like Jude, though his constant pain carved a permanent scowl upon his once-handsome features and his fine golden hair was thinning somewhat and had lost its sheen.

Neither did I possess the face of Adonis-like Father Christian, whose female parishioners adored him as if he were an Old

Testament idol. His eyes, deep set, dark and fathomless, worried me. If they be the windows of the soul, as it was said, what lay within my friend's soul I hardly dared think upon. And yet he seemed kindly, gentle and caring, as a priest ought. I could find no fault in him.

I tipped our little coffer of money from the shop, emptying the contents on the bed, spreading coins across the coverlet, sorting pennies from groats.

'How much should I give to Margaret...'

'Meg.'

'I beg her pardon. How much money should I leave with Meg for household expenses, do you think?'

'Half a mark will be more than enough, I should think. After all, there will be four fewer mouths to feed with us away and there isn't room enough at Friday Street to have a crowd to dine on the Lord's Day, as we usually do.'

'Aye, Thaddeus must find his own dinners in our absence but I would have Marg... Meg to see Old Symkyn gets a good meal under his belt, all the same. He will be needful of all his strength to survive the cold months to come upon the street, if his prophecy be correct – and it usually is.'

'He foretells another harsh winter, then? Worse than the last with those weeks of snow?'

'So he says. A long, hard frost with the river frozen over be his prediction. I pray he has it wrong but 'tis rare for him to be much mistaken concerning the weather.'

'How does he know, Seb? I think even Almighty God must have difficulty foreknowing our fickle English weather.'

I laughed.

'Aye, mayhap the Lord should consult Symkyn's bunions. He says they tell him the truth, unfailingly, if it will rain, snow, blight us with gales or bake us like the deserts of Araby. Fortunately, he foretells mostly sunshine for our pilgrimage and quite windy but likely clouding over for our return journey with possible showers along the way. I believe that to be the best we might have hoped for this late in the year.'

'But we should still take our winter cloaks. If we don't need them in the daytime, they will serve us as blankets of a night. It turns chill when the sun goes down.'

'A wise precaution, Rose.' I kissed her cheek as she stepped back from pummelling the bag of linen clouts into a better shape to fit in the hand cart.

'What was that for, husband? Do you expect bed sport tonight with so much yet to do?'

'Of course not. Not on a Sunday. But you look right comely, all flushed and unkempt from your labours. How may a man resist?'

'No wonder you feel you must humble yourself as a pilgrim with such sinful thoughts filling your head. I think you ought to make the entire journey on your knees, there and back.'

'Oh, come, my sweet, if I did that, how many pairs of hose would require darning and patching? How much mending would you have to do?'

'Do it bare-kneed.'

'Heartless jade! I ne'er realised I had wed so cruel a wife.' I held her close in my embrace and kissed her cheek again, soft as petals.

'Are you sure about making this journey, Seb?' she asked, snuggling into my fine wool doublet. 'You know a pilgrimage means denial of all bodily pleasures along the way. We're supposed to turn all our thoughts to spiritual matters for the benefit of our souls.'

I sighed and loosed my hold, turning away.

'I know. And having you close will make a far harder penance of it.'

'Is that why you want me to come with you? Just to make it the more difficult? How perverse you are.'

'Nay. That has naught to do with it. You and the children cannot bide here whilst Stephen bludgeons great holes in the walls and, I thought, you might like to visit Canterbury again…

your birthplace and childhood home. That was my reasoning, dearest one. I hoped to please you was all.'

'I told you: I care not a jot for seeing Canterbury again. And as for my family, they mean less than a clipped ha'penny to me. I would not give them 'good day' if we passed in the street. But, if you want my company, I suppose I cannot gainsay my husband.'

'Indeed you can, Rose. I shall not force you. You must do as you desire.'

'Even at this late hour?'

'If you do not want to come with me, I shall understand. Say me 'nay', if you will, and I shall bear no grudge.'

'Truly?'

I nodded reluctantly.

'Aye. Truly.'

'Then, of course, I shall come with you, Seb.'

'Thank you,' I said, mystified as ever by a woman's logic but inordinately pleased, all the same.

Chapter 3

Monday, the twenty-third day of October
The Pilgrimage begins

I OPENED THE door to be greeted by a fellow I first took for a stranger, hid 'neath a wide-brimmed leather hat as he was. The saffron-hued doublet glimpsed under a fur-trimmed travelling cloak further confused me.

'Father Christian? Is that you?' I queried.

'Who else are you expecting at this absurdly early hour?' he growled. 'Even the damned sparrows aren't awake yet and I've been up an hour at least, packing. Haven't broken my fast either.'

'Nor have we,' I said, ushering him across the threshold with his hefty pack. 'We were to St Michael's first thing to receive Father Thomas's blessing for our pilgrimage, although I suppose you could have supplied that… maybe?'

He saw me looking at his attire. No priestly garb whatsoever but stout boots to the knee and thick worsted breeches. A leather jerkin, as yet unlaced, overtopped the bright woollen doublet.

'I'm a common pilgrim for this next fortnight coming, not a priest. And don't address me as "Father Christian" either. I don't want anyone extending special privileges to me, you hear? I'm just an ordinary fellow.'

'In a saffron doublet?' I grinned. 'Come, Rose has oyster pottage for us.'

'On a Monday? 'Tis not a fast day.'

'Every day should be a fast day whilst upon pilgrimage.'

'But we haven't set foot upon the way as yet. One last

decent meal…'

'Cease your grutching, Fa… oh, er, Christian. Oyster pottage or naught? 'Tis your choice.'

'Kit. Call me Kit, as they did when I was a student at Oxford. Christian suits a priest well but not a common sort.'

'You will have to keep your hat on, within doors and out, else your tonsure will betray you,' Rose said as she ladled pottage into our bowls, steaming and savoury.

'Fear not, Mistress Rose,' he removed his hat. 'This coif is as good as glued in place, so none shall know my secret.' A snowy linen cap flattened his luxuriant curls of red-brown, the colour of a fox's pelt.

'We are first bound for *The Tabard Inn* across the bridge in Southwark,' I said, guiding Julia's pottage spoon in the correct direction towards her open mouth. She showed four white pearls of teeth, top and bottom. A pretty little lass: her only fault those mismatched eyes – one hazel-green, the other blue – that told the truth of her begetting to any who recalled my one-time journeyman, Gabriel Widowson. Fortunately, fewer did remember him with each month's passing, it being more than two years since he last troubled London, seducing my Emily into sin. And she paid the ultimate price: dying in childbed, whilst he – so far as I knew – yet sailed the Seven Seas, free as a bird. The wretch.

But now was not the time for such thoughts.

'At the inn, we may meet with other pilgrims forwhy 'tis the gathering place for such as we,' I continued. 'Likely, not so many as there would be in spring but enough to make for companionship on the road and safety in numbers. This book,' I held up my little volume *A Guide for Pilgrims*, 'Tells that 'tis customary to stop in Deptford for dinner at a tavern there, *The Greyhound*, but I have written to Dick Langton, asking if we might visit him for an hour or two.'

'How lovely, Seb!' Rose clapped her hands in delight. 'We haven't seen him, Bella and the children for so long. I must tell

Bella what we are doing to this house. Our friend Isabel was born here,' she explained to Christian. 'It belonged to her father then. Seb served as his journeyman for a time... until his, er, somewhat untimely death.'

'I be sure Christian does not wish to hear our ancient history,' I said. As with Julia's birth, how I came to purchase this house was not to be dwelt upon at a time when our thoughts should turn to higher matters. 'Come, break your fast, all of you. We must be departing. Say your farewells in haste and don your cloaks.'

In truth, only Margaret and Nessie were there to wave us 'Godspeed'. The others were yet abed at such an hour, for it was still dark in Paternoster Row, the sky showing only the faintest glow to the east, beyond Aldgate, foretelling sunrise. Even that brightness was made the less certain by a thin veil of mist that hung from the gables, crept from dark alleyways and shrouded St Paul's steeple, concealing more than half its height from view.

Nessie was sobbing into her apron as though we were leaving forever, foolish maid, but Margaret was right stern with her and told her to cease wailing and go prepare a breakfast of bacon for the others – no fasting fare for them on a Monday morn.

'I wish you a safe journey, Master Seb, Mistress Rose. And you also, Father Christian.' Margaret kissed us all most formally afore hugging Dickon and Julia close, each in turn. 'Have a care and return safe soon.'

'Thank you, Meg,' I said, returning her kiss. 'You, too, take care and remember to see to it that Symkyn has bread and meat, as I told you. I have left you coin enough.'

'Fear not. I shan't forget him. And I'll look to Pen Hepton also, if she needs help with her babe.'

'That would be a kindness. I thank you for it.'

I settled Julia in the cart atop the heap of our belongings, wrapping the sheepskin close about her. Rose had endless last-minute instructions for Meg concerning who knew what? All those matters which fill women's lives, I suppose, whilst

Christian and I huddled in our cloaks and stamped our feet on so chill a morn. Dickon, young and impervious to the cold, damp airs, danced about the wet cobbles, impatient and eager, insisting he would walk, rather than ride like a babe. I wondered how long it would be ere he changed his mind. Afore we reached London Stone in Candlewick Street, probably.

'Be you ready, Rose?' I urged her. 'I would cross the bridge afore it becomes too crowded.'

'Aye… oh, and Meg… don't forget what I said about buying cheese: don't get it from that dreadful besom in Paul's south aisle. The last portion from her was rancid. And Tom Codling by Ironmonger Lane has the sweetest apples… excellent for baking with honey. And remove the spice pots from the kitchen. Put them safe in the knife box before Stephen even thinks of taking a hammer to the wall. And the drying herbs must come down from the rafters – I forgot about them.'

'Rose. Wife. Margaret will manage. Now come. The longer we delay, the worse the crowds on the bridge will be.'

'I am ready,' she announced, even as she bent to wipe Dickon's nose upon the hem of her apron. 'Do you have our penny toll to pay at the bridge?'

'Nay. We need it not. Remember, as pilgrims, we offer our prayers at St Thomas's Chapel halfway across instead of paying the toll.'

'That's a benefit, then. But how do the toll-gatherers know we are pilgrims? Anyone could say they were just to avoid payment.'

I frowned. Rose was correct, as ever.

'Father Christian will vouch for us.'

'And who will vouch for him without his cleric's gown?'

'Fear not, Rose. They know me well enough, even in doublet and breeches. No one will challenge us, I promise you,' Christian assured her.

With which, Christian took up the wooden handle on the cart's shaft and our pilgrimage commenced as we trundled along to Cheapside's Cross, turned down Bread Street, then onto Watling Street by All Hallows Church. Along the way, a few of our early-rising neighbours wished us 'Godspeed'.

'Come, Gawain, keep close,' I told my dog.

Watling Street became Budge Row until we reached London Stone by St Swithin's Church.

'This stone marks the centre of the city,' I told Christian, a hint of pride in my voice, thinking that he, as an incomer, would not know. 'It has stood here since Brutus conceived London as the New Troy, a thousand years before the Romans trod these streets, so the history-recorders tell.' I put my hand to the lichen-dappled limestone, rubbing it for good luck where it was worn to purest white by the hands of all those who had done the same down the centuries.

'I didn't know that, Seb,' Rose said. 'Should we all touch it for luck?'

'Aye, 't'would be as well, would it not?' I lifted Dickon so he could pat the top of the stone, which stood waist-high to a man.'

'Superstitious nonsense,' Christian mumbled even as he did likewise.

Candlewick Street led onto East Cheap. Unbelievably, *The Boar's Head*, a disreputable ale-house by all accounts, was already open for business at this hour. Mayhap it never closed, for it had customers aplenty, most of them fishmongers and fishermen, to judge by the stink of rotten herring emanating from the open door. We hastened by, turning down Fish Street towards London Bridge.

Here, closer to the river, the mist was thicker, minute droplets clinging to our cloaks, hats and hair in a glistening sheen and sparkling on Gawain's ears and tail. We stopped at the toll gate beside the church of another martyred saint, Magnus.

'We are embarking upon a pilg…' I began to explain to the fellow there, the City badge displayed upon his tunic as he sat well back within his wooden niche with a brazier close at hand, giving a rosy glow of heat.

'Good day to you, John,' Christian greeted him, removing

his hat to better show his face.

'Ah, Kit! A right early visit this? We don't usually see you at this hour.'

'Indeed not. Neither would you this day except that my friends here and I are off to Canterbury, to the Holy Martyr's shrine.'

'What you! On a pilgrimage? What have you done, Kit? Swived the lord mayor's daughter, if he's got one, and must flee the city? Or is this just a ruse to avoid the toll, you tight-fisted miser?'

'We be *bona fide* pilgrims,' I began, anger swelling in my chest. But both Christian and this John were laughing.

'I wouldn't tell you if I had swived her,' Christian chuckled. 'Else the whole of London would hear of it before supper, you old slack-jaw. And, by the by, the mayor has two daughters…'

'Aye, so they would, Kit. I could have free ale for a fortnight with such a tale as that. Now, get you gone. I've a queue of proper toll-payers waiting.' With a grin, the fellow waved us through the raised bar and we were on London's famous bridge.

But if I hoped to avoid the crush of folk betwixt the shops and houses, taverns, chapel and privies, we were too late. I lifted Dickon in my arms, away from so many booted feet. It was my custom to carry him upon my shoulders but the narrow passage passed 'neath the hanging signs and jettied upper storeys and he might be struck by a dangling sign or a window flung wide without due care. The bridge was crammed, not only with humankind but with a flock of geese destined for Poultry and wayward goats escaping a young goatherd and his dog.

One goat overset a huckster with her tray of apples, sending fruit rolling every which way whilst the woman screeched and shook her fists at the goatherd. Meanwhile, the goats munched the scattered apples. Urchins also made the most of this unexpected bounty. The goatherd's dog chased an errant beast down a gap betwixt a cobbler's workshop and a pie stall just as we drew level and I was forced to restrain Gawain from joining the pursuit. Folk were laughing, enjoying the sport but, well, what can I say? We saw an unfortunate fellow squatted at the far end of the narrow way, bare backside exposed out over the river foaming below. The goat butted him squarely at the knees and, with a terrible cry, the poor man disappeared from sight, pushed off the bridge. The merriment should have ceased forthwith but it did not.

'Hush, Dickon,' I rebuked my son, who chortled as loud as any. I suppose the sight of a fellow upended with his hose about his ankles was amusing but knowing his likely fate… Of course, my son was too young to realise the consequences but I would not have him become accustomed to mocking others in their plight.

'Funny man, Papa,' he giggled, pointing towards the scene where the goat bleated, the dog barked and a single shoe was all that remained of the poor fellow.

'Nay, lad. Do not laugh. Let us away to the chapel over there. See the bright painted figure of St Thomas Becket above the door? I believe he smiles at you.' I tried to distract Dickon with higher things but I fear I failed. We all crossed ourselves. It was no auspicious beginning to our journey.

'What chance does he have in that turmoil of churning waters?' Rose asked softly so the children should not hear.

I gave no reply. Very little, by my reckoning, even if he avoided hitting one of the great stone starlings which supported the bridge, splitting the Thames into a score of separate raging torrents and, presuming he could swim, if a passing wherryman might fish him out. I made the sign of the cross again. In truth, his chances were slight indeed.

'Should've used a proper privy,' was Christian's uncharitable comment.

We reached the Chapel of St Thomas Becket in the midst of the bridge despite the goats' best efforts to the contrary. Within the door, we blessed ourselves with holy water from the stoop afore moving towards the chancel screen to make our reverence and say a prayer. Incense hung in the air, thicker than the mist outside, causing Gawain a fit of sneezing. Mayhap God's house be no place for dogs, although Gawain survives his visits to our own parish church well enough.

I was about to put a coin into the alms box, as was required: a groat but then reconsidered and dropped in a penny. Who could say how many chapels and churches, abbeys, priories and hospitals would demand a donation afore we reached Canterbury? My purse was not infinite and I thought how poorly it would look if, as we neared journey's end, I had exhausted my coin and could not pay. I argued with myself that if I were over-frugal now, I might make amends upon our return if I yet had money to spare. Aye. That would be for the best. Then I noticed Christian persuading a handful of coins through the small slot in the box, putting my offering to shame and I felt badly about it again.

As we crossed the drawbridge section towards the Southwark side, Dickon was intrigued by the gaps betwixt the boards underfoot where the river frothed and foamed like fresh-poured ale. He wanted to poke his fingers into the torrent, misjudging how far beneath us it roared and churned. I snatched him up afore he should get his little hand stuck or be trampled by hastening feet. In the nick of time, I prevented him from being run down by a fine gentleman on horseback who was utterly oblivious to a small child crouched in the midst of the way. 'Twas proving a dangerous journey and we had not yet departed the city.

More horror was to come. My son saw the severed heads on spikes at the southern end of the bridge afore I could turn him away. Foolishly, I had quite forgotten that dreadful sight would likely await those who failed to avert their eyes.

'What them, Papa?' Dickon asked, craning his neck to look up at them.

'Food for the crows is all,' I told him, shielding him from the sight in the folds of my cloak. Most of the traitors' heads were too far gone to be recognised for what they were. At least I hoped that to be the case but my son used his new-coined phrase and laughed:

'Funny man!'

Was I mistaken in bringing my children upon pilgrimage? Should I have made this journey alone, leaving my family safe in London? Nay, I decided: they must begin to learn the way of the world, that not all was love and kindness. As somewhat of a cripple child, at Dickon's tender age I had already felt the sting of cruel mockery, folk who stared and shunned me and laughed at my lameness. It was only by God's miracle that I was made straight five years before – yet another reason to make this pilgrimage, to give thanks for it.

At last, we were clear of the bridge. Although the crowds were no less, at least the street was wider but folk were still queuing to cross into the city. A fellow pushed through with a yoke slung over one shoulder from which hung a lidded basket at either end. Every passerby was in danger from the ends of his long pole. His merchandise was chickens, which squawked and clucked within the baskets, leaving a trail of feathers in his wake. Dickon made a grab for a feather floating in the air and nigh had me off balance. Christian steadied the pair of us.

'*The Tabard Inn* is farther along this street, so I've heard,' he said. 'Want an apple?' He offered each of us a fruit from a stash hidden 'neath the sheepskin in the cart, no doubt purloined during the unfortunate apple-seller's encounter with the goats.

'I thought only street urchins benefitted from such mishaps,' I said. 'Are priests not more honest than they?'

He shrugged and bit into his apple with strong white teeth.

'They're good and sweet but if you don't like the thought of eating something not paid for, that's your loss. The fruit would have either gone to waste or been eaten by someone else probably less deserving than we.'

I understood his reasoning and accepted the apple. He was correct: it was sweet and delicious and I shared it with Dickon.

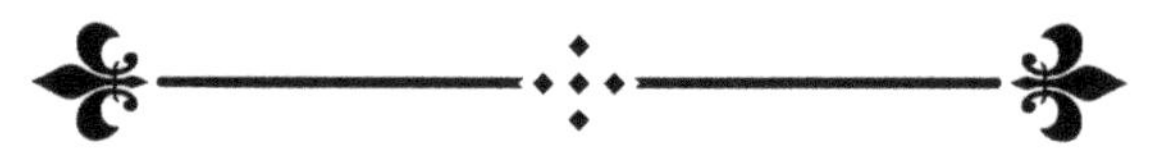

The Tabard Inn was the customary meeting place for Canterbury pilgrims and had been so for a century at least, as Master Chaucer tells us in his famous *Canterbury Tales*. And no wonder forwhy it was an impressive building with tiled roofs and tall chimneys constructed on three sides around a cobbled courtyard on the east side of the street beyond the hospital of St Thomas. The long eastern wing opposite the wide entrance appeared to provide accommodation and the upper gallery was swathed with bed linen put to air. The southern wing was taken up with stabling, ostlers tending beasts which varied from a humble donkey to a splendid gelding, ready-saddled, and all nature of mounts in between. But most folk were coming and going from the northern wing, ale cups in hand, sitting on benches outside, enjoying the sun breaking through the thinning mist, warming the day.

Free of the pressing crowds outside, I set Dickon down, for my arms were aching, but kept hold of his hand, what with horses prancing and pulling, eager to be off. We were not here to join a party of pilgrims travelling on horseback, else we would never maintain their pace. We wished to join a group with most of their number going afoot. I was considering how best to make this known when Christian let go of the cart handle and cupped his hands around his mouth.

'Anyone here walking to Canterbury?' he yelled. 'We would join you… and pay our way besides.'

At first, none seemed to hear but then a fellow lounging upon a bench beckoned us over. He looked to be of middling years, his beard showing grey. He wore travelling clothes of reasonable quality, if not the best, for his boots appeared to have done a great many miles and his leather hat – not dissimilar to Christian's – was misshapen and battered. A pilgrim staff, propped beside him, bore badges: St Peter's keys signifying a pilgrimage to Rome, a scallop shell denoting St James of Compostela and three crowns for the Three Kings' tombs in Cologne. Other badges on his staff were unknown to me but he was a well-travelled man, obviously.

He looked us up and down, considering: two men, a woman, two small children and a dog.

'Young, aren't they?' His eyes indicated Dickon and Julia, the latter sitting up in the cart, proud as any queen in her gilded chariot.

''Tis a family pilgrimage,' I said.

He raised his eyebrows.

'Can be dangerous on the road.'

'I know. 'Tis the reason we would travel with others like your good self.'

'I don't deal with infants. I don't have the time. Find another party to join.'

Rose stepped forward.

'Sir, we wouldn't expect you to have any dealings with the children. We will see to it that they don't slow you down. We want naught but safety in numbers and I see by your staff you well know this art of pilgrimage.' My wife held out her hands in supplication and smiled her most enchanting smile. 'Please?'

I swear I could see his heart succumbing to her womanly wiles, poor fellow. Most sane men were unable to resist.

'Art, you say, mistress? Aye, well, I suppose 'tis as much a sacred art dedicated to Our Lord God as carving saints and glazing church windows. But what of travelling? Are you prepared for the hardships and discomfort?'

'I have walked the length of Watling Street before, sir. I was born in Canterbury,' Rose spoke truthfully.

'With babes?

'No, but I have two strong men to aid me now.'

The fellow glanced at Christian and nodded, then looked at me. I could see grave doubts reflected there concerning my person.

'I be stronger than I appear at first sight,' I said, though why I felt the need to justify myself, I knew not. 'Besides, the sick, the blind and the lame make pilgrimage.'

'Not with babes in train.'

'Nonetheless, sir, we be Canterbury-bound, with or without your aid. We shall find another group of pilgrims to join.'

'At this tail-end of the season? Unlikely. Most folk here are travelling upon business and will be in all haste to reach their destination. Many are merchants and dealers in trade making for the ports of Sandwich or Dover. The monks there –' he nodded towards a band of holy brothers clad in brown habits of the Carmelite Order, assisting an aged cleric to mount the donkey '– are going only as far as Aylesford Priory. As for them…' A wave of his hand dismissed a pair of young men laughing as they ordered the ostlers in the saddling of two fine horses. 'As useless a pair of popinjays as I ever saw. They're going to Canterbury, if you think they'd wait for you… if you'd trust them with a clipped farthing… which I wouldn't.'

I had to blink as I looked to the youngsters forwhy it seemed I suffered double vision of a sudden. They were, mayhap, approaching a score of years in age, or thereabouts, tallish, gangling-limbed as unbroken colts, their red hair worn long and curling on the shoulders of their identical dark cloaks. When they turned, I saw two pairs of pale eyes in freckled faces, full lips and snub noses – handsome after a fashion, I suppose, or mayhap, 'twas the bloom of youth and good health upon them that made them appear so. Twins, for certain, and 'twould be a wonder if any but God Himself could tell one from the other.

'We'll walk with you, sir,' Christian said. 'If we fail to keep up with you, then leave us behind.'

I clutched Christian's sleeve.

'That would be most unwise…' I began but he shook me off. To me he said:

'But we won't fail to keep pace. Look. The brothers with the donkey are waiting, waving to this fellow who seems to think he has power over all. If they're of our party, even Dickon could keep up with slap-footed monks waddling along.'

At length, the pilgrim drank the last of his ale and bestirred himself, gathering up his scrip and taking firm hold of his staff.

'Come then. Let us away.' He beckoned to others who, likewise, rose from their stools. Some had bundles 'neath their arms or hoisted upon their backs. There was a deal of kissing and leave-taking and it was not yet apparent who would be of the party and who was here simply to bid farewell. Tears were shed, kerchiefs fluttered, kisses blown, yet, even so, some followed us out of the inn courtyard and trailed down the street, crying blessings in our wake. It seemed an excess of grief for a fortnight's absence, so perhaps some were destined for pilgrimage farther afield, to Rome or even Jerusalem, although this was not the time of year to set out upon a long sea voyage. (In truth, to my mind, setting sail at any time of year was utter madness. I could not bide a boat ride across the Thames without puking and thinking death would be a mercy unto me.)

By the time we turned eastwards onto Watling Street, otherwise called the Dover Road, our group of pilgrims devolved from the well-wishers into an odd assortment of folk. Apart from us, our self-appointed leader, four monks – one of whom was astride the donkey but seemed like to topple off at any moment – and, surprisingly, those youthful twins on their fine horses, there were five others.

One was a musician of some sort with a selection of instruments slung across his back. I smiled, thinking he would likely provide merriment for the dark evenings with his crumhorn and tabor. He looked a lively fellow, skipping along, dancing to music heard within his head, so it seemed.

Another was an elderly woman, somewhat bowed, clad in a ragged tangle of clothing, but she appeared nimble enough, though her gait rolled like that of a mariner late from the sea. She carried a basket from which peeked a whiskered face every now and then, setting Gawain to growling. Why would anyone take a mouser upon a pilgrimage? A dog could be our defender on the road but of what use be a cat to a traveller? Oh, well, each to his – or her – own, I suppose. In truth, I felt a wariness of the crone. Might she be a witch and the cat her familiar? But why would such a one go on pilgrimage? I was mistaken, no doubt, but would keep Dickon and Julia well away from her, all the same. I glanced at Rose, wondering what her opinion might be of the woman but my dear one was striding along, turning her face to the sun and looking happy at her release from household chores. To judge by her gladness, this day could be a holy day and, in some ways, I suppose it was.

Another of whom I felt a certain wariness was a gaunt, pale-featured man who wore a surly visage indeed but, since his right arm was supported in a grubby sack-cloth sling, I doubted he could do much harm. And there were two others: men of learning by the look of them, who talked together in undertones as they walked; the occasional gesture, all-encompassing, suggested they discussed some matter of great significance.

Once we left the hubbub of Southwark behind, the crone lifted her cat from its basket and spoke to it in gentle wise, though I could make out no words. Then she set the creature, sin-black as it was, upon the road and it walked before her, a bell about its neck tinkling with every movement. Well, it would catch no mice whilst wearing that device and, in truth, I feared the tinny jangling would become irritating all too soon – another cause to keep away from her.

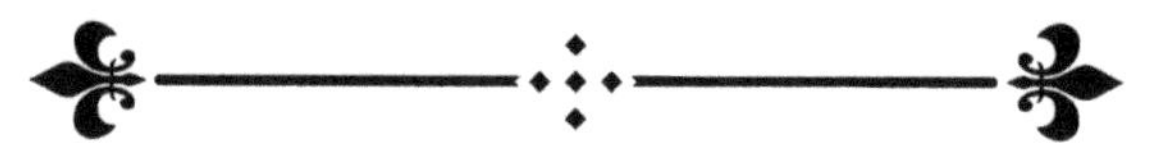

We passed through the village of Bermondsey, crossing a little stream which our knowledgeable pilgrim told us was named St Thomas' Watering. I had read of this place forwhy 'tis mentioned in Master Chaucer's *Tales* where they water their horses. Predictably, the aforementioned twins let their horses drink there, rejoining us at a trot as we kept to Watling Street.

I noted another large inn; its sign board denoted it as *The Thomas Becket*. It appeared that the martyred archbishop would be with us at every step. I took the opportunity offered by a bench beside the inn door to sit and take Dickon upon my knee. He was complaining of a 'hurty foot' and I suspected a stone in his shoe to be the cause, as proved to be the case. But a woman bustled out from the inn.

'You buying ale or not?' she demanded right rudely.

'Nay, mistress,' I said, touching my cap. 'I was but refastening my son's shoe.'

'These benches is fer customers only. That'll cost yer a ha'penny.' She held out her hand for a coin.

'We be pilgrims bound for Canterbury and I owe you naught.' I set Dickon down. 'Does your shoe feel comfortable now, lad?' I asked him, hastily rising from the seat.

He nodded, testing his foot on the ground before scampering off to join the others.

'A farthing, then,' the woman demanded of me, her hand still held out 'neath my nose. She stood so close I smelled onions on her breath.

'I told you 'nay'. I shall not pay you for two moments upon your bench. Desist, woman, I bid you.'

'Wretch! Tight-fist!' she screeched after me as I walked away. 'We got t' make our livelihood too, you scapegrace pox-monger.' I could but hope her kind was not so common in the county of Kent. I did not want an argument, name-calling nor demands for coin every time I paused along the way.

'I should've warned you of Hetty Barnaby,' the pilgrim said as I caught up with him. 'She'd charge you for farting on her premises, she would, if she could. That's why we don't stop there. It's dinner at *The Greyhound* in Deptford. The innkeeper is a decent sort, quite the opposite of that money-grabbing jade back there.'

'We shall be dining with friends in Deptford and shall follow on after, by your leave, master… I fear I did not hear your name.'

'Worthy Tanner, at your service.' He swept off his brimmed hat and bowed low as a courtier before the king, propped up by his staff. He chuckled. 'A foolish name, I know. Call me 'Tanner' as most do. And yours?'

'Oh, aye, forgive my lack of courtesy, Master Tanner...'

'Just Tanner will do.'

'Tanner, then. I be Sebastian Foxley of Paternoster Row in the City of London. You may call me 'Seb', I suppose. My goodwife be Rose; my son Richard or Dickon and my daughter there in the cart be Julia.'

'And the fellow pulling the cart? Who's he?'

'Our friend, Fath..., I mean, Chr... er, Kit. He prefers to be known as Kit,' I confirmed.

'Your friend, you say? Yet you hardly remember his name? Seems a strange sort of friendship to me.'

''Tis Kit. Most certainly.'

Chapter 4

The Langton House by Deptford Quay

DICK LANGTON was not yet home for dinner when we arrived at the master shipwright's house by Deptford Quay. 'Twas a tall, narrow building and I saw Dick kept it in good repair. Paint was fresh on the door jambs and window casements and, despite its proximity to the River Thames, no sign of mould or mildew besmirched the lime-washed plasterwork.

Dick's wife, Bella, opened the door to our knocking. She was the daughter of my one-time master, Matthew Bowen, he who had owned our house in Paternoster Row and come to an ungodly end five years since. But that horror was in the past. Even so, straightway, I thought matters must weigh heavy upon Bella's thin shoulders, or was it just that she was great with child again.

Her daughter, Janey, came rushing to greet us, embracing my knees with such fervour that I was hard put to keep from toppling over the threshold.

'Janey! Mind your manners.' Bella spoke sharply. 'This is no way to greet your godfather. Now make your courtesy as I showed you.'

The five-year-old made her wobbling courtesy, fair curls bobbing, afore grabbing my legs anew.

'Papa-Seb!' she squealed, calling me by the name she had invented in babyhood.

'God give you good day, Mistress Langton,' I said, removing my cap. 'Bella. You be well?' I stooped to Janey and untangled myself from her grasp whilst Rose and Bella greeted one another and Dickon and Julia were ushered forward in turn. 'You be much grown of late, Janey,' I told the lass and it was so. 'Do you help your mother and give eye to your little brother?'

'No, Papa-Seb,' she said right boldly. 'Mattie went to Jesus last week.'

I was taken aback by the child's plain speaking and Bella's sobs confirmed that Janey told true.

'Bella… Bella.' Rose edged past me and held the bereaved mother close, stroking her back. 'Come, let us sit awhile. May we bide in the kitchen? Let me pour you ale. Shall it help you if we pray together? Seb knows the Latin…'

I herded all three children towards the kitchen at the back of the house, following the women.

Rose guided Bella to a bench at the board and sat beside her, putting a strong arm about those juddering shoulders. Heads bowed together, they spoke in whispers.

I espied an ale jug and cups and poured measures for us all, watering the children's drinks as necessary. I knew not what to do for the best, wanting to keep the little ones quiet in this house of sadness. Being somewhat familiar with the Langtons' place, I was aware that it lacked a garden plot where children might play, the backyard being a timber store for Dick's shipbuilding trade. So I sat them on the floor mats in the entrance passage with Gawain as guardian and fetched a stool for myself.

To amuse them, I told them a foolish tale of three mice who went to sea in a pottage bowl, weathering storms and tempests, encountering mermaids and fishes which flew. (I had heard of such fish from Gabriel Widowson, once my journeyman and now a sea captain, but whether such creatures existed, I could not say for certain. He was ever a man of vivid imagination, as attested by the wondrous marginalia he used to create.) The children laughed and clapped as the mice defeated a sea serpent, beating it with a wooden spoon.

My story could have continued indefinitely but for the smell of savoury pottage, which first inspired my tale, becoming the tart odour of scorching meats and hot iron. I hastened to the kitchen, finding the women gone and the pottage burning. 'Twas not my place to attend such matters but a ruined dinner and the possibility of a house catching afire made it my business. I took the fire irons and moved the hottest embers aside in the hearth, away from the cauldron. Thinking to lift it from the heat altogether, the pot handle glowed a dull red, warning me not to touch it. Instead, I used the ladle to stir the pottage but the oatmeal stuck to the bottom. Spoiled, for sure.

The sound of soft voices betrayed Rose and Bella, outside among the great baulks of timber and lesser spars stacked high to season, the stink of tar and turpentine, the more pleasant scent of fresh-sawn wood. Rose glanced up at me from their seat on the back step.

'Bella needed the cool air,' she said. 'Are the children behaving well? Lordy! I smell burning.' She leapt to her feet.

'Fear not.' I held her arm. 'All be safe, though the pottage has caught, somewhat. Gawain be guarding the little ones in the passage, away from harm.' I lowered my voice to a whisper: 'What of Bella? She seems… unwell.'

'Weary.' That was all Rose said but her expression told more.

Dick came home then and the house was all noise: his great boots clumping along the floor boards and crushing the woven mats, his greetings loud and boisterous as he enfolded all three children in his embrace and kissed them heartily as Gawain barked his welcome. All was merry for a few minutes as Dick and I laughed together, until his eye alighted upon Bella. In most gentle wise he held her close and whispered words I could not make out. Whatever he said to her, his wife dried her face upon her apron, braced herself and forced a smile of sorts.

'Forgive me,' she said. 'What manner of hostess forgets her guests in this way? Give me but the space of five Paternosters and I shall have dinner set out upon the board. Help yourself to ale as you will. Janey, fetch a clean towel that our visitors may wash their hands. Make haste now.'

To a casual onlooker, the meal may have appeared a joyous gathering of friends but the undercurrent of sorrow could not be denied. Our laughter rang false, our exchange of news half-hearted and our jests hollow. Bella laboured valiantly but her grief sat upon her like a malevolent miasma of which she could not be free.

After we had eaten – none of us making mention of the bitter taste of burned pottage – as Rose aided Bella to clear the board and scour the pots, Dick and I took our ale out to the yard. The children came too, playing in the sawdust, which caused their faithful guardian, Gawain, to sneeze repeatedly.

'I be so sorrowful, Dick, learning of your loss. Little Mattie was a dear lad.'

'Aye. He was so.' Dick heaved a sigh. 'And his passing made no sense.'

'Can you speak of it?'

'Not much to say.' Dick hitched his hip to sit on a protruding beam. 'Before dinner, he was chuckling and playing… the next, Bella found him turning cold and stiff in his cradle where she'd lain him for his afternoon nap. Lifeless as a stone. Neither priest nor surgeon could explain it. God wills it, was their answer. But that's no answer for my Bella… or me. Now she fears the same may come to pass when the new babe is born. That God shall take that too. She's bereft, Seb, drowning in grief, fading even as I watch… In truth, I fear I'll lose her also, as you lost your Emily. What's a man to do?'

He paused, shaking his head and staring down at his gnarled hands.

'I feel helpless as a kindling stick in a storm,' he continued. 'The priest tells us prayer helps but Bella is too angry at God. I don't incline to praise Him either, not now. What sort of loving God takes an innocent child from his family like that? A heartless God, that's what. It makes it hard to believe in His mercy… to believe in a Divine plan that snatches a babe from his cradle. How can we pray to Him? How will it serve?'

'You both be deeply grieving, my friend. 'Tis not easy, I know. I, too, found it so hard to credit that God saw fit to deny two infants their mother. But… time heals. To you, that seems unlikely now but it does. You and Bella will soon have a new life to cherish.'

'To fear and fret over, you mean.' Dick sounded angry. 'And always supposing God sees fit to spare my dear Bella… if He deems her worthy of surviving her time of travail…' He kicked at a spar and the pile of wood began to slip sideways. 'Damn it all!' He leaned his weight against it and steadied the pile, bracing it with short lengths of timber. 'I must get this restacked,' he muttered, 'Before it kills someone.'

There was naught that I could think to say. Father Christian – Kit – and our companions at the Greyhound Inn across the way would have finished dinner and be upon the road once more but it seemed wrong to depart, leaving our friends in such distress. But Dick had not forgotten:

'You must go, Seb. I'm keeping you from your pilgrimage with my groaning and grouching. How are you travelling? The Long Ferry stops at the wharf here, if you signal to it. I can do that for you. The tide is turning and the boat will be passing within the hour… have you disembarked at Gravesend before dusk. It'll save you a deal of walking.'

'Nay, Dick. I thank you but a pilgrimage is intended to be arduous, else where be the point of it? Besides… you know my aversion. The Long Ferry would be as torture to me. I should rather face every cutthroat, flea-infested inn and yard of pot-holed road betwixt here and Canterbury than a single moment in a storm-tossed boat.'

'Storm-tossed? Pity's sake, Seb, the river is flatter than a duck pond today.'

'Even so…'

'Ah! Forgive me. I forgot you get sick just looking at a ship moored alongside. Poor Seb. In which case, I'll bid you fare well upon the road. Take good care of Rose and the little ones.'

'I will.'

'And Seb…' Dick unlatched the purse at his belt, took out a coin and pressed it into my hand. 'Light a candle for my Bella. Say a prayer…' He wiped his eye upon his sleeve and choked back tears.

'I would do so anyway, Dick, without this.' I looked at the gold half-noble resting in my palm. 'I will use this to purchase a vial of Holy Water and St Thomas's badge and bring them back to you, as well as paying a priest to say more efficacious prayers than mine alone.' I smiled, hoping to reassure him, relieved that he still believed in the power of prayer despite his earlier declarations of doubt.

As we departed the house of sorrows, Rose and I exchanged glances. There was no need of words: we each knew what the other was thinking concerning Bella.

From Black Heath to Shooters Hill

We met up with the rest of our band with little effort forwhy they had sat overlong at their ale after dinner at The Greyhound. Apparently, the innkeeper was 'as fine a fellow as you could wish'. No doubt his free round of ale for all pilgrims had much to do with this worthy appellation. We caught them up as they crossed Deptford Bridge over the muddy waters of the Ravensbourne River.

We came to a place called Black Heath yet it was a green enough stretch of common grazing land dotted with a few goats, geese and a small flock of sheep. Our fellow pilgrims on horseback watered their mounts at the wide pond beside a long, high wall. Ignorant, I enquired of Tanner what lay beyond the impressive barrier behind the ironwork gates with gilded spikes.

'That's the king's palace of Placentia at Greenwich, down the hill, towards the river. You never seen it?'

I shook my head.

'I have not travelled this way afore, although my goodwife has done so one time.'

'Black Heath saw the likes of Wat Tyler and, later, Jack Cade preparing their rebel bands for the assaults on London and Harry the Fifth assembled his army here before the Agincourt campaign back in '15. I should like to have seen such days but naught of the kind happens in these tedious times.'

Tanner's eyes were staring afar off, his countenance wistful. For myself, I was right glad we had peace in England nowadays. I did not relish conflict of any kind and the very thought of battle made me feel queasy.

With wide expanses of open pasture on either hand – Woolwich Common to the left, then Eltham Common to the right, as Tanner informed me – we came upon quite a commotion of banging, yelling, sawing and cursing. Eltham Palace was a scene of such industry not unlike our own house in Paternoster Row but on an incredible scale. Hearing pulleys shrieking in protest, I watched a mighty stone being raised on high by two men pacing in a tread-wheel. Both were red of face and sweating, shirts discarded and naked torsos glistening as they toiled in unison, grunting at the effort.

'Funny man, Papa.' Dickon made use of his most recent favoured phrase, pointing at the men.

'See how strong they be, lifting that great stone. Is it not a marvel, Dickon, that they have such power, like Hercules or Sampson?'

'Just mechanics,' Kit said, appearing beside us, pulling our little cart with Julia sound asleep within.

'Aye, they're building the king's new Great Hall,' Tanner added. 'Costing a fortune, no doubt.'

The surly fellow with his arm in a sling was also viewing the spectacle.

'I suppose if King Ned lives his full span of three score and ten years, he might get his money's worth. If he survives that long…' The man spat into the grass and turned away: no supporter of York he, obviously.

'Who is he?' I asked Tanner, who shrugged.

'Calls himself George Glassman, joined with me at Walsingham and tagged along ever since. That's the most words he's ever said together at one time. Come along now. If we climb to the top of Shooters Hill before dark, I'll show you a real sight to wonder at.'

'Have you read Euclid?' Kit asked me as we trudged along and the road began to incline more steeply uphill. Carrying Dickon on my shoulders, I was beginning to sweat like the fellows in the tread-wheel.

'Nay. Naught by him has crossed my desk that I can recall. Is he a poet or priest?'

'No. He was a mathematician in Ancient Greece who wrote a vast work on geometry.'

'I know of Homer who wrote the tales of Troy. He was a Greek, was he not?' I loathed to reveal my ignorance.

'He was. What about Archimedes? You must have heard of him.'

'Nay, I fear not.'

'Euclid and Archimedes understood how pulleys work. Did you know the more pulleys you have in a sequence, the greater the weight a man can lift? Ingenious, isn't it?'

'I know naught of such things, Kit,' I said, pausing to catch my breath. 'But I can tell you young Dickon becomes heavier at every step as this hill gets steeper. Is that not so, my lad?'

Dickon chuckled and clung the tighter to my aching shoulders.

'Put him in the cart with Julia and we can pull it together.'

I did as he suggested but the respite was momentary afore my shoulders were put to pulling the cart with Kit like oxen yoked to a plough.

'Did you never hear of such things at the university?' Kit asked. Quite how he had breath enough for speech, heaven knows. I was gasping like a fish stranded in Thames mud and could make him no answer. In truth, I was in no hurry to explain my education to him, or rather my lack thereof. I simply shook my head and took another pace, the child-laden cart trundling behind.

I noted the monks and their donkey turning aside from the road.

'I wonder where they be bound?' I said, determined to change the direction of our conversation.

'There's a grange in the woods a half mile along there.' Kit appeared to know everything. 'They will prefer to pass the night with fellow monks and lay brethren. A common inn is no place to observe Vespers, Matins, Lauds and Prime, is it now? I expect they'll rejoin us in the morning but they'll have this hill to climb first thing.'

'At least they will be refreshed… by a night's sleep… Phew! This be hard going, Kit,'

When the little cart suddenly lurched sideways in a pothole we had failed to avoid, nigh spilling the little ones into the road, we had to stop. I put stones behind the wheels so it would not roll back down the hill whilst Rose tended the children. Julia had awakened with a start but come to no harm, though her wailing advertised some terrible catastrophe befallen. Dickon, who had been sitting upright, toppled out, grazing his cheek on the road. He, too, howled fit to raise the Last Trump but Rose found a sweetmeat in a box and peace was restored.

'Told you not to bring children,' Tanner reminded me as we breasted the hilltop at last. He planted his staff firmly in the ground and leaned upon it. Mayhap Shooters Hill had bested him also. 'How good are your eyes?'

'Keen enough.' I mopped my brow with the sleeve of my jerkin and felt grit scraping my skin. Likely, I now had smears of dirt across my face.

'Turn around then. Look back at the way we've come. Now that's as fine a view as you'll ever see.'

I did as he suggested. Off to the west, the sun was sinking, casting golden light across the land. In the distance, it glittered on water, turning the Thames into a gilded serpent. It sparked on pinnacles and towers: the churches and fortresses of London. Highest of all was the spire of St Paul's, picked out in gleaming gold. At home, that spire seemed to touch the heavens but, at this distance, it was but a gleaming spindle point.

'That's the last you'll see of London. What a sight, eh?' Tanner commented, nudging me familiarly. 'And Englishmen built it all. Makes you proud, don't it?'

I said naught, having no desire to gainsay him but I thought otherwise. 'Twas as if God was reminding us how insignificant are even the greatest of our works compared to His vast Creation. I felt diminished by the exquisite tapestry of fields and trees, interlaced by rivers, all laid out before me, by the stars appearing in the eastern sky like jewels sprinkled upon black velvet. Humbled, not proud.

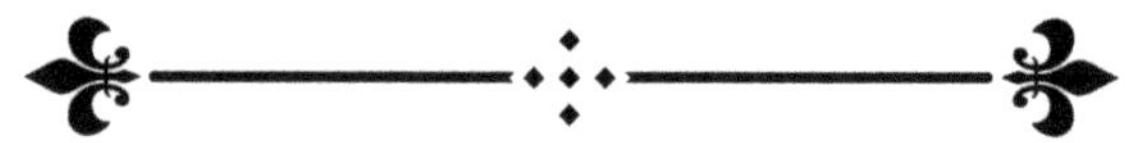

Gladly and with relief, I turned away to the less intimidating prospect of the commodious inn on the summit of Shooters Hill, neath the ill-conceived sign of some creature or other. It might be a fat goat on trestles or a snub-nosed horse of indeterminate breed. Tanner said it was an ox, but I remained unconvinced. Whoever had painted it was no artist. We pushed wide the heavy oaken door to be greeted by warmth and the cacophony of myriad voices.

Washed clean of dust, we supped together at a long refectory board. My shoulders hurt and my feet were sore but such niggling matters were easily ignored when the mutton pottage was thick and savoury with herbs and onions, the bread wholesome and the ale more than welcome.

I sat betwixt Rose and Kit. Rose chatted merrily with that old crone to her left who, all the while, fed tit-bits to her evil-eyed cat. Kit conversed with one of the learned-looking men to his right hand and they seemed deep into some earnest subject or other. Opposite, were the twins who sniggered together behind their hands, casting glances all about. Were they mocking me or another or simply sharing some privy jest?

Thus excluded, I shared pottage-soaked bread with Gawain neath the board. I had thought to acquaint myself with our fellow pilgrims once the children were settled in their bed-upon-wheels, but now I felt too weary and could not make the effort, though I determined not to fall asleep at the table.

A fist banged the board, jolting me awake.

'Hey! You deaf? I said pass the ale jug, you selfish oaf. You can't keep it all to yourself.'

'I beg pardon,' I said, blinking. Somehow, the jug had come to stand afore me. I moved it across to the twins, who waved it away, guffawing at my confusion and pointing to their neighbour, a man I did not recognise as one of our band. He scowled at me and beckoned to the jug. His surly mien and a vivid scar slicing across his cheek did naught to reassure. I passed him the ale and looked to Rose, hoping for a pleasing countenance but she was still talking with the old woman, both of them petting the cat.

I wondered how long I had slept. No more than a few moments, surely. Then I noticed the tapers had burned down somewhat, the cheap wicks guttering, in need of trimming, yet they had been lit as our supper was served. I must be more weary than I realised and was eager for my bed. Or any bed. I vowed I would get to know my fellows on the morrow.

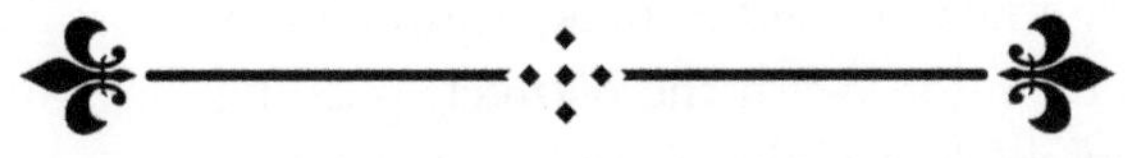

We were assigned to a communal room and I wondered how I would fare, sleeping with strangers all around me but then I had managed well enough in the clerks' dormitory at Westminster last winter. As the first to seek my bed, I had the choice of straw-stuffed palliasses and picked out the two plumpest for Rose and me. Likewise, I selected the least moth-eaten and smelly of the blankets provided and took them to the corner farthest from the door where Rose had put the cart. Dickon and Julia slept sound within, head to toe. I rearranged the sheep's fleece coverlet and tucked it close about them, for Dickon had kicked it aside, leaving his naked legs exposed to the night's chill.

I laid our straw beds side by side, close to the children, and put my scrip 'neath one to raise the end as a pillow, putting my boots and jerking under the other in likewise, as I removed them. Upon spreading the blankets, thinking Rose and I could share a double thickness, I found them too narrow – in truth, barely of sufficient width to cover one body. I had not had cause to wear my travelling cloak this day and, thus, it was yet in the cart, serving as a mattress upon which the little ones slumbered and I would not disturb them to retrieve it. I must hope that Rose beside me and other bodies sharing this place would provide warmth enough without it but the blankets were pitifully thin. A sheet of parchment had more substance to it than these bed covers. At least Gawain would see to it our feet did not get cold. He was already sprawled across both palliasses.

Some of our fellow pilgrims followed my lead, coming to devise their beds and retire. I was glad to see Rose among them but she was still talking with the old woman and leading her by the hand. Fortunately, I saw no sign of that evil-eyed cat of hers but my wife aided her in making her bed, laying the palliasse too close to ours for my peace of mind.

Having knelt beside our makeshift bed to say our Aves and Paternoster, I got 'neath the blanket, pushing Gawain to the bottom of the bed with my feet, and watched Rose removing her boots, apron and day cap, discreetly replacing this last with a night kerchief. It would not do to appear a harlot with her hair uncovered in public – and this rapidly-filling chamber was most definitely a public place – especially since pilgrimage be a holy endeavour. Her items of discarded apparel were neatly folded and joined mine in making a bolster for our heads. Smoothing down her skirts so they should not become any more creased than could be avoided, she called out to the old woman, asking God's blessing upon her through the night.

By this time, a solitary cresset lamp by the door was all our light, casting long shadows. Outside, in the refectory, other, hardier members of our fellowship were laughing and carousing. Kit must be among them, I realised, for he had not joined us, and that minstrel was banging his tabor and folk were applauding. Likely, someone was dancing or turning somersaults or some such. I hoped they would tire of it soon and not disturb us when, at last, they saw fit to come to bed.

As Rose curled close to me, I felt it imperative to make known to her my distrust of the old crone and how I wished she would not consort with her kind.

'And what "kind" do you think she is?' Rose pushed herself up on one elbow.

'Shh. Lie down, you be letting the cold in. In truth, I mislike her and as for that darkling familiar of hers…'

Rose did not comply and her tone of voice, even in a whisper, was blade-sharp.

'Her familiar? What? You believe she's a witch?'

'Who knows? But I do not trust her one iota and I do not want her near the children nor you.'

'Oh, Seb, I'm so disappointed in you. You're too quick to judge. That's not like you. Mother Thorogood is no more a witch than I am.'

'Mother Thorogood, is it? Well, a more inappropriate name be hard to conjure. Thorogood, indeed!'

'Stop it, Seb. She was a seamstress until her sight began to fail. This pilgrimage is her last hope of a miracle to save her sight that she may earn her living again. She has no family to support her.'

'But what of that mouser? Horrid black creature. Gawain hates it.'

'Gawain is a dog: he's supposed to hate cats. But why do you?'

'Feeding it at the board like a child upon her lap. Disgusting! It should be out, hunting rats and mice…'

'Which it is, right now, so you can cease your fussing, husband. It isn't going to abduct your soul in the middle of the night, if that's what you fear.' With which declaration, Rose turned her back upon me, dragging both blankets with her.

As I considered pulling the blankets back again – in childish pique, I admit – Rose turned to me once more:

'And just so you know, the cat is her eyes. If you troubled to take notice, during the day, Mother Thorogood ties a little bell upon a ribbon about its neck. The cat is trained to follow the path ahead and she follows the sound of the bell. At night, she removes the bell so it can go off and hunt. And she wasn't feeding it at the board, or whatever you thought she was doing, she was trying to undo the knot in the ribbon, which she can hardly see to do, so I helped her. So if you think all that must make her a witch, then you're an unfeeling wretch and a fool and I'm ashamed of you, husband.'

Once again, Rose turned away from me and rightly so, perhaps.

'By the way, the creature is called Lucifer, which should please you immensely,' she shot back over her shoulder afore settling, rustling straw.

Mayhap I had leapt to ill-founded conclusions about the old woman but I was perfectly correct in striving to protect my family from evil, was I not? My concerns were justified in the face of such odd behaviour. Why did she name it "Lucifer" if it was not the devil's own disciple? Aye, of course it must be. My wife was too trusting of strangers and it was within my responsibilities to warn her and keep her and the little ones safe. That was a man's duty, I confirmed to myself.

Yet the disagreement with my dear one sat heavy upon me like an ill-digested repast. I could not sleep and lay, listening in the dark to the snores, grunts and farts of my fellows. Mayhap I should awaken Rose and make my apology, then might I sleep, but I doubted she would thank me for rousing her from her much-needed slumbers – it had been a long first day trudging the road. My feet attested to that. In the morn, I would don a second pair of hose. The last thing I wanted was blisters to impede me.

I was still awake when the late-sitters came to find their beds, including Kit and the minstrel who dropped his instruments with such a clatter as to bring a deluge of curses from those disturbed. In the darkness, I could not see where my friend spread his palliasse and blanket and, in truth, I did not much care. Kit had pulled the little ones' cart without complaint, for which I was most grateful but, elsewise, he had discomfited me.

I ne'er accounted myself a man of learning exactly but reckoned I was a man of some knowledge at least. I expected this pilgrimage to be an uplifting, spiritual experience but, thus far, it seemed more as though it simply held a murky mirror to my life in which I saw, reflected, naught but mine own ignorance of the world.

Kit's astonishment that I had never heard of Euclid nor that other... Archie whatever... made me feel of so little account. He caused my wonderment at watching the work of the masons at Eltham Palace seem a childish thing and now, as if to prove his case, I suffered the childish traits of resentment and humiliation when I knew I should embrace such new learning. I was worse than a sulking scholar who had failed to take his lessons to heart and felt angered when his shortcomings were found out.

I resolved to do better on the morrow and glory in new discoveries along the way.

Chapter 5

Tuesday, the twenty-fourth day of October
Shooters Hill to Dartford via Lesnes Abbey

I WAS FROM my bed right early, although I had not slept well. The palliasse had been hard, the straw compacted into lumps and – worse – I had been bitten and the bugs must have been starving, for they had made a right good meal of me. Doing my utmost not to scratch the red weals, I went outside, tip-toeing around those yet sleeping – which was nigh everyone, even my Rose. Only Gawain bestirred himself and followed me.

In the cold morning air with the first fingers of dawn-light brightening the eastern sky, what a wondrous sight met my eyes. Every fence post, bush and clump of grass was spangled with draped cobwebs, each a wheel or necklace of diamond droplets. That humble spiders, so universally despised, could create such beauty overnight was yet another of the miracles of the Almighty's Creation. What purpose could such ethereal loveliness serve except to remind mankind of God's artist's eye and His pleasure in simple things wherein lie such marvels?

Before the street door to the inn was a horse trough, and I washed thoroughly in the ice-cold water, paying particular attention to the itchy bites to cool them whilst Gawain lapped thirstily. Then, refreshed but without a towel, I returned within to retrieve the rest of my attire, for I had stood in the street clad in only my shirt, nether clouts and hose. Fortunately, none had seen me. Shivering, I dressed in haste in the near dark of the sleeping chamber, remembering to put on my second pair of hose to protect my feet from blisters afore pulling on my boots. Wearing my jerkin, I was warmer but would have wished for my cloak also had it not been serving as the children's mattress.

I took my scrip from beneath the palliasse and went out. Likely, my companions would doubt my sanity if they knew, but I sat by the roadside and sketched a group of cobwebs along the crossbars of a field gate. They were not an easy subject, for no charcoal, chalk nor silverpoint was fine enough to depict the strands of the webs, each thinner than a hair. So I smeared the paper with charcoal dust and then drew into it with the edge of my fingernail, making fine white lines across the dark dust in the pattern of the webs. To indicate the silvery droplets, I took one of my artist's brushes – a stiff, short-bristled one of badger hair used for stippling – wetted it in the dew, and used it to flick water over my marks in the charcoal. Where ere the water splashed, a small white dot was created in the grey dust. I could not match Nature's beauty but it made a pleasing design and would serve as a reminder to me to be thankful for such wonders, freely given, to be enjoyed. I dare say little else on this journey would come without cost.

'What are you doing, Seb?' Kit saw me as I was packing away my stuff into my scrip. He, too, had come to wash in the horse trough but, unlike me, he had a towel to dry himself vigorously. 'Not drawing? I thought this pilgrimage was to be dedicated to higher matters, not to your work.'

'I saw the cobwebs and was reminded of the beauteous Creation of God. I thought to capture them, though my efforts be poor, as a prayer of thanksgiving of sorts, acknowledging God's gifts.'

'Pah! You've brought your drawing equipment with you, not to praise God but because you can't exist without it ever to hand.'

'Aye. I suppose you be correct. 'Tis second nature to me. I could no more leave it at home – where, I might add, it would risk being damaged during the building work – than I could discard my own skin. Mind, at this moment, I might gladly leave off parts of my skin forwhy I was so bitten during the night. Have you suffered likewise, Kit?'

'Nay, I think not,' he said, pulling up the sleeves of his shirt to inspect his arms. 'No. not a one. You must be of sweeter flesh than I am. Have you said your 'Angelus' yet?'

'Er, not as such. My drawing was...'

'More urgent? Naught is more urgent than prayer. And we are on pilgrimage.'

'As I said, my drawing be a prayer...'

'But not the prayer the Church requires at daybreak. Let's pray together, you and I. on your knees, Seb, and face the rising sun. Come. *In nomine Patris et Filii et Spiritus Sancti...*'

I joined Kit, kneeling in the wet grass at the roadside. I was surprised when he added to the *Paternoster* and *Ave Maria* a prayer in English, a favourite of mine which I usually recited in Latin: "I rise and pledge myself, Lord, that this day I shall do no evil deed but offer every moment as a sacrifice to you. I blush when I remember my sinfulness; I shudder when I recall how I have betrayed you. Yet you know that now I want only to serve you. Make me this day your devoted servant. *Amen. Gloria Patri et Filio et Spiritui Sancto, sicut erat in principio et nunc et simper et in saecula saeculorum. Amen.*" He made the sign of the cross, as did I.

The chorus of voices repeating the 'Amen' revealed that we had been joined by others in our dawn prayers. No doubt that be why Kit said the most suitable but less familiar prayer in English. We all got to our feet. Now was I eager to break my fast.

'Thank you, Kit,' Tanner announced, levering himself off the ground with his pilgrim's staff. 'That was a goodly prayer you made. I believe I've heard it before.'

'It was written by St Gregory of Nazianzus more than a thousand years ago. I deemed it appropriate to the occasion,' Kit said, brushing the detritus of fallen leaves from his fine hose though the dew had made wet patches upon his knees and shins.

'Folk might take you for a priest,' Tanner added, raising an eyebrow in query.

'I suppose they might,' my friend said with a shrug, which ended that conversation.

'Right, collect your belongings, everyone. We're bound for Lesnes Abbey next.'

'What, no breakfast?' the twins asked in unison and others nodded in agreement. I admit, I was likewise disappointed, for my belly felt empty.

'Later, after we've heard Low Mass at the abbey, then we can eat,' Tanner assured us.

'Gawain's hungry, Mam,' Dickon said. This being his lately accustomed way of saying what *he* wanted and, of course, the requirement to fast afore mass did not apply to children. Nor dogs.

'Let's find you an apple, shall we?' Rose said, 'I think there are still a few left of those Fa… Uncle Kit collected yesterday.' She rummaged through our baggage in the cart and found a costard apple. 'Here you are. It's somewhat bruised, I fear, but will serve. And here's one for Julia, too. That's fortunate.'

Mother Thorogood came over with her cat and Rose bent and tied the bell about its neck. They smiled and shared a jest, laughing as my wife released the creature which wound about her legs, purring in mock affection. I did not trust the beast with its luminous yellow eyes which, I swear, glared balefully at me. It liked me no more than I liked it.

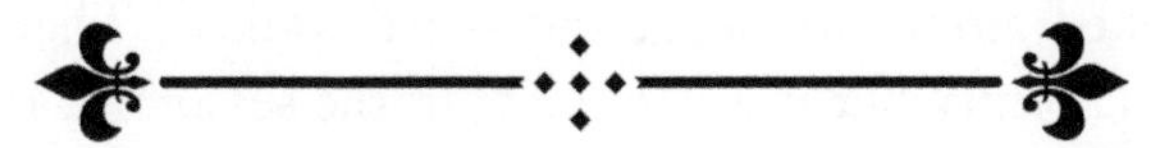

As the four Carmelite brothers joined us, puffing and wheezing from climbing Shooters Hill, having to persuade the recalcitrant donkey with its aged burden every step of the way, our pilgrim band set off for Lesnes Abbey. The twins surged ahead, their fine steeds eager for exercise, but they swiftly returned to ask of Tanner the way to the abbey.

'Along a little farther, you'll see a chapel upon your left hand

and a lane turns there, northwards, towards the woodland but have a care: it's boggy underfoot in places.'

The twins galloped off once more whilst the rest of us negotiated our way down the hill. Kit found it easier to turn the little cart around, using the shaft to hold it back from careering down the steep slope. At present, the cart was empty of toddlings, for Rose was carrying Julia as she ate her apple in a neat and ladylike manner as usual. Dickon trotted beside me, one hand in mine and the other holding Gawain's tail, his apple finished and the core discarded a quarter mile back.

'Papa, Gawain's still hungry.'

'I know and he did not have an apple as you did.'

'But it was a little, little apple, Papa.'

'We shall all break our fast in a short while.'

'When?'

'Soon. Look yonder, Dickon. What do you see?' I said, pointing, hoping to distract him.

'Trees.'

'Above the trees. Do you not see that cloud shaped like a duck?'

'Where?'

'There.' I pointed again. 'Is is not like a duck? Or a swan, maybe?'

'Nay. I'm hungry, Papa.' My son was not to be diverted from thinking about his stomach.

I looked along the hedgerow as we walked. There were brambles aplenty but it was too late in the season for there to be any blackberries remaining. Likewise, the hazel bushes had long since been stripped of nuts, either by squirrels or local folk. Rose hips and hawthorn berries glowed like rubies and we disturbed a group of thrushes feasting on them. Dickon let go of my hand and ran to pick some for himself.

'Not the rosehips,' I warned him. 'They be hairy inside and unpleasant 'til cooked. You may eat the darker, round haws if you must.'

He did so but spat them out, pulling a face, returning to the hedge to find something more palatable.

'Not that!' I cried in alarm. 'Never touch those black, shiny ones. Dickon. I know they look good but the Devil be in them. They be deadly nightshade. Touch them not. Best to leave all the berries for the birds, eh? We shall find you something better in the next village, I promise.'

As I took him by the hand and crossed the road, I noticed the minstrel, instruments clattering together at his back, go into the bushes, no doubt to relieve himself, as we all did as the necessity arose. I drew close to Rose now that the old woman was more concerned to listen out for her cat's bell tinkling and they had parted company by a little.

'Sweeting?' I began. 'I would apologise for last eve. I was overly stern with you. My anger was but grounded in keeping you safe, yet I spoke more harshly than I meant. Will you forgive me?'

'Of course. I forgave you there and then, knowing you were tired.'

'As were we all. That was no excuse for us retiring on a sour note due to my sharp words.'

'Ah, well, husband, I see you have been punished anyway.'

'Punished?'

'You've been scratching like a fleabag mongrel all the while.'

'I was bitten in the night.'

'Aye, and had you not turned your back upon me in bed…'

'I turned away?'

'Had you not done so, I was about to offer you the lavender water I brought with us for the very purpose of avoiding bugs, fleas and whatever other horrors lurk in public sleeping quarters. And see now how you suffer for the lack? Tonight, I'll sprinkle your clothes and skin for you so that you will not be punished further.'

'I shall be grateful for it,' I said, purposefully pulling my sleeve to cover the most irritating of bites on my forearm such that I could not scratch them, aware they were inflamed already.

We followed a path through a wooded valley. Ancient beech trees, grey-barked, still clung to their old leaves, refusing to part with them as misers keep hold of their coin. Neath the rustling canopy of dried bronze foliage, the narrow way squelched under our boots. We went in single file and Kit and I had to lift the cart betwixt us as its little wooden wheels became mud-caked. Dickon was not pleased at being made to walk since I could not carry him and the cart. He hated the dry bracken still standing chest-high to a man alongside the narrow path. To a child, it loomed overhead, bobbing and bowing in the rising breeze, and I understood well why he was afeared of it. Rose had Julia in her arms and told Dickon to grab hold of her apron and keep close. But this did not allay his fears.

I was much taken aback when Mother Thorogood lifted my son above the bracken and wiped away his tears. I wanted to take him from her, prepared to drop the cart if necessary, but Kit was ploughing onward. I had no choice but to follow him, looking back over my shoulder frequently to assure myself of Dickon's safety. Was it any wonder I tripped on a tree root and nigh sprawled headlong in the mud? Indeed, I should have, if not for gripping the cart otherwise held firm by Kit. I recovered my balance and paid more heed to the way ahead. I be uncertain whether my pounding heart was due to my sudden near falling or for fear of my son in the old woman's clutches.

Lesnes Abbey was a small religious house, nestling in a hollow betwixt wooded hills and the distant River Thames, this latter glimpsed occasionally as a silver ribbon through the trees.

'This abbey,' Tanner announced as he knocked loudly with his staff and we queued at the gatehouse, awaiting entrance, 'Is dedicated to St Thomas Becket, so it's fitting that we pray and pay our respects here. When mass is done, you can claim your bread and ale at the dole table just within this gate if you're too hungry to wait until we reach Erith. But I warn you about the ale here. I guarantee Becket wouldn't drink it, else he'd suffer a second martyrdom.' Some of our number laughed at his jest as the porter opened the gates to us.

I wondered if the ale truly was so bad, for I was right thirsty and would welcome a decent brewing.

The Office of Low Mass was short and, I regret to say, uninspiring. The priest mumbled so, his chin buried in his vestments, making such haste to reach the *Gloria*, I suspect he was as eager as we to eat. We pilgrims had stood mute and respectful at the back of the abbey church. No doubt, it was once a fine foundation but the wall paintings were faded and mildewed, the gold leaf dulled with layers of dust none had thought to wipe away. I saw Rose run her finger along a window ledge and frown at the dirt thereon. I had to squint at one mural for some little while afore I could make out that it depicted St Thomas Becket's martyrdom. He being the abbey's patron saint, this image at least might be expected to be in good order. Yet the paint was flaking so badly, parts were impossible to discern and only the gold of his halo suggested where the martyr's face used to be. The vermilion blood had turned black long since, as is sometimes the way with that contrary pigment if 'tis neighboured with white lead, and I suspected this was the case here.

The abbey ought to employ a decent artist to repaint the whole image – if not the entire church – one with a good understanding of his craft and of pigments, which to employ where and knowing those intolerant of each other that must not lie together. Whoever painted this was ignorant indeed but, mayhap, it was done long ago, afore such matters were properly realised. However, looking closer and wiping away centuries of grime with my sleeve, I discovered the dreary bluish pigment was, in truth, the priceless lapis lazuli! How could the brethren here so neglect such treasures? What an insult to God, to the Holy Martyr Becket and to the patron who had paid for the image!

'Seb! Are you coming?' Rose pulled my arm. 'You're not here to assess their murals, are you? Let's put our offering in the alms box, light a candle and collect our dole. The children are impatient to break their fast and so am I.'

'Such sacrilege to let a holy image moulder like that. I wonder a thunderbolt has not struck this place down forwhy they would deserve it and it might serve to rouse them from their sluggard ways.'

Rose laughed.

'Oh, Seb, you attend their church for less than one hour, examine one mural and all but condemn the house to hell's mouth for their shortcomings. Mind, I agree that their housewifery skills are lacking indeed. There are more cobwebs in here than were on the hedgerows earlier and the dust lies that thick…' She used her fingers to demonstrate the depth of dirt.

Out in the courtyard, we both washed our grubby hands in a water conduit and the children's also afore joining the line to take our dole. I hoped Tanner's opinion of the ale was in error and that it would be drinkable at least. I found it to be thin and upon the point of turning sour but I had tasted worse. The bread compensated for the poor ale, being fresh, still warm from the oven and delicious, likely made from grain recently harvested. The young brother who set the tray of small loaves upon the dole table bade us take one each but it took not the sharpest wit to see there were more loaves than pilgrims but insufficient for two each.

Rose and I took four and retired to a corner of the yard to eat them. Rose broke one in half for Dickon and Julia to share and she and I bit into our bread with relish but I saw my son eyeing the fourth loaf as it lay on his mother's apron, stuffing his bread into his mouth, the sooner to eat the next.

I was about to deplore such a lack of good manners when, upon an instant, the loaf was gone and Gawain hastened away to skulk 'neath a wooden stairway, his prize clenched betwixt his jaws. In two swallows, the bread was devoured and the dog regarded me warily, awaiting reprimand. The canine thief knew full well his error. Realising the poor beast must be as hungry as we were, I said naught. Instead, I took from my scrip *The Guide for Pilgrims*, intending to learn what we should expect at this next place, Erith, or Eareth, as it was written in the book. "A busy village where pilgrims from the Eastern Shires may take the ferry to cross the River Thames to join the way to Canterbury. 'The Half Moon Inn' provides hospitality at a fair price or else 'The Lamb and Flag'. The village has a licence for a Tuesday market, a water mill and a hythe."

As I sat reading, an argument ensued among the pilgrims, betwixt the surly fellow with his arm in a sling – whose name was George Glassman as I recalled – and the twins, whose names I had yet to discover. They were arguing over the last two loaves upon the tray. Tempers were rising and, likewise, the wind, which sent dry leaves skittering and whirling in circles about the courtyard. Old Symkyn had foretold that the weather would be breezy during our journey and, as usual, it appeared he was correct.

Tanner pulled Glassmen away from the twins afore matters grew overheated, reminding all three that they were pilgrims and should avoid conflict.

'Quarrelling is unseemly and an insult to the Almighty. Now behave yourselves as befits pilgrims or go home. You're not fit to bide with our party if you can't be courteous, each to the other. Understand?'

Glassman wrenched his cloak from Tanner's grasp, turning away, but the twins now insisted to Tanner that they had the right of it: the loaves were their due dole portion.

Tanner merely gave the pair a clip round the ear each, as if they were disobliging scholars, and ordered them to fetch their horses. Whether they wished to continue the journey with us or go their own way, he cared not, so he told them. Their mutinous scowling faces were mirrored images but gave no indication of what their decision might be, only told of grave displeasure. Therefore, as we left the abbey, turning eastwards on the road, I was surprised when the two did likewise rather than riding in the opposite direction.

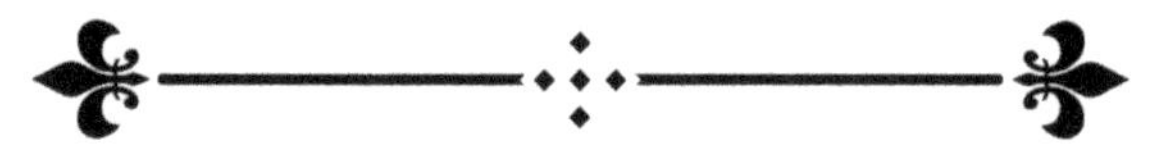

With little Dickon now perched upon my shoulders, I joined Kit. He pulled the cart in which Julia rode, sitting like a noble lady, proud as the Queen of England herself, gazing about at her humble subjects.

'Kit,' I began, 'I think I should set matters straight betwixt us. You seem of the opinion that I must have studied at the Versity of Cambridge or Oxford or else in some other land. I did not. Even a song school, like St Paul's, refused to have me.'

'Really? With your voice? Why ever would they not pluck you from your family at the first opportunity?'

'That be another story, Kit. For the present, I will tell you my father – a stationer – taught me to read and write in both English and Latin. At fourteen years, he apprenticed me to Master Richard Collop who had me learn French as well as all the secrets of my craft. I read every book that he gave me to copy.' I adjusted Dickon on my shoulders to a more comfortable position.

'Some scribes,' I continued, 'And my brother Jude be among them, can copy an entire text without actually reading a single word. Their eyes observe the exemplar and their hand makes marks with the pen accordingly. The words ne'er touch their mind, nor heart nor soul. But I absorb every word of a text. Jude says it makes me a slower copyist but I do not think that be so. What I be attempting to tell you, Kit, is that my education be but rudimentary. I know not of Euclid and some others, which surprised you yesterday. I-I felt belittled, shown in my ignorance and...'

'I'm sorry, Seb. I didn't intend to discomfit you. In truth, hearing how you have come by your knowledge, I would be proud indeed, if I were you. Now, take a-hold of this handle, will you? I need to…'

Kit disappeared behind an elm tree at the roadside and I continued on, carrying my son and pulling the cart. Rose hastened to assist me.

'Is Erith much farther, do you suppose?' she asked as we pulled together along the rutted way like yoked oxen. 'Julia will need her tail-clout changed.'

'Not far, I think. I espy smoke through the trees there.'

'Aye, the market's round the next corner,' a stranger said, pushing by with a willow basket on his head. 'If you want parsnips and turnips, come see me. Best in Kent are my wares.'

'Thank you,' Rose called out as the fellow hurried on. Not that we would be buying worts for the pot, not to lug all the way to Canterbury but, maybe, upon our homeward journey, we would purchase "the best in Kent", if indeed they were.

Erith was bustling and noisy. The market was spread in haphazard wise, a motley assortment of stalls lining the main street and spilling down byways and alleyways. A potter sold his wares beside a cheesemonger and a cobbler shared a bench with a poulterer. We sought out a pie-seller and purchased three mutton pasties and three apple turnovers. Kit consumed one of each whilst Rose and I shared ours with the children.

Rose found a secluded corner to change Julia's wet clout and, having all partaken of a jug of fresh spring water from a water-seller's tun, we were satisfied and ready to follow Tanner upon the next leg of our journey along Watling Street.

For a while, the way was level, rising but a little above the wide stretch of marshes which led out to the Thames. We crossed bridges and fords over little rivers all wending their circuitous paths across the reedbeds like numerous silvery serpents to join the great river in the distance. Marsh birds called, wild ducks paddled and I pointed out to Dickon a grey heron fishing in a pool, patient as a saint's statue. We all got wet feet at the ford across the River Cray, apparently deeper than Tanner said was usual. But after that, the road climbed gradually towards Dartford although, with such a name as that, I expected our next destination would again be low-lying. I never knew Kent was a shire of so many hills.

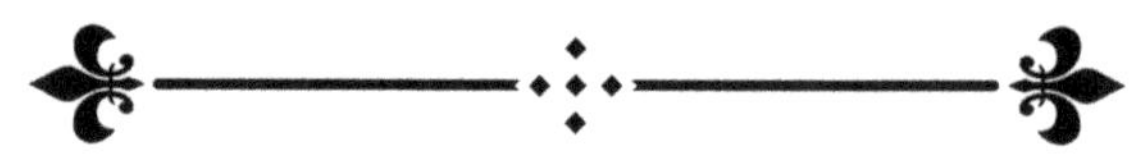

We breasted a high point and there, below us, lay Dartford. Halfway down the steep hill, upon the left hand, stood the grey stone buildings of the priory and in the valley below rose a square church tower beside another river. Like the Cray, this disappeared into the marshes, its course untraceable among the sedges, rushes and occasional stunted, salt-blasted tree.

Once within the gate of Dartford Priory, the difference here in comparison to Lesnes Abbey was obvious. No skittering leaves, no dirt nor cobwebs. Was this because it was a house of women, I wondered? A black-clad woman of middling years hastened towards us, smiling, her hands outstretched in welcome.

'May the Blessed Virgin's grace be upon you all. Come this way to the guesthouse. You are in good time for dinner. I am Sister Beatrice Eland, one-time prioress here and now having the honour of being the guest-mistress and cellaress. If you are in need, let me know.'

Sister Beatrice led us to a cavernous building but instead of entering the great double doors, she went up the stone steps outside.

'That is the storehouse below,' she explained, 'The guests' refectory and lodgings are up here. I'll show you where you may leave your belongings and wash away the grime of travel, then dinner will be served.' She turned to Rose and Mother Thorogood particularly. 'Have you come from London? Do you know it well? Prioress Anne Barn and I are London born and bred and ever crave news of it.'

'Aye, Sister, my husband and I have a house in Paternoster Row by the cathedral,' Rose said.

'Then shall you dine with the prioress and me and tell us everything. Men may not, unless they are of the cloth, of course, but women pilgrims are rare…'

'I must see to the children…' Rose began.

'Bring them too, mistress. Children are an even rarer joy.'

Rose turned to me, her eyebrows raised in silent query.

'Go,' I said. ''Tis an honour indeed to dine with the prioress.'

Sister Beatrice smiled broadly as Rose accepted the invitation in courteous wise before we went to the laver bowls to wash. I saw to it that Dickon had a thorough wash with the warm water, fragrant with lavender, despite his wriggling and protests as I scrubbed his neck and behind his ears.

'Too rough, Papa,' he complained, doing his utmost to fend off my ministrations. 'Gawain hates washing.'

'I shall not have you shame the name of Foxley in this spotless house, Dickon. Clean you will be, like it or not. And do not speak unless you are spoken to and remember your manners, as we have taught you.'

Meanwhile, Rose prepared Julia, who made not the least fuss, afore attending to her own ablutions most assiduously. She tidied her hair and donned a clean cap, as well as changing her apron.

'How do I look?' she asked me, smoothing out the creases where her apron had been folded in our baggage pack.

'You are a credit to me as ever. Now go. Do not keep the prioress waiting. And send Dickon back here if he fails to behave as he ought.'

'I'm sure he'll be good, won't you, my little man?'

'Aye, Mam. I'll be sooo good,' my son assured her.

Mm. I had heard that upon other occasions and knew full well the lad's short memory concerning such reassurances. Likely, they would be forgotten upon a count of five but there was naught I could do about it once he was out of sight.

The rest of us – menfolk all, including the four brethren – were served in the guests' refectory. At first, after the aged brother had said grace, the presence of the monks at the long communal board had a restraining influence. Speech was quietly made, the subject matter reserved and all courtesies observed. But everyone was hungry and wine was served along with the bacon pottage, white bread and roasted marsh birds: curlews and bitterns. We were informed by the lay sisters who brought the birds in upon a pewter charger that we might serve ourselves. The sight of glistening, succulent meats made certain persons forgetful of their manners and etiquette was discarded along with the bird bones.

The youthful twins were amongst the worst offenders.

'Look at those two… the twins, I mean: like swine at a trough,' I whispered to Kit beside me upon the bench. 'Did their mother not teach them any better?'

'They haven't had a mother,' Kit said betwixt spoonfuls of pottage, 'Not for many years, at least. Though I know that's no excuse for ripping meat off the bone with their teeth, as Troilus is doing.'

'Troilus?' I repeated the outlandish name.

'Well, it could be Tristan: the Warenne boys. I can't tell the pair apart. Can you?' Kit turned his attentions to untache a curlew, removing the flesh from the bones as was required of a lord's carver. I had seen it done properly at that marvellous feast at the Duke of Gloucester's house in Bishopsgate a few months before and it seemed Kit was no stranger to this art.

'I did not know their names 'til now, nor their situation.' I took a bird from the platter and attempted to copy what my friend was doing – with rather less elegance and dexterity, I have to admit, grease running over my hand and dripping on the spotless cloth. I hastily arranged my napkin to hide the blot. 'But I can tell you that one twin has a narrow white line through his left eyebrow. A scar, I suppose. But which one that be, I know not.' I glanced up at the young men, greedily dipping meat into the honey and ginger sauce which had been provided as an accompaniment. 'There. The one licking sauce from his fingers has the scar. Do you see it?'

'Hardly. I know you have sharp eyes, Seb, but I would never have noticed it if you hadn't drawn my attention to it. I think that's Tristan. Maybe.'

'Where did you learn to untache a curlew?' I asked him, changing the subject as I, too, dipped a piece of succulent bird into the sauce. I learned the correct term from an instruction book I had once copied but knew little of the actual procedure. The book had not revealed those secrets.

'My father had ideas that I should become an esquire to some nobleman or other one day. My mother would have it otherwise… that I would be a priest. You know who won that argument but I learned to take both parts: esquire and priest, to please both my parents, whosoever was present or in the ascendant at the time. There are days when I wish my father had been the victor but my mother outlived him, so it was an unfair contest and the priesthood won out.'

'But your heart is not in your vocation?' I suggested, feeding Gawain 'neath the board with a piece of flesh without sauce. His hot, wet tongue licked my fingers, eager for more.

'I do what's required and do it well enough. Baptising, burying and reminding my flock of their erring ways upon every Lord's Day.' Kit shrugged and reached for the wine jug. It was nigh empty and I declined when he offered it to me, watching as he poured the last of it into his cup. It proved little enough – a trickle and no more. I felt it was too early in the day to be partaking of wine, else I should be befuddled by afternoon, and drank the ale instead, it being my preference in any case.

Chapter 6

Tuesday later
Dartford

WE WERE walking down the steep way into Dartford village. Tanner said we would pass the night at The Bull Inn at the foot of the hill and I think we were all glad not to have to go any farther, what with having eaten so rich a dinner. Most looked right ready for a nap.

'I assure you, Seb, Dickon was an angel,' Rose said. 'He behaved perfectly, even when the prioress insisted on feeding both him and Julia with titbits from her own platter, as if they were her pet lapdogs – of which she has three – treating them all alike.'

'Like lapdogs!' I echoed.

'Aye, but she was most kindly and wanted to hear all about your work. She was impressed to learn of your royal commissions… even mentioned that the priory is in need of a new Gospel Book. I think there might be the possibility of another commission for you. She said she would speak with you upon our return journey… if she remembers.'

'Well, what a clever wife have I? When our new workshop be set up, we shall have room enough to take on more projects of that kind.'

'And new scribes, maybe?' Rose suggested. 'You work too hard as it is.'

I laughed.

'I doubt that Adam sees it thus. He regards me as too

wayward, ever busying myself with matters other than our work. At least he has changed his mind concerning a return to Norfolk; God be praised. Young Hugh will be qualified in a few weeks and may serve as a full-time journeyman. But… aye, mayhap another journeyman would aid us all. I shall think upon it, Rose. Well done, though, for raising the subject with the prioress, even if naught comes of it.'

She smiled and squeezed my arm.

'Perhaps, in Canterbury, I can persuade the archbishop to order a new Bible from you… and an antiphon and a reredos and a mural or two…'

'Have a care, lass. Would you work my fingers to the bone afore I achieve my third decade?'

We entered The Bull, laughing together, glad to be out of the wind which pulled at our clothes and blew my hair in my eyes. Rose's apron was whipped about her legs, nigh tripping her as she carried a sleeping Julia within. In my embrace, Dickon was out of humour and tired, too, telling me how Gawain so hated the wind.

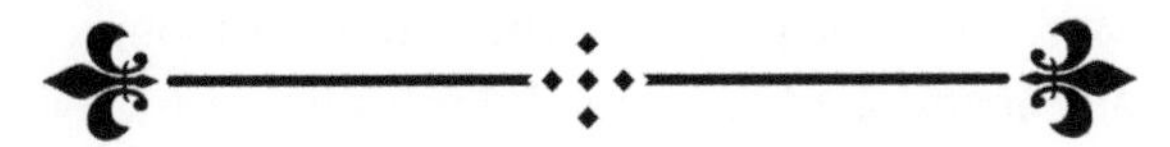

The Bull Inn appeared to be a clean enough place with room aplenty for our pilgrim band. However, we were not the only party seeking accommodation and I expected the dormitory would be right crowded this night. A group of well-dressed merchants were at meat when we entered the high-ceilinged refectory. They ignored us, discussing business in voices so loud any might learn of it.

A florid-faced man with a sizable belly and a turban-style hat of green velvet was waving his arms about, boasting of the profits he would make in London on the imported Burgundy wine he was shipping up the Thames from the port of Sandwich. One of his fellows, equally loud and gaudily clad in crimson, was insisting his profits on glass from Bohemia would be by far the greater. The other two members of their group, drab by comparison in plunket and grey wool, appeared to be doing their best as peacemakers, attempting to calm the other two who might come to blows at any moment in their heated – and somewhat drunken – exchange.

We avoided them as Tanner introduced another group of pilgrims who intended to join us, having come from Essex, crossing the Thames by means of the Erith ferry that morn. Two fellows, one of middling years, the other a lanky youngster, carried a third man on a makeshift litter constructed of two poles lashed to a bed of intertwined willow withies and a woven rush mat. I could not see what ailed the invalid forwhy he was covered with moth-eaten blankets but, whatever his malady, it did not stop his mouth. Indeed, he had strength enough to constantly berate his litter-bearers, complaining of their mishandling and lack of consideration in words so foul no pilgrim should ere give utterance to the like. Yet the pair bore his tirade in patient silence. I admired their steadfast attendance upon the fellow. Whatever his affliction, I could not have withstood his vile tongue without some response. Likely, I should have abandoned the wretch long since, which does but prove those two be more worthy Christian souls than I.

Rose put Dickon and Julia in the cart in one corner of the communal dormitory to have a nap and said she would be glad to take off her boots for an hour. Mother Thorogood was already nodding upon a bench, her cat curled in her lap, looking all innocent this once.

I turned to Kit – as I be getting used to calling him – and asked if he had a mind to explore the village.

'I noted a stone church down by the river,' I said. 'Tanner is planning to visit it on the morrow for Low Mass, for it has a chapel dedicated to St Thomas Becket but we shall be hastening on after and I would prefer to spend a little more time there. Will you come with me?'

Kit agreed and we put on our cloaks, for the wind was

considerable now and chill, cutting through my jerkin and shirt as if they were of no more substance than cobwebs. Then, with Gawain trotting beside me, we crossed the marketplace and made towards the church.

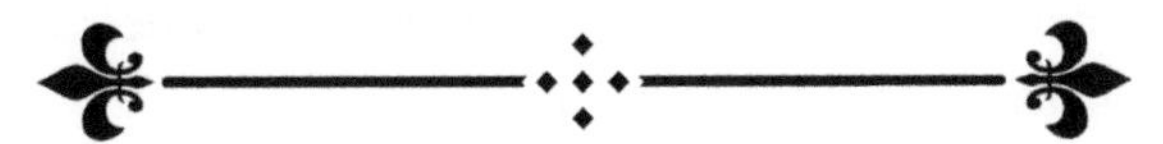

The church of the Holy Trinity had a sturdy square tower and a chequered design of dark flint and pale stone upon its crenellated walls. Aged, indeed. Tanner had mentioned something about King Harry stopping here, having a Mass of Thanksgiving said for his triumph at Agincourt and, once more, resting the night here as a coffined corpse. Mayhap it was true forwhy the church stood upon Watling Street and would have been convenient.

The River Darent flowed hard by with both a stone bridge and a ford. The road beyond then climbed a hill to the east even steeper than the one we had descended earlier by the priory.

The wind whipped at the water, creating wavelets that sparkled silver in the fleeting moments of sunshine betwixt scudding clouds. We stood on the bank, watching as a fellow leaned from his little boat to pull up a fish trap, hoping to have caught something. He spilt shiny, flapping fish into a basket afore replacing the trap.

'You have a goodly catch?' I asked him.

'Could be better,' he grumbled. 'Fish laying low, I reckon. Don't like this wind churning the river. Nor do I. It'll be a rare storm tonight, mark my words, so tie your thatch down and say your prayers.'

'Good fortune with the fishing,' Kit said as we waved our farewell, adding, 'What a miserable old Jonah. This weather is bracing… marvellous for raising the spirits.' My friend took a deep breath of the cold air and exhaled noisily. 'Marvellous,' he repeated. 'Come on, Seb, race you to the church door.'

Kit sprinted along the street and Gawain chased after him,

ears and tail flying. He knew full well I was never a runner, having been lame until God granted me a miracle a few years back, wrenching my left hip and shoulder into their rightful places after so long amiss. Although I walked well enough these days, in any race, a man like Kit could beat me, unless his knees be tied together. I caught them up in the porch.

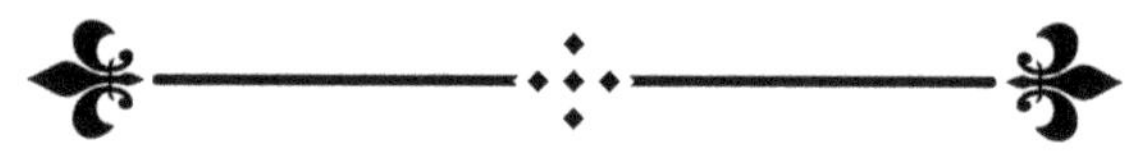

Out of the buffeting wind, all was silent at first until I heard the murmur of voices carried on a draught of incense-laden air. Chantry priests at prayer, mayhap? We entered the nave and blessed ourselves with holy water from the stoop by the west door. I went up to the arch in the rood screen, removed my cap and bent the knee, making my reverence to the gilded cross, glimpsed at the east end of the chancel. Kit did likewise, murmuring a Latin prayer. I saw that the screen looked new made, or freshly painted, at least.

I could hear the voices to our left hand in a side chapel off the north aisle.

'I recognise those, I think,' Kit said. 'That must be the Becket Chapel, for that's Tanner, I'm certain.'

I agreed but whereas Kit went to join our fellow pilgrims, I made for the south aisle and the Chapel of Our Lady and such a joyous sight greeted me there. Atop a spindly and precarious tower of wooden scaffolding poles stood a limner, painting a huge mural which covered the width of the wall behind the altar. I was about to hail him but, at that moment, he reached up high to apply pigment to the likeness of a city wall in the distance and I feared startling and oversetting him if I did. Thus, I should wait until he stepped back to assess his work and, in the meantime, make my own deliberations as to its merits.

''Tis well done, good master,' I said as he paused and washed out his brush. 'St George be drawn wondrous well and his horse a fine beast to the life. You have observed them accurately indeed.'

'You know about such things?' he answered, cracking a fresh egg, breaking the skin of the yolk and mixing pigment into it without glancing in my direction.

I was unsure of his tone, whether enquiring or sarcastic.

'Aye. I be a member of the Limners' and Painters' Company of London.' This was true since August last, when I was forced to pay them my fee to avoid any future court cases being brought against me for painting coats-of-arms, shop signs and the like. I begrudged them every farthing.

'Ever done a mural like this?' he asked, returning to his work.

'I've repainted a St Christopher and redone a much-faded Day of Judgement at a church in Norfolk but never one entirely new like this.'

'What do you think of my dragon, eh? Difficult to paint it against the light from that window but I think it'll afright the congregation well enough.'

'It most surely will. Those teeth… the claws… the serpent-like scales… Most impressive.'

'And what of George? I based his likeness on Sir John Hornley – without the wrinkles and the bent back, of course – so what think you?'

'I do not know Sir John.'

'He was our priest here 'til he died two… no, three years ago now. Father John was a good man; he bequeathed money for this work in his will and for the rood screen. I thought he'd appreciate having his likeness as a man in his prime up here forever, or for as long as the pigments last, at least.'

'No doubt but he would. What pigment did you employ for the red cross upon the knight's surcoat?' Mentally, I crossed my fingers, hoping he would not say vermilion.

'Red lead on white lead with a crimson wash overlaying. Why? Do you think I'm fool enough to put vermilion with white lead, knowing it'll turn black within the year?'

'Er, no, of course not but I cannot tell from this distance, in this angle of slanting light. Others have made that mistake in the past.'

'Have you?'

'Certainly not. Never. My master taught me better than that.'

'Glad to hear it. You want to share a jug of ale at The Sun Tavern across the way when I'm done here? The light'll be fading all too soon and Sir John will have to wait until tomorrow to slay his dragon. The name's Miles. Just ask for me in the tavern. I'll be there 'til they lock up.'

'Sebastian Foxley. They call me Seb. I cannot promise to join you in the tavern forwhy I be with my family and a friend on pilgrimage to Canterbury but I wish you well with your mural. I shall call by upon our return to see how it progresses.'

'Safe journey to Canterbury then, Seb. God speed.'

'I thank you, Miles, and may God bless you and your work.'

'Seb! Where are you?' Kit's voice rang out.

'Here,' I called. 'My friend,' I told Miles. 'Come, look at this wonder, Kit.' I beckoned him over.

Kit came hurrying.

'We've been waiting for you to join us in the Becket Chapel, Seb. What are you doing?'

'Watching a skilled craftsman at his work.'

'Work? Oh, I might've guessed: a man painting. We're meant to be on pilgrimage, not inspecting the building. Forget your craft this once.'

'But look at it, Kit. Is it not a marvel of the limner's art?'

My friend glanced up momentarily, shrugged his shoulders and grunted.

'Mm. I suppose so. Now come along; the priest is waiting to bestow his blessing on our journey and endeavours.'

'You'd better go, my friend,' Miles called from his high perch. 'Father Gurnes doesn't exactly have the patience of a saint as Father Hornley did, God rest him. Maybe I'll see you later in the tavern, Seb, eh?'

'Maybe.' But, in truth, I doubted it. Neither Kit nor my Rose would approve of me sloping off to drink with my new acquaintance.

The Bull Inn

As I expected should be the case, the refectory was crowded at suppertime. The Warenne twins – as I now knew them – were vociferous as usual; the merchants were louder than ever, still arguing, and the newcomer upon his litter continued to berate those who cared for him at the top of his voice. Naught amiss with his lungs, whatever else ailed the old curmudgeon. And then, atop the din, our so-called musician added his off-key caterwauling, banging his tabor. Mayhap I would visit the Sun Tavern after we had eaten, for I knew not how long I could withstand this flood of noise.

As if the guests did not make racket enough, the wind was strengthening outside, rattling doors and shutters, creaking under the roof tiles and howling down the chimney, sending smoke the wrong way, out into the room to make eyes water and set the company coughing.

When the meal was served – pottage, bread and small ale being our pilgrim's fare – another argument arose. The florid merchant was shouting that he was no pilgrim and expected a decent supper of roasted meats, not this 'pig's swill'. Aye, that was how he called it, yet it was wholesome pottage and the bread fresh. The innkeeper's wife answered him back as she served him, telling him he could either be content with pottage, like everyone else, or go hungry and she didn't much care which. Then he slapped her face. She screeched at him and hit him with the now-empty tray – a solid piece of oak board.

Chaos erupted as others joined the affray on the far side of the refectory whilst we kept our heads down. It would not do to involve ourselves in the brawl, being pilgrims upon our godly errand; rather, we gave the food our fullest attention.

Except for the Warenne twins.

I might have supposed youth would find the commotion

impossible to resist, pilgrims or not. They leapt from the bench opposite and, with joyous countenances, jumped over stools and other men's bags of belongings to join the fight. In their absence, the musician took their place at the board and inspected their half-empty pottage bowls, giving one a stir afore changing his mind and leaving the seat. George Glassman, with his arm yet in a sling, sat and poured himself ale one-handed.

'How fares your arm, Master Glassman?' I enquired in friendly wise. I had not spoken with him previously, for he seemed disinclined even to so much as exchange a greeting. As proved the case now forwhy my few words drove him away without his troubling to reply. I shrugged off his rudeness but did not repeat my error when another took his place: one of the men of learning. He also helped himself to ale and a heel of bread afore he also went to observe the fight more nearly.

However, in the crush of wiser folk now moving to our side of the room to avoid the conflict, benches and bowls being hard to come by, the two who cared for the miserable invalid, the man of middle years and his lanky young companion, took the opportunity to sup in comfort. Being late-comers to the meal, they took up the abandoned spoons, put more pottage from the shared pot into the twins' bowls and began to eat. I wondered what the fiery young pair would have to say concerning their lost supper but, if they preferred fighting to eating, then so be it.

The innkeeper himself quelled the riot, cuffing ears and banging heads together until the last combatants thought better of continuing with their disorderly behaviour. It was impossible to gainsay the innkeeper who came as close as any man I had ever seen to matching the mighty King Edward in height, girth and, mayhap, surpassing his Grace in his breadth at the shoulders. Only the most foolhardy would dare challenge such a one as he.

Peace returned, briefly, if we paid no heed to the wind battering the building, screaming like a demon in defiance when it was denied entry. The fisherman was correct in predicting a storm this night. My dear friend, Old Symkyn, had rightly foretold that our journey might be breezy but I did not think he meant we would encounter this roaring gale.

Of a sudden, the man across the board from me began gasping, struggling to draw breath. His eyes bulged with fear as air was withheld from his lungs. His features contorted in desperation, yet his hands hung slack, neither grasping at his throat nor clutching his belly. What strange ailment was this?

The younger man beside him cried out to us to aid his father. The bench overturned as both the afflicted and his son went on their knees in the struggle for life. The elder man collapsed, foaming at the mouth as the younger tried to help him, pleading with him to breathe. His suffering was done in silence but for a faint clicking in his throat, as if he would breathe if only he could recall how it was done.

Kit and I rushed to his side but in the time it had taken us to come around the long table, the man ceased his gasping and lay still.

'No, no, Father!' the youngster sobbed. 'You can't die. Not now. Father! Speak to me.'

'He cannot, lad,' I said softly, holding him. 'Your father be gone.'

'But he can't be. We have to carry Grandfather to Canterbury. How can I do that alone?'

I had no answer to that as Tanner came to us, taking charge of the distraught lad. Beside me, Kit was kneeling to tend the deceased, closing the man's clouding eyes for the last time.

'What's your father's name?' he asked the trembling lad.

'Alfred… Alfred Denny… like me… like Grandfather. We're all Alfred…'

Even as I watched, my friend subtly transformed from Pilgrim Kit to Father Christian and began reciting the Last Rites and the Office for the Dead, calling upon Our Lord Jesu to accept the soul of our brother, Alfred, lately a pilgrim in His Holy Name.

'I knew there was more to you than you were telling,' Tanner said. He stood behind Kit, having led the lad aside and handed him into the care of Rose and Mother Thorogood. Kit was still murmuring Latin and making the sign of the cross over the cooling body. 'He's a priest, isn't he?' Tanner asked me.

'Aye, and a good one. And when his work be done, we must summon the constable, if Dartford has one?'

'Why? The fellow suffered an apoplectic seizure. I saw it myself. No need to trouble the law for that.'

'As with my friend, Kit: I be another who has not entirely revealed himself unto you, Tanner. Back in London, I assist the coroner and the city bailiff in cases of unexpected death, as has occurred here.'

'But apoplexy's always unexpected.'

'This man did not die of so natural a cause. I believe he was poisoned.' I spoke upon a sigh. Thaddeus was correct: trouble did follow me and being upon pilgrimage did not prove sufficient to avoid it.

'Poisoned? That's ridiculous, Foxley, and don't you dare spread such malicious rumours among the others.'

'But this man was murdered as surely as if a blade was plunged in his guts.'

'I see no such injury,' Tanner persisted.

'Of course you do not, forwhy he was poisoned. 'Tis an unlawful killing all the same. This man and his family deserve justice.' I became right heated in this exchange.

Tanner grabbed the front of my jerkin, pulling me close.

'Listen to me, Foxley. I don't care who or what you are in London, here, you'll do as I say, elsewise you're banished from our fellowship. He died of an apoplexy. Understand?'

'But 'tis not right nor lawful…' I protested.

'Do you understand me?' Tanner repeated, his voice a hiss, his eye hard as granite.

I nodded reluctantly. In truth, even in London, I was but Thaddeus's unofficial assistant and here, in Dartford, I held no position nor authority whatsoever. It was not my place to investigate the death of a man I had never seen afore this afternoon and whose name I did not know 'til after he was dead.

Even so, the fact that a Christian had been denied the full and rightful term of his life by another's hand did not sit well with my conscience. It never would. But what could I do?

'He was poisoned,' I whispered to Kit when he was done with priestly concerns.

'As I heard you tell Tanner. Why do you think that?'

'Foaming at the mouth.'

'As can happen with any seizure, like the falling sickness.'

'But he was not convulsing otherwise. In truth, his limbs were not obeying him.'

'As with apoplexy.'

'Nay. That afflicts but one side of the body and the mouth droops lopsidedly. 'Twas no apoplexy. Whatever it was stopped his breathing, yet he did not cough and choke as though something lodged in his windpipe. It seemed to me that, of a sudden, his body forgot how to breathe… or was unable to do so. Certain poisons can do that, as I have read in books concerning medicine and the apothecary's art.'

'You think the food was bad? What of the rest of us?'

'There was naught amiss with the food and drink. Look around. Everyone else be fit and hale. But I think *his* pottage or ale was tampered with; no one else's. Just his. He must have enemies here. Someone who hated him sufficiently to…'

'But he only arrived today, as we did. When could he have made so fearful an enemy?'

'Mayhap this is not his first visit. Or suppose he brought his killer with him?'

'His son, do you mean? No. I won't believe that. The lad's devastation and grief are real enough. He didn't do it.'

'The testy grandsire, then?'

'How? He can't leave his bed. How could he have poisoned the pottage? He wasn't even here but in the dormitory.'

'Well, I know not how it was done nor by whom but Alfred Denny's death was murder. I know that much.'

'Forget it, Seb. We're on pilgrimage. You're not following at Thaddeus's heel now. It's not your business. Nor mine. Tomorrow, we'll be on the road to Canterbury and Alfred's death will be but a sorrowful incident which happened on the way. Now, say no more of this. Tanner's correct, you mustn't afright the others on this our godly pilgrimage.'

'Aye, I suppose you have the right of it, Kit.'

As instructed, I told not a soul of my suspicions, not even Rose, but that night, it was not the howling wind alone which kept me from sleep. If only I had gone to the tavern to drink with Miles, I should not have witnessed the death and never supposed it to be other than an untimely but natural passing. Whereas now I knew it was not.

In the night, there came a thunderous crash which shook the very building in which we lay. All but the soundest sleepers were wakened, including the children who required much consoling. Others left their beds to see what had come to pass but returned, reporting that naught appeared amiss in the darkness and we all attempted to resume our slumbers.

Wednesday, the twenty-fifth day of October Dartford

Disaster! Unforetold by the stars. No other word can describe such a scene as met our eyes next morn. The street in front of the inn, leaf-strewn yesterday, was now littered with entire branches snapped off, lumps of thatch, broken tiles and even someone's window shutter, ripped from its hinges by the storm's blast.

We stepped out warily from the sanctuary of the inn which, at first glance, leastwise, appeared to have survived intact, looking upwards, fearful of more tiles or trees crashing down upon us. But the wind, having vent its wrath upon the world, now sighed, gentle and innocent as a virgin, afore fading away to a whisper barely able to stir a dried leaf.

'Merciful Jesu. Look there.' Rose pointed to that which last evening had been a house and shop facing towards the inn across the marketplace. Now it was a roofless ruin, half collapsed and only maintained in place forwhy its neighbours allowed not room enough for it to fall. Yet the buildings on either hand remained upright, though one had a gaping hole in the thatch. The other was untouched. The cause was a great beech tree lying amidst the shattered roof beams of the middle house. One side branch had pierced the neighbour's roof.

'That tree… no doubt but that's what wakened us all last night when it fell,' someone remarked.

We all made the sign of the cross and said a prayer for those who were asleep in the upper room last night. We could but pray they knew naught of it when the tree crashed down and shattered their home and, likely, their lives also.

Rose was in tears at sight of it but, being a woman of resolve, she swiftly dried her tears upon her apron.

'We must help them, Seb. Never mind our pilgrimage for now. As true Christians, we have work to do here, aiding our neighbours, as we are taught.'

'Aye, lass, you be right. Let us organise folk to rescue those trapped or to begin clearing up the mess. What say you, Kit?'

My friend agreed and began rolling up his sleeves there and then.

I turned to our self-appointed leader, who stood beside me, staring at the scene. 'Tanner? For certain, you cannot intend to make for Canterbury this day, abandoning these people in their plight? Get the others from their beds – those that can – whilst I find out who be parish reeve here, have him allot tasks and get spades, saws and axes. We shall have to cut that tree into pieces and dig out the survivors. And heaven alone knows what other disasters have occurred elsewhere.'

Tanner did not give answer but returned within the inn,

hopefully to fetch more hands to this huge task.

Meanwhile, I made my way to the church, having to climb over fallen debris and beware of more which might come down upon my head. As I passed by the market cross, a cascade of loosened tiles slithered down a roof close by and crashed at the foot of the cross, setting my not-so-brave Gawain to whimpering. I was unharmed, apart from coughing on the cloud of red dust thrown up as they smashed on the ground, but my heart was set hammering by the near miss.

At the church, Father John Gurnes – he who had blessed us in the Becket Chapel yesterday – stood in the road, staring up at the church and wringing his hands.

'Curse the devil who sent that wind,' he yelled as soon as someone – me – was close enough to hear. 'Look at the cross atop my church! So bent it looks like some heathen symbol. It won't do. It really won't do. Get somebody up there to straighten it. Now!'

'Forgive me, Sir Priest,' I said with due courtesy, 'But your parishioners be more in need. A house has collapsed in the marketplace and folk may be trapped within.'

'What of it? Who are you? What do you expect me to do about it?'

'If you will direct me to the reeve so matters can be organised, tools gathered…'

'We don't have a reeve, not now. He ran off with the proceeds of the market fees a month ago. Haven't seen him since.'

'So who has charge of affairs here?'

'I do. So, as the authority here, I demand that you – whoever you are – find someone to mend that cross!' He pointed to the angle at the top of the chancel roof with a finger so forceful it looked to pierce the blue skies overhead. But it did not pierce my heart nor my determination.

Close at hand, a crowd had gathered but not to bemoan the damage to the cross. Instead, they were all staring at the river. Or they would have, had there been a river to see. Instead, a muddy and gravelly bed lay 'neath the single arch of the stone bridge with but a trickle of water making its way downstream. Fish lay stranded and locals were gathering them up in baskets, not wanting them to go to waste, Wednesday being a fish day. Gawain went down the bank, his paws squelching in the mud, and helped himself to a crayfish or two for breakfast. I could not think when the rest of us might have the chance to eat but no matter.

'Mam, where's the water gone?' a little lad asked his mother.

'I don't know. Father John tells us we're all sinners and God will punish us. Maybe this is God's punishment: He's taken our river away.' Both mother and child broke down and wept. This was Father John's doing. I had no liking for a priest who cared more about a piece of wrought metal than he did for his flock. I went over to the woman.

'Fear not, mistress, your river will return. Trees have fallen and likely one has dammed the river upstream. The water will flow anew when the blockage be removed.'

'You're sure, sir?' she asked, hope shining in her eyes.

'As sure as I may be without seeing the problem for myself. But whilst I be here, can you tell me who leads your villagers in times of strife?'

'Father J…'

'Other than your priest.' I did not disguise the despairing tone in my voice. 'There must be somebody else?'

'Miles Paynter. He should be around here, or maybe he's gone to paint the church, as usual?'

'On such a day?'

'Oh, of course, that's not likely. Ah, I see him there, on the other side of the bridge.'

'Fear not, folks,' a familiar voice spoke out. 'A whole stand of alders has fallen across the river up by the mill. They've caused a land slip which has cut off the water and is flooding the pastures beyond. Now, everybody who can, bring your tools, whatever you've got is bound to be useful, and come with me. We've got a deal of work to do this day.'

'Er, Miles, if I might speak?'

The limner noticed me then.

'Ah, Seb. You never came to the tavern. I missed your company. Is all well at The Bull Inn?'

'Aye, well enough but a tree brought down a house in the marketplace and we fear folk maybe trapped under the rubble. We require aid to get them out. Can you spare a few men or at least tools to help?'

Miles did not waste words but looked around the villagers. He waved to a group of three stout fellows.

'Harry, Ralph, Tom… there's another task for you. Go with Master Seb here; he'll tell you what needs to be done in the marketplace where a house was knocked down by a tree with folk inside. Do as he says. He's a good man, being a painter like me.'

Who knew if I might live up to Miles's expectations? What did I know of digging folk out of ruined buildings? At least he had given me three strong-looking men, all of them carrying axes, pruning hooks and spades.

Back at the marketplace, Kit had organised a few local folk, women among them, and some of the pilgrims and they were lifting away shattered beams and lumps of thatch. Rose was there, skirts kilted, balanced on the rubble, throwing aside broken wattle and daub.

I saw Mother Thorogood had charge of Dickon and Julia and they were out of harm's way, so I, too, joined in the rescue attempt, along with the fellows Miles had sent. As I lifted away a beam, with Kit taking the other end, I asked if he had seen the innkeeper. A man of his size would be right useful, hefting such weight as we struggled with now.

'Haven't seen him. Nor Tanner. But the Warenne twins are over there, making use of a couple of spades to shovel rubble. They're not so bad as they seem. I saw Glassman earlier… can't see where he's gone now… hey, Seb! Watch out!'

With a thundering roar, the back wall of the house came

down. We dropped the beam and jumped clear. Safe. But within an inch of our lives.

'Rose! Rose, where are you, lass?' I cried in a panic.

She came, coughing, through the cloud of dust, wiping her face on her now-filthy apron.

'I'm here, fear not. But one of the men… he's there.'

A booted foot waved through a gap that was lately a window in the back wall but now seemed as a trap-door in the floor. Our frantic hands clawed and dug at the debris. The fellow was calling out. Others helped and we got him free of his rubble tomb. He was dusty, badly bruised and had a gash across his forehead which bled profusely, as such head wounds do, but he insisted he'd do well enough after a cup of ale in The Bull.

We continued to dig and discovered a mound of bed covers.

'Have a care now,' I warned everyone. If the occupants of the house were abed when the tree fell, likely, we would find them here, 'neath the blankets.

We lifted the bedding away. I braced myself for a gruesome revelation. A man and a woman lay side by side, naked as God made them. The man was dead – no doubt of it – but the woman stirred a little and moaned softly, turning somewhat and revealing a babe, swaddled, lying betwixt them.

Rose lifted it away and it began to cry. The woman opened her eyes at the sound of the infant's wail and struggled to sit up.

'Rest easy,' I told her. 'My goodwife has your babe safe. We needs must get you out of here.' I tore a length of blanket from the bed and wrapped it around her to cover her nakedness. But then she espied the man beside her.

'Walter, wake up. Wake up.' She looked to me as Kit and I were freeing her legs from a heap of roof thatch. 'I don't know what's happening. Why is Walter not at his forge?'

'In the storm last night,' I explained, 'A tree came down upon your house… but you and the child be safe now.'

'Walter?'

I shook my head. There was no gentle way to tell her, for he lay there beside her, cold and stiff as stone. A rafter had struck his skull.

'He would have known naught of it,' I assured her. 'An instant death. Come now.'

Kit and I lifted her free and, with her neighbours' aid, we carried her to a house across the way. Rose followed us, the babe nestled in her arms. As we settled the woman with her friends, I enquired whether anyone else was in the house last eve. When she shook her head, we all breathed a sigh of relief that we need dig no more. Only the body of Walter, the blacksmith, remained to be freed. I prayed his soul was already flown from earthly concerns into God's care, and Kit insisted on returning straightway to minister to the unfortunate.

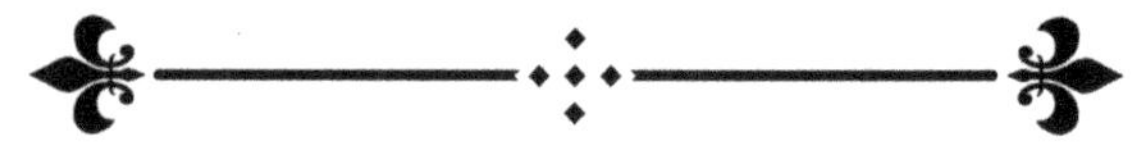

Throughout the day, we all worked to set Dartford aright. We discovered that the innkeeper, Tanner and others had been rescuing the horses from the stables behind the inn and attempting to fashion some shelter for them forwhy the roof had been quite ripped off and lay yards away in the lane behind. The poor beasts, mad with fear, had trampled each other as they attempted to escape. Two had to be put down; another was injured but would likely recover.

The Warenne twins were right concerned for their fine steeds but their fears proved groundless. Those horses had come through, white-eyed with terror but unharmed. Though I would ne'er ill-wish any of God's creatures, it seemed right, somehow, that the horses which had to be put from their suffering belonged to the boastful and quarrelsome merchants. God works in His mysterious way, as it is written.

Chapter 7

Wednesday, late

AFTER A cobbled-together supper at The Bull Inn, most had retired early, exhausted by a long day of digging, lifting, sawing and chopping, rescuing folk and livestock. Rose and the toddlings were asleep already and Kit was chatting with the two scholarly fellows when those wretched merchants began berating and cursing the innkeeper, demanding he pay them the price of their horses.

'They were in *your* care in *your* stable. If you'd built it as you should, our horses would still be alive,' one shouted, poking the innkeeper's broad chest with a skinny finger. A risk indeed, as I thought, but the innkeeper did not retaliate. He looked weary as the rest of us – except the merchants who had not once sullied gown nor hand to help anyone.

'That animal cost me five pounds, six shillings and eight pence,' yelled the one in the green turban hat. 'I demand compensation, you oaf. Apologies won't amend my account book. I want my money and extra beside for the inconvenience you've caused me.'

'You have until midday tomorrow to pay us,' said the fellow in crimson, 'Else we'll see to it no other London merchant ever gives you custom here in future.'

I suppose it was an improvement of sorts that the two merchants were in agreement this once as the pair shouted down the innkeeper's protests. But I was too tired to abide their quarrelling. A headache threatened, so I called Gawain, took my cloak and walked out.

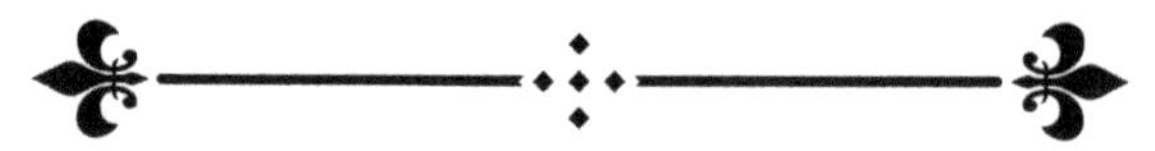

I strolled to the river to observe whether it flowed or not. It did, though perhaps not so deeply as afore. I gazed up at the moonlit, star-studded sky. Heaven looked to be so peaceful a place compared to our troubles this day.

'Seb Foxley! I was wondering if you'd come. I was looking out for you, hoping you would.' Miles Paynter sounded merry enough but, even by moonlight, I could see the lines of weariness drawn stark upon his face, his mud-plastered attire.

'You succeeded in clearing the river upstream,' I said, gesturing towards the dark water, the joyous sound of it dancing over stones once more.

'Aye, somewhat. There's still work to do tomorrow to have it flowing full again. But you'll be gone by then, I suppose.'

'Tanner would have us on the road for Otford soon after cockcrow to make up for a day lost. Not that I consider it lost,' I added hastily, fearing to offend my new friend.

'You saved Blanche and her babe, for which we are all grateful. Saving lives can hardly be accounted a wasted day.'

'Nay. Were other lives lost, apart from the blacksmith's?'

'Jed the shepherd and his lad… their shack came down on them. The other shepherd was trying to save the sheep from the flooded pasture. Drowned he was whilst the sheep swam to safety. But I suppose that's the way of life. Contrary. But let's not dwell on that. I've earned a jug of ale and so have you.'

Miles led the way to a house full of candlelight and laughter, even if the laughter sounded somewhat forced. The Sun Tavern was crowded with men and women, many of them still mire-spattered and unkempt from their struggles to restore the river and rescue livestock. Miles took me to a table by the hearth. Everyone turned and cheered, raising their cups to him.

'Hail the hero!' someone cried and others took up the chant. 'Ale's on the house, Master Paynter, for you and your friend.

He's the one saved our Blanche, 'ent he?'

'Aye, he saved her,' Miles agreed.

'I had a deal of assistance,' I said. No matter. An ale jug and cups were put before us, as well as bread, cheese, onions and apples.

One by one, the other drinkers came over and clapped Miles upon the back or shook his hand, everyone giving him thanks. I wondered what he had done to earn such acclaim. He was grinning but I could tell the commendations embarrassed him.

'What did you do?' I asked him quietly as we shared our unexpected free supper. Gawain certainly appreciated Kentish cheese, so it seemed.

'Nothing really. I'm in haste to get back to painting my dragon. You know how it is.'

'Aye, tempera dries in a ridge and it be difficult to hide if you leave it overlong.'

'Exactly so. Mind, it's probably too late already. I'll have to scrape it back.'

'Pity, after all that fine work,' I said, munching a sweet apple. 'So how come you be Dartford's man of the hour?'

'What else would I be? I brought the, er, ladies safe out of The Broken Heart House upriver. They were flooded and climbed onto the roof, what with the water all backed up by the landslip. I remembered they might be underwater and went to see what I could do.'

'You saved everyone's favourite tavern? Little wonder they're pleased.'

'I wouldn't call it a tavern. It's more of a house of pleasure.'

'A house of… oh, I understand.' I felt my cheeks redden.

'And the whole valley is flooded higher up. Trees down everywhere, blocking the road. A fellow from Shoreham managed to get through but had to use a rowing boat as far as Eynesford and again at Sutton.'

'Is that anywhere close to Otford?' I asked, cutting more cheese to share with Gawain.

'Aye. It's all the same road along the Darent valley. You're supposed to be going there tomorrow, you said?'

'I did. That be the plan forwhy it is the pilgrims' road but now…'

'You'll not get there for at least a week and likely longer than that, not with trees fallen across the way all along and blocking the river.'

'I shall tell Tanner but he will be displeased.'

'Can't be helped, can it? But you can go by way of Gravesend and Rochester, carrying on along Watling Street. You can follow it all the way to Canterbury.'

'Truly? Then why do pilgrims go to Otford?'

'Because the archbishop owns all the inns and resting places between his palaces at Otford and Wrotham and so on. It means he gets a share of all the money the pilgrims spend. Also – and you must mark my words on this – there is the benefit of his peace-keepers making the way safe. The one thing to beware of on the road from Gravesend to Rochester is thieves in the woods who waylay travellers but, if you're a good-sized party, I doubt the miscreants will dare trouble you.'

Thursday, the twenty-sixth day of October
Dartford to Northfleet

Tanner was quite discountenanced when I informed him of what I had heard: that the pilgrims' road to Otford was impassable at this time. He grumbled at this cause for further delay.

'Miles Paynter says we may simply follow Watling Street and it will take us all the way to Canterbury.'

'And who's this Paynter fellow?'

'A friend.'

'Some friend,' Tanner scoffed. 'And did he tell you about the outlaws, footpads and rogues who haunt the woods along the way?'

'He mentioned the possibility, aye.'

'And you would risk it? With your goodwife and children?'

'Do we have a choice, unless we abandon our pilgrimage? I have no intention of turning back now.'

'We can each arm ourselves with stout staves,' Kit said, joining our conversation.

'The women also?' Tanner looked doubtful.

'My Rose be adept at dealing with ne'er-do-wells. I cannot speak for Mother Thorogood but it would be a rash fellow who attempted to challenge that cat of hers. Have you seen the length of its claws and razor-sharp teeth?'

And thus, it was decided. The Carmelite monks rejoined us, leading the donkey bearing their infirm brother, having passed their sojourn in Dartford at the priory. The convent had suffered some damage – a deal of mess but naught which threatened life or limb, God be praised – and the monks had spent yesterday assisting the nuns and lay sisters in putting God's house to rights. Now they were eager to reach their own priory at Aylesford, undeterred by the enforced change of plan. Even the mention of outlaws did not concern them, so they said, for the Lord Jesu Christ Himself was their staff and protection.

Tanner's final problem – that of the Alfred Dennys, grandfather and grandson, and who could assist the youngster in carrying the old man's litter – was solved even as we attended the hasty dawn burying of Alfred Denny, deceased, in the churchyard of Holy Trinity. The two men of learning, Kit's friends, offered to take turns helping young Alfred on the condition that the grandsire held his tongue. One foul word and they would abandon the litter by the wayside.

I thought this a right Christian act on their part – the offer, not the threat – and said as much to Kit who grinned, looking pleased with himself.

'Aye, my honeyed tongue can be most persuasive when I have a mind to it.'

'You persuaded them? That was well done indeed.'

'Michael and Jonathan are fine fellows when you can drag them from their disputations on Aristotle, even though they're Cambridge men, not Oxford like me. But we can't all be perfect and must be allowed to make one mistake in life,' Kit added with a chuckle.

'I have not spoken with them as you have… not being learned and knowing naught of – who is it? – Euclid and Aristotle?'

'Aye. I hope your lack of knowledge hasn't kept you awake at night.'

'Hardly, but apart from the storm, something else be troubling me.'

'Oh?'

'Alfred Denny's death. I like it not that we must let the culprit run free.'

'If there was one? I'm not convinced it was anything but natural causes.'

'Well, I be certain it was not and I have recalled the likely poison employed: deadly nightshade. I remember its symptoms, which tally most nearly with what we observed. And the way Tanner threatened to banish me from this company if I spoke to any of my suspicions… to my mind, he cast aside too readily the possibility of death by some unnatural means.'

'He didn't want you upsetting others nor causing delay to our journey.'

'I do not trust him, Kit.'

'Surely you don't believe Tanner killed Alfred? That's absurd, Seb. You go too far. I'll not countenance such a ridiculous notion. Forget it. Say not another word upon this matter. Save your breath to climb the next hill.'

With that, Kit strode from the churchyard, crossed the bridge and began the steep ascent of the long hill to the east of Dartford, pulling the cart behind him. Since both children sat within, riding like royalty in a carriage, the cart was heavy indeed and I hastened to assist him, vowing to say no more about the sudden death at The Bull. But I made no such vow as regard thinking on it.

But then, a pleasant surprise raised my spirits. My new-found friend, Miles Paynter, came from the church, pigment pot in hand, to bid us farewell and God speed. A kindly gesture indeed. I would not forget the limner.

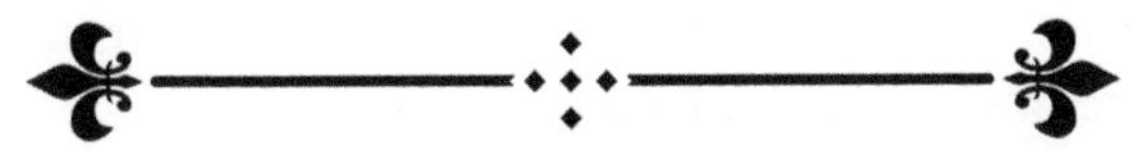

Watling Street turned somewhat inland after we left Dartford. Now we were upon high ground, the River Thames but a grey streak in the distance against a pallid sky of thin cloud and, for a mile or so, the road lay flat and we made good time. Tanner was obviously cheered by this and sang as he led us along, his voice booming out, scaring a crowd of starlings into taking flight from the bushes. I recognised the song and joined in – somewhat more melodious than he, if I do say so myself. Others also took up the refrain as our merry band ambled along.

As we followed the road, there were trees down and the woodland on either side of the road closed in. It appeared this stretch of Watling Street ahead was little used, as brambles and briars encroached. Through the now-bare trees – the gale having torn away the remaining leaves – we saw smoke. A hamlet in the woods? Charcoal burners, mayhap? After a brief consultation, Tanner decided it might be the smoke of a fire in an outlaws' camp and to be avoided. Thus, we retraced our steps a quarter mile or so and turned down a winding lane to the north.

We passed a little wooden chapel and a shrine dedicated to St James, to judge from the carved image of the saint in his niche, scallop shells at his feet, where we paid our respects. Then on to the Bishop of Rochester's church at Stone. Dedicated to St Mary, its timbered spire pointed heavenward with its cross aloft – having survived the storm blast in better case than the one at Holy Trinity.

Within, Tanner allowed us so short a time, barely long enough to recite a Paternoster and an Ave, yet I espied the murals of the Virgin and Child and the Martyrdom of Becket. Both were exquisitely wrought by limners who had excelled at their art long ago but the fingers of the faithful must have touched the face of Becket so frequently – it being within easy reach – that the archbishop's features were quite worn away. A job for the talented Miles Painter, I thought.

Tanner insisted we hasten onward, making for Gravesend, seven miles distant, in time for dinner, he said. This lower road to Canterbury and Dover ran through several hamlets and villages. Thus, it was travelled more frequently than the straighter Watling Street these days.

'More folk about so it's safer and more taverns and inns when we need them. We should have come this way to begin with,' Tanner apologised.

Downhill and up again, through the village of Swainscombe with its squat-towered church of St George. I wondered if Miles may have painted a mural here, or might do so in future but there was no time to enter the church to discover it, if he had.

One of the twins had reined in his horse beside the lych-gate and dismounted to inspect its right fore hoof.

'Be aught amiss?' I asked him, content to stop and catch my breath after another long climb with Dickon upon my shoulders. Kent was proving too hilly a shire for my liking. I saw the road afore us had a sharp descent, then an equally steep ascent once more from the valley below.

'A loose shoe,' the twin said. 'I'll have to walk him until we can find a smith or farrier to put him right. Damn shame. Trist has just challenged me to a race but now…'

I looked at the lad's eyebrow. No trace of that thin white line, so now I knew: this was Troilus; Tristan bore the tiny scar. Now I could tell the pair apart, one from the other.

'Likely, there will be a smith in the village down there,' I said, pointing to a huddle of buildings in the valley. 'Your horse be a handsome beast. I should like to draw him some time.'

'Draw him? How d'you mean?' Troilus appeared startled at my suggestion.

'With charcoal and chalk upon paper,' I explained.

'Thank God! I thought you meant to draw out his guts like a fish or drag him on a hurdle like a man condemned.'

'Naught so final as that, I assure you,' I laughed.

'Horsey, horsey,' Dickon chortled, pointing to the beast, meanwhile using my hair as reins and urging me into a trot.

'Papa be unfit to trot at present,' I told him. 'Leave go of my hair, if you will. Papa be a blown and spavined nag this morn. You must have a little patience.'

'You've brought your whole family with you on this pilgrimage,' Troilus observed, changing the subject as we began the walk downhill.

'Aye. My goodwife has kinsfolk in Canterbury and we could not leave the little ones in London as our house is in the process of being rebuilt after a fire.'

'So you're not really on pilgrimage then?'

'Indeed we are. I come on my brother's behalf. He suffered a serious injury to his knee last winter. It has crippled him and I would pray for his recovery whilst giving thanks to the Almighty for sparing his life. 'Twas a close call for him. I feared he would die. What of you and your brother?'

Troilus shrugged.

'We're on pilgrimage in our father's name and making the best of it whilst we can. He's a sick old tyrant; he treats me and Tris worse than scullions ever since our mother died. Yet we're his joint heirs. One day soon, his wealth and estates will be ours but then we'll be tied down with the responsibilities of it all. First thing though, when he dies, we'll send that bastard brother of ours on his way. Fenshaw's older than us and father's favourite but he can't inherit, being baseborn. Father threatens to strike us from his will unless we make this pilgrimage to beseech God, by way of the Holy Martyr, to prolong his life and health. In which case, if we don't, he will name Fenshaw as his sole heir, bastard or not. Thus, we have no choice but to do this. We are praying that he lives long enough to know we've completed the pilgrimage and that he'll honour his pledge and complete his will in our favour. The law's on our side but Fenshaw's a…'

'Troy! What're you about? I've been waiting to begin our race, you dunderhead.'

Tristan rode up on his equally fine horse.

'Cass has a loose shoe. We'll race later, when it's mended. Let me mount up behind you, Tris. I'm not of a mind to walk and ruin my decent boots.'

Lithe as a deer, Troilus leapt into the saddle behind his twin and they went off down the hill at a trot, the other horse, Cass, following on upon a leading rein. Our conversation was at an end.

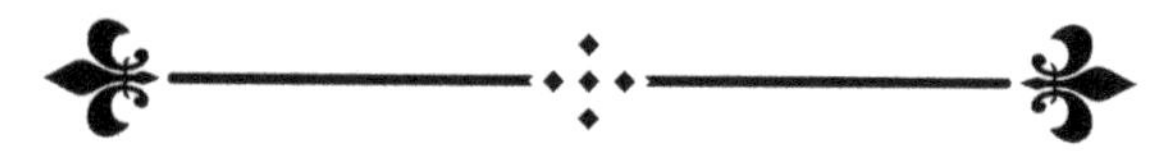

It proved a deep valley with a river at the bottom, fast flowing and clear as crystal. To our left hand, its waters snaked out to join the Thames. Shipwrights and carpenters were working to repair boats and fashion new vessels all along the banks. Nowhere near so busy as Deptford but a scene of great industry, nonetheless. The sounds of sawing and hammering, shouts and laughter among those labouring and the clang of metal on anvil rang in the still air.

Here, trees were upright, the last leaves yet clinging to them, telling of a quieter night past. No storm damage in this place that I could see.

'Is this Gravesend?' Kit wondered aloud, inspecting the palms of his hands. They were blistered and raw. I realised I had been shirking my share of cart-pulling. Across the river, another steep hill awaited our struggles.

'No, this is Northfleet,' Tanner said. 'And that's the River Fleet – not the size of London's, I know, but the water is sweet, straight from the springs over yonder. I advise you to fill your water-skins since there's none better to be had for miles. And when we cross, make use of the bridge, for the current will sweep you off your feet if you try to wade through it.'

I was aiding Kit in binding his hands with linen. Fortunately, Rose had thought of everything needful but my friend had been foolish, not bothering to wear the stout gloves we had brought with us for the very purpose of pulling the cart. For the moment, she was keeping both children well away from the river bank. Little ones being attracted to water like iron to a lodestone – except when it be time to wash – she held both firmly by the hands.

There came a sudden splashing and commotion, a deal of shouting and neighing. A horse was thrashing in the river. I left Kit's bindings dangling and ran to see if aid was required.

How it had come to pass, who could say? The twins' horses were both in the water and folk were dragging at their bridles and saddles. Would it not be better to give the beasts a chance to right themselves, unless they be too sore injured to do so? But then I realised that the Warenne twins were caught 'neath the struggling horses.

I slid down the chalky bank into the icy turmoil of water. It took my breath away. Others were there afore me, pulling and tugging, one horse screaming. Then it was on its feet and being led away – Troilus' steed, the one with the loose shoe. A man's head broke the surface, tousled hair soaked and obscuring the face.

'Help us!' came the spluttering cry afore the head disappeared back into the water.

I waded to him, water to my hips. The current was strong indeed but the other floundering horse was taking the brunt of its force and I kept downstream of it, avoiding flailing hooves.

The musician fellow was there, trying to rescue one twin, so I aided the other, grabbing his clothes and pulling with all my strength. I succeeded in raising his head, sufficient for him to suck in a gasping breath and held him there whilst Kit, Tanner and young Alfred Denny wrestled with the horse which held him trapped beneath it.

Gawain was barking frantically from the bank, running up and down, and I bade him 'stay'. I did not want my faithful dog washed away if he leapt into the river, thinking to save me. He be foolish and loyal enough to do so but he obeyed me – this once – thankfully.

Of a sudden, the horse was up, releasing the rider.

Kit helped me drag the half-drowned lad to dry earth, where he choked and spewed out water afore lying still. Alive, God be praised. But the other was yet under water. The musician was having little effect in aiding him. So I waded back in to help. This second twin hung limp when Tanner joined me. The current was threatening to sweep us off our feet but eager hands were held out and we reached the bank in safety, giving the second lad into the care of others. His case appeared doubtful for some little while but the efforts of Rose, Mother Thorogood and his brother, this latter now beseeching God upon his knees in the midst of the road, brought him back from the brink.

We all gave hearty thanks for four lives preserved: two of humankind and two animal with surprisingly few hurts, mostly bruises and gashes. But the Warenne twins were much in need of rest, refreshment and dry clouts, as was I.

As Tanner led us across the narrow bridge of crumbling stone, in far from good repair, I wondered how the mishap had come to pass. But I required to re-assemble my wits, only recalling my distrust of water after the near-fatal event and I began to tremble as with a palsy. The chill of wet attire upon a cold day was not the sole cause. What madness had possessed me in those moments? Others could have done as I did but not many had waded in so promptly, except the musician whose attempts at rescue seemed to have come to naught.

Tanner led us into The Plough Tavern and, God be praised, a good fire snapped and crackled in the hearth. He pushed the twins and me onto benches beside the blaze and I held my hands to it and my feet in sodden boots.

Rose came with towels for us three, begged from the ale-wife, and dry clothes for me.

'You were so brave, my Seb, for all your dislike of water. You saved Tristan's life… or mayhap it was Troilus'.'

'Whichever it was, he looks right poorly.' I nodded to where the brothers sat across the hearth from me. One leaned heavily against the other, his countenance grey as dishwater.

'But he's alive. He owes you that,' Rose insisted, passing me a cup of mulled ale sweetened with honey. Oh, how it did me a world of good and I blessed the ale-wife and the unknown inventor of so fine a drink. The nectar of the gods could taste no better nor prove a more excellent restorative. A second cup gave me strength enough to change out of my dripping shirt and nether clouts, concealed 'neath a towel, of course.

A row of wet boots was lined up around the hearth, each stuffed with straw. Kit and Tanner had put theirs beside mine and those of the twins. But a pair was missing. I looked around the tavern but could not see the musician. For certain, he must be as soaked as I, his boots, likewise, in need of drying out.

'Tanner,' I called out, still towelling my hair, 'Have you seen the musician fellow? He was in the river but I see him not. He has not come to grief, has he?'

Tanner glanced around, then shrugged.

'Not here, so far as I can tell. He'll be around somewhere, quaffing ale like the rest of us. Likes his ale does Hugo Harper.'

'He was doing his best to aid the twins. I pray he be safe.' Hugo Harper… quite a name to conjure with and this was the first I knew of it. Hugo the harper, the tuneless minstrel. 'Tis quite a merry jest.

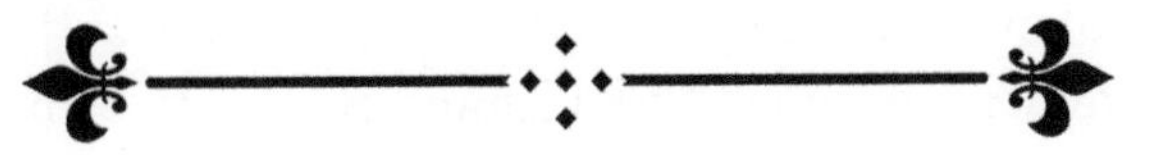

With all of us somewhat restored, though my boots were still quite damp, we climbed yet another hill. The blacksmith sought by Troilus for his horse had his forge atop that hill, beside the church of St Botolph, as the ale-wife told us. It seemed inevitable that it was so and this hill was longer yet than those we had trudged up previously. The cheering and strengthening effects of the mulled ale swiftly dissipated as I toiled upward.

Half way, I lifted Dickon from my shoulders.

'Sorry, little one. Papa be spent. Hold my hand and we shall walk together.'

For fifty paces or thereabouts, my son was content, pointing out a group of youngsters racing after a barrel hoop as it gained speed down the hill. But he wished to join the game, pulling me back.

'Nay, lad. Do not…'

The word 'nay' was sufficient to set off a screech of protest and my son sat down in the midst of the street and refused to get to his feet and walk another step.

'Richard!' I said sternly – the times I used his proper name within a twelvemonth could be counted upon the fingers of one hand. 'Get up now.'

He did naught but thrust forth a mutinous bottom lip.

'Then we shall neither of us go anywhere,' I said, sitting in the dirt beside him. 'And no dinner either.' I rested my weary head upon my knees whilst Gawain licked my face as if to revive me. From the corner of my eye, I watched my son. His features were as an open text and I read it well enough as he considered the undesirable possibility of foregoing a meal. Dickon was ever a good, if messy, trencherman and no mistake.

'Gawain wants dinner,' he said plaintively, and likely it was true. 'Get up, Papa.' A toddling of three summers be no match for a man's weight, yet he grabbed my wrist and attempted to pull me to my feet. His valiant efforts were in vain and I had to offload my scrip from my shoulder and rise of my own accord. 'Twas more of a struggle that it ought to be but I succeeded, much to my son's delight. 'Papa, run like me,' he shouted, racing ahead as if the road lay flat as a Lenten pancake. I shook my head in despair. Such be his youthful agility and liveliness as I might never match, afore or since.

Chapter 8

Thursday, after noon.
Gravesend

THUS FAR, we had followed the Thames for much of the way but as we departed Northfleet, high chalk cliffs fell to the river far below. Sheep cropped the turf, the only paths across being those made by the flocks. Gulls swooped and cried; choughs wheeled, red of beak and leg against soot-black feathers.

We turned southward, away from the river, Tanner assuring us that this was still the road to Dover, down another, if somewhat gentler, hill and back up the other side.

Orchards of pear trees grew on either hand. The sun came out and skylarks trilled in the wide sky. We were all of us hungry, our promised dinner in Gravesend delayed by the mishap that occurred earlier. Thus, I was right glad to see a woman with a basket of fruit upon her head.

'Do you have pears for sale, good mistress?' Kit asked her afore I did. 'We're all famished.'

'No, master. These are windfalls after last night's gale. They'll go for the making of perry, not for eating. Too hard and sharp tasting and now bruised. But if you go farther along Perry Street, there...' She pointed to a shack with a blue door, its paint mostly scoured away by wind and weather. 'Marjorie has pears for eating.'

This Marjorie, a plump, smiling woman, made a goodly profit from our pilgrim band. Every one of us purchased a fruit or two from her golden store. The pears were sweet and delicious and even the dopey, last wasps of summer who would share our bounty were tolerated with patient humour.

Much cheered, we made our way up the sloping street – not worthy of being called a hill, God be praised – and reached Gravesend. A fine old church of grey stone, moss-clad, stood at the crossroads, children played, ducks swam upon the pond and a sizeable inn awaited us. The Warenne twins caught up with us there. Their horses had had their cuts and grazes tended by the farrier back in Northfleet and the loose shoe was put to rights. But Tristan's pallor was ghastly as he sagged in the saddle. He needed rest and time to recover from his near drowning.

When the so-called musician, Hugo Harper, arrived – in an ill-humour, I noted, as he cast a stone, for no reason at all, at a too-friendly mallard duck and yelled abuse at the youngsters playing five-stones – our pilgrim band was complete once more, including the Carmelite brethren and their donkey. Harper kept glancing at the twins, glaring at them. Mayhap he regretted now his efforts to save them from the Fleet since, at every step, his boots squelched audibly, leaving wet footprints in his wake even after a couple of miles of walking.

We ate a belated dinner of mutton pie and worts but every one of the locals, from the innkeeper to the potboy, was urging us to make haste and not dawdle over our meal. Some occurrence or other was to take place that very afternoon, down by the hythe and the air of excitement was tangible, such that the children made quite an ado, insisting upon viewing the forthcoming spectacle, whatever it might be. So long as it was not a hanging, I should make no objection to their seeing it.

Tanner explained that although he did not know Gravesend so well, since he seldom frequented this way, to his knowledge, there was a decent inn down by the river, used by pilgrims who came this far by boat. The Long Ferry, he called it and I remembered Dick Langton had suggested we paid our sixpences for a quicker means of travelling this far. Of course, I had no intention of making our pilgrimage more convenient. That was not the way to go about a holy journey… my great dislike of boats being an irrelevance.

We followed the crowd wending its way along the road. St Mary's church was upon our left hand and Rose, Kit and I paused to bow our heads, as was proper for pilgrims, and say a prayer. But Dickon and Julia, both on foot for now, pulled at us, urging us to make haste.

Upon our right hand stood a flint-built manor house, smoke rising from two chimneys, one at either end of the gabled roof, and glass glinted in the arched windows which faced the road through a square gatehouse, likewise of flint. It stood amidst pastures where cattle grazed, content. Lesser buildings of mostly wattle-and-daub lined the way, single-storeys with thatched roofs but, here and there, taller houses with tiled roofs proclaimed owners of greater prosperity.

Down at the riverside, the Thames spread wide. On the distant Essex bank, the dull waters blended into grey mudflats and a vast expanse of salt marsh, sheep-dotted. Curlews called, bitterns boomed and oyster-catchers piped. But this side of the river was thronged with folk both on land and water. Small boats fought the tide to keep station for the best view of whatever was about to come to pass.

The road turned right to follow the bankside and I was surprised to see the ruins of such a grand manor it must have once been nigh a palace. A royal coat-of-arms hung crooked and much faded above the gatehouse where oak doors sagged and swung, blackened by fire. I peeked through the gap, curiosity having got the better of me, and espied ruinous buildings, half robbed of their outer stones, broken window embrasures, the place now open to the sky, roofless. Choughs perched on empty window casements. Neither quite crows, rooks nor jackdaws, these birds seemed right common here.

But my son dragged me onward.

In amongst ramshackle houses, little better constructed than the privy at the end of our garden plot, endless nets were hung to dry. They were of finer mesh than those I saw at Billingsgate and Southwark and I wondered what tiny fish they were meant to take. Dickon would be right pleased if his favoured whitebait was the catch. The smell of fish was so strong here it took my breath away.

Dickon held his nose.

'Stinky,' he proclaimed and I agreed but the locals seemed oblivious as they pushed and shoved, elbows out, jostling to see what was going on. As late comers at the back of the crowd, I could see little and lifted my son onto my shoulders. Though I doubted it improved his view by much, at least he was not in danger of being trampled underfoot.

'I'll take him. He'll see better from up here.' Troilus bent from the saddle of his horse, arms outstretched to take Dickon. I hesitated forwhy I barely knew the youngster. Should I trust him with my precious child? But it seemed my son would decide for himself, reaching out to Troilus' open arms. And he was lifted from me, squealing 'Horsey! Horsey!' in great delight. I dared not take my eyes from him but Troilus was urging his steed forward through the throng, leaving me far behind.

My anxious gaze lost sight of them just as that dread question was asked:

'Where's Dickon?' Rose stood at my elbow.

'With Troilus... on his horse,' I replied, feigning confidence.

'Is he safe?'

'Less likely to be crushed by so many feet.' I hoped my tone was nonchalant so as not to cause Rose the least concern. I worried enough for us both. 'What is happening? Do we know?' I changed the subject but stretched my neck, hoping to glimpse Dickon's whereabouts. I could not.

'Tanner said something about ducking. That's all I know.' Rose shifted her hold on Julia.

'Let me have her: rest your arms a while.' I lifted my daughter high onto my shoulders. 'A duck hunt, mayhap? That would explain the nets hung all about. I thought they were for fishing.

The stench here suggests that to be the cause: fish, not fowl. Julia will love watching ducks fly; will you not, little lass?' In reply, she did but chuckle and push my cap down over my eyes. Such is life for a fond papa.

The crowd, having waited patiently if noisily thus far, was now bestirred in expectation. Voices hushed.

'Make way! Make way for the mayor!' came the cry, accompanied by the beating of a drum. 'Make way there.' A young man in a particoloured tabard of blue and white was banging his instrument with much enthusiasm, bellowing fit to burst as a great gilded mace appeared off to my left, being used as a battering-ram to force a way through. The fellow wielding it was pock-marked with the eyes of a startled hare. The mace seemed too heavy for him, his cheeks red and sweat-streaked with the effort of it. I half expected him to drop the cumbersome thing at any moment.

Behind the mace-bearer strode the mayor, decked in crimson robes with a golden chain of office about his neck and a plumed hat. A man of middle years, puffed with the pride of a fighting cock, he would likely make good use of the tall, silver-topped staff in his hand. Almost as I thought this, an urchin, leaning out from atop a precarious tumbledown shack, threw a rotten fish at the dignitary. Upon the instant, the mayor changed his stance and the rod was hurled with the precision of a Roman javelin, knocking the miscreant from his perch with a cry as the staff clattered to earth.

I could not see what happened to the lad but I saw well enough the smirk of satisfaction upon the mayor's face. Not a man to be crossed: that was my assessment of Gravesend's magistrate. A priest and a brace of clerks walked behind him, followed by a trio of rough-looking fellows. One of them exuded an air of menace like a foul odour – not that I could smell aught but fish – but which sent a shiver down my spine. The other two dragged a reluctant donkey with a cart behind upon which was a wooden cage, ill-made.

At first, I could not see what manner of beast it housed but, as the crowd cheered and shouted, I saw it was no beast but human. Clad in naught but a filthy, ragged shift, a woman cowered in the corner. Folk hurled rotten fish and mouldy fruit at her. Although the cage protected her from most of the missiles, yet she flinched each time one battered the slats of her tiny prison. Her hair hung loose and matted, more grey than dark, so far as I could tell 'neath the dirt. Poor soul. What had she done to deserve this humiliation?

Behind the cart walked one more in this strange procession: a man, ill-kempt and uncertain upon his feet. He might have been a casual drunkard staggering along behind, curious as to what was afoot, but since others made way for him, I suspected he was more than that.

'Yer for it now, woman… getting' yer deservings. That'll settle yer, yer ol' bitch,' he bawled at the woman, hitting the slats with a stick. 'Call yerself "wife", yer fat sow. We'll sees about that now.'

Above the heads of the crowd, a great beam leaned, not unlike the cranes of the Steelyard back in London, yet I realised this was not about to off-load cargo from a ship forwhy some kind of chair hung from the end. Slow-witted this once, light dawned eventually: no fowls were about to be pursued for the pot; rather, the woman was destined to be ducked in the river. This be the punishment for a scold, a nagging wife. But, in truth, having observed her man, the vile sot, my sympathies were all for the woman.

'Oh, Seb, how can they do this to her?' Rose whispered, clinging to my arm. 'I'd be a scold if I was unfortunate enough to be wedded to his kind. She doesn't deserve to be punished. It should be him strapped to that chair, then the cold water might sober the wretch. You hear the names he calls her?'

'Aye.' I pulled my dear one close, vowing I should ne'er give her cause to become a scolding wife. And even if, no doubt rightly, she did nag at me, I would not make report of it to the authorities. Was this not a matter to be resolved at home, behind closed shutters, not bandied about the town to the utter humiliation of all involved?

Even as they strapped her, shrieking, into the chair, we turned our backs and forced a way free of the throng. Neither did we look around when the crowd cheered madly as her screams were muted by the water closing over her head. The crowd fell silent as if it also held its breath 'neath the waves, but the cheering resumed, louder yet, as the chair was raised aloft once more. But I did search out my son with Troilus upon his horse.

To my great shame, I saw Dickon, like Troilus, laughing and cheering as the ducking chair plunged into the river for a second time. I wanted to grab him away. He ought not to be enjoying this piteous spectacle but, of course, he was too young to understand. All the same, I was surprised by Troilus. Did he have no sympathy for the woman's plight after his own half-drowning in the Fleet this morn and his brother's even closer encounter with death?

Whatever my opinions, I could not reach either of them through the jostle of folk. I consoled myself that at least my child was safe, though that was no salve for my conscience. I wished we had not come to bear witness to this but we had no choice now but to stay until I could retrieve my son.

The Three Choughs Inn
Gravesend

Three Choughs were the arms of St Thomas Becket and fitting indeed where such birds were numerous as rooks in London. The inn of that name, where Tanner had now made arrangements for us to sup and sleep, was hard by the ducking chair, such that the crane could be seen from the window. Though the unfortunate woman was now gone from the chair, released into her husband's custody – no less a punishment, as I believed likely – dozens of folk now crammed into this nearest house of refreshment to end the day in revelry. They behaved as if it were a matter for celebration, an unexpected half-day free from labour upon a Thursday, which it was, I suppose.

With Dickon restored to us, unharmed but over-excited, we huddled in a corner with our ale, doing our utmost to close our ears to the raucous voices all about, discussing in lurid detail every aspect of the afternoon's "entertainment", as I heard it described. How the poor woman had looked, cried out and writhed within her bonds in a futile effort to escape, how the water had streamed off her. Her choking, then spluttering protests as her punishment was repeated – three times in all. Drinking themselves into a frenzy, collecting their wagers: those who had reckoned she would drown counted their losses. Those who wagered she would survive collected their winnings, all the while relishing how close it had come to ending otherwise.

Earlier, I accounted Gravesend a good place to spend the night but now I was right impatient to leave it. The morn could not come quickly enough. They say Time waits for no man but upon this occasion, I did not want to wait upon Time, dragging its feet. But I had no choice.

Kit joined us in our corner, bringing his own ale and a bowl of cooked shrimps.

'Well, that was a different way to pass an afternoon,' he said. His expression was bland and blank, such that I could not gauge his thoughts upon the matter. 'Here, have some shrimps: Gravesend's finest, as I was told, the town is known for them. They're not bad. Help yourselves.'

Rose and I did as bidden, removing the spiky heads, holding them by the tail and biting off the rest in one small mouthful. I admit they were tasty. Dickon enjoyed them also; Julia not so much, spitting out the scales of the shrimps' casings.

'We lost sight of you in the crowd,' I said, equally without any suggestion as to whether I approved or disapproved of the happenings. I peeled a shrimp for my daughter and she preferred it thus, though it was now reduced to a mere morsel. 'And it would appear others had little liking for this afternoon's so-called entertainment.' I nodded towards Hugo Harper, sitting morose and subdued over his ale. 'Is it because he be upset by the ducking or forwhy it reminds him of this morning's wetting when he attempted to save Tristan?'

'The latter,' Kit said. 'He's looked forlorn ever since.'

'He's still wearing those same garments and shoes,' Rose said, 'So little wonder he's miserable, clad in damp clouts. Mayhap he has naught else to wear? He seems to carry no baggage but his musical instruments.'

'Then he should unburden himself and leave them by the wayside. We all of us know by now that he's tone deaf and tuneless as a cat on the privy roof,' Kit mumbled through a mouthful of bread and shrimp, short on sympathy for the minstrel. 'It would be a Christian act indeed if he spared us all the torment of his efforts. And if he hopes to earn a living from music-making, it's going to be a short life before he starves to death.'

'Mayhap, 'tis his reason for making this pilgrimage, if his musical skills have been lost to him and he wishes to have them restored,' I suggested.

'Is that possible: to lose a God-given talent?' Kit asked.

I shrugged.

'I pray it ne'er happens to me. What would I do if I could no longer draw or wield a pen? Or if I awoke one morn and my singing voice was gone? I, too, should be a lost soul… like Hugo Harper there.'

Having finished our shrimp supper, the little ones were yawning and Rose settled them down in the cart to sleep. Kit sought out his learned friends, no doubt intent upon some long disputation concerning that Euclid fellow or some such ancient Greek or other of whom I be utterly ignorant. Not wishing to embarrass myself by demonstrating my lack of learning, I left Rose chatting amicably with Mother Thorogood about how best to remove this or that stain from various types of cloth – another subject of which I knew naught – to join the twins upon their bench in the corner.

Troilus looked well enough but his brother did not. He was slumped back against the wall, eyes closed. Even in the dim light, his colour appeared little improved from earlier, if at all.

'How does Tristan fare?' I asked Troilus, who shook his head.

'Not so good are you, eh, Tris?' Troilus tucked a blanket closer around his brother who, I realised, was wearing a cloak beneath that but was visibly shivering nonetheless.

'Would mulled ale or wine be of help?' I suggested.

'We tried that… didn't make him feel any better but churned his belly. Reckon he swallowed too much water.'

'Mayhap he should be abed. I will aid you with him, if…'

'I'm well enough here,' Tristan mumbled, stirring without opening his eyes. 'Just let me be.'

Troilus rearranged the blanket again, then left the bench, beckoning me to follow him. We left the inn and went outside, looking across the river as it reflected the warm gold-leaf afterglow of sunset up river. It was a fine eve but turning chill.

'You were there, Seb,' Troilus began without preamble, gripping the sleeve of my jerkin. 'Do you know what happened at the river this morn? One moment we were both on Tris's horse, the next we were under water. How did that come to pass? Did you see?'

'Nay, I know not. The first I saw was the splashing and turmoil. You were already down in the river.'

'You came to aid us, I realise, but Tris be right confused. He says it felt as if someone held him down.'

'The weight of the horse…'

'Not that. He insists it was hands clutching his shoulders, forcing him under. I told him he's mistaken, that those hands were pulling him clear… saving him… and me. But he refuses to listen. I think the water must have gone in through his ears and addled his brain. Can that happen?'

I shrugged my jerkin higher about my neck and fastened the top lacing.

'Being neither a physician nor surgeon, I am not the man to ask. Mayhap it can but I have ne'er heard of such a thing occurring. Ask the two Cambridge scholars; they be well learned in many things, perhaps in medicine also.'

'I shall. At least our horses have recovered well. The farrier at Northfleet looked them over and, to be certain, I asked the ostler here to tend them closely. He says they're fine. And that's another thing amiss with Tris: he hasn't once asked me about them, yet our horses are like close kin to us. More than family, in truth. I'm worried about him, Seb. I think he's quite sick, worse than he admits if he has no thought for Goodwin and Cassidy. The horses,' he added, as I was about to ask to whom he referred.

Friday, the twenty-seventh day of October
Gravesend to Rochester

The morn was gloomy, mist-shrouded and cold. Our first prayers of the day hung like damp smoke from our lips. But we had slept well and I felt enlivened with new vigour after yesterday's drenching, the weather notwithstanding. I admit my surprise at seeing Tristan breaking his fast with the rest of us after his woebegone condition last eve, but that be the way of youth: quick to mend and recover, God be praised, though he spooned the eel pottage with less enthusiasm than his twin.

We returned to St Mary's Church by the crossroads to hear Low Mass and put our donations in the alms box and then we were back upon the Dover Road.

'At the first chance, arm yourselves with stout staves for later, when we reach Cobham Woods. Who knows what ill-starred wretches may lurk there in the greenwood; outlaws all,' Tanner instructed us as he strode ahead, already with his trusty pilgrim staff in hand. His words recalled a song to mind and I began singing 'Under the Greenwood Tree' as others joined in.

Troilus and one of the Cambridge men had especially fine voices. Tristan did not sing, having all to do to sit his horse, so I thought. The so-called minstrel also remained silent – a blessing indeed. Our music passed the miles through Milton, Denton – hardly a hamlet – Chalk, Merston, Oakleigh and Higham. Merston and Oakleigh were but a handful of dwellings yet Merston boasted a fine church. Perhaps the hamlet had once been larger, in times afore the plague.

Here we paused – sadly, no inspiring murals for me to admire, although there was a handsome wooden carving of St Christopher to whom I lit a candle, beseeching him to guard us this day upon our journey and keep us safe from harm. Others may arm themselves with sticks, I would trust to Our Lord Jesu and St Christopher's protection. As did the Carmelite brothers.

By the time the trees closed in around us, most of our band had cut staves to beat off any attack. Even Rose had a whippy hazel branch in hand. Kit wielded a hefty ash branch, carrying it over his shoulder in the manner of a club. Dickon demanded he should likewise go armed and I broke off a twig for him.

'Big stick, Papa, big stick,' he insisted as he cast the twig aside, finding a fallen branch for himself. It was two yards long at least, its shrivelled leaves dragging the ground as he attempted to pull it free of the brambles. I took my knife and cut it to less than half the size – easy enough as it was mostly rotten – and my son was content to stagger along with it. No doubt, he would tire of its cumbersome weight right swiftly.

As matters turned out, prayer proved sufficient and no staves were required. It seemed the outlaws were elsewhere this day, bothering others, maybe, but leaving us in peace. Dickon – as I predicted – abandoned his stick, swapping it for a length of fluffy traveller's joy, tickling Julia with the 'old-man's-beard' seed heads, making her laugh. Our toddlings' merry chuckling echoed through the dour woods, cheering everyone.

Out among fallow fields once more, we descended another long hill towards a wide river. Not the Thames, as Tanner informed us. This was the Medway, which made Kent a country of two halves. I took care crossing the marshy way, it being my turn to pull the cart in which both children now rested. Kit's blistered hands were sore, he having forgotten to wear gloves until it was too late, whereas I had a stout pair made for me by Rose that served right well to prevent blisters. We kept to the path marked by painted poles, making for the stone bridge. A tumbledown building, roofless now, had once been a Chapel of Ease, according to my *Guide for Pilgrims*, as I had read last eve. Now, it could hardly pass for a cattle byre. My book also told that tolls would be demanded in order to cross Rochester Bridge.

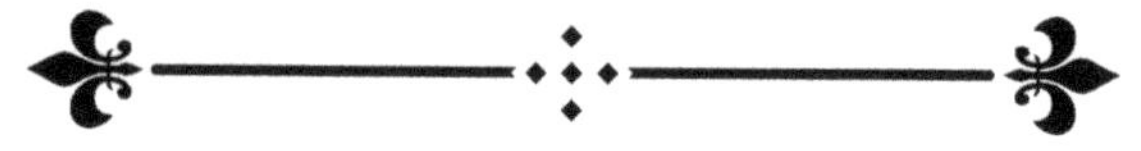

Overlooking the river, a mighty square keep loomed large, guardian of the bridge, although the castle be a deal older than the bridge. I paused to select coins from my purse for the toll.

'And no allowance made for pilgrims!' the officious bridge warden said. 'Otherwise every damned traveller claims he's on a bloody pilgrimage.' I paid him two pence for Rose and myself and went to walk on. 'Hey! It's a penny for that cart, too.'

'What? For the babes? They go upon London's bridge for naught.'

'Well, this ain't London, is it? Laden carts are charged a penny, no matter what the load: hogsheads of ale or children, they wear out the bridge just the same.'

I suppose he had a point but it was such a little cart.

'Buckle your purse, Seb,' Kit said, pushing in front of me. 'Now listen, here, you fat oaf, we are pilgrims bound for Canterbury and the whole of Christendom knows that pilgrims pay their dues in prayer, not coin. Now return my friend's money or…'

'Or what?' The warden sized up to Kit who topped him by

half a head, although the fellow was broader and stoutly built.

'Or I'll personally report your offence to the Bishop of Rochester. Return the money to everyone in our pilgrim band or suffer the consequences.'

The wretch laughed aloud.

'And why would the bishop listen to you, eh?'

'Because the new bishop, Edmund Audley, happens to be my uncle.'

'I don't believe you.'

'No? Then believe *this!'* At which Kit balled his fist and struck the warden squarely on the nose. Blood spurted.

'The bailiff shall hear o' you,' the fellow muttered from behind his gore-soaked hands, staggering back.

'And Bishop Audley shall hear of you… from me. Now return our coins… all of them.'

The warden was too slow to oblige, more concerned for his broken nose, so Kit took a handful of silver from the box and distributed it among us: a penny for everyone on foot, tuppence for those on horseback and for the monk upon his donkey. The remainder he returned to the toll-box.

'And forgive us our trespasses, Oh, Lord God, as we forgive those who make trespass against us,' I heard Kit say under his breath as he crossed himself. When he looked at me, he wore the grin of a mischievous schoolboy.

'Be it true? About the bishop being your uncle?' I asked.

'Maybe. Who can say what relation he could be? My mother knew a lot of churchmen in her younger days,' he added wickedly.

Gawain came trotting back from somewhere or other, his fur befouled with mud.

'You foolish dog,' I remonstrated with him. 'What have you done? Look at you, you filthy beast. Nay, keep away from me.' Despite my command, he then shook himself, splattering Kit and me, yet had the temerity to wag his tail after. If dogs may have facial expressions, I would hazard that the impudent creature looked most pleased with himself. I wiped my face upon the hem of my cloak. 'You shall do penance for this, Gawain: no cheese for you this day nor tomorrow.' He continued to wag his tail joyously. Likely, he comprehended the word "cheese" and naught else and now expected his favoured treat to be forthcoming. In which case, he would be disappointed.

Kit was still grinning even as he sucked at his bruised knuckles. He seemed unmindful of the muddy droplets besmirching his attire.

We made our way across the long bridge. Unlike London Bridge, there were no houses nor shops erected upon it and the way was broad enough for us to walk abreast, which was fortunate forwhy a small band of pilgrims was coming the other way. We greeted them in the midst of the bridge, wishing each other Godspeed. One who spoke with us was plump as a pudding; his companion, thin as a stick, looked most unwell, jaundiced and hollow-cheeked. I wondered how he had managed to reach Canterbury but his pilgrim badge proclaimed that he had. Would he reach home, if he should survive so long, poor man? His efforts to please Almighty God did not look to have met with success – at least, not as yet. Mayhap miracles took a little time. The others of their party looked both hale and whole, thankfully.

Rochester

We collected our customary pilgrims' dole at the Priory of St Andrew. The ale was good, the bread wholesome and we lingered under the gate arch to consume it. The market in the main street was bustling 'neath the shadow of the castle's outer curtain wall. A knife-grinder was plying his trade upon a whetstone and I paid him a ha'penny to sharpen my knife and Rose's whilst she purchased a few sweetmeats for Dickon and Julia to reward their good behaviour thus far. We could overlook my son's little tantrum at Northfleet yesterday, for he had long forgotten it by now.

The mist was thicker by the river, lacing the bare branches of the willows and alders along the bank. Cattle grazed in the meadow, half-shrouded, moving ghost-like, lowing and blowing clouds of wet breath. I pulled Dickon's cloak close about him and chafed his little fingers.

'Keep your mittens on,' I told him, putting them on his hands for the third time – or was it the sixth – knowing full well they would be off again and dangling from their cord afore I could say a Paternoster. 'Come, let us enter the cathedral. Mayhap there will be a brazier to warm us.'

There were no braziers, unfortunately, and the stone nave with its great rounded pillars was colder yet than outside. We followed Tanner and the others in silent procession to the shrine of St William of Perth – a place in faraway Scotland, apparently. It stood in the north transept. As we knelt to beg the saint's intercession, Rose asked me in a whisper who was this William? I explained to her that, according to my informative *Guide for Pilgrims*, he had been a humble baker come upon a pilgrimage on his way to Canterbury nigh three hundred years ago.

'So any ordinary one of us can become a saint,' she whispered back. 'How marvellous is that?'

'Not so marvellous, in truth. He earned his sainthood by being murdered here in Rochester.'

'Oh, indeed then, I shall pray that none of us earns sainthood that way.'

'A fellow pilgrim, suffering some affliction, found the body and, upon touching the same, was instantly cured of whatever assailed him. 'Twas deemed a miracle.'

This set me to thinking about Alfred Denny's death back in Dartford. Mayhap Mother Thorogood should have touched his corpse and her sight could have been amended forwhy I be certain he too was murdered. St Alfred of wherever he came from. Had we been in company, however briefly, with a saint? If we had, naught came pass to indicate the sanctity of poor

Alfred. No miracles apparent. Yet he had died a pilgrim like this William.

In the south aisle, I admired a mural of Dame Fortune's Wheel, well done, if not to such a high standard as those done at the church in Stone and not displaying Miles Paynter's degree of accomplishment either. But it reminded me of how fickle life can be: all well one day, calamity the next. Our one and only certainty is Almighty God.

We ate a hasty dinner of bread and herring in the priory's guest house as Tanner was right eager that we should spend this night at Boxley Abbey.

'It's not so far,' he announced as we were finishing our ale. 'Though there is a right steep way down Bluebell Hill, it will be worth it, as you'll see.'

'So there's yet another hill,' Kit muttered gloomily and I wondered if our irrepressible priest was coming to regret his impulsive decision to join us.

'As Tanner says, it will be worth it. My *Guide for Pilgrims* tells of wonders to behold at Boxley,' I said, attempting to cheer him.

'Unless these wonders include new hands and feet for me, I have little interest in them. My blisters are a plague.'

'Two pairs of hose have worked for me and remember to wear gloves when pulling the cart.'

'Aye, I'll try putting on extra hose right now. As for the cart, I leave that to you this afternoon.'

I nodded. Had Kit not accompanied us, I should have had to pull it every step of the way and had been prepared to do so. I was grateful that he had spared me much labour thus far.

Chapter 9

Friday after noon
To Boxley Abbey

IN TRUTH, 'twas a long, gradual ascent up the escarpment to the top of Bluebell Hill and thus not so arduous as we feared. The weather had cleared and the view from the summit showed a wide valley spread before us. I likened it to a tapestry in shades of green, brown and gold against a pale sky with the River Medway appearing occasionally as a silvery skein glimpsed among the naked willows that marked its path. Smoke rose from scattered houses below and Tanner pointed out the more substantial buildings of Aylesford Priory to the west at the foot of the hill whence the Carmelite brothers were bound. A little to the east, he directed our gaze to a cluster of stone buildings and a square church tower.

'That's Boxley,' Tanner said, pointing. 'The Cistercian brethren there have such miraculous things you'll find hard to believe. The Rood of Grace quite robbed me of speech the first time I saw it. And the image of St Rumbold will put you to the test for certain.' He chuckled and thumped Kit on the shoulder. 'It'll test your sanctity, Sir Priest, then we'll know whether you're worthy of the title or not.'

'I think this cliff will prove the greater task, whatever St Rumbold has in store for us,' Kit said with a sigh, peering at the chalk face which descended precipitously before us. 'How do we get down there?'

'There's a winding track, steep but possible, though I suggest you carry the children. That cart may well be inclined to run away with you. And should we meet anyone coming up, for pity's sake, don't impede them: if they stop, they may not get going again. You'll see there are a few levelled places where horses – or folk – may pause to gather their strength but you're right, Priest, it's a great task going up or down.'

The Carmelite monk on his donkey did better than any of us, the creature being sure-footed and seeming to know the best way forth. The Warenne twins had to dismount and lead their horses, the animals refusing at first to go down, tossing their heads and whinnying, pulling back. They required a deal of persuasion.

Kit carried Dickon, saying his hands were too sore to hold the cart from careering off the track, so that left me to wrestle with it alone. Rose had Julia in one arm and assisted Mother Thorogood with the other. Of course, her wretched familiar, that demonic cat, had no difficulty whatsoever in making its way down the hellish hill.

Halfway down, we met a waggoner, struggling to get his oxen moving again after resting to catch their breath on a flat, chalky area. I did not envy him or his beasts and wondered how we would manage upon our return journey. Mayhap there was another road, a different route we might take to avoid this climb.

I lost count of the times my feet slithered from under me as I struggled to restrain the empty cart and ended up sliding on my backside in the dirt. Others suffered similar mishaps. Kit chuckled into his sleeve when one of the Cambridge scholars pitched over – a less-than-Christian act on my friend's part, I fear. Rose slipped one time but managed to remain upright, although Julia cried out at her stepmother's momentary over-tight handling.

I saw Master Glassman – he who kept his right arm in a sling – suddenly forego the sling, windmilling his arms in an effort not to tumble and such language as he used did not belong on pilgrimage. Tanner grabbed him and saved him from a fall, brushing him down as the man returned his arm to its sack-cloth support. I wondered if he truly required its aid forwhy there seemed naught amiss with the limb. And how young Alfred Denny and the other scholar avoided tipping his grandsire off the litter and all three of them kept from rolling down hill, I know not.

A curse and a clatter drew my attention even as I struggled with the cart, which suddenly had a mind to go where I did not intend. Hugo Harper – it was he who was cursing – took a tumble and landed on his back, crushing the musical instruments slung over his shoulder. His elbow went through the parchment skin of his tabor and his curving crumhorn fell in three pieces. Back upon his feet, what he did next shocked me: he flung both instruments off the side of the hill, putting all his strength behind each throw! What manner of artist treats the tools of his craft, his livelihood no less, with such contempt? Most probably, the tabor could be repaired with new parchment and a good joiner may have been able to mend the crumhorn. I treasure my drawing stuff, pens and pigments as if they be family members and I could not understand such wanton destruction. How would the minstrel earn his bread now? Mind, in truth, a less talented musician may be difficult to find and the Warenne twins cheered his desperate action, knowing we would be spared any future "entertainment" from Harper. I, too, was not entirely sorry to see the instruments gone.

At last, we were at the hill's foot. Mayhap the Almighty and all His saints were watching over us, for if there ever was a miracle at Boxley, it must be the fact that all of us arrived whole. No broken bones or twisted limbs: that I did account miraculous indeed.

'Now you understand why I wanted us to come by way of Otford and Wrotham, along the proper Pilgrims' Way,' Tanner said. 'We could have saved ourselves this hazard.'

I did not remind him that we had no choice since the Otford road had been flooded. I was more concerned to get back my breath.

The Carmelites with their donkey turned right at the bottom of the hill, taking the sunken lane towards their priory in Aylesford. The rest of us went west along a broader way 'neath bare oaks, our feet hushing through the carpet of fallen leaves. Acorns lay scattered everywhere. The swineherds should bring their pigs to fatten on this bountiful harvest.

Boxley Abbey

The abbey gatehouse stood four-square, mighty and impressive as a castle keep. Only the gilded rood above the double doorway proclaimed it a religious house, not a fortress. Tanner knocked at the small door cut into one of the greater oak doors. It opened straightway but we had to stand aside as a group of pilgrims was leaving, chattering and proclaiming the wonders they had witnessed within.

'Make sure to see the Rood of Grace,' one said, clutching my sleeve as he passed me. No greeting whatsoever yet he behaved towards me with more familiarity than a close kinsman! 'It comes alive. Christ Jesu lives within this place, I tell you.'

We were every one of us weary from our travail and suppertime was nigh. Even my Gawain lay panting at my feet. All we desired was rest and refreshment – at least I did. But Tanner was already speaking with one of the monks, persuading him to direct us into the abbey church immediately, so eager was our leader that we should witness the wondrous Rood afore we ate.

'Come, come,' he said, beckoning us to follow him. ''Tis arranged and cannot wait. You'll see. You won't be disappointed at this reward for our efforts this day.'

'It'll have to be something marvellous indeed, else I'll be most disappointed, as will my feet and my belly,' Kit muttered as we crowded through the west door into the candlelit gloom of the church. I agreed but the children were eager for some new excitement. They were not so exhausted, having been carried all the way.

As my eyes adjusted to the dimness, we were told to look at the Rood above the screen dividing the quire from the nave. The Crucifixion scene was vividly painted with a deal of gilding shining in the candlelight but not so well carved as others we had seen. The one at Stone was done in far greater detail and that at Dartford was better painted, mayhap by Miles' hand. The Virgin's blue gown was dusty, a cobweb hanging betwixt her veil and the foot of the cross. St John had lost the toe of his sandal.

I looked at Kit and he glanced at me, shaking his head. Was this Boxley's wonder? The figure of Christ Jesu, crowned with thorns and draped in purple, hung in pain and sorrow, eyes closed. But, as we watched, Our Saviour turned His head; His eyes opened. Our Lord looked straight at us!

We gasped, crossing ourselves. Some fell upon their knees.

Then His lips moved:

'Repent ye, all ye sinners, and ye shall be forgiven!' His voice rang clear, echoing through the silent nave. Then His eyes closed once more and all was as before.

It truly was a marvel and I could not help myself: I was moved to sing in praise of this miracle we were so privileged to see. I sang the *Gloria*, pouring my heart, my very soul into every word, oblivious to those around me, aware only of Christ upon the Rood of Grace above me. Such a moment I had ne'er experienced afore. Tears of joy ran down my cheeks. Upon the last, long *Amen,* others repeated it and I came to myself as one waking from a dream.

'Seb, that was beautiful.' Rose touched my arm. 'I've never heard you sing quite like that before.'

'I have not felt such a depth of love for Our Saviour before.' I wiped my cheeks with my sleeve and looked back at the Rood, the dust, the cobwebs and the unimpressive carving. The miracle was ended but my heart exalted still.

'Good Pilgrim,' a monk addressed me as I stepped away. 'I'm Brother Oswald, the Precentor here. You have a fine voice indeed. Might I prevail upon you to sing the *Gloria* for us at Vespers?'

'I, er, of course, Brother Precentor, 'twould be an honour and a privilege indeed.'

'Excellent. Vespers begins in a half hour. I'll speak with you before then. I suggest you refresh yourself in the refectory first. Washing water is provided,' he added, noting my grubby, travel-stained apparel. No doubt my face was dirt-streaked also. 'The refectory is to the right of the courtyard. I'll find you there.'

My fellow pilgrims congratulated me. Well, most did, including the Cambridge scholars, which pleased me particularly. Hugo Harper ignored me utterly, jealous of my gift, I suppose. Master Glassman had naught to say but Troilus and Tristan also – the latter being much recovered from yesterday – cheered me heartily. Young Alfred Denny bubbled with enthusiasm and Mother Thorogood could not praise me enough, dabbing at her tears with her apron. Incidentally, I noted her cat had not dared to enter the church, the devilish thing.

I called Gawain to heel, took my son by the hand and led the way outside to the bright courtyard and thence to the refectory with the prospect of a welcome cup of ale.

'Gawain's hungry, Papa,' Dickon said, not the least overawed by miracles.

'Aye, I know. Mayhap there will be a wafer or some such to content you until supper after Vespers.'

'Gawain wants supper now!' My son stamped his foot.

'Do not be peevish. I fear Gawain will have to wait a little longer.'

'I have a sweetmeat here,' Rose said, coming to my rescue, timely as ever. 'Shall I give it to Gawain?'

'No. Dickon wants it,' he said, truthful now, reaching out with both soiled hands.

'Then what of your manners?' Rose queried.

'Please, Mam, Dickon wants a sweetmeat.' He received his reward and it was gone in an instant. Of course, Julia had to have one also and peace was restored for the moment.

Bowls of water and towels were provided, set out upon a laver board. I washed my hands and face thoroughly whilst Rose found a fresh shirt for me in our bundle. It was somewhat creased but clean. Mother Thorogood aided Dickon to wash, which was a kindly act. Rose turned her attention to my jerkin, shaking off the worst of the chalky dust from the descent of Bluebell Hill, doing all she could to have me look respectable enough to sing in the church. She also handed me a comb to do what I might with my tangled hair. I do not remember giving it the least attention since we set out from London. Be that a virtuous act, to have turned from my one vanity? I pray that it may be regarded so and not as a neglect of decent and proper cleanliness.

Kit, may God bless him, brought me a cup of ale. I was much in need and grateful for it, drinking it down in one draught. Kit promptly gave me his cup, yet half full, and went to fetch more.

'Can't have our sublime chorister croaking for want of liquid sustenance,' he said, grinning. 'You've made quite an impression, I think. Here comes Brother Oswald, looking well pleased.'

'Are you ready? Forgive me. I didn't ask your name.'

'Sebastian Foxley of London,' I said, laying aside the comb and fastening the last points on my jerkin.

'Father Abbot has given permission for you to stand in the quire with the brethren. Not in the stalls, you understand, but close at hand. You will not join in the psalms and responses, being but a layman, but we will be pleased if you would sing that fine rendition of the *Gloria* as a solo. I'll indicate to you when to sing it, so watch for my sign towards the end of the office. Did you compose the piece yourself?'

'Nay, I cannot claim such mastery of music. 'Twas written by the Precentor of St Paul's Cathedral where I be a chorister.'

'I'll have to write to him, ask his advice on certain motets I have composed. Now, come this way, Sebastian. I'll show you to your place before the choir monks assemble.'

'Aye, Brother.'

The church was aglow with candles. A brother was lighting the last few upon a great iron contraption, the size and shape of a cartwheel with more than a dozen sconces around the rim. With all candles burning steadily, he waved to another who pulled on a rope – with pulleys, I noted, understanding such things now following my introduction to Euclid and Archie Whoever – to raise the wheel high above before securing the rope around a large hook in the wall and making it secure. Four similar wheels were already in place above the nave's central aisle, providing light aplenty.

The congregation bustled in, assorted pilgrims and local folk. Members of our band were much to the fore, in particular those who knew of my appointment to sing with the expected absentees who did not care to hear it. Rose was there, shushing the children. Kit had Gawain upon a lead, Mother Thorogood stood smiling – without the cat – both Cambridge men, young Alfred Denny with his grandsire lying on the litter, the Warenne twins and Tanner, of course.

The abbot processed the length of the nave, preceded by an ornate, bejewelled cross which looked to weigh more than the little crucifer who carried it. With acolytes on either hand, the obedientiaries were followed by the choir monks and the novices, the only music the sound of sandaled feet upon encaustic tiles and the murmur of prayer. They filed 'neath the rood loft and took their places in the quire whilst the abbot, the sacrist and others went into the chancel. All made a low obeisance before the altar and Vespers commenced whilst I stood just beside the arch in the rood screen, aware that the miraculous Christ Jesu was right above my head, fully illumined by the nearest candle wheel.

The Office of Vespers was well done. I think the choir monks get more practice than the choristers at Paul's. When Brother Oswald nodded to me to begin the *Gloria*, I breathed deeply to steady myself, closed my eyes, raised my head high and sang. I gave it my all but I suspect that the incredible depth of feeling that had given the first rendition such joy and poignancy was somewhat lacking. In truth, I fear I shall ne'er attain the like again. But I trust it was good enough to please the abbot, which was all Brother Oswald said he required of me.

As I let the *Amen* fade into the incense-perfumed air, I caught a movement from the corner of my eye. I know not what I saw precisely but then came a whooshing sound, a loud clattering and a mighty clang and thud. Someone cried out and, of a sudden, all was panic in the nave. And there before me, but five paces away, lay a great candle wheel, its iron frame buckled. Candles were strewn upon the smashed tiles, a few yet burning but most extinguished by the rush of air as the wheel fell. But what of that? More importantly, one of the twins lay sprawled upon the floor beside it. I could not see which of them it was.

Sweet Christ Jesu be merciful, I prayed under my breath as I hastened to aid whichever twin it was. His brother was beside him.

'Troy! Troy, speak to me!' The prone figure stirred and his brother assisted him to sit. Then I could see no more as everyone crowded around the lad.

'He's fine,' I heard Tanner's voice. 'Move back and let him have space to draw breath.'

By which time, the abbot had come through the screen, demanding to know what had come to pass. The candle wheel had fallen – that much was obvious – but how and why: they were the abbot's main concerns after the wellbeing of Troilus Warenne.

Having directed the Brother Infirmerer to take charge of the unfortunate young man, the abbot began interrogating us all, in particular the monks responsible for lighting the candles earlier, but members of the congregation also: had we seen anything untoward? Was the rope frayed, the pulley broken or the hook come loose from the wall? These questions were swiftly answered as the mechanisms were inspected for damage. Naught was amiss. Had the rope been properly secured? This was impossible to confirm forwhy the rope now hung loose, dangling from the top-most pulley.

The abbot began berating the brothers involved in tending the candle wheels, accusing them of carelessness, negligence, idleness and every other fault he could think of, telling them the penances to follow would be extreme indeed and teach them a lesson they would ne'er forget. In the meantime, they were to complete their duties, clear up the mess, collect any usable candles and sweep away the broken floor tiles, then snuff all the other lights bar that on the high altar. After that, they must prostrate themselves before the altar and remain there overnight, supperless.

'Twas a harsh punishment and none of my business but I felt sympathy for the monks as the possibility niggled me that they might not be to blame. I recalled that movement I had seen from the corner of my eye in the moment afore the wheel crashed down…

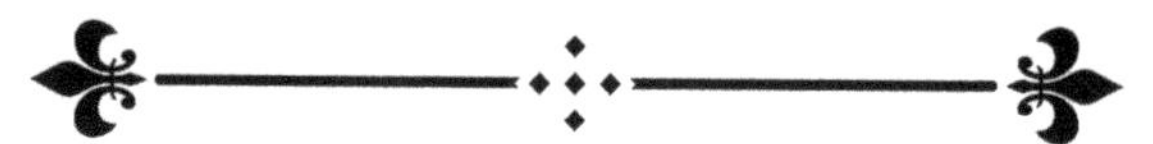

Supper in the refectory was salt herring – again. Whenever Rose prepared a similar dish at home, she soaked the fish beforehand to wash away most of the saltiness and served it with a parsley or chive sauce to improve the taste. Here, we were served the fish plain, so salty it dried our mouths and led to a deal of ale being consumed until it ran out and I was still thirsty. Dickon complained that Gawain wanted more sweetmeats to take away the taste. Julia refused to eat the fish after a single mouthful and ate only bread dipped in ale to moisten it.

'The twins are fortunate,' Kit said, pushing his platter aside with half a herring remaining.

'You think so? Sweet heaven, Kit, an inch or two closer and the outcome does not bear contemplating: a young life ended afore it has hardly begun.'

'True, but it didn't end so and those in the infirmary are permitted meat on fast days. It might be worth our while to stub a toe or complain of an aching head in hope of a decent meal.'

I ignored his words, not daring to tempt fate just to avoid more salt herrings.

'Were both the twins injured then?'

'I think not. The iron wheel caught Troilus a glancing blow to the shoulder, as far as I could make out, knocked him down. But it must've hurt and been a great shock to him. He'll be a mess of bruises by morn but I pray there are no broken bones. Tristan refuses to leave his side, which, I hope, earns him a wholesome supper, too. They deserve something good to happen to them after so much ill-luck thus far.'

Dame Fortune's Wheel leapt to mind once more. The twins certainly seemed to be caught upon its lowest point. In which case, their situation could only improve from now on.

Supper was not pleasant but at least the palliasses in the guest dormitory were comfortable, the straw stuffing being fresh and free of bugs. The blankets were of some quality and we were all of us exhausted by the day. I should have slept sound but I awoke in the dark, startled by a bad dream in which Fortune's Wheel came hurtling towards me like a runaway cart, then plunged off the edge of a precipice, taking me with it. I woke afore I landed, sweating and shaking. At least I did not disturb Rose forwhy, this being a religious house, women and children slept in a separate chamber, far removed from us menfolk and any unholy intent.

Saturday, the twenty-eighth day of October Boxley Abbey

’Twas morn but it seemed the sun had forgotten to rise, so dour was the light. The windows of the dormitory looked out onto the courtyard but, when I opened the shutter, there was naught to see below. The earth was shrouded in thick fog, a heavy grey blanket which clung damply, concealing everything more than an arm’s length distant.

‘Shut the bloody window,’ somebody shouted at me. ‘You’re letting the cold in, you damned fool. Go back to sleep.’

‘Nay. It be time for Low Mass,’ I said, closing the shutter. ‘They rang the *Angelus* bell a while since. Did none of you hear it?’

‘Low Mass be damned. I’m staying in bed,’ the fellow said and turned over. Others were of a like mind but, one by one, those of our little band bestirred themselves and prepared to face the day – what little could be seen of it.

‘Come on, you idle wretches. Get your selves out of bed,’ Tanner ordered, poking Hugo Harper with his boot. ‘We’ve got St Rumbold to contend with before we depart.’

‘Bugger Rumbold, whoever he is,’ Harper muttered, throwing off the blanket and pulling his jerkin over his head, having not bothered to unlace it when he removed it last night. ‘I wager he never had to traipse across half England on a supposed holy errand.’

I raised my eyebrows at this. Why had the minstrel come on pilgrimage if he thought it not worthwhile?

We went down the chill stone stair to the refectory, out across the mist-swathed courtyard, towards the barely-visible church for Low Mass. Rose joined us at the doorway and I kissed her heartily, earning a scowl from the monk who saw what I did. There be naught sinful in greeting a loved one so and, I suppose, if I had but brushed her cheek with my lips, that would have been acceptable. But having missed her overnight, I pulled her close and lingered long over kissing her sweet mouth. After which, I smiled at the disapproving brother in mischievous wise. *Mea culpa.* I admit my fault but did not feel the least remorseful.

I greeted the little ones in a more comely fashion – unlike Gawain, who gave both Dickon and Julia a thorough lick and wash – and gave Mother Thorogood my best smile whilst casting my eyes about, searching out that cat, the better to avoid any close encounter unexpectedly. There it was, lurking 'neath its mistress's skirts. Would it dare accompany her into God's house? Indeed it did, blatant and bold, tail held high. I wonder it was not struck down by a thunderbolt.

'Twas fortunate that the office was brief, forwhy we all were eager to break our fast. It being a Saturday, we hoped for a generous portion of something better than over-salted herring. The presiding Guest Master recited a long Latin grace and dishes were brought in by a motley group of lay brothers, some very young, others ancient, tripping on their tattered gowns. But the aromas rising from the steaming pots did not hold much promise.

Fish. Pickled herrings this time, served with dark bread. No sauce but the sour pickling verjuice. Little wonder Boxley Abbey was said to be right wealthy. They certainly wasted not a farthing on feeding their guests.

Little Dickon shuddered visibly at his first bite of the fish. Julia cried over hers and Gawain – wise dog – refused my offering, an event not known afore.

'Leave it,' I told them in a whisper. 'We shall buy something in the village when we depart.'

'Sweetmeats?' my son suggested, hopefully.

'We shall see.'

'Anything is preferable to this,' my wife said. Ne'er one to complain, if Rose commented thus, the food must be dreadful indeed.

'Pigs wouldn't eat it,' Kit admitted as we sat, looking at our hardly touched platters, awaiting the final grace, which seemed irrelevant in any case. Who would give thanks for a meal so inedible? Etiquette and piety required we wait but not all were so well-mannered.

A handful of pilgrims – their badges marking them as having visited Canterbury already – rose from the benches, muttered a few words that may have been a grace of sorts and walked out. The Guest Master was left spluttering in outrage at such disrespect but, realising folk were done breaking their fast, he stood and said a brief prayer of thanks afore dismissing us with a curt nod.

'Gawain wants sweetmeats,' Dickon announced loudly the moment we left the refectory.

'Soon, soon, little one,' Rose assured him as she settled Julia in the cart, wrapping the lass warmly against the chill of the fog, droplets of moisture already forming on the sheep skin coverlet.

But Tanner was not ready to leave.

'Come. We have yet to behold the marvel of St Rumbold. Back to the church, everyone.'

In two minds, I was unsure whether this saint, whose name I had not heard until I read my *Guide for Pilgrims*, was more important than a fat pasty for our rumbling bellies. But the guide book said the saint tested folks' degree of piety by some means, without giving further details. I admit to being curious as to the method employed but uncertain as to whether I wished my own piety to be tested and made known to all. How embarrassing it would be if I failed.

A monk led us to a side aisle where the saint's image lay upon a plinth. Expecting the likeness of an ancient bishop or some such, I was surprised to find a swaddled babe carved from alabaster, painted and gilded.

'This most holy infant,' the brother began, raising his eyes and outstretched hands to heaven, 'Is an example to us all. Upon the very day of his birth, he cried out that he was a devout Christian, demanded he be baptised with the name "Rumbold" and preached a sermon...'

At which I glanced at Dickon. A babe, newborn, able to speak a solitary word would be wondrous indeed, but an entire sermon? Hard to believe.

'...Telling others to forsake their pagan idols and worship Christ the Lord. He foretold his own death within three days and directed his place of burial...'

'Here at Boxley, no doubt. Died of a surfeit of fish,' old Alfred Denny said from his litter.

'No. At Buckingham,' the monk answered, sounding impatient. 'Now, who will be the first to demonstrate his piety and righteousness of spirit? 'Tis easily done: simply lift the little saint from his resting place.' He stepped forward, close to the plinth, took hold of the image in both hands and raised it high, then replaced it with care.

None volunteered, despite it seeming an easy task.

'I'll do it,' Tanner said.

'Good but first make your offering. Put your coin in the dish provided.' The monk pointed to a sizable wooden platter set upon a shelf beside the image. A few coins lay upon it.

Tanner unfastened his purse, took out a groat and placed it in the dish. Then, with a nonchalant grin, he made to lift the image. It did not move. Tanner tried again, putting in more effort but the saint refused to budge even so much as a hair's breadth.

'I lifted it the last time I was here,' Tanner said, grunting as he struggled.

'Then you are less righteous now than you were before. Reconsider your sins, is my advice.' The monk beamed, self-satisfied at Tanner's failure. 'Who's next?'

After that, others tried. Only one of the Cambridge scholars passed the test, his righteousness proclaimed by the monk; the other failed, as did young Alfred Denny, who ought to have succeeded if for no other reason than his saintly patience shown towards his grandfather. Master Glassman and Hugo Harper did not bother. The twins had not yet appeared. Mayhap poor

Troilus was too sore to leave the infirmary and they would remain here for a few days that he might rest and recover. I should be sorry to lose them from our band.

'I'll have a go,' Kit said with a shrug, 'Sinful as I am.' He tipped coins into the dish and took a firm stance. When he made to lift St Rumbold, the image moved so easily that my friend – expecting it to be difficult – nigh toppled back and I had to steady him.

'God be praised. We have another righteous pilgrim amongst us!' the monk declared.

'Well, that wasn't so hard, was it?' Kit said. 'Why don't you try, Seb?'

I shook my head.

'You're a righteous man,' Rose told me. 'How can you fail?'

Oh, aye, I could fail right easily and feel an utter fool. I had not forgotten that kiss at the church door.

'You sang that beautiful *Gloria* last eve, didn't you?' the monk said. Was he implying that my singing must make me more righteous somehow?

'I did but…'

Kit leaned close and whispered in my ear:

'Put at least six pence in the dish and you'll have no trouble.'

I frowned at him but he nodded and nudged me with his elbow. I fished a groat, a half groat and a penny from my purse – seven pence in all – placed them in the offertory platter and reached for the saintly babe. It weighed so little as I raised it up. Sweet Jesu be praised that I had not failed. How come Kit was so certain I should succeed? I must ask him later.

'May I try?' Rose asked the monk.

'A woman?' The monk sounded incredulous.

'A woman can be as pious and righteous as a man,' she told him. 'I haven't always lived a righteous life, I admit, but my husband set me upon the narrow way and I've tried so hard to make amends for the past. I wish to know if my efforts and prayers to Our Saviour are sufficient to begin to earn my redemption.'

'Let her try,' Mother Thorogood insisted, 'On behalf of womankind.'

'Then she will undoubtedly fail,' the monk said. 'But do as you will, mistress.'

Rose put a few coins in the dish but I could not see how many since there was now quite a heap of silver. As she made to take hold of the image, I saw Kit standing so close to the monk, he must surely be treading on the brother's feet. The monk grimaced and pushed Kit aside even as Rose lifted the saintly babe aloft.

The monk did not proclaim her but glared at her. Even her winning smile did naught to assuage his obvious anger. I could not understand it. Should he not delight in the proof of another worthy soul? Especially that of a woman in this abbey dedicated to St Mary the Virgin? Perhaps, long ago, a woman had upset him and he took refuge in holy orders but could not forgive that lost love, venting his chagrin on all women?

'Twas time to depart Boxley and purchase a goodly breakfast.

Chapter 10

Saturday morn
From Boxley to Chilham

In Boxley village, praise be, there was a man with a tray of pies. Mutton, beef or chicken? We could choose which. Anything but herring! Everyone bought pies of some kind and the man went on his way with an empty tray, whistling as he disappeared into the fog. We all felt much improved for a full belly but Rose purchased a pot of quince jelly from a woman with a basket by the village green.

'In lieu of sweetmeats, just in case,' she assured me.

Surprisingly, the Warenne twins joined us, mounted upon their fine steeds.

'How do you fare, Troilus?' I asked, seeing he nursed his arm somewhat as he sat in the saddle.

'I'll mend,' he said cheerfully, although the grin required effort, I thought.

'And you, Tristan?'

'Same here. Better than yesterday. The infirmerer said I'd swallowed too much water. Gave me a remedy to ease my belly. It worked well.'

'I be right glad to hear it,' I said.

'Be sure to take good care, both of you,' Rose told them in motherly wise. 'Look after each other.'

'We always do.'

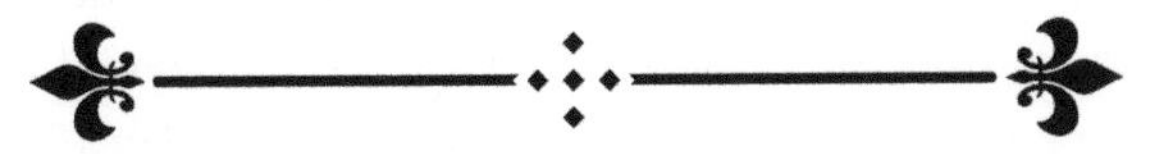

We now followed the Pilgrims' Way proper to Harrietsham. Tanner was more at ease on this familiar track, telling us the way would be safe now, patrolled by the archbishop's men and we could make good time on this better road. However, it was a score or so miles to Chilham, where he determined to pass this final night afore we reached Canterbury, and the fog was dense at ever. We kept losing sight of each other and even Tanner took the wrong path once or twice.

Lenham, our intended place for an early dinner, became, instead, a hasty stop for a belated dinner. We saw naught of the village but Tanner pointed in the direction of the church that we might offer an appropriate prayer or two afore hastening on.

Then Mother Thorogood's cat went astray for a while. I thought – nay, hoped – the creature was gone forever. The old woman was sobbing, at a loss without her bell-tinkling guide, though it was difficult to hear it, muffled by the fog. She begged us to search out the creature and I was right torn betwixt my desire ne'er to set eyes upon it again and sparing my ears from her heartrending wails of distress.

My soft heart won the day and, in truth, the wretched Lucifer was easily discovered, sitting in the church porch, tail neatly curled over his paws. Picking him up was another matter. Well aware of my deep dislike of its evil yellow eyes and black-as-sin fur, it hissed at me, ears flattened, backing away, its fur on end. As I grabbed it, it yowled, twisting in my arms, lashing out with its dreadful claws. I cursed as it tore the end of my jerkin sleeve, drawing blood from my hand and justifying every ounce of my loathing.

Mother Thorogood heard the commotion and hastened to its source.

'Puss, puss,' she coaxed, 'Come here, my dear.' And there it went, meek and mild as a saint, into her welcoming embrace, rubbing against her as though with real affection. The monster.

I sucked at my hand, hoping the triple gouges would not turn morbid, praying there was not poison in those claws. I should have kept my gloves on – those I wore when pulling the cart – but I removed them to eat my bread-and-cheese dinner. Too late, I put them back on, covering the scratches.

Both children slept in the cart as we trundled on. Kit aided me in pulling it, his blisters much better now, he insisted. At least the hills were gentler and less frequent but we all required some respite at Charing.

The fog thinned a little and Tanner led some of our band to the church there to see the block upon which John the Baptist was beheaded and promising they should see another marvel alongside the magnificent Archbishop's Palace – Becket's favoured abode, as my guide book informed me. But I had not the heart for it.

Rose and I retired to the Saracen's Head Inn so she might tend my injured hand. Their first sight of it, still bleeding a little and already inflamed, caused much consternation among the women. Mother Thorogood deluged me with apologies, claiming her cat must have been greatly affrighted else it would not have behaved so, being such a friendly creature. This statement I received with – as the old saying goes – a pinch of salt. Both women applied every ointment and salve they had with them afore winding layers of linen and bindings about my hand. 'Twas my left hand, God be thanked. Had it been my right, the cat could have ended my livelihood with its act of foul wickedness. Even so, if ever it came within a knife blade's length of me…

Kit returned with Tanner, the Cambridge scholars and both Alfreds from the church.

'Did you see the marvel, whatever it is?' I asked him as I

drank my ale.

'Aye. It's a clock. We went up into the bell tower where you can watch the cogs and gear wheels turning and see how one causes the next to move. Most informative.'

'A mechanical marvel this time, not a divine one as at Boxley, then?'

Kit sipped his ale and then looked me straight:

'You know St Rumbold's miracle was all mechanical, don't you.' he said.

'Nay. 'Twas a test of piety…'

My friend snorted.

''Twas a trick. That's what it was. A test of the giver's generosity, not his piety. Those who donate six pence or more can lift the image; less than that and it stays firm on its plinth.'

'Then is that not also a marvel? That the saint knows how much you gave.'

'Oh, Seb, how gullible you are. The saint knows naught. The monk sees how much you put in the offertory platter. If it's more than whatever amount he decides you can afford, then he steps upon a pedal at the base of the plinth, releasing the mechanism which clasps the saint in place.'

'Truly? Nay. The monks would not… 'tis a fraudulent act. I cannot believe they would do such a thing.'

'Oh, indeed they would. I watched exactly what that monk did every time someone succeeded, and he would never have allowed Rose to lift it if I hadn't stamped on the pedal.'

'You did that? Oh, Kit, you'll tell me next that the Lord Christ on the Rood of Grace did not look upon us and speak to us… He did, I know for certain.'

'Mm, I wonder if you do,' Kit mumbled and turned his attention to refilling our ale cups from the jug.

'Make haste, everyone, we're leaving now,' Tanner called out from the door onto the street. 'As it is, it'll be dark by the time we reach Chilham. Come. Move your lazy backsides.'

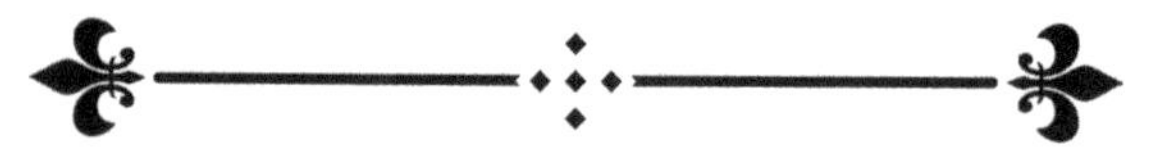

In truth, it was half dark now, though the midday *Angelus* had rung not so long since. Gauging the hour by the sun was impossible through the yellow-grey gloom which shrouded everything. No bird sang. Likely, they were all gone to roost, reckoning it was dusk already. Not a breath of wind disturbed the pall of fog.

We trudged along, doggedly determined to reach our destination but there was no joy in our journey. Few words were spoken. No songs were sung nor jests exchanged. Neither did we pass another soul upon the road. Anyone with the sense God gave a sheep was indoors beside a goodly fire, except us.

I should have been content to remain at The Saracen's Head over night, even if that meant an extra day upon the road but Tanner was insistent. We could have defied him but then we would be travelling without a guide tomorrow and lacking the safety of numbers.

Trees closed in about the way, mere shadowy forms yet making the day ever darker. We came to a shallow stream and crossed it by way of stepping stones, having to each take our turn, which strung out our party, particularly as Kit and I had to lift the cart across, matching our steps to maintain the cart's length betwixt us. The stones were green and slippery and much care was required. Meanwhile, the twins simply spurred their horses through the water and went on to join the others. I had been following their horses' tails, making certain to keep them in sight but now our efforts with the cart left us trailing behind at the back of the group. Only Mother Thorogood was still with us.

A flock of starlings burst from the bushes in a flurry of feathers.

'What disturbed them?' I wondered aloud.

'A fox, maybe?' Rose offered. 'Or a Foxley, at least.'

Then we heard shouts up ahead and hastened onwards to discover what was happening. Closer, we made out cries of alarm and the clash of staves. A horse whinnied and the sound of running feet accompanied the snapping of twigs and rustling undergrowth. We came upon a scene of chaos.

Outlaws were attacking our band.

'Stay back, Rose. Guard the children,' I told her afore grabbing a staff which lay dropped in the road. 'Come, Gawain: do your duty, lad.' I ran after Kit into the fray.

Ne'er a fighting man at heart, I would protect my loved ones to the last breath in my body. I laid about me with the staff, hitting out, uncaring what I struck so long as it was a stranger's head, back, arm or knee cap. Gawain leapt, snarled and probably bit whilst I fought like a demon. Who knew I was capable of such ferocity?

Then, as suddenly as it had begun, the attack ended, the brigands fleeing into the woods from whence they came.

I leaned upon a tree trunk and closed my eyes, saying a swift prayer of thanks for my survival afore taking stock of the damage to others. My first concerns were for Rose and the little ones. They were hale and whole, God be praised, and though Julia was crying in the cart, Dickon – my little warrior – was on his feet, waving a stick and shouting with excitement. Secondly, I looked to Gawain. Although I had to pull the shreds of some fellow's hose from betwixt the dog's teeth, all was well with him also. But where was Kit?

I went to aid Tanner, who was struggling to get up, and I realised it was his staff I had used as a weapon. With its aid, Rose and I got him to a log that he might sit and recover his wits. A bruise the size of a duck's egg was already turning black and blue upon his forehead.

'Bastard cut my purse,' one of the scholars cried.

'He didn't get mine,' his companion declared, 'But received my knife in his arm for his trouble. You should've been quicker.'

'It was all so sudden.'

Tanner noticed then that his purse was also gone.

Grandfather Denny began shouting, instructing everyone as to what they should have done and how, in former days, he would have gutted the miscreants personally without anyone else's aid.

'Hush, Grandfather, 'Tis done now. Don't upset yourself further,' young Alfred was saying, still brandishing a stout stick and I noted he had a gash upon his cheek. The lad must have defended the old man right bravely and taken the wound for his efforts.

'Where is Kit? And the twins?' I asked, accounting them friends more than the rest of our band.

Kit and Master Glassman came from amongst the trees. Kit paused to rub his hands with a tuft of wet grass afore gripping Glassman's shoulder in a comradely fashion and exchanging glances. Without a word, the older man dropped the stolen purses on the road. His sack-cloth sling hung loose about his neck and he used it to wipe gore from the long-bladed knife in his supposedly-injured hand. Both knife and hand were then placed back in the sling. Well, it was an unusual place to keep a weapon but his actions had been timely. But none had answered my question about the twins' whereabouts and Hugo Harper was also missing.

'Are you hurt?' I asked Kit. He shook his head, grinning. 'And Master Glassman?' He shrugged.

'Why ask me?'

'You seemed companionable just now.'

'I don't know him no more than you, Seb, but he looks well enough to me. His injured arm doesn't appear to hinder him in a fight, does it?'

'No, it does not. But you and he…'

Unaccountably, Kit glared at me, so I pursued the matter no further.

Rose and Mother Thorogood set about dispensing salves for bruises and binding cuts. Tanner was looking better 'neath the old woman's ministering hands.

A clattering of hooves heralded the return of the twins.

'Get off me, you damned idiot!'

'Leave my brother alone!'

Hugo Harper was clinging to the back of one twin, a knife in his hand. The other brother succeeded in wrenching him away, so the minstrel fell in the bushes.

'What's amiss with you, Harper? Are you blind or stupid or both? We're not the outlaws. We were trying to run them to ground and then you attacked Troy. Why?'

'I thought you were... outlaws, I mean,' Harper said, brushing his clothes free of leaf litter. 'An easy mistake to make in the heat of the moment.' He shrugged, retrieving his knife from the wayside and putting it back in its sheath on his belt afore slinking away to hide behind the nearest tree.

'But we're mounted; the outlaws weren't. Are you unhurt, Troy? I'll slay that fool if he's harmed a single hair of your head.'

'No. I'm fine. My bandaged shoulder made it harder to... fight him off but I...' Troilus's voice faded as he slipped from his horse to tumble into the road. Tristan leapt down, kneeling at his brother's side, just as he had last eve at Boxley. The lads' run of ill-luck continued.

But Troilus recovered swiftly, as youngsters do, revived by a draught from the wine skin the elder Denny had kept hidden under his blanket all this while, insisting his swoon was but a momentary thing of naught account. Nonetheless, as Tristan helped him back into the saddle, we would all keep a close watch upon him.

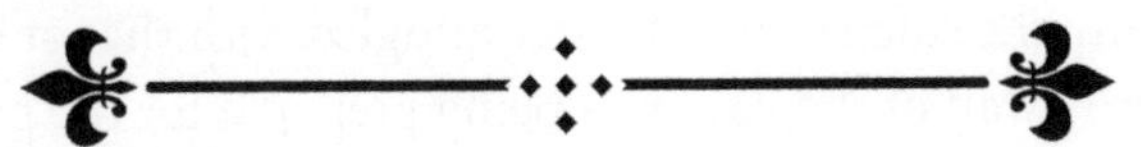

Somehow, we reached Chilham. It was nigh true dark by then and we had no light. We found the way only because the road was chalk-dust white beneath our feet. It pains me to admit this but that hateful cat aided us all as we followed its tinkling bell, cats being keen-sighted in the darkness. Mayhap even Satan's minions have their uses.

Our night at Chilham be somewhat of a blur unto me.

We ate; we drank. Wounds were tended and then we slept but I was that weary and aching, I recall little of it. I do remember giving thanks unto God that we all survived but then exhaustion must have claimed me.

I suppose Rose took care of the little ones as always. Did I feed and water Gawain? Who can say? I suppose I did or mayhap he found sustenance for himself from someone's platter or other.

I can say little more concerning Chilham except that, by morn, we were all of us still breathing, even that scapegrace, Hugo Harper, whom we all assiduously ignored.

Sunday, the twenty-ninth day of October Chilham to Canterbury

The Lord's Day dawned misty but bright. The horrid fog was gone for the most part, like a malevolent sprite retreating to its lair. I hoped it would stay there. My cat scratches were sore but looked to be healing. Yet I had bruises aplenty I did not recall afore. Kit admitted to the same. Others were even worse afflicted, groaning at every move. Tanner especially complained of a headache and little wonder with that great ink-black lump above his eye. It made me wince each time I saw it.

We attended Low Mass in St Mary's Church. My *Guide for Pilgrims* told of its ancient foundation but much of it be but lately built.

Within, the smell of new plaster mingled with that of incense as an entire wall of the nave was being prepared for the painting of a splendid – and very expensive – mural of the Virgin and Child, so the rector informed us proudly, his eyes constantly flickering towards the offertory platter. I observed the teetering scaffolding, relieved it was not my task but fearing for the safety of the unknown limner upon that uncertain edifice, which did not appear in the least well constructed.

I admit my contribution to the rector's heap of coin was meagre, not so much because my purse was growing somewhat lighter than I wished, though it was, but forwhy I did not take to the man: a priest whose thoughts were all for coin. Mayhap I was mistaken in this – in which case, I crave his pardon – but my feelings were what they were.

After a less than inspiring Mass, we returned to the inn – named for St Peter's Keys – to break our fast. Bacon collops, eggs and good white bread! What joy. Not a herring in sight. I be certain everyone's case was much improved by this hearty fare. I know my spirits were raised. Folk smiled again and the children laughed.

Tanner was complaining to the innkeeper that something ought to be done about the outlaws in the woods, saying the archbishop was responsible for ensuring the safety of pilgrims betwixt Otford and Canterbury. The innkeeper – obviously the archbishop's man – argued that since our band was travelling outside the proper season for pilgrimage, 'twas our own responsibility and we should have hired an escort of armed men. Had we come betwixt Easter and Michaelmas, the archbishop's patrols would have protected us.

'But what of merchants, traders and messengers?' Tanner insisted. 'Such folk journey all year round.'

The innkeeper shrugged.

'They hire escorts, go by river or take the old London Road: Watling Street, as they call it. It's none of my business.'

'Well, it should be. Wouldn't you make more money if more folk travelled this way in safety, whatever the season?'

'His Grace sees me right,' the innkeeper said, wiping up an ale spillage with his apron.

'The king?' Tanner asked.

'No. Archbishop Bourchier, of course.' With that, the innkeeper went off about some other pressing business.

Having overheard this exchange, I turned to Rose and Kit: 'That determines our homeward journey, does it not? We shall go all the way upon Watling Street. If we avoid this supposed 'pilgrims' way', we may spare ourselves the danger of outlaws and that devilish climb up Bluebell Hill. I have no desire to even make an attempt upon that perilous incline. What say you?'

They both agreed, which contented me well.

'Twas but seven miles from Chilham to Canterbury and we would attain our goal by mid-morning, Tanner said – a cheering prospect at last. What with so many incidents and mishaps along the way, I had nigh forgotten our ultimate purpose.

Once or twice, I had almost despaired of seeing Canterbury but as we stood upon the high plain of Harbledown, the last tendrils of mist dispersed, the sun broke through and the city lay before us, bathed in light. The holy city of Jerusalem it was not but this was as close as a humble London stationer was ever going to come to witnessing such a sight.

Some few of us – Kit, the Cambridge scholars and I – ventured to St Nicholas Lazar House close by. If we feared that there might be lepers within, our anxieties were soon put to rest.

'Only those infirm with age dwell here now,' the young Benedictine brother told us with a smile. 'There hasn't been a leper since the Black Prince – may God assoil his soul – paid for this hospital to be rebuilt. I am Brother Luke. Will you take ale first or would you wish to see St Thomas Becket's slipper directly?'

'Becket's own slipper?' Kit queried.

'I thought the relic was your reason for visiting,' the monk said.

'We did not know of it. Tanner, our guide, hasn't mentioned it.'

''Tis but a footnote in my *Guide for Pilgrims*, I fear,' I added.

'Ah, me,' the monk sighed. 'Little wonder we've had fewer pilgrims stop by this year. Are we becoming forgotten, do you suppose? That would be a pity, for we do good work here, caring for those no longer able to care for themselves. One poor soul is convinced he's Richard the Lionheart, leading his knights against the Saracens. Another believes he can fly like a bird. We have to watch him closely. More than once of late, he's climbed onto the roof, determined to leap off and take wing. Shall I serve you ale? I brewed it myself two days since.'

'I would appreciate a cup of your ale, Brother Luke, if it please you?' I said. In truth, I was not thirsty but it seemed churlish to refuse, almost as though he had brewed his ale especially for our coming.

'It's made with sweet cicely and meadowsweet for flavouring,' he said as he poured us each a generous measure in wooden cups.

'That's the best I've had since I last drank my mother's own brewing,' one scholar admitted.

Brother Luke laughed.

'Aye, mothers know how to brew as no other can. This is made to my mother's receipt and she the finest brewster in Kent. Come, let me show you the Blessed Martyr's slipper. 'Tis in the chapel. Then you may have more ale. With so few pilgrims passing by, it'll only go sour and be wasted if you don't drink it. I ever brew too much for the few of us here. Oh, excuse me…' The monk suddenly ran off. 'Alan, Alan! Nay, I pray you. Do not pierce Michael with your lance. Come, meet our guests. They've come especially to greet you. Michael, you come also and you can have ale.'

Brother Luke ushered two ancients before him, one wizened and wrinkled as last year's apple and armed with a broom handle, the other wearing a vacant expression.

'Bid our visitors welcome, Alan.'

''Tis Richard!' the old man said in a surprisingly powerful voice.

'Oh, aye, forgive me, Highness. Gentlemen, may I introduce unto you King Richard the Lionheart, lately victorious over the Saracen host.'

We exchanged grins, the monk, Kit and I, afore I stepped forward, bowed low and said:

'My hearty congratulations upon your great triumph, sire.'

'Mine also, Your Highness, most esteemed prince,' Kit said, bending the knee. 'I hear those Saracens are the most devilish enemy of all.'

'You speak true,' the man said and, of a sudden, he clouted both of us upon the shoulders with the broomstick. 'Arise my goodly knights and bear arms forever in the service of Christ – and me, your noble king!'

'Enough, my king. You'll not get your ale if you strike our visitors. Treat them gently. Come, you two, drink your ale in the garden. The sun has yet some warmth. Brother Geoffrey will fetch your cloaks.'

In Brother Luke's brief absence to escort his elderly charges elsewhere, we laughed over the good ale and our newly bestowed knighthoods.

'My father would be delighted to know I've risen so high,' Kit chuckled. 'It was always his wish for me. And what of you, Sir Sebastian? Rose is now a true 'lady', though I'm not sure you'll make much of a noble knight. I can't imagine you charging about on horseback, wielding a broadsword. A pen, but not a steel blade.'

'My deepest apologies, gentle pilgrims,' the brother said upon his return. He looked somewhat flustered. 'I shouldn't have encouraged Alan. He's unpredictable at the best of times. I hope he didn't hurt you?'

'It's worth a sore shoulder to receive a knighthood from our hero king,' Kit assured him. 'May we see Becket's slipper now, please?'

'Of course, of course. How remiss of me. You can't waste the whole day here. The chapel is this way.'

The little Chapel of St Nicholas was simply furnished with a spotless linen cloth upon the altar. There was no silverware, no gleaming gilt, only lovingly polished treenware candlesticks, pix and chalice. Christ on the Rood, also of wood, had a gentle smile for us, His agonies set aside. A quiet sense of peace washed over me and I knew this to be a kindly place to end a man's days.

Brother Luke took the relic from its locked box upon the altar and held it out to us. Of faded damask with traces of gold thread, it was well-worn, trodden down at the heel, the fur lining thin with age: a most believable relic. The monk put it into my hands, trustingly.

'You see the Blessed Martyr's blood stains at the toe? At Becket's death, his slipper fell from his foot. A woman from Harbledown, she afflicted with a palsy, saw the murder happen and picked up the slipper, kissed the still-wet blood upon it and was instantly cured. She brought it back home and a child who had eaten poisonous berries was revived by its touch and, most importantly for us, a man who had lost his wits had them restored when he put the slipper upon his own foot. We've tried this cure with Alan, Michael and others here without success thus far. But we trust in Our Lord's unending grace and St Thomas's intercession and one day, we may be deserving of a miracle, God willing.' The young monk smiled. 'Until then, we care for them and keep them safe.'

Warily, I put my lips to the dried blood stain.

'For Jude,' I whispered, 'That his leg maybe healed and without pain. I ask this in the name of Our Sweet Saviour and the Martyr St Thomas. Amen.' I returned the slipper. 'My thanks, Brother Luke. I pray your work here shall be forever blessed.'

Afore we departed, I put a handful of coins upon the altar. I felt this little hospital deserved more than any other place we had visited thus far. The simple devotion of Brother Luke and his obvious love for those in his care was an example to us all who would call ourselves Christian. And, by the by, his ale was excellent also.

Sunday, mid morn
Canterbury

Having traipsed uphill and down – Tanner warned us that local folk called Harbledown 'Bob-up-and-down' – at last, we reached St Dunstan's Church and turned to the right at the ancient, weathered cross, following the wide street towards Canterbury's great West Gate. The way passed betwixt two round towers of considerable height and I was yet craning my neck, attempting to estimate the standard of craftsmanship of the coat-of-arms thereon of our mighty King Edward IV – whether it was as good as those I had done for his esteemed brother Richard, Duke of Gloucester and Lord Howard – when, without the least delay, we were waved through the gate and entered the city. No payment was required from pilgrims on foot, though the twins had to pay one penny each for their horses to enter, this being half the usual price, apparently. Had they ridden humble donkeys, like Our Lord, there would have been no charge, so the gate-keeper told us. The pair laughed loud at the foolish notion that they might come all this way astride asses.

And here we were, in Canterbury at long last!

The streets were thronged, despite it being the Lord's Day, and not only with folk hastening to or from High Mass in the numerous churches. London was famous for its cacophony of bells but Canterbury must come close. Bells chimed on every hand, discordant, as each place of worship would out-do all its fellows.

Most prominent upon the street were hucksters bearing trays of ready-cooked food stuffs: roasted apples seeming popular and also chestnuts. But I was surprised at the number of hawkers and street-sellers offering a vast assortment of small lead bottles in so many guises, all purporting to contain drops of Becket's blood, the Virgin's tears or Holy Water at the very least. Could one man's martyred body ever have contained so much blood that they were still selling it more than three hundred years later?

Tanner directed us to St Thomas's Hospital astride the bridge over the River Stour on St Peter's Street. Here, he said, we could pay our four pence in advance to reserve a bed for the night or take our chances in finding lodgings elsewhere. We agreed, Rose, Kit and I, that, for a groat each, it would be worthwhile to have beds assured for our first night in the city and paid the Guest Master accordingly, giving our names. The others of our band did likewise.

The brother told us we were fortunate, just in time afore the last beds were spoken for, yet was this not outside the usual season for pilgrimage? In season, I imagine many must spend the night hours bedless, sleeping on tavern benches, in cowsheds or even on the streets.

At leisure now, we three, with the little ones, strolled along High Street, gazing at the buildings, from tumbledown hovels crammed together to magnificent stone constructions four storeys high. Just beyond the fine guildhall, to our left hand on the corner of Mercery Lane, was a place familiar to me, by name at least: The Chequers of Hope Inn, where Master Chaucer's pilgrims stayed, according to his *Canterbury Tales*.

I had imagined a huge inn surrounding a courtyard on three sides, similar to *The Tabard* in Southwark. But at first sight, there were simply long street frontages both on High Street and Mercery Lane. I could not see any entrance passage whereby horses might be led to stabling at the back, though we later saw the way lay betwixt this building and The Crown Inn, next door, closer to the cathedral.

A doorway stood wide and inviting and tempting odours wafted there from: of roasting pork and beef, of onions and herbs. How could we resist? Dinner at the famous Chequers Inn: our first taste of Canterbury.

A fellow – fat as an ox, so a fine advertisement for the food available – hailed us at the door.

'Come in, come in. Welcome to The Chequers of Hope, where you'll get the best hospitality in town: fine food, excellent drink, comfortable beds and we throw in merriment and laughter for free. What more could you wish for?'

'A comely woman,' Kit suggested, raising his eyebrows.

'That can also be arranged, should you require it,' the fellow said, speaking quietly.

'Kit, you rogue,' I said, nudging him. 'We be upon pilgrimage,' I told the fellow. 'My friend jests so. But we be in want of a goodly dinner. Tell us your bill of fare, master, if you will?'

He recited a lengthy list. We could choose from pork with crackling, apple sauce and savoury dumplings. Or beef in a coffin with cheese and onion fritters and roasted parsnips in a mustard sauce. Or mutton pottage with peas, leeks and crisp fried worts, all served with best white bread. Or almond tartlets with cream or baked pears in wine. Did we want ale or wine – Malmsey or Rhenish – by the cup or the jug full?

My mouth was already watering at the mention of pork and by the time he spoke of pears in wine, we were his willing servants for life. The choice of herrings salted, herrings pickled or herrings plain was a rapidly fading unpleasant memory.

Afore I could speak, Kit ordered a mess to share consisting of every dish and my heart sank a little, considering the cost. My purse was becoming rather thin and I might have regretted what coin I put in Brother Luke's bowl earlier. But how could I? St Nicholas's Hospital was a most deserving cause.

With our first hunger pangs somewhat satisfied, as I assisted Dickon with his pottage and fed a strip of pork crackling to Gawain 'neath the board, I began telling Rose about our visit that morn; how impressed I had been with the love and care afforded to the aged. Thinking, wrongly, that it might be a leprous place, I had not allowed her or the children to come there.

Rose wished to hear about Becket's slipper also and I described it in detail.

'And you say the poisoned child was revived by its touch. What a miracle that must have been?' she said, giving Julia a piece of pottage-soaked bread to chew upon before taking and munching a cheese fritter. 'We could have needed a like miracle if you hadn't been so quick to notice Dickon about to pick those nightshade berries on Shooters Hill.'

'Aye, that was fortunate, indeed.'

As I set my spoon to the almond tart, watching the children at their pottage, I recalled the death of Alfred Denny, the father, at The Bull in Dartford. Thinking upon it, had he not sat and spooned pottage from the same bowl from which one of the twins was eating afore the scuffle began?

At the time, I was certain that food had been tampered with but could the twins have been the intended victims, not Alfred? And following that thread of supposition, had Tristan's survival at the river been a miracle granted because he was on pilgrimage? What of Troilus's encounter with the candle wheel? Was there a pattern here with the Warenne twins at its heart?

Pushing the last empty dish aside, as Kit leaned back and patted his contented belly, I put these possibilities to him.

At first, he laughed into his cup of sweet Malmsey. Rose and I preferred ale.

'Your imagination runs wild, Seb. Are you suggesting that there is some mischief afoot? A conspiracy to kill the twins? What utter nonsense. Who would want them dead, upon a pilgrimage, too?'

'Those lads do seem to have suffered one misfortune after another,' Rose said. 'Maybe Seb is right and somebody wishes them harm.'

'And most likely 'tis one among us,' I added. 'In which case, this may be the felon's last chance whilst we be all together at St Thomas's this night. I believe the lads to be in danger.'

'Absurd. Ridiculous.' Kit finished his wine and beckoned a tap boy to bring more.

'Kit, I know both you and Tanner insist that Alfred Denny died of natural causes, so I shall discount that but consider this: after their near drowning at Northfleet, Tristan said he felt hands pushing him under the water, holding him down, rather than attempting to pull him free of the floundering horse. Suppose someone purposefully tried to drown him whilst it would seem to be an accident?'

'Why? They're just a couple of lads, boisterous, probably not short of money, but harmless enough.'

'Money is often the cause of ill-feeling,' Rose said.

'Then at Boxley, when the candle-wheel contraption fell… in the moments afore that, as I ended the *Gloria*, I thought I saw something from the corner of my eye, over by the nave wall where the rope was wound about the hook…'

'What did you see? The Devil at work, no doubt.'

'The more I have attempted to recall what I saw, the more convinced I become that somebody unfastened that rope at that moment forwhy Troilus stood 'neath the iron wheel. That it failed to kill him when it fell be yet another miracle.'

'So many miracles beggar belief, Seb.'

'Aye, Kit, or could the would-be assassin simply be utterly inept? Whatever your opinion, this night I shall endeavour to keep a watch on the Warenne twins for fear their luck thus far will run out.'

Chapter 11

Sunday after noon
Canterbury

THE MIDDAY *Angelus* was ringing as we departed The Chequers, having taken long over our excellent repast and then, on my part at least, spent a deal of time attempting to persuade Kit that my concerns for the safety of the Warenne twins were based upon facts and not simply the conjuring of my overly active imagination. I determined to say no more of that matter for the present.

As we walked down Mercery Lane to the Buttermarket, who did we see but the twins, leading their horses into the passage betwixt The Chequers and The Crown next door to the stables behind?

'The food here is of the very best,' I told them. 'I recommend the pork and dumplings. Have a care, both of you.'

'Are you going to the cathedral now?' Troilus asked. 'The queues are longer than serpents' tails. We waited for an age, but our hunger got the better of us, so we left. The brothers there say Monday is a quieter day, so we'll try again tomorrow.'

'My thanks for the advice,' I said. Even so, we continued the few yards farther to the Buttermarket, intent upon viewing the cathedral through the gateway, if no more than that.

Christ's Church Gate was impressive indeed; the great statue of Christ the Redeemer stood atop the cream stone arcading, gilded and sparkling in the chill sunlight, noble yet compassionate. I wondered who carved such beauty centuries ago – my *Guide for Pilgrims* did not say. Angels, wings spread, supported the pinnacles on either side and beneath the Christ, upon a shield, I could make out the Three Choughs of Archbishop Thomas Becket, the paint much faded now. Did he have this magnificent gateway erected, or was it raised to honour him once martyred? A frieze of kneeling figures, so worn I could not determine whether they be saints or sinners, either praised or made supplication unto Christ above the heavy oak doors. These last being silvered with age but their ironwork polished and gleaming.

Both doors stood wide and we gazed through to the cathedral itself. I was eager to be impressed but, in truth, found it somewhat disappointing. I realised that our own St Paul's stood taller and larger. Here, the solitary southwest tower cried out for a partner upon the northwest corner, giving a lop-sided appearance. Beyond that, the barely begun central bell tower was wreathed in scaffolding. Of course, no work was in hand on the Lord's Day but, on the morrow, it would probably be as a hive of bees labouring – much as we saw at Eltham Palace. I hoped I should find the interior of this, the Mother Church of England's Christianity, more awe-inspiring but, to those who knew not our own beloved St Paul's, no doubt it was a building of some magnificence.

There, by the cross in Buttermarket, we saw our failed minstrel, Hugo Harper, being harangued by a stranger and getting the worst of it. Had it been any other member of our band, I may have been tempted to intervene on his behalf. But his foolhardy attack on Troilus yesterday had earned him little favour with me or anyone else.

Now, it appeared he had upset a good citizen of Canterbury within hours of our arrival. I could not but note the man was handsome of feature with long reddish hair and a beard of matching hue. His distinctive likeness appealed to me and I thought to make a sketch of him sometime.

'I see Harper's making yet another friend,' Kit said wryly.

'What a popular fellow he is.'

'I fear the fellow lacks the skills for making friendships as he does for creating music. I ne'er met another so sullen as he,' I replied.

Having looked long enough upon Christ's Church Gate, the little ones were growing fractious.

'Rose,' I said, 'Would you wish to show us where once you lived? Is it far?'

'Oh, what? I, er… I suppose so. I haven't thought on it. Who can say if they live there still? They may have died or moved away. Or be out and about somewhere…' Her voice trailed off.

'Lass, if you do not wish to see your family nor enquire concerning their situation, then say and we shall speak no more of them. I understand your reticence, I truly do.'

'Aye. I'm so unsure what I want to do.'

I kissed her hand to reassure her.

'Mayhap, if 'tis not so far, we could find the place. If it seems deserted, then so be it, but it cannot hurt to take a look. No need to go to the door.' In all honestly, I admit I was curious, if Rose was not, to see where she was born and passed her childhood. But, considering how her father had treated her, blaming her when the apprentice had defiled her and throwing her out upon the street when she proved to be with child, would any lass wish to return to the scene of so much unfairness?

'It's not far at all. If we return to High Street and go a little farther, right opposite the Shambles is Rose Lane, by the Cloth Market. We lived in Rose Lane. They even named me for it as I was born soon after my father took the lease on the workshop and house there.'

'Will you guide us, then?'

'Aye. I suppose I shall.'

'Whilst you're visiting family,' Kit said, 'I'll take a look around the city and search out some decent lodgings for tomorrow night. St Thomas's Hospital looks too cramped for more than one night. But, who knows, maybe you'll be staying with your kinfolk?'

'I doubt it,' Rose said quickly. 'The place never was much of a size.'

'I'll meet you back at The Chequers in time for supper, then,' Kit proposed. 'Let's hope the meal is as good as dinner and I'll sleep sound tonight on a full belly. I shan't even care if there are fleas feasting on me at the hospital, for I shall have supped right well already.'

We agreed and he went off along Burgate whilst we returned up Mercery Lane, back to High Street. The little ones rode in the cart. Julia was asleep and Dickon's eyelids drooped also as they snuggled 'neath the sheepskin. Rose led the way whilst I pulled the cart behind, aided – or more like hindered – by Gawain bouncing along beside my feet.

The street was somewhat less crowded than earlier and within a few minutes, we were at the Shambles. Though closed now, the reek of the place broadcast the market's daily fare of meat and offal, the gutter dyed dark with old blood.

'And this is the Cloth Market,' Rose said, indicating a grand timber-framed building opposite, raised up on stout wooden timbers, forming a covered area where stall-holders could set up and merchants conduct their business whilst sheltered from the weather. 'My mother has a stall here to sell the gloves whilst my father runs the workshop. At least, that used to be the way of it. Who knows how it is now? Stop here, Seb.' Rose held my arm and I could feel a slight tremor in her hand. 'That's the house there, three doors along.' She pointed across the way. 'You can see the glover's sign still hangs outside. Naught changed there: the same old faded sign on its squeaking hinges.'

As we watched, the door opened and a woman stepped out. Of middling years, she was also of middling height, respectably clad in a good woollen mantle of dark green. I exchanged a glance with Rose.

She nodded.

'Aye, that's my mother.'

I saw my dear one purse her lips, square her shoulders and raise her chin in determined wise. I knew what she was about to do must take all her courage.

'Mistress Glover,' she called, leaving the shadows of the Cloth Market and advancing into the lane. 'Mistress Glover,' she repeated.

The woman looked over and frowned.

'Do you not remember me: your own daughter? It's me, Mam. Rose.'

'Rose? Is that truly you? Rose! I can't believe it. Rose. I never… I can't… You're here. I never thought… Let me look at you, girl. You're wearing your hair covered.'

'Aye, Mam, and a ring. Look. I'm a married woman now.'

'Are you home to stay?'

'No, 'tis a brief visit is all. But meet my family… This is Sebastian Foxley, my goodman and husband. Seb, this is my mother, Clare Glover.'

There, beside the empty Cloth Market, I was introduced to my mother-by-marriage. I bowed and greeted her with a smile, though I know not whether it was convincing. Gawain, tail down, a soft growl rumbling in his throat, was likewise unsure, backing away. She regarded me warily, assessing me, looking me up and down like a horse for sale.

'He's handsome enough, I suppose,' she said, hands on hips. 'Is he kind to you? What manner of trade does he have? Does he work hard and earn a good living?' she asked Rose as though I could not answer for myself. 'I wouldn't have my daughter wed to an idle wretch. And children,' she cried, espying Dickon and Julia asleep in the cart behind me. 'Grandchildren! How wonderful.' She clapped her hands in delight, beaming now: an utter change of demeanour. 'Rose, bring the children indoors. We'll have ale and wafers and exchange tidings.'

'Is my, er, father at home?' Rose asked, a quaver in her voice. 'I would not put you to any trouble.'

'He's down at the tavern as always on a Sunday afternoon.

You know that's ever his way.'

'Aye, I suppose…'

'And, of course, it's no trouble. I must get to know my grandchildren. What are their names?'

Rose glanced at me, the question unspoken: should we disabuse her mother of the idea that these were Rose's offspring? I shrugged, then shook my head. Let her believe them to be of her own flesh and blood; it could do no harm, forwhy the acquaintance would be but brief.

'This is Dickon – Richard – and this is Julia,' Rose said, gently rousing the little ones. Dickon yawned, rubbing his eyes. 'They shall greet you properly in a few minutes when they're fully awake. We're upon pilgrimage from London; it's been a long journey for them.'

'Well, come along in. We can't have the babes catching cold out here. Come, Rose.'

The woman's earlier errand, whatever it was, looked to be forgotten as she herded my family towards her door. I noted the invitation did not seem to include me and wondered if I should follow. Would I be welcome? Of course, simple Christian charity ought to mean anyone deserved a token of hospitality but…

'Seb,' Rose beckoned to me, thankfully solving my dilemma.

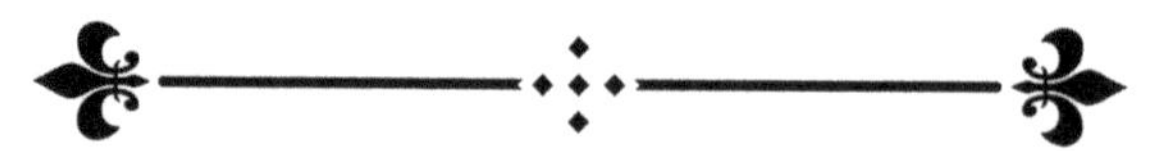

We passed through a small workshop. I noted it as tidy, tools, each in its proper place, the floor swept and the smell of fresh leather pervaded all from a pile of tanned hides, dyed and ready for use. Finished gloves – from heavy labourers' ones of thick leather to dainty, kid-skin gloves for ladies – were set upon stands for display when the shop opened upon Monday morn. Other pairs lay in baskets, ready for sale. Whatever my previous opinions of Master Glover as a father, he seemed a reputable and skilled craftsman, undoubtedly knowing his business right well.

Beyond the workshop was the living area, again small but

clean and neatly kept. No wonder my Rose be so particular about keeping house. She had learned her lessons in housewifery from her mother.

'Sit, sit.' Mistress Glover waved us to a short wooden settle squeezed in beside the hearth. A leather cushion made it comfortable. 'Shall you have ale? And I have wafers, baked yesterday.' We agreed to both and she bustled about, fetching cups down from the shelf, setting wafers on a platter, throwing questions at Rose all the while: Where did we bide? What manner of house? What age were the children? Did they know their *Paternoster* and *Ave* yet? How long had we been wed?

Ah! That was a dangerous subject indeed.

'Four years,' Rose said boldly, looking into her ale cup.

'I see,' her mother said. And I wondered if she did see through this untruth so easily. For some minutes, silence ensued. I sipped my ale, awkward as I was with my cup since my left hand was yet in bandages from the cat scratches.

Rose set her ale down upon the hearth and picked up Julia from the floor where both children were sitting with Gawain. She set her upon her feet, facing our hostess.

'Julia, greet your granddame,' she instructed. 'Can you make your courtesy? I know you can.'

After a brief hesitation, Julia bent both knees and bowed her mousy curls in a somewhat wobbly obeisance. Mistress Glover clapped her hands in delight.

'What a clever child! Come to your granddame and you shall have another wafer.' She held out her arms and Julia tottered forward, eager for the treat.

'Gawain wants another a wafer, too,' Dickon said plaintively.

'Then you must also make your courtesy and remember your manners, Dickon,' Rose told him.

'Aye, Mam,' he said, getting up and facing the woman.

'Brush those crumbs off your jerkin first,' Rose said, smiling, clearly relieved at his calling her 'Mam'.

My son obeyed and executed a most passable bow

afore asking:

'Please can me and Gawain have another wafer…'

'Granddame,' Rose added.

'Can we have another wafer, Granddame… please?'

'Of course you may, my little man. Help yourself. Who's Gawain?' she asked, pushing the platter across the board so Dickon might reach it.

'The dog,' I said, speaking for the first time since I had made my thanks for the drink.

Rose glanced at me with an approving smile, no doubt pleased that I deigned to join the conversation at last. Mayhap I should have made reply to some of the earlier questions but, in truth, I felt utterly out of place. I could more easily speak with a royal duke than with my wife's mother, finding my noble patron less intimidating than this ordinary woman.

Questions continued to flow like a river: in one direction only. Rose made her replies short and to the point, fidgeting all the while with a loose thread upon the hem of her apron. My wife was hardly more at ease than I.

'Cease fiddling with that, Rose,' her mother barked. 'You never could keep still and you haven't changed on that score, so I see.'

'Twas as if my dear one was, of a sudden, a child again. I could see the downcast look in her eye at this chastisement. Oh, how I wished to speak out on her behalf but could not think what to say. If Kit were here, or Jude, neither of them would be lost for words. I decided we should take our leave and stood, ready to thank our hostess for her hospitality and make our farewells but, as I did so, there came the sound of a door opening, the thud of boots, men's voices and laughter.

Rose and I exchanged worried glances. Her father! It had to be. I had hoped to avoid this.

'John, we have visitors. You'll never guess…' Mistress Glover began, her excitement palpable as she jumped from her stool and hastened to drag the newcomer into the room.

He was tall and broad in the shoulder, more like a blacksmith than a glover. Yet he had ripe-corn-coloured hair – though streaked with grey – and hazel eyes. There was no mistaking that he was Rose's sire. But he was not alone. A younger man stood beside him: shorter but as strongly built, dark of hair. He bore no obvious family resemblance.

'It's our Rose, John. Our daughter,' his wife explained.

He barely glanced at my dear one.

'I don't have a daughter.' He took the ale cup I had left on the board and refilled it, emptying it at a single draught.

'But we have grandchildren, John. Is that not a marvel after our Michael's wife lost so many babes? John?'

'Hush your mouth, woman. See them from our door.' The man went up a stair in the corner, taking his ale.

The younger man remained. He, too, poured himself ale, as if he belonged but he was looking at Rose as a wolf might look at a lamb.

'Rose, we must take our leave,' I said.

The fellow came over to us, blocking our way, standing far too close. To my horror, he reached out and stroked Rose's cheek.

'Get away from me, Watt Saunders, you devil,' Rose said, moving behind me.

'How dare you lay a hand upon my wife, you rapscallion,' I cried, bunching my fists.

'Wife, eh? Did she tell you she's a whore?' He turned back to Rose. 'Come back for more, have you, you hussy? Tired of your milksop bedmate, eh?' He glanced at me, contempt in his pale eyes.

I am not a man of violence but what happened then, I cannot explain. The next I knew, the wretch lay upon the floor, bleeding from nose and mouth, cursing and spitting teeth. My unbandaged hand was throbbing of a sudden. Even so, I was slow to realise that the fellow's ruined face was my doing. I put the little ones into the cart and, with my arm around Rose, pulled it towards the street door.

'I bid you farewell, Mistress Glover,' I said as we departed with as much dignity as we might, Gawain following on.

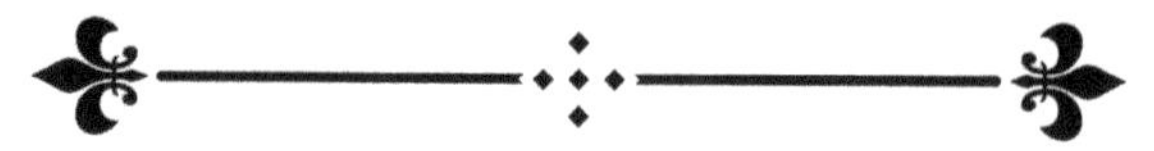

Outside, I hastened back to the Shambles and turned into High Street. There, my knees betrayed me, folding under me, forcing me to sit upon the ground, leaning back against the wall of a shop, eyes closed.

'Seb, Seb, what's amiss?' Rose said, fussing.

'Papa's tired,' Dickon decided, climbing out of the cart to inspect me, slumped there like a sack of mouldy grain.

'Aye… tired,' I admitted. 'Give me a few moments…'

'You hit him: that hateful wretch who robbed me of my honour all those years ago. Did you know it was him?'

'How could I? I have ne'er seen him 'til a few minutes since.' I breathed deeply, keeping my eyes closed against lights that spun around me.

'But you struck him such a blow. I'm so proud of you, Seb. You avenged my honour.'

'I did? In truth, I know not what came over me. I loathed the wretch at first sight.'

'Somehow you knew…' Rose took my right hand in hers and held it to her breast. 'Does it hurt you very much?'

'Nay. I think not.' I blinked and the circling lights dispersed.

'You are so courageous,' she said, aiding me as I determined to stand. Sitting in the gutter was hardly dignified and I felt steadier now. My heart ceased to race like a felon pursued and my head was no longer swimming in a fog but the kiss she gave me in full view of any who cared to see nigh set my senses spinning anew.

I had failed to notice the little crowd gathering but they cheered her kissing me. My ears burned upon hearing their lewd comments – upon the Lord's Day, too – and my face flushed hot.

'Not here, Rose,' I whispered.

'I care not, husband,' she said loudly enough for all to hear. 'You earned that kiss.'

'Go to it, lad!' someone shouted. 'Wish I had a wife who paid me like that.' A deal of raucous laughter ensued.

'Come away, Rose. 'Tis is privy matter,' I said. The crowd mistook my meaning.

'Aye, find a quiet corner. There's an empty barn behind the Shambles. That'll be the place.' More laughter. 'I'll wager he can't manage it, though. A groat says he's too drunk.'

'Sixpence says he can, seeing his woman's so willing to help.'

'Rose! Come now, for pity's sake,' I urged. 'Dickon, make haste.' I lifted him back into the cart beside Julia, deaf to his protest that he would walk. 'Gawain, here.'

I strode away, pulling the cart as swiftly as I dared. Never had I suffered such embarrassment. I could not believe that Rose had made of me a laughing stock. So long were my angry strides, she had to half-run to keep up but my flaming anger lent wings to my feet. I turned into a side street, neither knowing nor caring where it led.

'Wait! Wait, Seb, please...'

I refused to slow even as I became breathless, a stitch in my side.

'I'm so sorry,' she called out and I realised how far behind I was leaving her. 'It was all my fault. Forgive me, Seb. Please!'

I heard tears in her voice – my beloved lass who wept so rarely. It had been an occasion of raw emotion for her. What manner of heartless beast would not harken to her pleas? I ceased my flight from ignominy and turned to wait for her.

'Nay, sweeting, I be at fault. I should ne'er have persuaded you to show me the place where you were so cruelly used. I ought not to have subjected you to the risk of so vile an encounter with your tormentor. And I suppose I was also at fault for knocking him down.'

'No, no, that was the right thing to do. He has deserved it

all these years. My father ought to have done it and thrown him out long ago but, no. Instead, I see they've become drinking companions, friends rather than master and 'prentice. He's probably a journeyman by now: Watt Saunders; the devil take his name.'

'Forgive me my churlishness concerning the kiss. You took me unawares and…'

'Like this?' She kissed me again but this time it was a butterfly's wings brushing my cheek, not hot-blooded passion searing my mouth as afore.

'Aye. Far more seemly, lass. That I can deal with.' And I kissed her likewise as we strolled along together.

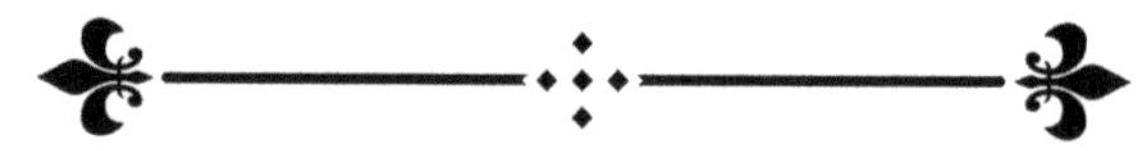

We returned to The Chequers. 'Twas not yet suppertime and there was no sign of Kit. I should not have been in need of more ale and yet, after the shock of encountering that vile knave, Watt Saunders, I determined that we both were in need of a restorative and ordered a jug of best ale from the tapster.

Rose was silent even as she attended to changing Julia's tailclout, a task which was usually accompanied by playful words, tickling and laughter. But not now.

I had no urge to speak either, at a loss for what to say. Should the afternoon's events be discussed? Or was it better to pretend they had ne'er come to pass and say naught of the matter? I would leave that decision to Rose.

So with naught much to occupy me, having played cat's cradle with Dickon, employing a length of string he found on the floor, until he tired of the game, I took my drawing stuff from my scrip and began to sketch.

The inn was busy and there were plenty of subjects to engage my skills. The innkeeper was a hearty soul with ruddy cheeks and a thatch of unruly curls surrounding his bald pate like a monk's tonsure. The tapster, hastening to and fro, refilling jugs, was a skinny streak of a lad with an engaging grin and large dark eyes, the latter reminding me of Gawain at his most pleading. A prosperous-looking merchant had an interesting countenance. He sat with his wife – if indeed she was his spouse – much younger than he and pretty. Mayhap, she was his daughter or niece, since they shared the trait of blue eyes, although hers were the more striking. Unfortunately, my red and white chalks and charcoal did not allow me to document this, the young woman's most outstanding feature.

'Her breasts are bigger than that.' Kit was at my elbow of a sudden, watching as I drew.

'Oh. Do you think so? I noted her eyes rather than…'

Clearly, Kit had noticed a different feature.

'Make them larger anyway and the lascivious old sot will pay you well for her likeness.'

'I had not intended to make money of a Sunday,' I said. 'Or at all whilst we be upon pilgrimage.'

'As you will,' he said with a shrug. 'Did you find Rose's family's house?' he asked, having called for another cup and poured himself ale from our jug.

'Aye, but the less said of it…' I whispered, taking a fresh sheet of paper to begin a new sketch of a priest seated by the door, accompanied by a small wiry-haired dog that was upon the board, lapping ale from his master's cup. The pair made a good composition and the dog's coat was a challenge to depict in life-like fashion.

'Well! Would you ever have guessed that was possible?' A customer passed by, making to depart, but he saw my sketch of the comely woman with the merchant which happened to be lying by cup upon the board. 'Look at this, Hamon,' he called to a fellow near at hand, picking up my sketch. 'That's her over there, isn't it? No doubt about it. You're a clever one, aren't you?' He nudged me. 'How much to make a likeness of me, eh?' He struck a pose, laughing. 'Handsome devil, aren't I? The perfect match for her.' He waved my sketch of the lass. 'I'll give you a penny for this and one of me.'

'Tuppence each,' Kit said, butting in. 'And another jug of ale.'

'Who are you?' the fellow enquired.

'The artist's keeper of accounts,' Kit replied. 'I deal with the finances. So? Are we agreed?'

By this time, others were coming to look at my drawings, including the merchant and the woman.

'Hey! That's my Mary there,' the merchant said. 'Look, Mary, this fellow's drawn you.'

'You can't have it,' the first customer told him. 'I already agreed to buy it.'

'How much?' the merchant wanted to know. 'I'll double the sum.'

The two continued haggling with Kit whilst I ignored them, intent on completing my sketch of the priest and his dog.

By the time we were ready to order supper, Kit had acquired sufficient coin to pay for our meal with a small heap of pennies remaining upon the board and all my sketches gone, including a second likeness of the comely lass – this last done to avoid a scuffle betwixt our first two customers. Others had requested images of themselves, among them a pair of newly-weds and a woman who wished a drawing of her lapdog with which she was obviously besotted, willing to pay sixpence for my work of a few minutes. But after that, I had no more paper and had to turn away customers.

'He'll get more paper and draw your likenesses upon the morrow,' Kit informed them: 'Tell everyone: Seb Foxley – remember the name – will be here then, same time; same place. Bring your loved ones and he'll do family portraits, cheap at the price of a groat each.'

'Kit, we be here upon pilgrimage, not to set up in business,' I said, taking a spoonful of the delicious savoury chicken pottage. ''Tis immoral.'

'Never turn down an honest coin, Seb. You never know when you'll need it.'

I did not mention the fact but, in truth, my purse was much depleted, so I made no further objection. Mayhap that was wrong of me and what happened later was divine punishment.

St Thomas's Hospital upon East Bridge, Canterbury

After supper was done and we could find no more excuses to stay longer at The Chequers, we made our way back along High Street to St Thomas's Hospital, where we had paid our coin in advance to reserve us each a bed.

Mind, I should have been pleased to have wasted the groat in the case of Rose and the little ones forewhy I suffered a sense of foreboding of what should happen this night. Despite Kit's assertion that my fears for the Warenne twins' safety were groundless – the result of my wild imaginings and naught else – I could not shake off my anxiety concerning them. Too many troubling occurrences had involved Tristan and Troilus for it to be a matter of coincidence alone. I suppose I would have been relieved if Rose could have stayed with her parents but what with her father disowning her and the foul Saunders too close at hand, it was better thus that we were all together.

'Twas full dark and the torches were lit at the hospital. We made our apologies to the brother whom we had to rouse from his slumbers within the door but he took it in good part, saying we had caused him no inconvenience and pilgrims frequently arrived at all hours. In fact, he said we were not the last. Others who had reserved their beds were not yet come and, apparently, it often happened that some failed to claim their place at all, if they became too drunk or found accommodation elsewhere. The way he spoke of such 'accommodation' with the greatest disgust it was plain he referred to those who decided that sharing female companionship of the immoral kind was preferable to a monkish straw-stuffed pallet bed.

The pilgrims' dormitory was next to the river and the only source of daylight and fresh air was a shuttered opening, presently closed. This was the means whereby we could relieve ourselves, if needs be, directly into the fast-flowing water, as the brother explained. We could hear the river rushing by, washing the very fabric of the hospital. In such a situation, the stone walls were cold and slick with moisture, showing green in the flickering light of the torches placed in sconces at either end of the chamber. The flames cast strange, dancing shadows about the place. It smelled of mildew, damp and human sweat.

The stone floor was crowded with sleeping bodies upon narrow pallets, blanket-swathed and snoring, but it was as well we had arrived late since we were directed to take the beds by the door so as not to disturb others. This contented me as I had intended to find a place close to the entrance.

By torchlight, we settled Dickon and Julia – already sleeping – in as cosy a bed as possible in this dank chamber. Once Rose was comfortable beside me and we had said our prayers together, I kissed her and made the pretence of preparing for slumber. Kit fell asleep directly, keeping wrapped in his cloak and pulling the blanket over his head. But I did not, having no plan to do so.

Afore I made myself comfortable, I searched out the red-headed twins amongst the gloom and darker shadows. They were huddled together halfway along the opposite wall. Mayhap they were safe enough there, for I doubted any felon could reach them and do mischief without treading upon some other sleeper or tripping over a misplaced blanket or pair of boots. Even so, I would keep a watch.

Chapter 12

Midnight upon Sunday, the twenty-ninth day of October St Thomas's Hospital upon East Bridge, Canterbury

AT FIRST, I thought another pilgrim had come to seek his bed. 'Twas a late hour indeed: the dead of night. The torches were well burned down and would not last much longer. Twice, I had dozed and jerked awake, concerned that my vigil had faltered, but the twins appeared unscathed, as best as I might make out.

There came the faint squeak of hinges but what roused me to full wakefulness was the sudden icy draught as the door opened. The torch flames leapt wildly, then settled back as the door closed, casting the same shadows as afore. But as the newcomer passed the foot of my pallet, squeezing betwixt it and Kit's bed opposite, I saw what I had feared all along: the glint of a blade in the flickering light.

The felon had come, as I was certain he would.

Yet I had to be certain of his target. I peered over the edge of the blanket, watching as he searched out his victim – or victims. He was intent upon his wicked business and now had his back turned to me. Signing to Gawain to remain where he lay, silently, I slipped from my bed on hose-clad feet, nigh knowing where the wretch would pause. I saw he had discovered his quarry as he stopped, then moved betwixt the pallets, drew back the blanket and raised the knife.

I threw myself at him, yelling I know not what. He fell beneath me and I pummelled him, crying the alarum.

The chamber was swiftly in uproar. Some pilgrims came awake upon an instant; others dragged themselves groggily from their slumbers. But Kit was there to aid me, pulling the would-be killer to his feet. The twins were alert, unharmed – God be praised – but bewildered by the commotion beside their bed.

'He was attempting to murder you both,' I said, turning back the hood which concealed his face. 'Hugo Harper!'

There was much outcry at this revelation but his identity did not surprise me forwhy I had suspected as much for a while. But what occurred next was unexpected.

Our erstwhile minstrel tore himself from our grasp, ripping his cloak, leaving a length of it in Kit's hands, and raced to the shuttered opening onto the river. He hauled back the shutter and flung himself through, sending a cascade of water into the chamber. We all heard the splash above the rushing of the river.

The felon was gone.

Belatedly, the brother came running, roused by the ado, but 'twas over now. With Harper gone to a watery death, everyone calmed down as though we had suffered some communal nightmare and were gradually recovering. Folk were rightly concerned for the twins, gathered about their pallet, asking questions, reassuring the pair. The brother offered them ale to ease the shock of their close encounter with death. Yet they were unscathed and had almost no knowledge of what had come to pass.

I felt my heart slowing its rapid beat and, of a sudden, was taken by a fit of shivering. My feet were cold on the stone floor as I returned to my bed.

Rose, at least, was much concerned for me, holding me close, sharing her warmth but the noise had awakened the children and they were in greater need of consolation than I. Instead, I persuaded Gawain to lie beside me and recall little after that, sleeping better than I might have hoped.

Monday, the thirtieth day of October
Canterbury Cathedral

Here we were at last at our intended destination, standing in line awaiting the opening of Christ's Church Gate. There was an air of excitement about the crowd. Tanner was with us and old Mother Thorogood with her cat – I wondered if it would dare enter so sacred a place. The Warenne twins were eager, seeming none the worse after the midnight trauma, though both yet wore bruises, tokens of their previous assaults by Harper. Kit's scholarly friends were aiding young Alfred Denny with his grandfather's litter. I saw no sign of Master Glassman but, mayhap, he would join us later, if indeed he was a true pilgrim. I had had my doubts concerning him throughout our journey and, I admit, suspected him at one time as the twins' ill-wisher.

As we waited, shuffling our feet, kicking dust, of course the talk turned upon last night's occurrences. Tanner asked the question upon all our minds:

'Why would that devil-damned minstrel want to kill either of you?'

Tristan and Troilus exchanged glances.

'We've thought of little else since last night, haven't we, Troy? We never met him until he joined our band in Southwark.'

'Indeed not,' Troilus agreed. 'Did we offend him somehow in the meantime? It must have been some grievous insult to drive him to try to kill us but we can't think what we did to upset him so. All we could suppose is that we didn't thank him sufficiently after he helped save Tris at the river in Northfleet but that hardly seems…'

''Tis not the way of it,' I said. 'Harper was not aiding you in Northfleet but rather attempting to drown you. Neither was that his first attempt upon your lives. Afore that, at The Bull in Dartford, he poisoned your bowl of pottage with deadly nightshade berries. I be sure of that now. That was his intent but the unfortunate Master Denny ate from the wrong dish.

Do you believe me now, Tanner, as you refused to previously?'

Tanner rubbed his chin.

'Aye, I suppose. And you think all those other mishaps were Harper's failed attempts?'

'I do but that still does not explain why. Troilus, Tristan, it seems unlikely that Harper was doing this upon his own account. Could anyone else wish you so great a harm? In which case, Harper may have been paid to do it, however fortuitously inept he proved?'

Again, the lads exchanged meaningful looks:

'Well, there is one...' Tristan began but, at that moment, keys rattled and wood creaked as the great gates opened and the crowd surged forward. And we went with them in order to maintain our places in the queue. Shoved and jostled, we had trouble keeping our feet, what with carrying the little ones. I heard Gawain yelp as his paw was trodden upon, as were my own feet more than once. Kit held Mother Thorogood's arm so she should not be knocked aside in the crush of humankind so intent upon their purpose of visiting St Thomas's shrine.

Within the precinct, if we hoped to be greeted by angelic anthems and plainsong chants, we were disappointed. All the noise was of a building site: hammering, banging, the squeal of pulleys and a deal of shouting as the central bell tower inched higher by the day amidst its shroud of scaffolding. The labourers had the appearance of ants, scurrying hither and yon, climbing ladders with seeming ease despite carrying buckets full of mortar or heavy tools. A great, square block of pale stone was being winched up, many hands guiding its progress at every level and I feared for the safety of those beneath it as it hung there, above their heads. As it was lowered into place, I let go the breath I was holding, relieved none came to grief, yet this perilous act must be repeated a dozen times a day. It made me glad to be a scrivener with naught heavier to concern me than the possibility of a book falling from a shelf.

Black-robed brothers restored order with wooden staves,

directing us to form a line, commanding quiet and a respectful mien against the cacophonous background din. Even so, hucksters with their trays hastened among the waiting pilgrims, offering latten badges, tiny vials to fill with holy water and images of various body parts.

I made a number of purchases, most importantly, the pewter form of a leg as long as my thumb, representing the main reason for my being here: to request a miracle to mend my brother's knee and spare him a life of agony. I realised then how little thought I had given to Jude during our journey and felt a pang of guilt for my failing. How many prayers might I have offered on his behalf already, if my mind had not been constantly dwelling upon other matters, such as our own comfort and the solving of mysteries that were none of my concern?

I also bought four pilgrim badges: one for myself, one for Rose, another for Bella Langton, as I had promised Dick I would and, of course, one for Jude, if he would deign to accept it. Two flasks, for to fill with holy water – one each for Bella and Jude – completed my purchases made of the enterprising hucksters.

Slow as oozing treacle, we shuffled forward as pilgrims ahead of us were permitted to enter the cathedral. It would have been quicker had they walked but I knew we were expected to go upon our knees along the length of the vast nave. Little wonder then that this took time and it occurred to me that, despite such an expectation, old Alfred Denny's litter bearers would need to find some other way of carrying him. Mayhap they would be allowed to walk.

The little ones were already fretful with waiting as we reached the porch and the west door but I thought I might have a means of enlivening this next part of our pilgrimage as a brother directed everyone over to the north aisle.

'Dickon, Julia, can you show me how you crawl upon all fours? Your Mam and I need to learn the way.'

With a deal of giggling, they readily obliged us, Dickon on

his knees but Julia, preferring her feet upon the chill tiles, made her way, head down with her backside upper most. I fear such merriment – for others were laughing at her antics – detracted somewhat from the solemnity due to the occasion but 'twas better thus than tears and tantrums.

I, too, got down on my knees, hoping my left hip, which can be troublesome in cold weather, would not vex me in this unaccustomed position. Rose kilted her skirts, tucking the hems on either side into her girdle belt afore doing likewise with far more elegance and grace. Mother Thorogood managed the same with some difficulty, wincing as she lowered her elderly bones to the floor. Who was I to complain about an aching hip?

Dickon began making barking noises.

'Look, Papa, I'm a dog like Gawain.' To my horror, he went forth on all fours at a surprising rate and Gawain joined in the game, both barking.

'Hush, Dickon! Come back here. We must go quietly, like mice on silent paws.'

I suppose then that it was my fault when both children commenced squeaking loudly afore Dickon changed his mind:

'Run, Jul, I'm a cat and I eat mouses.'

Dear Lord, forgive me. The pair was off, my daughter toddling down the length of the nave, squealing and shrieking as Dickon ran after and caught her, making the pretence of eating her with great chomping sounds. 'You taste like sweetmeats, Jul. Yum.'

My embarrassment knew no bounds as I stood and hastened to retrieve my erring offspring. A brother came striding over, his frown threatening retribution.

'This is the house of God, not a menagerie. Control them or you'll have to leave.'

'You have my deepest apologies, Brother. It shall not happen again.'

'Your apologies are owed to God, not me. Now, resume your place or go.'

Meek as a duly reprimanded schoolboy, I took them each by the hand and returned to Rose's side. The children understood we were all of us in disgrace, even if they did not understand the reason, and were subdued and silent as we went on our knees once more. Julia, though, tired of the game ended so abruptly by adults, determined she would rather walk, flouncing out her skirts. Being so small, her mousy curls were hardly upon a level with my shoulder as I knelt and few would notice her refusal to comply. I tried to turn my thoughts to reasons why we were here.

Looking up, the vaulting of the nave soared heavenwards far above our heads, beyond the lingering blue smoke of incense, which rose slowly, taking our prayers with it on perfumed wings. The stained glass in the south-facing windows was catching the first of the early sunlight, casting rubies, sapphires, emeralds, topaz and amethyst beams across the aisle. I wished we might move more swiftly, knowing that now the huge east window, which I had read about in my *Guide for Pilgrims*, would be at its best with the sun streaming through. I feared our slow creeping would be outpaced by the sun and I should miss seeing the marvel at its zenith of glory. But we inched ever forward.

Young Alfred Denny and whichever of the Cambridge men was aiding him were allowed to walk with the litter bearing his grandsire. And, this once, the old man had ceased his constant recitation of complaints.

Through an archway and down a few steps, well worn by centuries' worth of pilgrims' knees – I discovered that descending steps whilst kneeling was no easy task – we entered the very place where Archbishop Becket was martyred. Here, the orderly line faltered as many broke down and wept, overcome by the awe of a martyr's death, the deep sorrow of it.

My throat was choked with unshed tears as I became overwhelmed, contemplating the sacrifice one man had made for the love of Christ, Our Saviour. 'Twas a moment so humbling yet awe-inspiring that Thomas Becket, a Londoner like me, had the courage to face death unflinchingly... nay, to welcome the sword that denied him his life. But how greatly in error was I, daring to compare myself to him? I was not the stuff of martyrs nor saints. This pilgrimage showed me for what I truly was: a man, fallible, frail and sinful. Yet I might be saved by Christ Jesu, Our Lord. All was not lost for my troubled soul.

I felt a hand squeeze mine. Rose, her cheeks tear-streaked, shared this blessed moment with me, our hearts and souls united.

Our wondrous reverie was broken by a brother tapping me on the shoulder with his staff.

'Move on now. Others are waiting.' He rattled a green-painted box 'neath my chin and looked at me expectantly, so I unfastened my purse and took out two pennies, putting them through the slot in the top. He repeated the gesture, obliging me to donate more coin. It was fortunate that Kit insisted I take payment for my drawings last eve, forwhy the brother was not satisfied until I had given seven pence – an amount I could not have afforded else wise. I suppose it put my somewhat immoral earnings to good use.

Reluctantly, we passed by the steps down to the crypt although it had marvels there I wished to see but, mayhap, that could be a pleasure for another day and I might come alone. I feared this present visit as it was would become overlong for the little ones.

Still upon our knees, we continued our increasingly painful shuffle along the north aisle, pausing to offer more prayers at the shrine of St Alphege, another martyred archbishop, slain by the pagan Danes long ago – as my *Guide for Pilgrims* explained. Here, another green box awaited prominently, padlocked to its plinth. No brother was watching, so I gave two pence and hoped that would suffice, for I knew there would be more to pay.

And then we saw it! The purpose of our pilgrimage.

St Thomas Becket's shrine gleamed and glittered in the light of a thousand candles, gem-studded and magnificent. 'Twas fitting then that, concealed within the choir screen behind us, the monks commenced to sing the office of High Mass and it seemed the angelic host of heaven gave voice above us.

As we approached, more brethren directed us into line and strict order was imposed. We waited at the foot of the steps, relieved to see that others were standing. How glad was I to be upright once more? We were waved forward to the altar where we laid our offerings. I lifted Julia so she might lay her specially polished silver penny upon the spotless cloth whilst Dickon managed for himself – just. Rose and I placed the little velvet bags containing our offerings of a quarter mark each with the pennies, having brought them from London for this moment. Beside my bag, I put the tiny pewter leg and took time to pray most fervently for Jude and for Bella and her unborn babe afore the brother moved us on, around the shrine.

Now we could look back and up, seeing the raised coffered lid above the shrine hanging from its chains. At night, it would be lowered over the martyr's coffin. The coffin was gilded and bejewelled, set upon a raised marble plinth. The plinth was itself upon columns, creating niches between and we were told we might reach in and be closer yet to the saint himself. We knelt and I stretched my hand into the void. It was dark as night within and I knew not what I touched but it was smooth and cold, sending a thrill through me, causing the back of my neck to tingle. Had I touched the bones of a saint?

'Papa, Gawain's hungry,' Dickon said in a whisper, meaning *he* wanted dinner.

'I know. Not long now,' I said. In truth, I wanted to make a detailed assessment of the huge windows of stained glass all around us but knew time was growing short afore the children could contain their impatience no longer. They had been models of propriety since that earlier misdemeanour but it could not last.

We returned by way of the south aisle, making our reverences to the Black Prince with his heraldic devices bright above the tomb and then to St Dunstan's shrine – and another donation. I must remember to regard every coin put in a green box as a tiny act of devotion.

Gazing up at the marvellous gilded arches of the nave, I noticed folk high above, walking along the clerestory passage, passing behind the spandrels that burst from each mighty column to create those arches.

Kit had caught us up and saw me looking.

'It's all a matter of geometry,' he said.

'Your old friend Euclid knew all about it, I suppose.'

'You want me to explain it to you?'

'Later, maybe. The children are hungry and then I must find a stationer's shop. I need more paper after your rash promises of last eve…'

'Oh, aye. I'd forgotten that. Should I apologise for having committed you to an evening of endless scribbling?'

I shrugged.

'The customers may not come. Folk will have forgotten since yester eve. Half of them were probably too drunk to remember.'

'I'll wager you a groat that you have a crowd wanting their portraits drawn. You may need more charcoal and chalks as well.'

Back outside, the sun was bright upon the long tail of pilgrims in the precinct still awaiting entry to the cathedral. If I intended a second visit by myself upon the morrow, I supposed I should have to stand in line again.

'Shall we return to The Chequers, Seb?' Rose asked. 'Julia needs a clean tailclout and we haven't yet reserved a bed for tonight. I would rather not go back to St Thomas's on East Bridge, not after what happened last night. Can we afford a room at The Chequers? The prices seemed none too steep and we know the food is good.'

At mention of the word "food", Dickon reminded us, right loudly, that Gawain was hungry. All the holy wonders we had experienced and now we had naught more sacred to discuss than tailclouts, food and a bed for the night. Should we not be pondering those marvels and considering more deeply the meanings and purpose of our pilgrimage? It seemed not.

As we dined at The Chequers upon rabbit in a coffin, cabbage in butter and a cinnamon custard, I saw that Rose appeared deep in thought.

'What do you think upon, sweeting?' I asked, expecting she would speak of Becket's shrine or the stained glass or some such.

'My mother,' she said. 'I was content to be with her yesterday until my father and that knave came home. I wished they'd stayed away longer, that I could have amended matters with Mam. She's a good sort at heart and I have no quarrel with her, if it wasn't for my father…'

'I know full well, lass, how hurtful a family rift can be. Have I not suffered the like with Jude too many times? You told me your mother has a stall at the Cloth Market. Could you not visit her there this afternoon? Mayhap you would have a chance to speak with her whilst the menfolk are occupied in the workshop?'

'Oh, Seb.' She flung her arms about me even as we sat at the board. 'How did you know those were my very thoughts? Would you mind if I went alone?'

'Without the children?'

She nodded.

'Aye. They could complicate matters, proving a distraction at the wrong moment or, if things should go awry and my father, or worse, if Saunders was to appear, I wouldn't want them involved. You do understand, don't you, Seb?'

'Of course. 'Tis a wise decision. I have my own errand to accomplish, purchasing materials for this drawing session Kit has arranged for later. The little ones may accompany me. I shall take the cart that they can nap if they feel weary.'

'There are clean tailclouts in the cart if Julia needs one and the pot of quince jelly if they become fractious.'

'Fear not; this be hardly the first time I have managed them without you. I am not incapable of changing a soiled clout if I have to. But you must have a care for yourself, sweeting. If you so much as espy that vile scoundrel in the distance, you must run, scream, do whatever it takes to call attention to your plight. I shall not rest easy until you return here safely and all of a piece. Would you consider taking Gawain to protect you?'

'This great soft bag of fur?' she laughed, stroking the dog's head. 'I swear he'd make friends with Old Scratch himself, given half a chance. No, keep him by you to guard the cart. It's more important to see the little ones safe. I will come to no harm, I promise you.'

'I shall most surely hold you to that promise, Rose.'

'I know you will.'

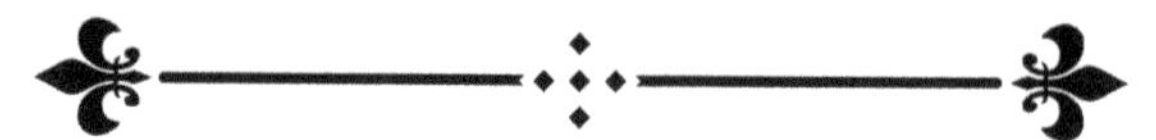

I spent the afternoon exploring Canterbury, pulling the cart behind me, Gawain at my side. We walked along the Stour, watching ducks dabbling, somehow avoiding the churning waters of the mill wheel beyond East Bridge. Last night, Hugo Harper had thrown himself in a scant few yards upstream in the dark. I doubt he could have passed by this great wheel. Would it have been working during the night? Most likely not, I thought. I wondered what had become of the wretch, whether there was any possibility that he had escaped with his life and, if so, where was he now?

Dickon and Julia watched in fascination and, in truth, the regular thud and turn of the wheel and the diamond lights on the water pouring from the blades lulled the senses. But a flash of blue and tawny roused us: a kingfisher darting from his perch on an alder tree, plunging into the river. A few heart-stopping moments later, he emerged, shedding silver droplets, a minnow in his beak, somehow taking flight off the river. Another of God's marvels. I did my utmost to preserve the sight in my mind's eye, that I might commit it to paper later, which recalled me to my errand.

Back in High Street, I searched among the hanging signs overhead, looking for some indication of a stationer's shop. An inky-fingered cleric weighed down with a portable writing slope and a bulging scrip seemed just the man to ask. He directed me down a narrow way beside St Helen's Church, said to turn right at the end, then left, then right again and I should come to Penman's shop behind the Rush Market. I couldn't miss it, he assured me.

Yet somehow, I did.

We were swiftly lost in a maze of winding back streets, each one seeming narrower and darker than the last. Few folk were about but an ancient, toothless fellow sat in the doorway of a tumbledown hovel, which made our privy at home seem a well-built dwelling. He was stripping rushes, preparing them for weaving into baskets and mats. I took this to be a good indication that we were close to the Rush Market but when I enquired the way, he only shook his head. I repeated my question but he put his hand to his ear, mayhap meaning he was too deaf to know what I said. With a sigh, I pressed on.

Down another passage, we were confronted by a large black pig and I retreated, knowing better than to attempt to squeeze past it with two children, a dog and a cart. A couple of urchins regarded us sullenly.

'A penny for you,' I said, 'If you direct me to the Rush Market.'

Eager hands stretched forth. I offered a half penny, promising another when we reached the place but one snatched it away and the pair disappeared through an unshuttered window. I suppose, to them, even a ha'penny seemed a fortune, especially since they had done naught to earn it.

'Where we going, Papa?' Dickon whined. 'Gawain's thirsty.'

'Gawain will have to be patient. 'Tis not far now.' I knew not whether this was true but prayed it was so.

We retraced our steps away from the pig, now rootling noisily in a midden heap. Or I thought we did but somehow we did not return to the same narrow way where we encountered the deaf old man. This alley was barely wide enough for the cart.

'Dickon, keep your hands within the cart, I pray you. These walls be so begrimed with filth. Gawain, let that vile mess be. Come away, I tell you. Let us sing a merry song: "There was a squire a-warring went. His steed was lame; his sword was bent. With a hey-ho, away we go to fight the lord king's foe." Join in, Dickon. You know the tune well enough.'

But my son's efforts were half-hearted. Then Julia began to grizzle. We were none of us at ease, lost in this foul place, and whatever I did to reassure the little ones failed utterly. And no wonder, forwhy I needed reassuring as much as they. I offered up a silent prayer to St Christopher to guide our steps upon what was become a perilous journey – or so it seemed to me.

The alley turned a corner and ended at a wall. Half stone, half rubble, it was in disrepair and falling down but a barrier all the same. Mayhap I could have climbed it and lifted the children over but not with the cart. Besides, who could know what horrors might lurk beyond? Again, we retreated.

This time, we came to a more likely way, broader, with the buildings in better repair. Eagerly, we hastened along and I saw it ended at a cross street with folk going about their business. Giving grateful thanks unto St Kit, we came out into the light, less than a stone's throw from Christ's Church Gate. The Rush Market was to our left and there was Penman's, the stationers, to our right, 'neath a sign bearing an ink pot, a quill and a roll of parchment. Until I saw it, I had nigh forgotten why we entered that labyrinth of squalor in the first place. Aye, paper, charcoal and chalks. But first, we were much in need of consolation.

A street-seller stood with her tray of baked and honeyed apple rings sprinkled with chopped hazelnuts, and I bought us one each of these well-deserved treats. How good they tasted, restoring our humours after that unpleasant interlude. I dare say we were ne'er in any danger but I had no intention of repeating the experience.

Penman's was a small shop. It did not sell finished books, as we did in Paternoster Row, but rather all the materials required by scribes, clerks and illuminators.

'God give you good day, master,' the proprietor greeted me: a hearty fellow with a grey thatch and beard and a friendly smile. 'How may I serve you? Whatever your writing requirements, Penman's can supply.'

'Good day to you also, master. I need paper, but not overly expensive, and drawing stuff.'

'How much paper?'

'Enough for an evening of sketching. I know not how many customers will come to have their portraits drawn. Maybe dozens, maybe none at all but the paper shall not go to waste since I use it constantly in my work as an artist.'

'It's cheaper by the ream.'

'Aye, but a ream weighs heavy and I have to carry it.' I was browsing the shelves, comparing the wares to our own back home. The choice of pigments was limited to a handful of cheap colours: white and red lead, verdigris and various ochre hues.

'Are you the fellow who's advertising his skills at The Chequers of Hope, promising to draw the likenesses of families for a groat this eve?'

'I – I suppose I am, aye.' Word seemed to have spread, surprisingly.

'So, you're Seb Foxley then?'

'Aye.'

'Not local, are you?'

'From London.'

'Staying long in Canterbury? It's a fine city, I can tell you.'

'A day or two more is all.'

'I might bring the wife along to The Chequers this eve and you can draw the pair of us. She's not such a bad looker and I'm right handsome. Obviously.' He chuckled at his own jest.

'I shall be glad to, Master Penman.'

'Nay. The name's Harry Thorn. Penman is the name of the shop, see? Clever, isn't it, advertising our wares?'

I agreed that it was as I purchased a quarter ream of reasonable quality paper – not the best but good enough for sketching – a bundle of small charcoal sticks and stubs of both red and white chalk.

'See you this eve,' Thorn called out as we left. Likely, then, that I should have one customer at least and a most voluble one.

Outside, we turned into Burgate. By the inn at the sign of The Sun opposite, I espied the Warenne twins, engaging two comely wenches in animated conversation, laughing and jesting. It seemed they were none the worse for the previous night's close call with Hugo Harper's deadly blade.

'Ah, Seb!' One of them saw me and beckoned us over. 'We're trying to persuade these two beauteous damsels to come and have their lovesome likenesses preserved for all ages. What say you? Such heavenly beauty is well worth saving forever, isn't it?'

'Indeed, it is, Tristan,' I said, smiling as I manoeuvred the cart, children and dog out of the way of passers-by. 'I shall be delighted to make images of both fair maidens.'

The maidens in question tittered behind their hands afore consulting together.

'We'll come,' they chorused. 'After supper, you say? At The Chequers? Joan can wear her new gown. Can't you, Joan? And I'll wear that necklace my godmother gave me.'

And so I would have three sketches to execute later.

Chapter 13

Monday eve
The Chequers of Hope Inn

AT THE Chequers, we exchanged tales whilst we ate. Rose told how she and her mother had got along well at the Cloth Market, acquainting themselves anew. She had successfully avoided any entanglement with her father or that wretched journeyman and hoped to see her mother again afore we departed for home.

Kit told us that he returned to the cathedral this afternoon to visit the crypt, recommending that I should likewise see for myself the wonders there, especially the murals in St Gabriel's Chapel. He doubted even I could better them, so he said.

As for my own story, I glossed over the fact that we had become lost in that foul maze of alleyways, making light of the extreme disquiet I suffered there.

'So many winding ways,' I said, 'But all was well. The little ones were quite unafeared, even when we encountered a pig… at a distance. There was naught to be concerned about, not in the least.'

The way Rose looked at me then, I wondered if I had protested too much in over-stressing the slight significance of our venture.

Supper was done and as I leaned back, satisfied, sipping the good ale, I saw that the inn was become crowded.

'More ale, Master Foxley?' the innkeeper enquired, holding out a brimming jug. 'It's on the house, seeing you've brought in a host of customers.'

'I have?' I held out my half-empty cup to be replenished.

'They've come to have you draw them.' He gestured towards the folk gathering in every nook and corner of the tap room. 'You did say last eve…'

'Oh, aye. I did.' Or rather, Kit did and the purveyor of my services was grinning at me over his cup rim.

'You're going to be busy, Seb,' Rose said. 'I'll go settle the children in the chamber above stair with Mother Thorogood. She says she'll watch them with me.'

'So long as her cat is not…'

'Lucifer has gone a-mousing, so you need not fear. I don't know why you hate that cat so.'

In answer, I held my left hand aloft, yet with a binding about the furrow-deep scratches.

'You hated the creature before ever it clawed you.'

'And, clearly, I was correct so to do.'

'I don't think it likes you either.' Rose left the bench. Taking Julia in one arm and Dickon by the hand, she made for the stair to the chambers above.

'Good,' I muttered. 'Then the cat and I be perfectly in agreement on that score at least.'

I set out my new half-ream of paper and drawing stuff upon the board and surveyed the crowd. I recognised the stationer, Harry Thorn, and beckoned him forward. We greeted each other courteously and he introduced a plump, smiling woman with apple cheeks as his goodwife. I bade them sit on two stools across the board and commenced to draw. This eve, I determined the procedure would be more decorous, none of the rowdy clamour of customers as upon the previous occasion.

I took somewhat more pains than usual with this first portrait, wanting to make it a good likeness and a work of fair quality. I felt folk edging ever closer behind me, wanting to watch as I drew.

'Move back,' Kit ordered. 'Give a craftsman elbow room,

can't you?' They shuffled to comply yet, nigh upon an instant, began to move in again. I ignored them until one came so near as to jostle me and Kit hauled him aside. 'Wait your turn,' my friend told him right sternly and the fellow slunk away. One fewer to sketch, I thought.

Master Thorn was well pleased with the portrait of him and his wife, side by side, each with a merry countenance. He paid Kit his four pence without quibble afore the couple left the stools vacant and went to order more refreshment. I, too, sipped my ale but every time I did so, the cup was full as ever, refilled. I needs must have a care not to become addled in my wits, having no means of gauging how much ale I consumed.

Next, I drew Tristan and his lass, though she was hard-pressed to keep still, fidgeting the while. Troilus's wench was calmer, the prettier and more assured of the two – a pleasure to sketch.

When those likenesses were done, much to the twins' satisfaction, a man lifted his lad onto a stool, instructing him to keep still. The child looked to be about six or seven, skinny, pale and terrified. He sat rigid, fists and teeth clenched, hardly daring to breathe.

I smiled at him, telling him the drawing would not take long. I portrayed him with an easy expression, not the fearful visage presented. His father paid the tuppence, telling us the child's mother wanted the likeness for fear the lad would not last another winter, he being often sickly. A sorrowful possibility.

Then, a fat blacksmith who had brought a hammer and tongs, furnace-black, desired his likeness to be preserved, along with the tools of his trade. Kit charged him three pence, jesting that the portrait of a man of such girth used up more chalk and charcoal. The smith did not query the additional penny.

And so the evening continued, peaceably but industrious. As I paused to sip my ale and flex my fingers one time, I was surprised to see Kit with Master Glassman conversing amicably. The man of so few words until now was animated, putting out a hand as though to prevent some action on my friend's part. I watched, intrigued, as Kit unlatched his purse and took out coin – a considerable amount by the look of it – and pressed it upon Glassman, who accepted it with a show of reluctance which I found unconvincing. I wondered much on this as I took up my charcoal once again and beckoned forth my next subject.

I was in the midst of drawing a youthful fellow who, in truth, appeared indifferent to what I was doing when, of a sudden, the hounds of Hell were let loose. The trestle board at which we sat was over turned with a crash. I tumbled off my stool, landing on my backside amid the floor rushes, paper, chalks and coins strewn all about.

Rough hands seized the front of my jerkin, dragging me upright. Utterly unprepared, I could not avoid the fist which smashed into my chin with the force of hammer upon anvil. Starbursts flashed across my sight. The room spun. At first, there was no pain, only shock, as I fell down, vaguely aware of the shouts and chaos around me. I heard a few words but they made no sense:

'You bastard, Foxley. You stole away my own flesh and blood. I'll have him back, you'll see. You and that whore can't take him from me.'

Mayhap whoever it was mistook me for some other, yet I thought he said my name. But with my wits reeling, I could have misheard.

The pain came thudding through my jaw, my face, my head. I felt nauseous and weak with it. I dared not open my eyes, for I knew the floor was tilting, the walls sliding sideways and, if I looked, I should be sick as on a boat at sea.

'Easy, Seb. Drink this.' Kit propped me up, holding a cup to my lips but I pushed it away, retching. 'Fetch a surgeon as well as the Watch. Keep a-hold of that devil.' Again, he offered me the cup and I sipped it. Strong wine. It restored me a little, as did Gawain, licking my face. 'Who is that scoundrel, Seb? How does he know you? What's his quarrel with you?'

'I know not,' I mumbled, holding my head in my hands in a vain attempt to prevent it from bursting apart like an overfilled pig's bladder in a Shrovetide foot-ball contest. 'I did not see... I need to lie down.'

'We'll get you to your bed.'

Later, the surgeon charged us eight pence afore announcing that my jaw was not shattered into a myriad of splinters, despite how it felt. Neither was it broken in twain. In fact, it was badly bruised and naught worse than that. I disagreed. My entire skull was cracked like a crushed egg shell, of that I was certain. The prognosis that I would probably have a head ache was irrelevant since I told him it was already throbbing like a bell tolling a death knell.

'How many fingers am I holding up?' he asked.

'Two,' I said, having to squint to focus my eyes.

'No need to summon a priest. You'll live.' With which bland reassurance, the surgeon departed, fee in hand.

Rose commiserated with me in my plight, mercifully providing a meadowsweet remedy for my headache. She had said little but wrung her hands all the while.

When Kit and Mother Thorogood left our chamber, having determined for themselves that I was not at death's door, Rose asked me outright:

'Was it Watt Saunders? It was, wasn't it?'

'As I said, I did not see aught afore I was stunned.'

'But you must have seen his face after.'

'Kit did. I was too befuddled to know what was occurring.'

'Kit has never met him. He wouldn't know.'

'And since I saw him for but a short space at your old home, I hardly know his face.' This was not true. My capacity to recall faces, their every delineation, meant I could have drawn Watt Saunder's hateful features unerringly. Not that I wished to. If I were able to forget it utterly, I would have done so.

'You saw it well enough to hit it.' Rose smiled at the memory. 'I suppose he came to return the blow.'

'Aye. Maybe. Some would likely say I deserved it.' But I was recalling his words – if I remembered them aright – when he accused me of stealing his flesh and blood. Yet Rose was not his sister and certainly never his beloved. What could he have meant? 'I needs must sleep now, sweeting. God keep you.'

Tuesday, the thirty-first day of October, All Hallows' Eve The Chequers of Hope Inn

I awoke late to the sound of Dickon singing yesterday's song about the warring squire with his lame steed and bent sword. Upon any other morn, I would have thought it a merry noise but not this day. I moaned and turned over in bed, burying my head 'neath the pillow to shut out the din.

'Hush, now, Dickon,' I heard Rose say. 'Papa needs his rest.'

'Papa tired,' he said and afore Rose could prevent it, he leapt upon the bed, bouncing up and down on my back, pulling the pillow aside. 'Wake up, Papa. Play horsey. Gawain wants to play horsey.'

'Ow! Not now,' I groaned, tugging the blanket over my head but my son had sharp eyes.

'Papa's face all dirty.'

'Aye. Come away. Papa will wash his face later,' Rose was saying. 'Let us go find Gawain something to break his fast, shall we? Come, Julia. Shall you like bread sops and quince jelly? There is yet a little in the pot.'

I heard the door close quietly. "Face all dirty", eh? Bruises more like. And if they were a match for my headache, they would be black as thunder clouds. Ah, me. I felt right sorry for myself.

Eventually, I decided I could not waste the day, lying abed, and sat up, carefully raising my head. Stars swirled, then vanished. I put my feet to the floor. A cup stood at my bedside

– Rose had left me another dose of remedy. My angel. I blessed her forethought as I drank it down. Every movement had to be accomplished slowly and gently. I was swaying as I made use of the piss pot. At a sudden knocking, I nigh dropped the jordan.

Kit strode in.

'Rose said you were awake. How are you feeling?'

'Fragile.' I set the piss pot down on the floor and the shooting stars flared again. I rearranged my breeches anyhow and sat on the bed, greatly tempted to lie down.

'Are you going to visit the cathedral crypt later? It's worth making the effort.'

'I have just made the effort to use the jordan, 'tis sufficient exertion for this morn. You do what you will. I shall stay here. Can you pay the innkeeper for another night?'

'Aye. You earned three shillings and seven pence three farthings last night before the rude interruption. Who was that drunken oaf?'

'I know not.'

'He seemed to know you. He called you by name.'

'Seven pence and three farthings seems an odd sum,' I said.

'Aye, well, it cost us four pence farthing to pay for the broken trestle and smashed cups and jugs. Oh, and then the surgeon's fee but we still made a profit. It could've been more but I suspect others helped themselves when the coins spilt everywhere as the board over turned. Now, turn your face to the light, Seb: let me look at you.'

'No need for that.' But Kit took my head in his hands to examine me close. 'Leave me be, I pray you.'

'Mm. You're black and blue, you know. Your jaw is twice the size it should be on the left side. Have you looked in a mirror?'

'There is no such thing here.'

'That's as well. You look ghastly.'

'Many thanks for your reassuring words, Kit. I feel so much better for knowing that. Please go away and leave me in peace.'

'What? To let you mope here, wallowing in self-pity?

No, indeed not. Come, I'll help you dress. Once you've got some bacon collops and a mess of eggs inside you, you'll feel much better.'

I was not convinced of the truth of this but allowed him to assist me into fresh linen, my good shirt and hose and to fasten my shoes. Especially this last since bending over made my head spin. He passed me my cap and nodded approval at his handiwork.

'You'll do. Just wear your cap low and fasten your mantle high under your chin and none will notice the damage.'

As it happened, the mess of eggs was good but chewing bacon hurt too much – Gawain delighting to oblige by eating the meat for me. However, every person who saw me stared long and hard at my ill-shapen features and dark contusions. Kit's certainty that none would notice was not the way of it. If a herald announced it with a trumpet blast, it could hardly draw greater attention.

The Cathedral

Kit determined he should take me back to the cathedral, to the crypt, insisting that, in candlelight, my ruined face would go unnoticed and I must see the limner's work in St Gabriel's Chapel there. Indeed, I formerly planned to go this day in any case, though I thought to achieve the visit alone in order to make an uninterrupted study of the artwork.

Meanwhile, Rose had more mundane matters in mind: washing our soiled linens. She had arranged to work with the innkeeper's wife, helping to launder the hostelry's bed sheets in return for having use of the hot water and butts to wash Julia's tail-clouts and all our other necessaries. Mother Thorogood was to assist by giving eye to Julia. This being women's work, Dickon would accompany Kit and me to the cathedral. It seemed a reasonable arrangement.

The moment we stepped from the shadowed way of Mercery

Lane into the open area surrounding the Buttermarket, my eyes were assaulted by the full light of day, sending daggers of pain through my head. I believe I must have staggered somewhat as I attempted to shield my eyes.

'Seb? Are you unwell? Should I take you back to the inn?' Kit's voice was all concern as he gripped my arm.

'Nay,' I said, thinking better than to shake my head. 'I shall do well enough out of this blinding sunlight.'

Kit looked up, as though to assure himself of this degree of sunshine. In truth, as I realised, the sky was a haze of thin cloud, veiling the sun in milky whiteness. Not a dazzling sunbeam in sight. I pulled my cap lower, almost covering my eyes.

'Come, then,' Kit was saying as we entered Christ's Church Gate, 'The priests' entrance is this way, so we need not join the queue of pilgrims as before.'

'The priests' entrance?'

'Of course, since I am a priest. I had a word with the prior yesterday, telling him of my illustrious connections with the Bishop of London, and gained permission to use this entrance to the cathedral. I have no intention of standing in line for hours as we did the first time.'

'But I am no priest.'

'You're with me. That's good enough.' He took us to the left-hand, to the north side of the cathedral.

'And what are your illustrious connections with the bishop? You have never said.'

'He's my, er, relative.'

'Truly?'

'An uncle of sorts, aye. It's a complicated story. I'll tell you sometime.'

It ever was a complicated story with Kit.

He led us to a side door, lifted the wooden latch and went inside, taking Dickon by the hand. I followed with Gawain at heel, relishing the blessed relief of a moment of gloom afore we stepped back into the daylight of the Great Cloister.

'We should not be here,' I whispered but Kit went boldly onwards. A pair of brethren looked about to question us but Kit strode forth with such an air of purpose that they did not do so. At the far end of the cloister, he turned to the right through an imposing doorway.

I followed and, having quite lost my sense of direction, was much surprised to find we were at the entrance to the place of Becket's martyrdom. Down a well-worn stair, we made our way to the crypt 'neath the cathedral.

'What do you think?' Kit asked, arms spread wide as if he would have my opinion upon some work of his own hands. At first, I made no answer. There were so many wonders to admire and study that I was rendered speechless. Down here, the columns were squat and round but each was painted in vivid hues: patterns and pictures, saints and wild beasts, angels and demons at every turn.

''Tis a marvel indeed,' I said, my voice hushed in awe.

'And you haven't seen St Gabriel's Chapel yet. That'll take your breath away.'

I was quite prepared to believe him forwhy it seemed impossible that any work of a human limner could surpass this. But it did.

Other pilgrims were crowded into the little side chapel such that, at first, I could not see the mural. No matter, as Kit pointed out to me, the capitals of the four supporting columns were each carved with fantastic beasts playing musical instruments. I lifted Dickon that he might see them too.

'Horsey,' he said, pointing at some strange winged creature playing a viol. A horse it was not but I could give it no better name. Setting Dickon down, I took my drawing stuff from my scrip, thinking how much young Kate would love to have seen this gathering of weird beasts that could so inspire her imagination. She might take ideas for her capital letters and marginalia and I knew customers would appreciate them, decorating future commissions.

Headache utterly forgotten, I sketched, drew and made notes until the other pilgrims departed and I might view the mural of St Gabriel unhindered. The life-sized archangel was clad in feathers of gold, crimson and lapis lazuli, hands raised in blessing, his feet upon a wheel. I admit, I did not know the significance of the wheel but what did it matter? His face was serene, beautiful as only an angel's can be. I gazed and gazed upon that haloed face afore attempting to draw it. 'Twas a nigh impossible task. The limner who painted it so long ago must have been inspired by God and, regrettably, I was not. But I did my best, creating a reasonable representation despite it lacking that divine spark and, of course, chalk and charcoal be no substitute for gold leaf and fine pigments. Nonetheless, it would serve to jog my memory.

'Dickon, come see this angel.' I looked around for my son but he was not in sight. There was no sign of Kit either, so they must have tired of watching me draw and gone to discover some other marvel. Gawain lay sleeping beside my scrip. 'Gawain, go find Dickon.' The dog raced off as I packed away my drawing stuff and followed at a more sedate pace, wary of rekindling my headache, which was so much improved in this calm place of dim light with the distraction of exquisite murals and carvings.

I found Kit upon his knees, offering prayers in The Black Prince's Chantry.

'Is Dickon with you?' I asked.

'He was with you.'

'No longer.' The first worm of panic began stirring in my belly.

'I expect he's wandered off. There's so much to see down here. He won't have gone far.'

Then Gawain returned alone, looking up at me with soulful eyes.

'I told you to go find Dickon,' I repeated. 'Go on.' I sent the dog off again, watching as he circled the columns, nose to the stone floor, round and round, afore coming back to me. His whimper said more than words could: my son was not here in the crypt. Dear God in Heaven, save us! My child was lost.

Kit looked perplexed, scratching his tonsured locks.

'He can't get far on those little legs, Seb. We'll find him. Perhaps he returned to the cloister, in which case those guardian brothers will have a hold on him. Don't worry.'

But I did. How could I not? So small a child wandering alone through Canterbury. My mind filled with legion horrors: the fast-flowing river, runaway horses, monstrous pigs, uncovered wells… The list of perils was endless. My guts churned. Stricken with dread, I knew not where to begin searching.

'Twas as well that Kit took the lead forwhy anxiety rendered me useless. I trailed my friend back up to the place of the Martyrdom, crowded with pilgrims. A child could be anywhere amongst them, trampled underfoot, crushed in the press of folk. But Kit returned to the Great Cloister and I arrived in time to hear him enquiring of the brethren there if they had seen a little lad alone. I saw the shaken heads. None had seen him here.

Back to the Martyrdom Chamber, I pushed through the throng, ignoring the brother with his green box demanding a donation.

'My child is lost,' I cried to any who would harken, 'A small, dark-haired lad, not yet three years of age. Richard, but answers to Dickon. He be clad in grey breeches, brown shoes and…' What colour was his tunic, blue or brown? Of a sudden, I, to whom the whole world be an intimate sequence of colours, could not recall what my son was wearing. 'A blue tunic… dark of hue, and a green cap. Has anyone seen him? I beg you… please…'

But pilgrims were busy about their own spiritual affairs. Besides, none wanted to lose their place in line after queuing for so long. I was wasting my breath.

'Any sign?' Kit arrived, breathless, from who knows where.

'Nay. Naught at all. Oh, Kit… what have I done? I was so entranced with the mural, I did not look to my son. *Mea culpa; mea maxima culpa!* Sweet Christ, forgive me. What am I to do?

'Don't despair. We'll find the little fellow. Like his father, he'll be enraptured by some stained glass or gilded candlesticks or some such, standing there with his head in the clouds, oblivious to the stir he's causing.'

'I pray 'tis so.'

'I'll go to the shrine; you make your way to the south aisle.'

I obeyed, not knowing what else to do. Every brother I passed, every concerned face I saw, I asked if they had seen him… my son, about so high; my little Dickon.

In the south transept, I had to pause, leaning against a tomb, nigh overcome. My limbs trembled as one with palsy. The monks were singing in the choir above. It must be the Office of Sext or maybe Nones. I had no idea what hour it might be. My strength was done; my being naught but an empty shell. I could not go on. 'Twas how I felt. And then I heard it. Or thought I did:

'Papa!' A single word. A cry. I was back on my feet in an instant, uncertain from which direction the cry had come or even if I had imagined it. But the dog's ears pricked, being sharper than mine.

'Gawain, go find Dickon.' He bounded towards a narrow stair set in the thickness of the stone wall. 'Up,' I said, nigh treading upon his tail as I followed so close behind. 'Up.'

The stairway led to the clerestory high above the nave where, yesterday, I looked up and saw folk squeezing along the narrow passage behind the mighty fluted columns. Now I realised there to be a little more width than there had seemed from below. But not so much that it was easy to make my way.

For a moment, yards away, I caught sight of a familiar little head, its green cap awry. Gawain set up such a cacophony of barking.

'Dickon!' I shouted. He looked back.

'Papa!' How that sound wrenched my heart strings. But then the devil carrying him turned also and I saw his face.

Watt Saunders had my son.

I forced my way along the passage against the tide of folk, the dog nigh entangling my feet in our haste.

'Stop that miscreant,' I cried aloud. 'He has stolen my child. Stop him, I say.' But folk looked at me, staring. Of Saunders and me, who looked the more likely felon: he with a swollen nose or me with my face black, blue and misshapen? To adjudge from the way I was regarded askance, my question was answered. I appeared more the criminal than he.

Then Saunders stopped.

'He's the thief,' he shouted, pointing at me. '*He* stole away my only son.'

I could hardly credit what he said. "*His* son?" Was he insane? He must be mad. What did he want with my beloved child?

''Tis a lie,' I told everyone. 'The lad be mine. Give him back, Saunders, for pity's sake.'

'Papa! Papa!' Dickon wailed, writhing in Saunders' arms.

'I am coming, son. Fear not, little one.' But some of the by-standers were purposefully hindering me, restraining me. I shoved them aside. 'Can you not hear? The child calls to me. Unhand me, I beg you.'

Just as I came within a few yards of my son and he was struggling to reach out to me, a brother entered the clerestory passage from the other end.

'Cease this disruption in God's house,' he said, raising his voice and banging his staff. 'What's all this commotion?' I recognised him as the monk who had silenced us yesterday when Dickon and Julia had pretended to be dogs, mice and cats.

Everyone began talking at once until the brother thumped his staff a second time.

'You!' He pointed the rod at Saunders. 'What's going on?'

'This wretch took my girl from me years ago. She was with child and this is the result: my only son since the woman I married instead proves barren. He's mine, I tell you.'

'You have the same colouring, I see,' the brother said. 'But then so does he.' The monk turned to me. 'What have you to say in this?'

''Tis a preposterous argument,' I retorted. 'The child is mine. Ask him, if you do not believe me.' I held out my arms to Dickon, who squirmed and cried out 'Papa'.

'Of course the child thinks he's his father,' Saunders shouted. 'He stole him away before he was born. He took the girl I loved.'

'You did not love Rose. You molested and violated her, you scoundrel. Besides, 'twas more than seven years ago. My child is not yet three years of age. How can he possibly be of your seed? How long may a woman be with child, do you think? You are a fool as well as a felon.'

'He's mine, I tell you.'

'Give the child to me,' the brother said. Saunders complied reluctantly as I moved forward to take him back. 'No,' the monk told me. 'We will uncover the truth here. God will decide whose son he is by right.'

I watched in utter horror as he carried Dickon to the balustrade and held him at arms' length, out over the nave. The little lad screamed in terror.

'Nay! Do not…' I screamed also. 'Do not hurt him, I pray you.'

'Christ shall have his soul now, if you two cannot speak true.'

'That's right,' Saunders said. 'If I can't have him as his rightful father, then neither should he.'

'Please, good brother, take pity on his innocent young life. I would rather Saunders has him if his life be spared. Have mercy, I pray you. Do not harm him.'

I went faint with relief as the brother stepped back from the balustrade, holding the sobbing child close now. I shut my eyes, unable to watch as my son was given into the keeping of another by Holy Church. But better that than see him plunge to his death. My poor dear one.

'Here, take him,' the monk said, giving him into my empty embrace. 'He's yours.'

'What? But I… after what I said?'

'The judgement of Solomon,' he said and I was too stunned to take his meaning. 'Besides, I now recall you and the child gave me cause to reprimand you yesterday. I hoped you would've learned how to behave in God's house but it seems not.'

A howl of rage and thundering footsteps betokened Saunder's departure as I held Dickon so tightly, clutching him to my breast until he protested, needing to draw breath. I kissed him and kissed him. Those around us cheered. Gawain yipped in delight. Tears flooded my cheeks even as I laughed.

'That was quite a scene,' Kit said, coming to stand beside me.

'I thought he would drop him,' I choked. 'Truly I did.'

Kit put a steadying arm about me.

'You did the right thing, Seb.'

'I did?'

'As the monk told you: it was the judgement of Solomon. Only the true parent would rather give up the child than see it die needlessly. You surely know the story from the First Book of Kings, the third chapter?' I must have returned him the blank look of a want-wit forwhy he explained: 'In the Bible… two women both lay claim to an infant. King Solomon ordains that it shall be cut in twain, so both may share it equally. The false mother agrees but the true one would rather forgo her claim than see the babe slain and gives it up. Solomon, in his wisdom, knew that would be the way of it. The infant was never in danger. And neither was Dickon – not from the monk, at least.'

'I shall not let him out of my sight ever again.'

Chapter 14

Tuesday, later
The Chequers of Hope Inn.

MY HANDS were yet unsteady as I drank the wine. Kit insisted I was in need of something stronger than ale to restore me. He was correct but I required it rather to brace myself than as an aid to recovery. I had yet to confess my failings to Rose. Though Dickon was not a child of her loins, she loved him as if he were her own. I dared not think how she would berate me and rightly so.

As I sat on the stool in the farthest corner of the tap room, my child upon my knee, I rehearsed how I should break the news to her.

'You don't have to tell her,' Kit said. 'She doesn't need to know of it.'

And I thought how little he understood my wife. She would see something amiss straightway. That Dickon nestled against me, still, silent, his eyes huge in a pallid face: she would know.

When Rose came in, a pile of laundered linen in her arms, I could not have counted beyond five afore she asked:

'What's amiss with Dickon? He's so pale. Is he sick?' She put the linen on the board and reached out for him. There was a moment of hesitation on his part but then, seeing her beloved face, he went to her, clinging tightly. She stroked his hair and felt his forehead. 'He's not feverish. What is it, my little one? What has upset you so? What has come to pass, Seb?'

I confessed all. My guilt poured out in a torrent of

recriminations against myself. There was no excusing my lack of care. No way to make light of the danger I had put him in; my child, *our* precious son.

'How may I ever make amends?' I asked, then lapsing into silence, wiping tears away with the back of my hand. What more could I say?

'Looking at you, I think you've suffered punishment enough already. And I know you'll never make the same mistake again, so you've learned your lesson. And God was merciful, sparing Dickon's life and us the greatest heartache.' Rose squeezed my shoulder. 'The nightmare is over for you both and he's safe, so thank Our Lord Jesu for it.' Then she went up the stair, carrying Dickon, leaving the laundry.

I deserved worse than that.

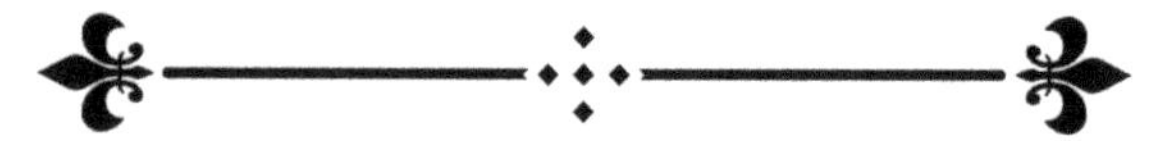

That night, the innkeeper and his wife went about the place, setting out numerous beeswax candles and lighting every one of them despite the expense. Then a priest arrived in full vestments, dispensing holy water all about. Having doused the tap room, the innkeeper took the cleric upstairs, who repeated the sprinkling along the way.

I looked to Kit for an explanation, he being a priest.

'It's All Hallows' Eve, of course. They must fear the intrusion of unquiet souls more here in Canterbury than we do in London. Blessed candles and holy water should fend off any troublesome spirits.'

'I pray that includes Watt Saunders also. I could not withstand another encounter.'

'You could draw more portraits; take your mind off him?'

'Nay, I have not the heart for sketching.'

'Lord save us, Seb! I never thought to hear you say such a thing. Do your injuries hurt you so badly?'

'Not so much as my conscience. Oh, Kit… the terrors my son

must have suffered… I cannot bear to think on them.'

'Then don't. Come, draw that fine fellow drowsing over his supper by the hearth. He looks prosperous enough to pay a goodly sum for his portrait and the money won't come amiss.'

'I suppose not, since you gave so much to Master Glassman last eve, as I seem to recall.'

Kit stiffened.

'Seb. You saw no such thing.'

'There was naught amiss with my eyesight at the time, afore I took that blow. But what does it matter? You do what you will with your own money. 'Tis no business of mine.'

'You saw no such thing,' he repeated, eyes blazing. 'You are utterly mistaken.' With which statement, he got up and left me, his wine barely touched.

I must have uncovered some delicate matter. Mayhap he owed Master Glassman money. A gambling debt, perhaps? The outcome of a vice he would rather conceal. That would be understandable in a priest and yet I knew what I had witnessed: Kit pressed Glassman to take the money. A loan? A gift? Was Glassman in need and did not want his penurious condition made known? Aye, likely that was it. In which case, why was my friend so angered that I saw his act of generosity? That he was angry – very angry, in truth – I had no doubt. I must guard my tongue in future. Money was a sore point: that much was obvious. Though he had admitted, finally, to the Bishop of London, Thomas Kemp, being his uncle, the mystery surrounding Kit now deepened all the more as I realised I did not even know his family name. To me, he was Father Christian when we were at home and, for some reason as yet unexplained, preferred to be known as Kit during this pilgrimage. Who was he? And mayhap I should ask also: who was the Man of Glass, the close-mouthed, unsociable individual, more soldier than pilgrim?

But the answers would not come and I retired early, joining Rose and the children in our chamber above stair. The day had been a long one, full of trauma and chaos. Exhausted as I was,

I feared it would be a restless night. If any unquiet spirits were abroad, no doubt they would intrude upon my dreams and make of them nightmares.

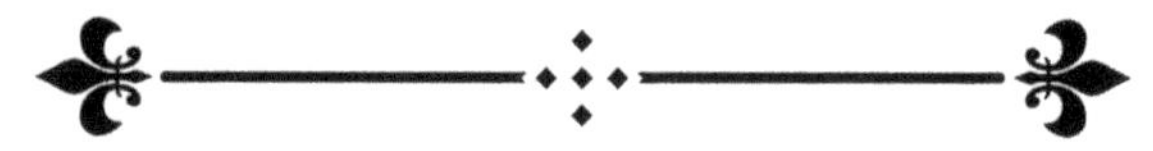

Much as I expected, I awoke in the night, sheet-entangled, but 'twas not a bad dream that roused me. A candle moved across the darkened chamber and I recognised a familiar outline.

'Kit, what are you about?' I whispered.

'None of your concern. Go back to sleep.'

But by now, I was sitting up, fully awake and I realised my friend was gathering his possessions together, stuffing them into his bag. He was already booted and cloaked.

'Where are you going at this hour of the night? Can your errand not wait until dawn?'

'You ask too many questions.'

'Are you in trouble of some kind? Mayhap I can aid you.'

He turned to me and I could hardly believe his next words:

'Let be, Seb, you don't want to make an enemy of me.' And with that, he departed, closing the door silently after.

Should I follow him, see him safe? I wondered. I left my bed and went to the window, opening one-half of the shutter. Our chamber overlooked the stable yard behind the inn. The night was clear and cold. A gibbous moon shone, sparkling on frosted cobbles. There was light sufficient to see Kit and another man mounting two horses. Kit leapt into the saddle with consummate ease. Why was I surprised at his horsemanship? Had he not said one time about being trained for knighthood in his youth? My friend was ever a fellow of mystery.

As they guided their horses towards the passageway betwixt The Chequers and The Crown next door, Kit's companion looked up, as though to gauge the hour from the stars or, mayhap, the weather. The moonlight showed his face clear as day for an instant: Master Glassman, though I had the feeling that was not his true name. At least my friend was not travelling alone.

Would we ever see Kit again? What was he involved in with Glassman? I closed the shutter and returned to my bed, shivering. Rose stirred in her sleep as I lay beside her, my chill flesh soaking up her warmth.

Of course, slumber eluded me, my thoughts swirling. Had this pilgrimage been naught but a ruse on Kit's part, a means of travelling to Canterbury in innocent guise? Had he made use of our friendship for some nefarious purpose? If he had, I was at a loss to suppose what his purpose could be but it seemed Canterbury was not his final destination. Where else might he go? Sandwich, Fordwich, Dover and other ports were not far – a few hours' ride at most. And from those places he could take ship to anywhere in the world… But why?

With which disturbing thoughts, I must have drifted off to sleep.

Wednesday, the first day of November, the Feast of All Hallows The Chequers of Hope Inn

When I arose, my thoughts continued to dwell upon Kit's actions last night, almost as though sleep had not interrupted my disquiet considerations. In daylight, I could see details I had been unable to discern previously by candlelight. My friend had not taken all his belongings as I believed. The coverlet and blanket upon his bed were rumpled, as though he intended the uninformed would think he slept there although, if I had intended such a deception, I should have made a hollow of the pillow where my head would have lain. There was none. But 'neath the bed were his walking boots. Surely, this meant he would return unless, wherever he be bound, he reckoned to have no further use for them. He was now mounted and horsemen have less need of such sturdy footwear.

'What are you doing, Seb?' Rose caught me inspecting Kit's boots as she came in with a bowl of bread sops for the little ones' to break their fast.

'Naught. I simply wondered if his soles be as worn as mine. I think I shall search out a cobbler this day and have mine re-soled afore we depart on the morrow. Do yours require repair also? Kit's do not seem too bad.' I replaced the boots precisely as found.

'Mine will serve well enough for the journey home. You can ask Kit concerning his. He's downstairs.'

'He is?'

Rose frowned at me.

'Why do you sound surprised? He's waiting for us, that we might attend Low Mass together, afore we eat. It is Wednesday, or had you forgotten the day?'

I hastened down the stair, requiring to see him with my own eyes, though why I should doubt Rose's word I cannot say – except that I realised I ne'er thought he would return. Yet there he sat by the hearth, still wearing riding boots, his cloak draped over the bench. Glancing about, I saw there was no sign of Glassman.

Of a sudden, I knew not how to greet Kit and he seemed likewise discomfited. For a few moments, we behaved like tom cats coming face to face, unexpectedly, in a narrow alley, unsure whether to fight or flee, as though we be strangers who knew not quite what to make of one another.

This was ridiculous. Yesterday, we had been close companions and I did not want others to see any change, Rose especially, but his words to me last eve made me wary and I could not unhear them: "You don't want to make an enemy of me".

'God be with you this day, Kit,' I said after due pause.

'And also with you,' he responded to my greeting as usual. And yet I sensed a lack of warmth or mayhap that was my imagination.

We waited, unspeaking, for Rose to bring the children. So many questions required to be asked but I kept silent.

Later, as he and I stood, side by side, listening to the priest conducting the office in St Andrew's Church in High Street, I tried to behave as usual but the strong whiff of horses, sweat and leather emanating from Kit's attire would not permit me to forget. Walking back across the way, I had to say something.

'Kit, I...'

'You haven't told anyone? It will be better for you all if you keep your mouth shut.'

'Nay, I...'

'Then see that you don't.'

'All I intended to ask is whether you wish your boots repaired afore our journey home. Mine need new soles and I must find a cobbler's shop this morn.' I shielded my eyes from the rising sun, low over the rooftops, and thus could not read his expression.

Back at the inn, others joined us in breaking our fast, though Kit chose to sit with his scholarly friends at the opposite end of the board from us. Mother Thorogood appeared in particularly high spirits.

'I'm sure it's working,' she told everyone gathered there. 'I'm so happy. It's been worth the long walk, every step of it. Master Tanner, you must tell future pilgrims of this.'

'What does she mean?' I asked Rose in a whisper as I broke off a heel of bread to eat with the sprats in chive sauce.

'She says her sight is improving after imploring St Thomas for a miracle. She thought it was a little better yesterday but now she's convinced. Is that not marvellous? We should all be so glad for her and give thanks.'

'Aye, I suppose 'tis a cause to rejoice.'

'Seb. What's amiss with you this morn, you old grouch? Are your bruises still paining you?'

'They be well enough. I need no further dose of remedy, if that be why you ask.'

'Kit's humour is no better than yours. He's hardly spoken a

word to me. Have you two quarrelled over some matter or other?'

'Of course not,' I said hastily – too hastily. I should have known Rose could not be fooled.

'You've had a falling out. I can tell. Was it about yesterday?'

I started, spilling sauce from my spoon. Did Rose know about Kit's late-night enterprise?

'Did he berate you after Dickon became lost?' she continued.

'What? Nay. 'Tis not his place to berate me concerning that. Rather, 'tis yours, sweeting, yet you have refrained.'

'As I told you, I think your conscience is punishing you quite enough without I beat you with more words of reproach.'

'Oh, best of wives… how I have been blessed with you.' I kissed her soft cheek.

'Enough of that, Seb, cease your flattery. It will achieve you naught. Make your peace with Kit as soon as we finish our meal. I will not walk all the way back to London in company with two men who refuse to speak courteously to each other. You're prickly as hedge-urchins, the pair of you. Worse than children.'

With which she turned her attention to wiping Dickon's face, all besmirched, and dabbing at Julia's sticky fingers. As usual, my daughter made less mess with her food than my son, who had silvery fish scales in his hair and a blob of sauce on his eyebrow.

The meal was done and I would attempt to obey my wife's instruction.

'Kit, may I speak with you,' I said as he rose from his stool, wiping his mouth upon his napkin afore discarding it.

'What?'

'Others are noticing the, er, change in our demeanour. If you do not want awkward questions asked, we best repair our friendship. Or at least make it seem as though we have. I will say naught and shall swear it upon the Holy Martyr's Bones if you want me to do so. Neither shall I ask you anything you do not tell of your own accord. Please, Kit, we needs must make some semblance of our previous comradeship.'

'Aye, you're right,' he said yet, despite that, he turned his back and walked away, joining the Cambridge scholars at the door. They three departed, laughing at some jest.

At least, I hoped it was at a jest and not at my expense.

Despairing, I searched out the innkeeper, asking to settle our reckoning for the meal and to pay in advance to reserve our beds for one more night.

'You paying for your friend as well?' the innkeeper asked.

'I suppose so.'

'Though he didn't sleep here last night, did he?

'Oh, I, er…'

'I saw him and that fellow with his arm in a sling – not that he did when he mounted one of my best horses. What's his name?'

'Glassman.'

'Aye, him. Both horses were back in the stable this morn, groomed, fed and watered, but you tell that friend of yours and Glassman they don't borrow my horses free of charge. Did they think I wouldn't know of it? They owe me, though God alone knows what they were about at midnight on All Hallows' Eve. Nothing good nor lawful, I'll wager, and I want my money before the law catches up with them and hangs 'em by the neck. Tell them what I said, Master Foxley. And…,' he bent close and spoke in my ear: 'Stay away from them, I would, if I were you. That Glassman in particular. I don't like his sort.'

'What sort is that?' I was intrigued. The innkeeper paused in his computing of costs due and tapped the side of his nose knowingly. 'Lancastrians,' he said and spat meaningfully on his fresh-swept floor.

'How can you tell?'

'Every night, last thing, I insist my remaining customers drink the health of our lord, King Edward – he being Canterbury's good friend – and two nights running, that fellow with the sling has done what I just did: spitting instead of wassailing the king. What else should I make of that, unless he's a benighted, bloody Frenchman?' He spat again. 'You owe me one shilling and sixpence ha'penny for bed and board for your family with a reduction of tuppence, considering your goodwife helped with the laundry yesterday… unless you're paying for your friend's use of my horses?'

'Nay. That be none of my business. You must deal with him in that regard.' I counted out the appropriate coins and smiled. Despite this, I felt deep unease on the innkeeper's behalf when Kit should discover last night's affairs were no secret. I prayed he would not think that I had broken my word, so lately given, and told of it.

Lancastrians. I might believe it of Glassman but Kit?

I returned up the stair to exchange my boots for my Sunday best shoes. I could not go barefoot whilst the cobbler made repairs. Mayhap Glassman was French? Was that why he spoke so seldom, that none might hear his accent? Mayhap I should term him *l'Homme de Verre* rather than the Man of Glass, as I thought of him.

A possibility struck me so forcefully that I stumbled, nigh falling on the stair.

De Verre! Or, rather, de Vere. The Earl of Oxford. The Lancastrian traitor imprisoned in Calais, though I seemed to recall tales of his escaping more than once.

No, it could not be. 'Twas an idea too absurd to give credence. Kit be as loyal to our Yorkist king as I. Why would he aid a traitor, giving him money for his treasonous cause? But the more I considered what I knew of Kit, the less evidence there appeared to prove him a Yorkist. On the other hand, there was no proof of any Lancastrian leanings either, not that I could recall.

'Seb, I would go to my mother's stall in the Cloth Market,' Rose said, intruding upon my ridiculous musings. 'I know you'll think I'm a lack-wit after what happened yesterday with little Dickon but that wasn't Mam's doing.'

'Maybe not but she must have revealed something of our history to that foul wretch, to make him believe Dickon could possibly be his.'

'I know, that's why I want to tell her the truth about the children not being mine, though you know how much I wish they were. I should not have told the lie: that we'd been wed for so long. I was wrong to do so. I'm sorry, Seb. Will you let me put this matter to rights and say my proper farewells this time?'

'Aye. I suppose you should. But do not take the little ones anywhere near the place where he could get his filthy hands upon them. Heaven knows what he thought to do with our son once he had him, though he mentioned a barren wife.'

'Mam told me that also, so it's probably true. For safety's sake, I'll leave them both in your care. I won't be long but keep a close watch on them.'

'I have learnt my lesson, Rose. Fear not. Two children have ne'er been guarded so closely nor with greater attention than these two this day. They shall not blink without my knowing.'

My dear one nodded and smiled, though I was unsure whether she wholly trusted me as afore time. Yesterday's failure yet weighed upon both of us.

'And look to your own safety, also,' I added, thinking that Saunders might mean her harm if he could not have Dickon. After she had gone, I began to think I ought to have accompanied her. But that would mean leaving the children here, alone, forwhy I would not let them anywhere near Rose Lane. Previously, I might have asked Kit to look to them but not now, which returned my thoughts to that thorny matter anew.

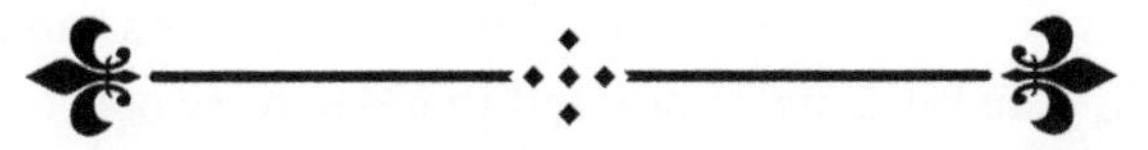

We made a brief foray – the children and I – to White Horse Lane, further along High Street, in the opposite direction from Rose Lane. The innkeeper recommended a good cobbler there who could re-sole my boots. I bought some sticky suckets from a street-seller for Dickon and Julia to content them. In truth, I yet felt guilty for my son's dreadful experience yesterday and would recompense him with a treat. And, of course, Julia could not be left without.

That the horror of abduction was not forgotten was evident in my son's long silences and unaccustomed listlessness. I worried for him. How long might he remain afflicted? Rose assured me he slept well enough last night, without bad dreams, insofar as she could tell.

Returning to the inn, which betwixt breakfast and dinner, was none too busy, I found a quiet corner and took out my drawing stuff, not for my own occupation but for Dickon. I gave him paper and charcoal and sat him amidst the floor rushes. Julia soon slept in the cart whilst Gawain sat guard and I ordered a cup of ale, prepared to make it last all morn. Peace and quiet were what we required at present: a day to recover afore the long walk back to London began upon the morrow.

Having made a few charcoal scribbles without much enthusiasm, Dickon curled up beside Gawain, using his furry flank as a pillow, and went to sleep – unusual at this hour. I reached down to touch his cheek, fearing to find it fevered but it was not. Mayhap he slept less well last night than Rose believed.

To my surprise, when Kit strode in, he came to join me directly. I was glad of it, so signed to the tap-boy to bring another cup of ale.

'How's the little lad faring?' Kit asked, looking to my sleeping child.

'Quiet,' I said. 'Too quiet, in truth.'

'The shock of it, no doubt. But a young one's memory is short. He'll be his usual, noisy self in a day or two.'

I nodded, hoping he was correct.

'Twas not the tap-boy but the innkeeper who brought Kit's ale and, to judge by his sombre expression, he was not best pleased.

'So, you're back then,' he said to Kit, setting the cup before him. 'I'm of half a mind to report you as a horse thief.'

I could tell my friend was startled by this, seeing his nostrils flare, but he maintained his composure, his eyes downcast.

'And why would you do that? Are any of your horses missing?' Kit's tone sounded mocking.

'No. But you know that full well. I'm talking about last night: you and that Lancastrian rascal borrowing my best mounts without a by-your-leave. You think I wouldn't know of it? I saw you. And now I demand you pay me. That's two shillings you owe me. Each.'

'Don't be so foolish. Such a sum could buy one of those sorry nags. As for riding one of them at dead of night, I wouldn't trust such a beast to carry me to the end of High Street in full daylight.'

'I'll wager you didn't think them so sorry when they were carrying you at full gallop all the way to Fordwich. Good enough for you then, eh?'

'I don't know what nonsense you're spouting.'

'No? Yet the Watch saw you and I have folks in Fordwich who tell me things. He sailed on the morning tide, your associate, on *The Margaret St John* with Captain Bartlett, bound for Bruges. See? You thought your doings were all so secret, didn't you? Oh, and the price has just gone up to three shillings since you insist on arguing the case.' The innkeeper held out his hand.

Kit stood up so suddenly, overturning the stool with a clatter. He slapped a penny upon the board.

'That's for the ale. Keep the change,' he snarled afore storming towards the door. But he turned halfway, his face suffused with anger. 'Speak one word of this… either of you…' He looked directly at me with a gimlet eye. '…And you'll suffer the consequences. You have been warned.'

'Lancastrian filth,' the innkeeper muttered, working up spittle and hawking it on the floor in Kit's wake. 'I told you to stay away from him.' He picked up the coin and went off, back to his ale barrels, whistling cheerfully as though the threat meant naught to him.

Being less of a phlegmatic humour than our host, I could not shrug off those words so easily forwhy I understood Kit made no idle threat. Though, plainly, I did not know him so well at all, yet I recognised true menace when I saw it and it had been there, black as sin, in his departing expression. I shivered, icy fingertips tracing a path down my spine.

I was meant to be upon pilgrimage but, somehow, trouble courted me at every turn. Thaddeus Turner had been right about that, as he warned me afore we left London. I found my thoughts taking me back home, to friends I could trust, folk I understood right well. How I wished to return to London, where I belonged. I would be glad, aye, and relieved to be away from Canterbury.

Rose returned, God be thanked, to spare me from further disturbing contemplation. She was smiling, so I assumed all was now set to rights betwixt her and her mother – no more untruths, leastwise.

'Did it go well?' I asked.

'Aye, well enough. Mam now understands about the children. She was greatly disappointed to learn they aren't her grandchildren but says there is much compensation in having regained her daughter. I promised to write to her by way of the priest at St Mary's, such that my father does not see the letters. She will need the priest to read them to her, anyhow. I'm not at ease, knowing we'll be deceiving my father but it serves him right, since he doesn't want to acknowledge that I exist. So there it stands!'

'You saw naught of that other?'

'Not a hair. And what of the children?'

'I have not mislaid them, not so much as a hair of theirs either.' I tried to make a jest of it. 'But Dickon has slept most of this while. I pray God he is not about to be laid low with some ailment or other.'

'Shock, I expect.' She picked him up and he came awake, yawning mightily, showing all his little teeth.

'Mam, Gawain's hungry,' he said, which I took to be a

good sign.

'Kit said the same… about the shock, I mean.'

'Where is he? Do you know? Is he joining us for dinner?'

'Best not to enquire, Rose, and I mean that in all seriousness. Things have been happening with him… inexplicable things. He warned me not to speak of such matters, saying it be for the best. I believe we may be returning home without him.'

'Oh, how we shall miss him. He was good company and a strong arm when we needed one. He is safe, isn't he, Seb?'

'In all honesty, lass, I do not know. I hope so. Come, what shall we have to eat? The partridges in a coffin with mushrooms and galingale sounds tasty indeed.'

The Warenne twins came as we were about to order our dinner and we sat together. I hoped with them, there would be some diversion to distract me from that disquieting exchange with Kit.

'You've been safe since we left St Thomas's Hospital?' Rose asked, 'Now that the minstrel is gone.'

Tristan pulled a face even as he chewed on a succulent morsel of partridge.

'If he is gone… Troy reckons he saw him since, hanging around outside Christ's Church Gate. Isn't that so, Troy?' He nudged his brother, who nodded, taking time to finish his mouthful of food. 'We thought, or rather hoped, the wretch was drowned but maybe he wasn't. Whatever is true, he's not attempted to injure us since. But what have you and Kit been doing, Seb? Did you get to visit the shrine? What a marvel it is. And we prayed for our father's recovery, as promised, didn't we, Troy? Not that the old curmudgeon deserves it but we did our filial duty as demanded. Now he can't disinherit us, as he threatened.'

'You think he'll keep his word, Tris?' the other twin put in, having finished his portion of coffin-filling.

'Why would your father even consider disinheriting you?' I asked, intrigued to hear their tale.

'Because he hates us, as does Fenshaw,' Troilus took up the thread of the story whilst Tristan ate his dinner. 'If Harper wasn't trying to kill us out of personal spite – which we can find no reason for – we both think Father, or more likely Fenshaw, sent him to do away with us. Paid him to be rid of us.'

'It's fortunate he was so inept as to fail at every turn.'

'Aye, true enough, Tris, but that last time... if it hadn't been for Seb, here, and his swift action, I think either one or both of us wouldn't be sitting at this board, telling our story. You saved us, Seb. We owe you...'

'Who is this Fenshaw who so hates you he would have you slain?' I asked, not wanting to hear myself praised.

'Our brother, Father's first-born son. He would inherit by right, except that Father never wed his mother, so he's bastard-born. He's almost a score of years older than us and reckoned he would inherit by default – there being no other relatives. Then Father wed our mother, though he was nigh unto three score in age and she was but fifteen – younger than we are now. But Father makes clear that Fenshaw's mother was his soulmate, not ours. When she died last year, he was glad, wasn't he, Tris? It gave him the chance to go back to Fenshaw's mother, even though she's an ancient hag.

'Meanwhile, Fenshaw runs the estates on our parent's behalf and won't let us be a party to any of it. Calls us "wastrels" and "useless popinjays" but we're not, if only he would give us some task about the manor. Then Father became ill – hardly surprising at his age – and threatened to rewrite his will, cutting us out because, so he insisted, we don't love and respect him as Fenshaw does.'

'So Fenshaw suggested,' said Tristan, taking up the tale,' If we proved our love of Father by undertaking this pilgrimage, praying for his health at Becket's shrine and bringing back Holy Water to cure his ills, the will would stand in our favour, as it should. But, of course, if we both should die in the attempt...'

'Fenshaw will inherit,' I said.

Both twins nodded.

'So, as you'll realise, if this has been Fenshaw's doing, we may not be safe yet. He could pay someone more efficient to do what Harper failed to do. Or maybe do the task himself as we travel home. The homeward journey could be just as perilous for us. What do you think, Troy? Naught may have changed except our would-be assassin's name.'

'What of this Fenshaw? How does he look that we may keep a watch for him?'

'He's much of our height and build and has hair like ours. We all take after Father in our colouring,' Tristan said.

'But Fen wears his hair long like some courtier's strumpet.' Troilus grinned at this. 'But with a beard. Of course, he's greying a bit these days, being older.'

A memory flittered like a butterfly afore my eyes and I took out paper and charcoal from my scrip and began sketching, delving deep, attempting to conjure a likeness from the briefest of glimpses a few days since.

'Could this be Fenshaw?' I showed the twins. Eyebrows raised in unison.

'You know our brother?' Tristan gasped.

'Nay, but if this is he, I saw him here, in Canterbury, upon Sunday, it must have been… aye, Sunday it was. More to the point, he was talking to Hugo Harper in a right-heated exchange with much gesticulation. Do you remember it, Rose?'

'I do. Kit remarked how Harper seemed to upset folk so readily.' She took the sketch. 'This isn't your best work, Seb. I recall that the man was more handsome than you show him.'

''Tis not meant to be a fine portrait,' I said, removing the drawing from her grasp and shoving it into my scrip, out of sight. ''Twas the observation of a few moments only, yet sufficient for Tristan and Troilus to recognise.'

'I never said it was a poor likeness, just that I thought him finer looking…'

'And you saw that upon the instant, I suppose? Trust a

woman to notice. Besides, he be an accomplice in multiple murder attempts.'

'You don't know that for certain,' she insisted and rightly so, I had to admit. 'And why would that make him more ugly? You've said yourself, many a time, "you cannot tell a felon by his face."' Then she kissed my bruised and swollen cheek. 'Surely you're not jealous, husband?'

'Of course not. Why? Should I be?'

She laughed.

'There's more to mark a good man than a handsome visage.'

Chapter 15

Wednesday, later

EXCEPT FOR collecting my boots from the cobbler, there was little else to do in preparation for our departure next morn. If Kit were here, he would likely have some matter in mind to occupy me, such as earning coin from my drawings or viewing more fine works at the cathedral. But, without him, my heart was not in it, even though I had promised myself more time to study the stained glass of the Becket windows in detail. After what came to pass when I examined the murals in St Gabriel's Chapel, I was not now so much inclined to do that either.

And now I was concerned anew for the safety of the de Warenne twins – not that I could do aught about it when the threat was so vague that it might not exist at all. Hugo Harper's encounter with their brother may have been but a chance meeting. The rogue could have insulted Fenshaw, an innocent passer-by, resulting in the altercation we witnessed. Yet I misliked such a coincidence. My friend back in London, Thaddeus Turner, spared no time for coincidences in his duties as City Bailiff and neither did I as his assistant – unpaid.

Therefore, when Tristan and Troilus suggested that we might go to the All Hallows revels beyond Queningate, I agreed. Apparently, there were going to be horse races and the twins thought their fine steeds stood a fair chance of victory.

Rose decided Dickon required calm and security to assure his recovery and although I was tempted to argue that watching horses galloping by at great speed might have pleased a little lad more than resting quietly, I bowed to her superior knowledge of such matters as the care of babes. Thus it was that just the three of us would go.

Having waited whilst the twins saddled their mounts in the stable yard behind the inn, we went along High Street, passed the Shambles and the end of Rose Lane, heading for Newingate by St George's Church. The twins led their horses on foot, though whether this was a courtesy to me and Gawain or to save the beasts' strength for the racing, I did not enquire.

Passing 'neath the gate arch, we turned to our left hand, following the city walls along, under two circular bastion towers until we reached Queningate, this portal being noted as a long-dead queen's privy entrance to the cathedral precinct, as it said in my *Guide for Pilgrims*, though which queen, it did not say.

Betwixt the walls and the Abbey of St Augustine beyond lay an area of common ground where the citizens held their revels in celebration of All Hallows. Back in London, we made little of this particular feast day but Canterbury did otherwise and crowds were gathering. Stalls were set up at one end of the green, selling all manner of wares, from saddles to sweetmeats, knives to nutmegs and, of course, the ubiquitous pilgrim trinkets.

The twins went off to give their names to the organisers of the races, leaving me to wander among the stalls with Gawain, enjoying the fair. A poppet show proved a marvellous distraction. How Dickon and Julia would have loved it. I was applauding right heartily and Gawain was wagging his tail. But, I realised, not because of the skills of the poppeteer. A hand rested upon my shoulder. It was Kit.

'Don't acknowledge me, Seb,' he said. 'Continue to enjoy the performance and listen to me, I pray you. I've been searching you out.'

'And now you have found me. Were you following me? What is it you want? '

'Seb, I'm sorry. I admit I've been less than honest with you, my friend.'

'We be friends still, then?'

'I hope so. I'm in trouble. Serious trouble. If you can forgive my devious use of you and your family, will you help me? I know I was wrong to involve you but your pilgrimage was a perfect means of my joining an old friend and aiding him.'

'Glassman,' I said, clapping a particularly amusing stunt as a poppet performed a cartwheel – I know not how it was done.

'Aye, we were supposed to meet up here in Canterbury. He'd travelled from the Midland shires with Tanner but my joining the pilgrimage with you made a good disguise. It gave us more chance to discuss his plans, aye, and to talk about the good times we once shared.'

'Is Tanner one of you also? A Lancastrian, I mean.'

'Aye, Tanner's been a messenger for the cause for years. He's well known as a pilgrim and can come and go throughout England and France as much as he pleases. How did you know?'

'Rest assured, your true purpose was not uncovered by me. The innkeeper be an observant fellow. He noted that Glassman ever refused to drink King Edward's health and suspected him of being a Lancastrian.'

'That was foolish of Glassman. I hadn't realised.'

'And if he supports the House of Lancaster,' I continued, 'Then you, who rode with him last eve, are likely to have sympathies for the same. And I thought maybe Tanner has also, forwhy it explains his great reluctance to involve the authorities after the death of Alfred Denny at Dartford. It would not do to have the King's Coroner asking too many questions, would it? But that is all by the way now. You say you are in trouble, Kit?'

'I know you're a Yorkist by sentiment, Seb, and I swear I've done naught to offend against the king but help a kinsman to safety.'

'Yet another kinsman?'

'On my father's side this time and but a third cousin…'

'Glassman is John de Vere, the Earl of Oxford, is he not? I unravelled that mystery for myself from the French.'

'Oh, you're a clever one, Seb. In my youth, seeming an age ago now, I was training as a henchman in his father's household until...'

'Until that earl and his heir were executed after the Battle of Barnet in '71?'

'Aye. So you know that, too.'

'Common knowledge.' I shrugged. 'Their heads were on spikes upon London Bridge for weeks.' I did not add that, as a youth with lurid intent, I made sketches of them at the time.

'What you don't know is that my own father was executed along with them.'

'What! Your father was condemned and executed as a traitor? Dear God in heaven, Kit.'

'Shh. Keep your voice down.'

'And you expect me to help you escape justice?'

'Come, let's move away; the show is done. Over in that stand of oaks... I'll meet you there in a few minutes.'

I obeyed despite harbouring grave doubts. On the way, I purchased a cup of bramble cordial, taking my time. Once amidst the bare trees, leaves crisp underfoot, Kit continued:

'I promise you that what I ask will do the Yorkists' cause no harm. This is now a case of saving my own skin. Someone betrayed us. Glassman escaped in the nick of time aboard ship from Fordwich but I was pursued over half of Kent by the port reeve's men, or so it seemed.'

'So the innkeeper and I are not alone in discovering the truth. He already told me about the ship, *The Margaret St John.*'

'How did he know that? Maybe it was the innkeeper who informed the port reeve there, or one or other of the Cambridge men. They openly approve of your patron, the Duke of Gloucester, since he is also Earl of Cambridge and has done a great deal to aid the university and the town. It's possible I said too much during our conversations. They have certainly been less friendly since we arrived here, avoiding me. But it doesn't matter who it was; will you help me now for friendship's sake?' He gripped my arm, withholding my drink as I was about to sip it.

'Suppose it was I who informed upon you?' I said, pulling free, resuming my drink.

'You didn't though, did you, Seb? You're too honest a fellow.'

'I am also loyal to my king. But, no, it was not I. And, if I may aid you without committing some treasonous act or other and it will prove no danger to my loved ones, then perhaps… What do you ask of me?'

'It's little enough and very simple, Seb, and will harm no one… I left papers and coin under my mattress at the inn. I dare not go back there now or the innkeeper or the port reeve will have me. I wasn't intending to flee the country but now I have no choice and I need the money and the documents.' He went on to instruct how and where this should be done and at what hour.

'I shall think on it,' I said, 'And I make no promises. If I do not come at that time, you will know I have thought better of it… or been caught in the process. In either case – and God help me, if 'tis the latter – you will be on your own.

'Now, if you will excuse me, I have a horse race to attend. The Warenne twins be taking part. Gawain, heel. Beware the flying hooves, lad.'

Wednesday eve
The Cathedral Precinct

Kit had instructed that I should enter the precinct by way of the postern gate beside Queningate. 'Twas not the most convenient way for me, having to walk from The Chequers, retracing the path of earlier in the day with the Warenne twins.

By the by, though they had not had the victory in the horse race, both acquitted themselves well. Tristan won a purse of one shilling for crossing the line in third place, neck and neck with his brother, whilst Troilus received a prize of two groats for the best turned-out horse. They were content with the afternoon's exploits.

Walking the streets of London after dark required citizens to carry a torch; elsewise the Watch be likely to ask questions or go so far as to make an arrest. Being unfamiliar with Canterbury, I feared the Watch here might be similarly vigilant but Kit had assured me it was not.

Thus, I crept like a felon without a torch, hoping I would not become lost. 'Twas as well I had walked this way in daylight but finding the postern gate without a light took time and every moment I feared discovery.

Kit's documents and coin were in my scrip, clutched tight, though I had forethought to put them in a canvas bag for his convenience. Alas, I was without Gawain, thinking he could attract attention, being inclined to bark at every nocturnal creature scurrying by. But I felt vulnerable, not having him at my side.

I found the postern gate. 'Twas neither barred nor locked, just as Kit said it would be, and I pushed it open. In the dark, the distant windows of the cathedral's infirmary showed clear. Otherwise, I found my way by starlight, following the pale gravel path through the monks' cemetery, showing white. By the old campanile tower – eventually to be replaced by the central bell tower when it was completed – I reached the place of assignation. The masons, carpenters and labourers had tidied away their tools and gone to supper long since. The skeletal outline of the scaffolding could be made out against the stars, spidery fingers of lashed poles and long webs of ropes.

Kit was not there but then the clock on the west tower had not yet chimed the hour of eight. I was a little early.

Great blocks of pale stone stood all around, some finished and polished smooth to the touch. My fingers, like everything here, came away covered in white dust. Other blocks were yet rough-hewn. In one corner, smaller pieces were partially carved.

Hard to make out in the dark, I thought for a moment I saw a spectral figure and jumped back afore realising I faced a nigh-life-sized stone saint, awaiting its feet and the hem of its robe to be released, chiselled from the rock. It gave me quite a start.

The bell chimed the hour. Kit was tardy. I sat upon a block to await him, wondering what madness had overtaken me forwhy what I was about was no less than treason. I wanted this over and done as swiftly as possible. Where was he?

Time dragged. How long should I wait? He could not expect me to sit here all night. I shivered inside my cloak, blowing breath to warm my hands. I leapt to my feet at the least sound but 'twas only a cat on the prowl, chasing after a rat or vole that set my heart pounding.

The bell chimed the hour of nine and to add to my misery, it began to rain; not a downpour but a steady, depressing drizzle.

I heard another sound: a distant shout. Probably some ne'er-do-wells about the town. More shouts. Louder. Nearer. The sound of running feet.

I hid betwixt two blocks, wedging myself into the narrow space. Whoever it was, I should not be here at dead of night. Torch-lights showed, outlining a black figure, cloak flying.

'Seb! Seb! For the love of God! Are you here?'

'Kit.' I came from my hidey hole.

My friend was panting. He looked back over his shoulder.

'You have my stuff? Give it to me.' He grabbed the canvas bag from me. 'Now run as you've never run before.'

Men appeared with torches… and dogs. Sighting their quarry, they began barking. There was no hope of outrunning four-footed pursuers. There was only one way: up the closest scaffolding ladder. I was ne'er one for climbing – nor running – but now I did both. Kit was right behind me as we scaled the first level of the masons' planking.

The dogs gathered at the ladder's foot, barking in their frustration. But the men came on up. We ran on, slipping on wet planking, to the bottom of another ladder. I did not dare think of the inevitable: that eventually, there would be no more ladders; nowhere else to go.

Rain dripped off my nose – or, mayhap, it was sweat – my hands were wet and a sure grip upon the rungs became less certain. My foot slithered sideways and Kit grabbed my arm to steady me as we mounted the second level. Here, we were as high as the clerestory where I had chased after my Dickon on the other side of these windows but our pursuers were gaining.

I wore my scrip with its strap across my shoulder, leaving my hands free, but the canvas bag had no such handle and encumbered Kit at every step. Yet I knew he dared not abandon it.

'Give it here, back in my scrip,' I said, holding it open so he might stuff his documents and coin within.

Another ladder. 'Twas as well that it was dark, I suppose, though it made matters ever more perilous, but at least, looking down, I had little impression of how far it was possible to fall. The only indication was the flickering of torches held by those who remained on the ground and the distant barking of the dogs – all of which awaited us upon our descent, if we made it so far.

My legs ached with effort as we ran along the third level of planking among a tangle of ropes, buckets, tools and sheets of canvas strewn with stone chippings. Here, the labourers had left their stuff, certain it was safe enough from petty thieves who would not trouble to risk climbing so high, in the darkness, in the rain.

But here we were, fleeing for our lives and yet I did not know from whom we ran. I swear the boards trembled under us and I heard the spindly edifice creaking.

'Who are they, Kit?' I gasped, wiping rain from my eyes with a sodden sleeve.

'Sheriff of… Kent's men…' he wheezed. 'Don't stop now. Betrayed…'

Betrayed, I thought? You but not me. I have done naught

amiss. Except now I was aiding and abetting a Lancastrian. Crime enough. I should have stayed at the inn, if not in London. I ought never have come. What of my family if I were arrested, tried and hanged?

We turned a corner and then another to the north side of the tower. The planking ended abruptly in a black abyss as we slithered to a halt. I grabbed at Kit, teetering on the edge of a chasm of darkness.

'When we're down, run for the inn. The sheriff doesn't know you and… I'm right sorry, Seb.'

'As am I. Where now?'

'Take hold of that rope and jump. The pulley will slow your descent. Go!'

'And you?'

'I'll use that rope there. See you at the bottom.'

As torchlight and black shapes appeared behind us and came thundering along the planks, I saw Kit swing up on the rope, kicking out at the nearest man, sending him flying over the edge, his drawn-out scream ending upon an instant. But as I stood, hesitating on the brink, Kit had another problem in that the rope was now tangled about him.

'Go! Jump!' he cried.

With my eyes screwed tight shut and a prayer on my lips, I obeyed, grabbing the rope, leaping out into nothingness, hearing the pulley clattering high above.

The ground came faster than expected, bone-jarring, knocking the breath from me. I hurt so much. Was I yet alive? A heavy thud a few yards away betokened Kit's landing like a stone. We had come down on the north side of the cathedral, away from the waiting dogs and men. I could see the lit windows of the infirmary across the way.

'Kit? Kit? Where are you?'

No reply, so I crawled to where I thought he landed, bruises throbbing with the smallest movement. Fearing ribs broken, I clutched my left side in agony. I felt his wet cloak, an arm.

'Kit, we must go now.' I knew not how: uncertain I could yet stand. 'Get up afore they bring the dogs.'

My friend did not move nor make a sound. He must be stunned. I groped about, finding his head, turning it so the rain might fall upon his face and revive him. Merciful God: do not let him be dead, unshriven…

An impenetrable blackness rose to our right hand, blocking out the thinning cloud and returning starlight. I dragged Kit towards it, scrunching through fallen leaves which had blown into the angle formed by the buttress and the cathedral wall. I prayed to St Thomas to hide us as I burrowed into the wet leaves, covering us as best I could, though with no way of telling if I made a fair job of it. I hoped the scent of mouldering leaves would disguise us from the dogs.

I lay utterly still, hardly daring to breathe. My heart beat so loud I feared the dogs, if not the men also, must hear it. And I knew not whether I held a dead man in my embrace. His skin felt chill but so did mine as the sweat of the chase turned cold. I was shivering, having to clench my teeth to prevent them from chattering. I heard the dogs barking and our pursuers shouting, but the sounds moved away until the night fell silent. They must think we were either long gone or dead from the jump, believing they would find our bodies come daylight.

Now what? Should I attempt to carry Kit to the infirmary not so far distant across the precinct or wait until dawn to fetch aid? I mustered my strength, shaking off leaves but, what with my own hurts, I found him a leaden weight. I might drag him a yard at a time but if he had broken bones, I would likely do him more harm. If I left him, he would certainly die of cold… if he were not dead already. Fearing to find out the truth, I put my fingers to the angle of his jaw, pressing against his neck, praying there would be a pulse. I thought there was but my fingers were nigh numb with cold and I could not be certain. I supposed I would know soon enough if *rigor mortis* began to set in but, as yet, his fingers flexed as I moved them.

The rain had ceased so I decided I would stay with him, there in our sheltered nook 'neath a coverlet of leaves. I lay back against the stone buttress, sharing my warmth, what little I had.

'Stay with me, Kit,' I whispered, chafing his hands. 'Don't leave me now, my friend. I do not wish to be here in the dark, alone. We are yet friends, are we not?' I realised there was some stickiness on his forehead: blood, mayhap. In the darkness, I could not tell. 'I care not what you have done... if you are for Lancaster or York. Just keep on breathing, I beg you.' I held him close, rocking him like a babe as we lay. 'S-stay with me.' And once again, my face was wet but not with rain.

Thursday, the second day of November

I lay abed in our house in London. My deathbed forwhy Rose lay beside me, holding me, weeping all the while. Her tears fell cold and wet against my cheek.

But not a few, quiet tears: a veritable conduit of water.

I came awake, realising I was not at home. Neither was I dead, though every part of me felt as though I was being dragged through Purgatory head foremost. 'Twas raining again and I lay 'neath a gargoyle spouting a torrent. And my bed-mate upon the hard ground was not Rose but the slumped form of my friend. He, too, was receiving a dousing and – glory be unto God and all the saints – he moaned and stirred.

'Kit, wake up. 'Tis morning. We have to get your hurts tended. Come, rouse yourself, elsewise I cannot carry you.' Our makeshift 'bed' was swiftly becoming a mud slick.

I wondered how long it would be afore the search party returned. That they would, I had no doubt. After all, we – or rather Kit – had killed one of them, kicking him off the scaffolding. For all I knew, he may have injured others among them during the chase aforehand.

In daylight, my friend's injury was all too plain. A great gash across his forehead continued into his hairline. The blood had crusted but now the rain was washing it down his face, so it looked to be bleeding anew. I wiped away the worst of the gore on a corner of my cloak.

'Come, Kit, the infirmary is not so far. There, you can rest, dry out and have your wound stitched. You will be safe with the monks. Take it slow… lean against the wall here 'til I get a better hold of you. Put your arm about my neck… easy now… one step at a time…'

By inches, we crossed the soaked grass. My ribs screamed for relief as I took his weight. Kit's feet dragged and we had to keep pausing so I might take a breath. I encouraged him constantly with meaningless words, yet he made no sound but his own laboured breathing. The infirmary door appeared as distant as ever.

'Wait here,' I told him, lowering him to the wet sward. 'Rest. I shall fetch aid…' I continued towards my goal. Even without my burden, I was slow of step, holding my ribs, lurching forward, stumbling. Once, I fell down, though I knew not why. Weary, I suppose.

It took a deal of effort to hammer on the door with my fist, calling out for succour. At first, it seemed no one heard. Nobody flung the door open to admit me.

'Help us!' I cried, sinking to my knees upon the threshold. Then, hands gripped me. The sheriff's men or blessed monks – I did not know nor care who. 'My friend… lies out there,' I managed to say, pointing vaguely. 'Sore hurt… '

Later
The Cathedral Infirmary

Wrapped in blankets, seated by the blazing fire, a cup of hot, mulled wine with restorative herbs in my hands, I felt better. My ribs were firmly bound and, though sore, were hurting less with each sip of wine. Likely, it contained something to ease the pain.

Kit lay abed behind me, still senseless, a brother attending him. His gash was stitched but, so they told me, he had other injuries beside. For now, I felt too tired to enquire the details. We were here, cared for and safe. That was all that mattered for the moment, though I must send word to Rose at the inn. She would be beside herself with worry. Last eve, I told her I intended a short walk afore bed. 'Twas all she knew of my night-time foray into deepest trouble. And we were supposed to be departing for London this morn. Oh, well, that must needs wait upon another day, at least. For the present, crossing this room seemed more than I could readily achieve.

A tall, stately brother swept in, fetched a stool for himself and sat facing me.

'I am Prior William Sellynge,' he said, smiling. His voice was soft but, even so, bore the mark of his authority. 'Are you well enough to tell what happened to you and your friend last night? I see he wears a tonsure.'

'Aye. Father Christian of St Mary Magdalen Church in London… my friend, that is. We be here upon pilgrimage, staying at The Chequers of Hope Inn in Mercery Lane. My name be Sebastian Foxley, also of London, and my wife and children await me at the inn. How may I send her word that I be safe?'

'I know the inn well. I'll send a lay brother with any message you wish. But it's a disgrace that two peaceful pilgrims aren't safe here in Canterbury. The archbishop shall be informed. Can you tell me what befell?'

Thus far, I had told the truth. What followed would be an edited version, though I hated having to lie to the prior.

'We were set upon by a pack of ruffians. I know not who they were. My friend suffered a bad fall during the assault.'

'At what hour was this?'

'Late. I wished a walk afore bed to stretch my legs. I paid little heed to the hour.'

'A sojourn after dark is never a wise thing but then two fit, young men should've been safe enough. Where did the attack take place?'

'My knowledge of Canterbury be limited but not far from the cathedral.'

'Can you be more precise? It might help us to uncover the evil-doers.'

'I came into the precinct by way of a small gate... little more than a wicket in a narrow opening in the wall.' That much was true, at least.

'The postern on the other side of the cemetery?'

I nodded.

'I think so.'

'So the attack did not occur within the precinct?'

I shook my head, keeping my eyes lowered as I finished my wine.

'You are certain of this? Thanks be to God for that, at least, since it means the crime doesn't fall within our jurisdiction. It's the mayor's responsibility but, since you're pilgrims, as I said, the archbishop must be made aware of this grave transgression. In the meantime, I'll send a scribe to you that you may dictate your message to your goodwife.'

'Do not trouble for that, Father Prior. I have paper, pen and ink in my scrip. I may write it myself.'

'Maybe you are capable but...' He rose and went to the hearth where our wet cloaks were spread to dry. He picked up a leather bag from which water dripped. My precious scrip. 'I don't think your supply of paper has survived the rain.' He took out a sheaf of sodden sheets. 'I will see you have what you require to pen your note.'

But what he showed me was not my paper. It was Kit's. In truth, I was utterly glad to see how the ink had run, turning the documents grey and making the writing illegible. I must have left the flap of my scrip unfastened and it had fallen open during the night and filled with rain water, perhaps from that gargoyle spout this morning.

With Prior William departed, I eased up off my stool, clutching the blanket about my nakedness, wondering what had become of my attire, that which was not drying by the fire. With utmost care, holding my ribs, I went to Kit's bedside, where a monk was washing a nasty wound on my friend's forearm.

'How does my friend fare?' I asked.

'He has received Unction,' the brother said.

My hopes plunged. Extreme Unction was only administered to the dying.

'So bad?'

'His skull is broken and dented, amongst other injuries. If he lives, it will be a miracle. And even so, he may not be as you knew him before. It's a serious hurt, you understand?' Having cleansed the wound on Kit's arm, he smeared a greenish ointment onto a linen pad and began binding it in place.

'You mean he may not recall what happened to us?'

'A loss of memory may be the least of his concerns. You did not mention the hound to Father William.'

'Hound?'

'This binding covers a dog bite,' he said as he knotted the ends of the linen strip. 'Those ruffians certainly meant you harm, setting a dog on you. You were fortunate indeed to come through with only a cracked rib or two, though you'll be sore for a few weeks.'

'Aye, my friend had by far the worst of it.'

The brother tucked the blanket more securely about Kit's immobile form.

'There. He rests in God's hands now.' He turned to me: 'But this isn't your first encounter with recent violence, is it? Your face tells the tale of injuries from a few days ago.'

'Well, I…' I put my hand over my misshapen jaw, still tender though the bruises were yellowing, as Rose had informed me yesterday when I insisted upon knowing.

'Did you think I was unlikely to notice? As the infirmarer here, I am constantly required to read wounds as others read words. And what of those nasty scratches, eh?'

I looked at my left hand, realising belatedly that the bindings were gone, lost during the night.

'A cat with a temper,' I told him. 'Naught more sinister.' I did not mention that, in my opinion, the God-forsaken creature was more sinister than the Devil himself.

'If I were you, Sebastian Foxley, whoever you are, I'd get me back to London as swiftly as possible since it appears our fair city is no place for you.'

I readily agreed with him, thinking he suspected our sorry condition resulted from more than a chance encounter with a couple of ruffians and their sharp-fanged dog.

Chapter 16

Thursday morning
The Chequers of Hope Inn

ROSE COSSETED me as I lay abed at the inn. She had come to me at the infirmary, having received my note. Exceeding anxious as she was, she knew not whether to scold me or love me upon seeing my condition. I deserved the scolding more than she knew, having endangered us all, but loving words came more readily to my dear one's lips. She could berate me later.

She brought me back to The Chequers with the assistance of two lay brothers who nigh carried me as I discovered my right ankle unable to bear my weight, though I failed to notice it earlier. The infirmarer had strapped it tightly as he did my ribs. I felt trussed up like a Christmas goose, hardly able to move.

'Forgive me, sweeting. Forgive my unthinking foolishness,' I said for the hundredth time as the brothers eased me up the stairs. 'I be that sorry,' I said as they assisted me into bed, wincing as I laid back against the pillows.

'Kit was in trouble and needed your aid. You helped a friend. I would expect no less of you.'

'Aye, but 'tis not a good thing that I have done.'

'It wasn't your fault Kit got hurt so badly.'

The lay brothers departed, their sandals pattering down the stair, and Rose closed the door after.

'I know but the reason why we were there... oh, Rose... 'twas a dire mistake on my part. This once, I should have refused to take any part.'

'Tell me later. Now you need to rest.'

'Where are the children?' I asked, seized by panic of a sudden. 'After what came to pass in the cathedral…'

'Fear not, they're perfectly safe, playing in the stable yard. Mother Thorogood and Gawain have care of them.'

'And her evil-eyed cat, I suppose.'

'Probably. Gawain gets along with the creature more peaceably than you do. Tristan and Troilus are there also, showing them the horses. They did well in the racing, so I hear. Now rest, husband, and you'll heal the more quickly so we can go home. I've been in Canterbury longer than I have a mind to and I've already said my farewells to my mother.'

'Aye, and I would have Dickon and Julia well away from here also… away from *him*. We shall leave in the morning, first thing.'

Rose raised her eyebrows at this. I suppose she doubted me and, in truth, I had yet to think how I might pull the cart up hill and down dale, all the way to London, without Kit's aid and my ribs afire. Aye, and what of Kit? Could I depart not knowing whether he would survive? And then a thought occurred: 'Rose, have you seen my scrip? Where did I leave it?'

'I don't know, Seb. Did you take it with you on your walk last eve? Maybe those ruffians you spoke of stole it?'

'Nay. I had it at the infirmary afterwards. I must have left it behind.'

'You certainly didn't carry it back here.'

'Oh, Rose, I feel lost without it. I shall have to go retrieve it later… after dinner.' For the present, after such a night as I had passed, sleep was all I felt fit for.

I awoke to the smells of meats cooking and pasties baking wafting up from the kitchen below and realised I was hungry – a fair sign of improvement in my condition. Or so I believed until I tried to push myself up into a sitting position and felt burning blades pierce my side. I cried out without meaning to, bringing Rose running and waking Julia from her nap in the blanket nest in the corner of the chamber.

'All be well,' I told Rose, holding up my hands to fend off her concern. 'I forgot my ribs is all… which shows how much better they be already.' I forced a smile. 'A good dinner will set me to rights, I know.'

'I'll go ask them to send up a tray.'

'Nay. Do no such thing, Rose. I be no invalid. I shall eat downstairs with everyone else.' Such was my intention but, until I made the attempt, I did not realise how much determination and gritting of teeth would be required. But I succeeded with Rose's aid, coming down the stair crabwise and then limping to the nearest bench. Despite my grave discomfort, once settled, I discovered I was hungry and set to devour the fried gobbets of pork in apple sauce with onion and fennel fritters, fine white bread and a quince cream served with hazelnut wafers. As ever, the food at The Chequers was excellent.

Mother Thorogood and the Warenne twins shared our mess, the youngsters laughing at some tale they related of a skinny merchant and his fat wife who had been here at the inn last eve. Amusing as it was, I dared not laugh – my ribs could not bear it – but it was difficult not to do so. Watching them in their merriment, 'twas hard to recall that, lately, someone had wanted them dead and I wondered if the threat truly had passed with Hugo Harper's fall into the river. I prayed it was so but feared the twins' journey home might yet prove perilous if their brother Fenshaw, possibly the originator of their intended demise, was here in Canterbury.

I told myself that the time at the horse racing yesterday had given Fenshaw plenty of opportunity for mischief, yet naught had come to pass. I was worrying about them without cause, no doubt, when I should be more anxious for Kit. If 'twas not for the effort required to walk to the infirmary, I ought to visit him. I had departed from thence, requesting that the infirmarer send me word if there be any change – for better or for worse – in my friend's condition but no message had come, so mayhap he was holding on to life, even by a thread.

In truth, I knew not what to do concerning him. He was a Lancastrian involved with nefarious deeds, so I risked much in even acknowledging him as an acquaintance but I could not so readily abandon a man who had been a friend, despite his keeping me in the dark as to his true self. I had yet to decide my feelings upon this tangled web of deceit and how it weighed in the balance against friendship. My fervent hopes were that Kit would recover and we could talk, forwhy, I realised, I liked him right well and did not want to lose him in such sorrowful wise, whatever his allegiance, preferring to reconcile our differences.

Mercifully, I had not yet made the effort to return to our chamber and was finishing my ale right leisurely when I saw a young lay brother hesitating by the inn door. He appeared breathless, flushed of cheek, his glance darting about. I caught his eye and beckoned to him even as my stomach tightened and heart beat faster, fearing he brought ill-tidings.

'You come in haste, Brother: what news?'

'Are you Master Foxley of London?'

I nodded.

'Have you brought my scrip?' I asked, hopefully.

'Your scrip? No, I know nothing of that. Prior William Sellynge sends you both greetings and apologies but asks that you come swiftly. I am to assist you. He says it's most important.'

'Has Father Christian awakened?' With care, I eased upright off the bench.

'Nothing has been said.' The brother observed my difficulties with a frown, as though I were a far worse case than he had been expecting. The prior must have made light of my hurts.

'What has Brother Infirmarer to say?'

'I haven't spoken with him. The prior sent me.'

'Ah. I see,' I said, though I did not see at all.

'I'll come with you, husband,' Rose said, taking my arm.

'Nay lass. Best not to. The children have need of you. The

good brother will help me. Besides, I feel stronger after that goodly dinner.'

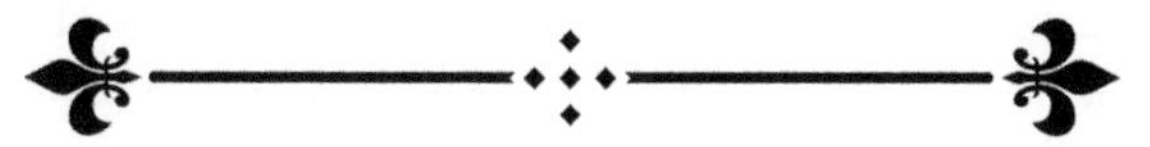

With infinite patience, the brother took me through Christ's Church Gate, past the waiting pilgrims, making for the priests' door where Kit had led me previously.

'This is a shorter way,' the lay brother explained. 'Not allowed normally but in view of your damaged ankle and the rest…' We cut through the cloisters but, instead of entering the cathedral, as afore, we went around the Chapter House to the Prior's Chapel beyond. Here, a stair went up to chambers above the chapel. I steeled myself for the ascent and managed it with my escort's aid and a deal of grimacing.

We entered an antechamber.

'Wait here,' I was instructed, being directed to a cushioned bench, for which mercy I was grateful, as the brother knocked upon an inner door which opened. He exchanged a few words in an undertone with whosoever was beyond afore leaving, neither speaking nor so much as looking at me, as though he was glad to be done with his burden. I felt a prickle of disquiet run up my spine.

I sat alone, waiting. I could hear voices on the other side of the stout oak door. Mayhap this had naught to do with poor Kit, languishing in the infirmary but what else could it concern? What business of mine had aught to do with the prior?

At last, having imagined any number of reasons for my summoning – none of them good – the door opened. A brother gestured for me to enter and I limped into the chamber beyond. Prior William Sellynge, I recognised, standing by a fine chair which reminded me of a throne. But more impressive was a tall, burly man of middle years clad in green velvet. He looked to be a prosperous merchant, plumes in his hat and shoes of Cordovan leather but his expression turned my blood chill. His stare was unyielding and claimed my rapt attention such that I nigh missed the introduction.

'Sheriff Brown, this is Master Sebastian Foxley of whom I spoke,' the prior said and then turned to me. 'Master Foxley, this is Master George Brown, Sheriff of Kent. Shall we all sit and I'll have ale served?'

'This isn't a social visit,' Sheriff Brown growled. 'I have questions and require answers concerning the safety of the realm.'

Dear God in Heaven! They must know about Kit.

Still standing in the midst of the prior's tiled floor, my knees threatened to buckle. I was aware of movement behind me but slow to realise that two fellows in red livery, with Kent's badge of the white horse rampant emblazoned on their tunics, had taken station either side of the door. The briefest glance over my shoulder confirmed it: both were armed.

I was trapped.

The sheriff wasted no time:

'I've been up all night because of you, Foxley, you and your Lancastrian scoundrels. You've led me on quite a chase and killed one of my men by throwing him from the tower but now I've got two of you, at least. Tell me, how long have you been plotting with the Earl of Oxford and Christian de Vere?'

'I have d-done no such thing,' I spluttered. 'In truth, I have not.'

'I admit your name was unknown to us until now but you're in league with the de Veres. Don't deny it: we have the evidence.' The sheriff picked up my scrip, which lay on the board, extracted the papers – those I previously believed to be illegible – and shook them in my face. 'It's all here, enough to see you die a traitor's death.'

'I-I have no knowledge of what be written there.'

'You saying you can't read? The prior tells me you read and write more than adequately. Are you denying it?'

'Nay, but…'

'This is your bag, isn't it?'

'Aye, and I admit the papers were in there but I was only the bearer of them. I ne'er looked at them, I swear. I still know not what they are.'

'Letters!' the sheriff roared. 'The schemes and machinations of Lancastrian dogs like you, intent upon bringing down our Sovereign Lord, King Edward, turning this blessed realm into a slaughter house again after nine years of peace.' He grabbed the front of my jerkin, dragging me towards him. 'I fought at Barnet Field and Tewkesbury, serving Edward and the House of York.' His spittle fell hot upon my face. 'And I won't have rogues like you undoing what we fought so hard for. I shed blood at Tewkesbury, as did my brother who died that day and I won't let his death be in vain because of you, you treacherous scum.'

'Hold, hold, sir.' The prior intervened. 'Release Master Foxley. I want no violence in my house.'

'Are you protecting him?' The sheriff dropped me in a painful heap, turning on the prior. 'Do I smell the foul stench of treason on you, too?'

'What an absurd notion. I serve God, not Lancaster nor York. God will still reign when they are gone and long forgotten.' The prior assisted me to my feet and led me to a cushioned settle. My ribs were an agony; I could hardly draw breath. He turned to face the sheriff: 'Now curb your tongue, sir. This man is a pilgrim and, as such, is under the protection of God, the Archbishop of Canterbury and this Priory of Christ's Church.'

'Pilgrim! Is pilgrimage now to be a shield for spies and traitors and murderers?'

'I am none of those things, I swear upon my soul,' I said, my voice pathetic and not in the least convincing.

'Do you deny knowing Christian de Vere?'

The question unnerved me. Should I deny him? Could I do as St Peter had done ere the cock crowed thrice and deny knowing my friend?

'I do not know any de Vere,' I managed to say. 'If you refer to my friend, you be mistaken. I know Father Christian as the priest at St Mary Magdalen Church in London. This, I freely admit. He determined to accompany me and my family upon pilgrimage as a friend and companion. I know naught of any de Vere connections.' This last was a lie and, usually, an untruth spoken coloured my cheeks crimson but I hoped my bruises would prove sufficient disguise.

'So why did you flee with him last eve, if you weren't privy to his secrets?'

'Why would I not, sir? As I explained to Father Prior, we believed you to be a pack of ruffians, armed and bringing dogs, pursuing my friend and me with intent to rob, maim and maybe kill us. Of course we ran. You did not cry your purpose as sheriff. How were we to know who you were? As for those incriminating papers, Kit – Father Christian – found them hidden in our chamber at The Chequers. Someone who occupied the bed afore him must have left them behind. He said they were of wicked authorship, though I ne'er read them myself, that we should hand them over to the proper authorities this very day. This we fully intended to do if you had not chased us and matters gone so awry.' I prayed my invented tale sounded plausible enough. At least the prior was nodding his approval.

'Then explain what you were doing, lurking in the cathedral precinct at dead of night? That was hardly the action of an innocent man.'

'Have I not explained that? We were fleeing from you, not knowing who you were.'

'But we were chasing one man, not two. You were here, by the masons' lodge, waiting for de Vere under cover of darkness, like the felon you are.'

'Nay, sir, you be mistaken. We were together, taking a turn about the town afore retiring to bed when you and your men set upon us.' I feared I was at risk here since I knew not the circumstances in which the pursuit of Kit had commenced.

I was saved by the prior:

'This concurs with what Master Foxley told me previously, Sheriff Brown, so desist from your interrogation. You made a mistake, thinking two godly pilgrims to be evil-doers, one of whom yet lies in peril of death in the infirmary. This affair has already cost the life of one of your own and I pray it does not cost a second. Now take your men and get out of my house.'

'I am the king's representative; I have his authority.' The sheriff stood tall, puffing his broad chest to the full.

'But in this precinct, *I* am God's representative and *His* authority outweighs the king's. In the secular world, kings are supreme but not here. Go! Or I shall inform Archbishop Bourchier of your gross misconduct and he has King Edward's ear as well as God's.'

The sheriff looked about to argue the point but must have thought better of it. With a parting glare at me fit to freeze the blood in my veins, he left, taking his men with him. Not only that but he took my precious scrip with those damnable papers. To me, it felt as though he had ripped out half my soul but I dared not protest. Tears sprung to my eyes as I watched it taken away in that infidel's grasp.

'You have my eternal gratitude, Prior William,' I said when the door closed on the red tunics and I could breathe easily again.

He made no reply but signed to the brother, who had stood silent and still as a carven saint all this while, to pour two cups of wine from a jug upon a side board. The brother served the prior and then handed me a cup.

'You may go, brother,' the prior said in dismissal. We were now alone. He drank his wine, all the while regarding me, looking me up and down. Such thorough scrutiny was disconcerting.

'I'm usually an excellent judge of character, Master Foxley,' he said at last. 'But I fear I should be doing penance for my actions today. I want no details but simply tell me this in all honesty, aye or nay: have I put my soul in jeopardy?'

'Nay, Father Prior. We be both of us genuine pilgrims.'

'Good. I hoped I was right to trust my instincts concerning you. As to your companion, I am as yet undecided since it's impossible to judge the character of one in his condition.'

'His condition? Has it improved?'

'Finish your wine and I'll take you to the infirmary; then you may determine for yourself.'

'But he lives?'

'Aye, he does and Brother Infirmarer has hopes that he will continue to do so.'

'God be praised!'

'Indeed, Master Foxley, but call to mind that mankind has little comprehension of the Almighty's Divine Plan, which doesn't always make sense to mere ignorant mortals.'

'What do you mean?'

'You'll see.'

The Infirmary

Matters appeared well enough. 'Twas the case that Kit's head was swathed in bandages, as was his arm with the dog bite, but he was propped upon pillows, being spoon-fed gruel by a lay brother. The improvement was heartening.

'Kit! Kit, my friend. How relieved I be to see you thus when I feared the worst.' We approached the bed. The lay brother wiped Kit's lips with a napkin, set aside the bowl and spoon and stepped away as I came nigh. I took Kit's hand – the unbandaged arm. ''Tis good to see you awake… and eating. It gladdens my heart.'

Kit said naught but looked at me, a strange, blank expression upon his features.

'We shall take you home soon enough… back to London… to your parish…' I continued but glanced at the prior.

'Now do you see?' the prior said. 'He hasn't yet uttered a word. I hoped he would respond to you as his friend but it seems not.'

'Is he unable to speak? Has he forgotten how? Or, mayhap, he cannot recall me?'

'Brother Infirmarer has not yet determined what is amiss but you can realise why I would not subject your friend to the sheriff's harsh questioning – questions he cannot answer for the present, at least. Whatever his allegiance, this is a sick human being not to be tortured by Sheriff Brown with his rough and ready, over-zealous enthusiasm for the House of York. The fellow is far too full of self-importance for my liking.

'Besides, ten years since, Master George Brown, vintner of Fordwich, was similarly enthusiastic in his support of Lancaster when the Earl of Warwick held sway so briefly. Likely, that's why he feels obliged now to support York right heartily.'

I let go of Kit's hand. He seemed not to notice, his eyes wandering, vague and unfocussed, as though there was naught of interest around him upon which to settle his attention.

'Can he see? The hurt to his head has not robbed him of his sight?' I asked as the terrible thought occurred.

'It's thought not, at least he flinches when a hand comes nigh but whether there is some degree of sight lost is hard to tell – so Brother Infirmarer informs me.'

In gentle wise, I took Kit's head in my hands and turned him so we were face to face.

'Look at me, Kit. You know me, do you not? I be your friend Seb Foxley. Do you recall me?'

He blinked and screwed up his eyes, squinting at me until his gaze focussed upon my face. I was certain he could see something.

'Touch my nose,' I said. ''Tis surely a target large enough.' To my delight, he obeyed; his unsteady finger touched the tip of my nose. 'There! He can see, hear and comprehend,' I declared in triumph. 'All will be well soon enough. Is that not so, Kit, my friend?' I let go of his head, a laugh upon my lips.

And then he spoke but in a whisper so soft I could not catch the words.

'What is it you say?' I asked.

'Who is Kit?' he mumbled, frowning at me.

'Why, you are, of course.'

'I know no Kit.' He looked confused, puzzling at his bandaged arm.

'Your given name be Christian but you prefer to be called Kit.'

'No. I-I am Alan… Alan, son of Richard… Aye, Alan Richardson… Lionheart.' He seemed to be testing the name upon his tongue.

The prior and I exchanged wary glances.

'Who is this Alan Richardson?' the prior asked me behind his hand.

'I have ne'er heard the name until now,' I admitted. 'He be confused, recalling some other he once knew, I suppose. We lately met a fellow by the name of Alan at St Nicholas Hospital in Harbledown who believed himself to be Richard the Lionheart. Mayhap therein lies the source of my friend's confusion.' And yet I wondered if, for the very first time, I was hearing the truth. Could 'Lionheart' be a nom de plume?

'I must excuse myself,' the prior said. 'I have obligations to attend elsewhere. I'll leave you and Brother Infirmarer to deal with this mystery. *Benedicite,* Master Foxley. I pray you get back to London safely without further mischance.'

'Thank you, Prior William, for all your aid in our time of trouble. Our pilgrimage has proved a trial indeed.'

'Gaining all the more merit for your soul then, I trust.'

I nodded but had my doubts on that score. Of late, I had committed too many unvirtuous acts and told too many lies for this journey to have benefitted my soul in any way.

With the prior departed, I thought to speak most seriously with Kit – or Alan Richardson, or Christian de Vere, or whatever his name truly was – and sort out this matter. But, upon returning my attention to the man in question, he was sound asleep and, mayhap, it was better thus. Oddly, in repose, though bandaged and battered, he bore the face of an innocent. I found it hard to credit him a traitor.

The Chequers of Hope Inn

Thursday's supper was, no doubt, good as usual but I was hardly aware of what I ate, my mind too full of questions regarding Kit.

'I'm so glad he's recovering,' Rose said. 'I feared we might have to return home without him. And his parishioners need him. It will be a fortnight or more by the time we get back. Do you think Stephen will have finished the building work on our house? I can't wait to see it, though Mother Thorogood says that when she had her roof repaired, there was such a deal of cleaning to do after it took weeks to be rid of all the dust. And likely, you'll have the same problem in the workshop, but all that extra space for the shop and room for more desks... I am so excited to see it all anew, Seb.'

I failed to note she had changed the subject, prattling on.

'I be uncertain of his returning to London with us, Rose. In truth, there is little certainty of anything concerning him and you must not set your heart upon continuing our friendship with him.'

'But he's our friend.'

'Our friend be a man known as Father Christian or Kit. And, in truth, sweeting, I think we may be utterly confounded by him. I have doubts as to whether he is a priest...'

'But he's tonsured, ministers a parish and the bishop is his godfather. Of course, Kit's a priest. He must be.'

'Afore he fell asleep, he was insisting his name be Alan Richardson.'

'The blow must have addled his wits, is all. He'll remember rightly in a day or two.'

The blow. Aye, more lies I had told. Rose knew naught of our perilous climb up the masons' scaffolding nor its painful ending.

Instead, she assumed those non-existent, so-called ruffians had beaten us and I did not correct her nor make any mention of Sheriff Brown and his men. My sole admission was that they – whosoever they were – had stolen my scrip. Also, I led her to believe that my afternoon summons by the prior had been concerned only with Kit's awakening, omitting entirely to speak of my suffering the sheriff's interrogation.

I once promised ne'er to keep secrets from my beloved but there was far too much to tell for now. When we were safe home, all dangers passed and the mysteries of Kit's true name resolved, then I should confess to her and explain everything. This I vowed but was guilt-raddled e'en so.

Chapter 17

Friday, the third day of November
The Infirmary

OLD SYMKYN, my knowledgeable friend back in London, had foretold, correctly, that our pilgrimage to Canterbury would be achieved in dry weather. He had said naught of our journeying homeward and the weather had changed these last few days. Rain fell and, with such a chill in the air, threatened to turn to sleet. Winter had come of a sudden.

Thus, wet and dripping, I made my way to the infirmary first thing without so much as attending Low Mass – it being a Friday – and, therefore, not having broken my fast but I could not delay speaking with Kit. I had to have the truth out of him, come what may.

Brother Infirmarer welcomed me, asking after my own hurts as he took me to Kit's bedside. I assured him I was mending, my ribs less painful this morn and my ankle not so bad.

'You must not tire your friend. Patients with head injuries need rest. Don't stay too long and don't upset or distress him.'

Kit was propped upon pillows as afore, staring at the wall opposite.

'God give you good day, Kit,' I said right cheerfully. 'How do you fare?'

'My name's Alan… Richardson.' Ah, so he had not changed his mind on that score. 'You were here yesterday.' He sounded dull, uninterested, but at least he remembered me, which I thought heartening, a good sign.

'I was.'

'I don't know who you are. What do you want of me?'

'My name be Seb Foxley and what I want of you be no less than the truth.' I perched upon the bedside but then realised I was yet dripping rain and wetting the blankets, so I removed myself to stand a pace away. 'I have known you for half a twelve month back in London. There, you serve as the parish priest at St Mary Magdalen's Church in Old Fish Street, being known as Father Christian.'

'How can that be? I'm not a priest. I'm a gentleman.'

'Feel the top of your head above the bindings and you'll find it to be shaven there, though your hair begins to grow back now. If you are no priest, why would you be tonsured?'

He did as I suggested, running his hand over the place, realising I spoke truly. He shrugged.

'I don't know why but I tell you this: I've never heard of Father Christian no more than I've ever heard of you. So leave me in peace.'

'If you be Alan Richardson, gentleman, tell me of yourself,' I said in an encouraging tone, refusing to be sent upon my way without answers of some kind.

'I am of Burnham in the Shire of Buckingham as the Richardsons have been for generations.' He sighed wearily as though he was telling this for the hundredth time. 'I'm my father's third son living, so of little account. I studied at Oxford and Grey's Inn, hoping to take up law. I have few prospects and little in the way of expected inheritance. That's it. That's my tale. Now I've answered your questions, so go away. I'm tired and in need of rest.'

'What do you know of…' I lowered my voice to a whisper and bent closer, 'John de Vere, Earl of Oxford?'

'Nothing,' he replied straightway, his eyes instantly intent upon a loose thread in the blanket as he plucked at it. 'Why would I know of him?'

I nodded.

'Thank you. I have my answers. I shall leave you to sleep now.'

Pulling my hood close, I made my way back across the precinct – no brother to lead me by way of the cloisters and thus was I subjected to the rain in full measure – to Christ's Church Gate. The weather had deterred Gawain from accompanying me but by no means had it deterred the pilgrims who formed the long, bedraggled line awaiting entrance to the cathedral. Upon reaching the gateway and attempting to go against the tide of folk eager to enter from Burgate Street, I was jostled by the crowd and elbowed in the ribs. My cry of pain went unheeded by the throng.

Despite my assurances made to the infirmarer concerning my recovery, my ribs were little better than yesterday and now they were an agony. Nausea threatened to overcome me as I staggered out into the street, clutching my hurts and barely able to stand. I found the nearest doorstep and eased myself down. With eyes tight closed, I prayed that the pain would pass swiftly.

I know not how long I sat there but, at length, I became aware of the drenching rain and that my boots were lapped by an ever-deepening puddle. Strands of hair had escaped my hood and clung to my face. Water dripped from my nose and soaked through my clothes. Yet still I could not move. If my ribs were only cracked afore, I felt certain they were splintered now, every shard of bone piercing my chest like a dagger from within.

'Twas not so far to the inn. Mercery Lane was but a few steps away but it might as well have been among the stars above for all the chance I had of reaching it. I looked about, through the pall of rain, hoping to see a face I recognised or a friendly Samaritan to aid me or someone to take a message to the inn, at the least. But everyone hastened by, hoods drawn close, heads down, eager to get within doors. No one so much as glanced at me: a huddled beggar crouched in a doorway. There were likely dozens of other poor souls on the streets of Canterbury, soliciting alms, utterly ignored on such a day. No doubt but I looked more like a drowned rat than a respectable citizen. No wonder none wished to help me.

At length, the pain was easing somewhat and, as I considered making the effort to stand, a man passed close. Like all the rest, he did not look at me but an unexpected torrent of water ran from the eaves of the house where I sat and, instinctively, he looked up to beware the source. I knew that face. Though previously I had seen him with reddish curling hair somewhat greying, now it was plastered flat to his head and black with rain but I knew him still: Fenshaw, he being half-brother to the Warenne twins and, possibly, the man behind the attempts made upon their lives. And he had a companion. I had to look twice, squinting and wiping rain from my eyes, but I felt nigh certain it was none other than Hugo Harper, he who we assumed to be drowned in the river by East Bridge Hospital.

That unholy pairing was yet at large in Canterbury. I must warn the twins.

With much wincing and groaning, I succeeded in rising from the doorstep, discovering my cloak weighed heavier than a millstone with rain-soaked wool.

The Chequers of Hope Inn

'Seb, you're hurt again,' Rose said, rushing to greet me as I entered the inn. I could not conceal the truth forwhy I needs must walk, favouring my injured side.

'It will pass soon enough, sweeting.'

'Let me put your cloak to dry. I must wring it out first. I'll have the innkeeper prepare you some mulled ale. Hey! You fellows by the fire: make room there for my goodman to get warm and dry himself.' I had nigh forgotten that my dearest once worked in a tavern, dealing with customers and that air of authority remained when need be. 'I'll fetch a towel for your hair.'

'Nay, lass. In a moment, I shall go up to our chamber, for I require dry clouts from top to bottom.'

'Then I'll have the tap-boy light the brazier up there. You have to get warm, else you'll catch your death. Oh, and how is Kit this morn?'

'Addled in his wits, I fear,' I told her, not knowing whether that be entirely the case. 'But growing stronger. I be sure he will recover, though his mind may take rather longer than his body.'

'Poor dear Kit. He doesn't deserve this.'

Precisely what "poor dear Kit" deserved, I could not venture an opinion. That he be the most consummate liar I had ever met was certain but was he also a traitor? And what traitors deserve did not bear thinking upon but 'twas a great deal worse than a gashed forehead and a dog bite. That he might be somewhat confused following such a blow, I could accept. As to his loss of all memory concerning the recent past, that I did not believe. He had reacted too swiftly in denying the Earl of Oxford, unable to look me in the eye. Such small things oftentimes betrayed the truth, as I had learned from working alongside Thaddeus Turner, London's City Bailiff.

'Where are the twins?' I said. 'I needs must warn them.'

'Warn them? Why? What's amiss now, Seb?' Rose asked as she set a steaming, fragrant cup before me, saving the tap-boy the trouble. My wife seemed to be well at home at The Chequers.

'No matter. Maybe naught. Are they out with their horses?'

'I doubt it in this weather. They were here earlier but went up to their chamber, as sensible folk do on such a day. I think I heard Troilus challenge Tristan – or maybe the other way around – to a game of chess, borrowing a set from the landlord.'

'Good. Then they be safe enough for the present.'

'Why?' Rose repeated, sitting opposite me. Her determined expression confirmed that she would accept no vague generalities nor partial truths.

I sighed.

'Forwhy I saw their half-brother just now and – you will find this hard to believe – Hugo Harper was with him.'

'The minstrel?' She leaned close, speaking low that none

other might hear. 'But he's gone… drowned… isn't he?'

'It seems not.' I sipped my drink, feeling the warmth flooding through my very bones.

'You're sure it was him, Seb? You could be mistaken in this rain…'

'Nay, lass. I know it was Harper with Fenshaw. I noted both faces well enough. The twins must be upon their guard as afore. I fear their danger has not yet past.'

'The twins? What of them?' Mother Thorogood came to join us, as did her feline companion, who hissed at me. Whatever the failing of her sight, which, she insisted, had been improving daily since her visit to St Thomas' shrine, there was naught amiss with the woman's hearing. 'What of those fine lads? I'll miss them when we part company. They remind me of my grandson – God love his soul.' She wiped her eye upon her apron hem.

'I be sorrowful to hear of your loss,' I said. 'How fare your eyes this day, Mother?'

'Good enough to see you're trying to avoid answering my question, young Sebastian. I asked you about the lads.'

'Aye, so you did and I suppose the more folk know of it, the more eyes can be keeping a watch: I saw the minstrel, Hugo Harper, alive and well not an hour since.'

'That scum-of-the-earth wretch? Did he not drown in the river by East Bridge Hospital?'

'So we thought but, clearly, he survived the waters.'

'I shall pray to St Thomas, who has served me so well, to make certain of the rogue's ending and save those good lads. You know Troilus – or maybe it was Tristan, since I can't tell one from the other – lifted Lucifer down from the tree in the stable yard the other day. Such a kindness when foolish puss got stuck.'

'Tristan bears a scar upon his eyebrow, just here.' I pointed to my own brow, all the while thinking how it would have contented me if the cat had been left up the tree; the higher, the better. 'Troilus does not.'

'Oh, I don't have the time to look for such little discrepancies,' she said, dismissing the matter with a wave of her hand, and I realised that so small a mark was likely yet invisible to her, despite her eyes improving somewhat.

With my restorative ale consumed, I set myself to the arduous task of climbing the stair and, having attained our chamber, the more painful necessity of undressing and donning dry clothes. Of course, my dear one aided me, observed all the while by Dickon and Julia. Unfortunately, the bindings about my body, which held my ribs secure, were as soaked as my shirt and had to be removed. Rose unwound them easily enough and put them to dry by the brazier but I felt worse without the support, wary of moving. Also, the bruising was awful and she kept from looking me straight so I should not see the tears in her eyes at sight of my discoloured flesh: a rainbow of livid, thunderous hues daubed across my torso in haphazardwise.

'Papa all dirty,' my son said, pointing a finger, his head upon one side in a gesture of curiosity.

'Aye, but this will not come off with a good wash,' Rose told him. 'You must be gentle with your papa, Dickon.' She helped me into dry nether clouts, followed by a shirt which required my biting my lips to keep from yelping. 'And you,' she turned to me, 'Will need to lie very still until the bandages are dried and I can replace them. Rest abed and we'll have dinner up here. And no arguments, Seb? You'll do as I say this once.'

'But I must warn the twins,' I protested.

'I'll do that. Now rest. Get some sleep, husband. That will serve you best and I'll bring you a remedy.' She wrapped me in blankets, straightened the pillow and closed the shutters upon the curtain of rain. Taking the children by the hand, she left me alone in the gloom with my bruises and disquieting thoughts for company.

Friday eve
The Chequers of Hope Inn

The rain had ceased and doors and shutters were opened on a chill but starlit night. There would be a frost afore dawn, freezing the puddles and making the ways treacherous.

Much recovered, I joined quite a gathering downstairs in the taproom. A few of our pilgrim party had ended up biding here since the food was good and the beds clean. However, Tanner had made other arrangements, staying with friends – possibly of the Lancastrian persuasion – in the town, so we had seen little of him once his duty was done in leading us here and making our first visit to the cathedral.

Now, he was come to bid us farewell, sharing supper and telling of his future plans to go to St James of Compostela in the spring. He was welcome to that: a journey I would ne'er risk. A ship all the way to Spain! I – who could not withstand a penny ferry ride across the Thames – would die of it for certain.

Of our original group, a few were missing: Kit in the infirmary and Glassman-de Vere gone for good, hopefully. As for Hugo Harper, the less said, the better. The Alfred Dennys, grandsire and grandson, had continued to sleep at East Bridge Hospital, it being cheaper than the inn, and we had lost sight of them, knowing naught of how they had occupied their time. But they were here now, along with the Cambridge scholars Kit had befriended, enjoying much knowledgeable discourse in their company. Those two were right sorry to hear of Kit's misfortunes and determined to visit him afore they departed upon the morrow, this despite my warnings that he might not recall them. Likely, it would do no harm and might serve to stir his memory, though I doubted that it was truly lost.

Lying in my bed earlier, I did little slumbering but a deal of thinking, concluding that Kit was pretending his witless state to spare us both further trouble with the authorities. Alan Richardson was an utter fiction and, though I found his part-playing irksome, mayhap 'twas a sensible precaution that I should encourage rather than attempt to refute. But that was a problem for the morrow. I attempted to put from my mind the dealings with the sheriff. I knew that the interrogation could easily have ended in my arrest had it not been for the prior – may God bless him eternally.

For now, I intended to enjoy good company and a hearty supper. Of course, Mother Thorogood and the Warenne twins had remained here at The Chequers all along with us and shared our board as usual. My only difficulty was avoiding excessive merriment since laughter caused such pain to my ribs and the Warenne lads and the scholars had a wealth of amusing tales with which to regale us.

Surrounded by merry faces, I thought to take out my drawing stuff and suffered such a jolt of realisation that my scrip was gone; everything lost. Ah, me. Though I might purchase a new scrip, it would ne'er be quite the same. That leather bag and I had shared many an adventure. It had been at my right hand through good times and bad, danger and hardship and no price could be put upon its loss, like that of a loyal friend.

Such was my self-absorption and sorrow that I missed hearing much of Troilus's amusing tale, which set the whole company laughing, rocking on the benches, spilling ale and slapping their thighs. The lad stood upon the stair, making use of it as a mountebank's stage, acting out the parts as he continued his story. He had a talent for it.

I caught something about a boastful knight trying to impress a lady by jousting against a gigantic snail, losing the contest and becoming slathered all in snail slime. I thought such an image might look right well adorning the margin of a manuscript – mayhap without the slime – and would have made a note of it if I had any paper and charcoal. This lack served but to add to my despair.

I noted that Rose did not laugh heartily with the others either, seemingly forcing a smile to her lips which touched not her eyes. I wondered what could be amiss with her. Was she so concerned for me? Or for Kit, mayhap? Or was one of the children unwell? I did not think this last to be the case forwhy both had partaken eagerly of honeyed bread and goat's milk afore Rose put them to bed, content. When I enquired as to what troubled her, she grinned broadly, shaking her head and declaring that naught whatsoever bothered her as she turned her full attention upon Tristan. He was now taking his turn, acting the fool, singing a lament over his cold-hearted lady who spurned him, preferring to take a wealthy miller, fat as lard, as her lover instead of him, the besotted wight.

But my eyes remained upon my dear one. How could she – who knew me right well – think I would not know a lie when I heard it upon her sweet tongue? What disquieting matter was she attempting to conceal from me? Did she not understand that the concealment of the truth might well worry me more greatly than the knowledge of it? When, later, I saw Mother Thorogood put a comforting arm about her, patting her hand, I knew I was not mistaken and determined to learn what she would keep hidden from me.

Then I heard a distant, plaintive wail. Not loud but of the kind that a parent will hear when others do not. Julia. Likely, her teeth were plaguing her again or a bad dream had disturbed her rest. I saw that Rose was alerted also but, since I was closer to the stair, I signed to her that I would attend Julia in our chamber. Better to reassure and settle her afore her noise wakened Dickon too.

I eased up off the bench, having a care for my sore ribs, and made for the stair, excusing myself as I edged past Tristan, now demonstrating his prowess with an invisible sword of gigantic and unwieldy proportions as he mimed it. Considering one injury to the exclusion of the other, I forget about my sprained ankle, which gave out, causing me to topple against Tristan, knocking him sideways as we fell in an undignified heap upon the stair. I heard a swishing sound and the company gasped behind us.

Full of apologies, I struggled to my feet in order to allow Tristan to rise. I had spoiled his fine tale and disappointed everyone. So I believed. Therefore, I was much surprised when a crowd gathered about me, congratulating me on an action so swift. Others were concerned for Tristan, so it appeared, though I was certain he was unhurt except for a minor bruise or two, perhaps.

But then I saw it. A few steps above where we had fallen, an arrow yet quivered in the wooden balustrade and I realised Tristan had stood there a moment since, playing his part. If I had not stumbled against him… the consequence did not bear thinking upon. But from whence had the arrow come?

A hue-and-cry was already being organised over by the door. Folk were hanging out of the unshuttered window, pointing and shouting, "There he goes!" Apparently, the shot had come through that window.

Above us, Julia renewed her cries with greater enthusiasm and I extricated myself from those who would continue congratulating me to go on up the stair. My injuries were sufficient to excuse me from joining the hue-and-cry. Besides, I knew they would be in pursuit of either Hugo Harper, the inept assassin, or Fenshaw Warenne, Tristan's and Troilus's half-brother. Or both of them. Who else would it be?

In our chamber, I lifted Julia from the nest of blankets. Dickon stirred and opened his eyes.

'Papa play horsy,' he mumbled.

'Not now, my son. 'Tis time for sleeping. Close your eyes.' The little lad obeyed, snuggling down to resume his slumbers.

Julia ceased her cries as I sat upon our bed and commenced to soothe her. One cheek burned crimson, a sure sign that a new tooth was the cause of her restlessness. I found the ointment which Rose used to ease sore gums and gave her the coral stick to chew on. I rocked her in my arms whilst singing a lullaby and soon she was asleep, the coral abandoned, so I returned her to her bed with Dickon. The pair looked like sleeping angels and I thanked God for the blessing of children, adding a prayer for their safe-keeping.

I did not return downstairs, which was likely empty of custom until the hue-and-cry apprehended the archer, whoever he was. Instead, I stretched out on the bed, taking my ease, until Mother Thorogood came in.

'You're missing a deal of excitement, Seb,' she said. 'But then, like me, you're hardly fit for the chase. I reckon you saved young Tristan's life – or maybe it was Troilus's – that's for certain. You're the hero of the hour, you know. There's free ale for you if you go down.'

'I have no desire to be anyone's hero, Mother, nor do I want ale, free or otherwise. I be too tired.'

'Then I'm sorry for disturbing you. I see the little ones are quiet now. I'll leave you in peace.'

'What of Rose?' I asked, forwhy I might have expected her to come see how Julia fared.

'She joined the hue-and-cry. Did you not realise? Banging pots and pans along with the innkeeper's wife, rousing the neighbourhood, as the law requires. I think she was glad of the excuse to do something vigorous and noisy.'

'Did they catch the miscreant?'

'I don't know but I pray they did. Poor Troilus – or Tristan – they're both good lads deserving of a long life.'

When Rose returned, breathless, she shared the good tidings that they had taken Hugo Harper – for it was indeed he who had loosed the arrow, as I suspected – and he now languished in Canterbury's gaol in the Donjon Tower of the castle. I prayed that would be the last we heard of the wretch. I might, likewise, hope that the twins were safe now but, knowing Fenshaw to be yet at large, that might not be the case if he determined to carry out his own vile deeds instead of leaving them to another so inept as Harper.

Later, in the privacy of our shared bed with the little ones in slumber deep and Mother Thorogood snoring softly across the chamber in her narrow bed, I broached the subject of earlier that eve, afore those startling events:

'Something has been amiss with you this day, sweeting. Do not deny it. Tell me what troubles you. Is it your family? Has that scoundrel Saunders been about?'

'No, Seb. I haven't seen him, nor my mother.'

'And the children be well, so you need not be anxious for them.'

'Aye, God be thanked.'

'Then tell me. And do not say 'tis naught, forwhy I know otherwise. Come, Rose, my dear one, share your trouble with me and halve your burden.'

'Oh, Seb… you know why I was right eager when you suggested I come on pilgrimage with you.'

'The possibility of seeing your old home and family once more.'

'Nay. That wasn't it.' She curled close to me, resting her head upon my shoulder. 'That wasn't my reason at all. Seb… I want so much…'

I realised then that she wept, feeling her tears wet upon my flesh.

'I want so much to bear your child,' she continued. 'And… in the six months since we wed, there has been no sign. You know I had a child before, conceived so swiftly, yet in all those years at The Pewter Pot, being forced to lie with so many men, I never got with child again and now I fear I never shall.

'Afore we departed London, about that time, my monthly flowers should have come upon me. But they didn't. I began to hope. And I prayed fervently at St Thomas's shrine that what I so desired had come to pass. And then this morn… I knew it was all in vain. It was not to be because the flowers came. Oh, Seb, I'm so sorry. I'm failing you as a wife… if I cannot give you a child.'

'My dearest Rose, never think that you fail me in any way.

You be my perfect wife. I could want no other.' I held her close despite my ribs protesting. 'God has blessed me with the best, my soulmate, my helpmeet. I love you more dearly than my life.'

'Which is why I want to bear your babe… give you a son, *our* son… or daughter. I love Dickon and Julia right dearly. You know that but…'

'But they are not your flesh and blood. I understand. We both be aware that Julia is not my flesh and blood either but I love her as though she were. We love the children God puts into our care but 'tis a human desire to see our own blood in the next generation. I watch you caring for the little ones – aye and Edmund and that young scamp Nicholas back home – as if they were your own. They all regard you as their mother, you know that, and they love and respect you as such. Mayhap, in time, God will grant our wish. Mayhap, in His wisdom, He thinks another babe will be too much for you at present. Have you thought of that? Besides, it took time after our marriage afore Emily conceived Dickon. Did she tell you that? Mayhap my seed is not so potent as some men's.'

'She didn't conceive because she took care not to. She told me she used a vinegar-soaked sponge as a preventive but never told you. She said conceiving Dickon had been a mistake, a moment of carelessness on her part.'

'She said that? She admitted defying God's will and the laws of Holy Church? I did not know; in truth, I did not. Why did she not want a child? Is that not the purpose of marriage?'

'Which is why I want a babe so much, Seb. Your child. *Our* child,' Rose sobbed as tears came anew.

Chapter 18

Saturday, the fourth day of November The Chequers of Hope Inn

WE SHOULD have departed Canterbury days earlier, yet Saturday came once more and still we lingered here, our money nigh all spent. Most of the blame lay with me and my injuries but I was undecided what we should do for the best regarding Kit, whether to wait upon his recovery that he might return to London with us or leave him here at the infirmary.

There were also his own desires to be taken into account. Mayhap he no longer thought of me as his friend, although I misdoubted he had truly forgotten who I be. If he determined to sever our acquaintance for safety sake – to keep me and my family away from his possibly treasonous association or for his own sake because he feared that I knew too much of his privy secrets and might betray him – I should let him alone to find his own way from now on. Such were my musings and predicament when I glanced from our chamber window that morn and espied Sheriff Brown and two liveried men-at-arms speaking with the innkeeper in the stable yard below.

Without knowing why he was come, to further interrogate me or to investigate last eve's attempt on Tristan Warenne's life, I thought it a wise precaution to make myself scarce, as the saying goes. Thus, I made haste down the stair, informing Rose as I limped from the chamber that I was to visit Kit. I left the inn by the street door even as I heard the sheriff's booming voice demanding the innkeeper's attendance as he entered by way of the back door from the stable yard. 'Twas a close thing as I made my hobbling escape.

I did indeed intend to visit Kit to see how he fared this day, but I also had need to purchase a new scrip despite the desperate few coins yet remaining in my purse. Thinking on it, I decided that if I only bought paper, charcoal and chalks and made more portraits to sell, I should then be able to afford a scrip of better quality later. That made good sense but I would have naught in which to keep my drawing stuff safe and carry it about, so I deferred my visit to the stationer's shop – hoping I would find it without getting lost as last time: I recalled the encounter with the pig with trepidation still – and made for the infirmary first.

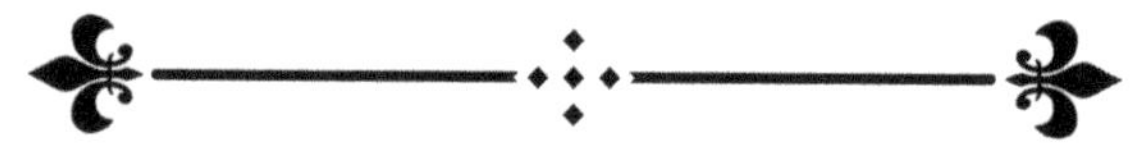

I eased through Christ's Church Gate with my arms wrapped about my ribs, wanting no repeat of yesterday's elbowing. I did not join the queue of pilgrims but went across the precinct, around the masons' lodge where men were busy raising stones, making clouds of dust and a deal of noise to skirt the east end of the cathedral and proceed to the infirmary.

Recalling what Kit had told me that day when we went in by way of the priests' door, I did my utmost to look purposeful, as though I rightfully belonged. And I must have succeeded in giving that impression forwhy I reached the infirmary without being questioned or attracting suspicious glances from the clerics and monks about the place. Or, mayhap, my continued limping made me appear a most likely candidate for Brother Infirmarer's attentions. My ankle had not improved significantly despite another night of rest, unfortunately.

The lay brother who opened the door to my knocking recognised me and ushered me in, telling me to sit and wait in the entrance hall and the infirmarer would see me when he could.

'I have not come for the good brother's ministrations but to visit Father Christian,' I explained.

'Oh. Brother Infirmarer is with him now. I'll ask if you may go in.'

He bustled off, dark habit flapping, in the direction of the tiny chamber in which Kit lay, separate from the common dormitory where other invalids were abed. The infirmarer had been wary of subjecting one with a head injury to the cries, wails and general disturbances of the sick bay, declaring his need for rest and quiet.

Thus far, such privacy had been fortuitous in regard to the thorny matters I had raised on my previous visit. It did not do to discuss possible treason where it could be overheard. But this day, I intended to talk of less controversial things, such as our journey home to be commenced whenever he and I were able.

I had thought much concerning our return and the safest way of achieving it. The Pilgrims' Way having little to recommend it now that we had seen the marvels of Boxley Abbey and the like, I thought the Watling Street would be a better road as the one that merchants most often use. With more travellers upon that course, there would be greater safety in numbers. I did not want to risk another attack by outlaws in which we might not fare so well as last time, being without Tanner and Glassman, and Kit and me being of little use in a fight at present. It would also avoid that dire precipice of Bluebell Hill, which I had no desire to attempt to ascend.

Kit lay back upon his pillows, his face pale beneath the swathe of fresh bandages about his brow.

'Ah, Master Foxley, how fare those ribs and ankle?' Brother Infirmarer asked, turning his bright eye upon me. 'Not so well, I see? You haven't been resting as I instructed, have you?'

I knew those eyes missed naught and could probably observe my bruises even through the bindings, my attire and my mantle.

'I try, good brother, but life has other intensions,' I said, making excuses. 'Two children, a living to earn…' I did not mention my fall upon Tristan, which had further hampered my recovery last eve, even as it saved his life. I had been avoiding the twins since forwhy Mother Thorogood said they were forthright in declaring me a hero and I knew it to be sensible to keep myself from notice, particularly from that of the sheriff. Besides, how could a clumsy misstep be construed an act of heroism? I did not desire such unwarranted acclaim.

'I fear your friend, Father Christian, is not so well this morn. Do not tire him. A brief visit is all I can allow.'

'My thanks, Brother. I shall not tarry long.' I took Kit's hand in mine but he did not respond. 'How are you, Kit? Rose sends her best regards and we have both been praying for your swift recovery. We shall all be going home soon… to London, that is… by way of Watling Street this time. What say you to that, my friend? Shall you be glad to go home? I know we shall…'

Kit opened his eyes, staring up at the roof beams, and I thought he was about to speak. His mouth moved but he emitted naught but a strangled, gargling sound. His entire body began to twitch, then to jerk violently, his back arched impossibly, his head thrown back.

'Brother Infirmarer!' I called out and he came in haste.

'A seizure… I feared this might happen. Hold down the blanket on your side; do what you can to prevent his flailing about and hurting himself. Brother Ignatius… Dunstan! Attend here now!'

Other monks came running and did what they might. Helpless otherwise, I kept my firm grip on the bed covers and watched in horror as my friend thrashed about, twisting his body into impossible contortions and then… it ceased. I would have been relieved but I was watching his eyes: staring and bulging one moment, then rolling up to show the whites only.

But as the fit ceased, the eyes were wrong. His right eye seemed to look at me, whilst his left was white, opaque, invisible. And then he lay still. Still as naught that yet draws breath ever can be.

I knew my friend was gone. His eyes glazed over; their light forever dimmed as his soul departed.

I stood back, shocked. I had ne'er witnessed a soul's passing so violent. Brother Infirmarer and the others did what they might to make things appear more seemly and sent for Prior William in haste to perform the last rites. None took heed of me, lingering in the shadowed corner, too stunned even to weep for my friend. I knew not what to do: stay or go; speak or keep silent.

The Chequers of Hope Inn.

'The funeral will be after Vespers this eve. He is to be buried in the Monks' Cemetery...' I said aloud for all to hear as I entered the door from the street.

Rose hurried over to me and took me by the hand.

'A funeral? Whose?' she asked.

I had returned to the inn hours later. It was nigh dinnertime and folk were gathered in the tap room, waiting for the meal when I entered, whey-faced and confused.

'His. Father Christian's. Kit's. This eve...' my voice trailed away. I could not think what to say.

'Kit's dead? Is that what's happened?' Rose was asking. 'How? When? Was he attacked again? In the infirmary? Sweet Jesu preserve us, Seb. What came to pass? Sit down; you need ale to restore you. You're stunned, I can see that.'

I was stunned. No doubt about that. I could barely keep a straight thought in my head and as for sensible speech, my tongue was unruly as that of a drunkard, tangling words.

'Oh, Rose... such a horrid end. Poor Kit. Right sudden, it was: twitching and writhing... I knew not what...' I slumped upon a stool, my head in my hands, yet still the tears did not come though my throat ached with the threat of them. 'Poor Kit,' I repeated.

'Did you light a candle for him in the cathedral?'

I shook my head. Such a thought had not occurred to me.

'You paid for a mass to be said, perhaps?'

'Nay.'

'Later then. We can organise matters after dinner, when you're more composed.'

'Aye. Later.' I took the ale she passed me and drank deep, hoping it would help. 'I would we could depart Canterbury this instant. 'Tis an unlucky place, I feel. We must delay our departing no longer. In the morn…'

''Tis the Lord's Day on the morrow, Seb.'

'Does it matter? I want to go home, Rose.' I must have sounded as a whining, petulant child but, at that moment, I cared not. Neither did I take into account our parlous state of coin nor consider how I would pull the cart with my lame ankle and injured ribs. Home was all I desired.

Saturday eve

As be so often the way of such things, Prior William conducted Kit's funeral in the rain. Torches hissed and guttered in the wet, wind-blown dusk as my friend, being honoured as a man of the cloth – whatever the truth of it – was laid to rest in the Monks' Cemetery within the precinct, ironically, within sight of the scene of his fearful fall which led to his demise. The weather also compared precisely to that fateful night, being rain-soaked and chill.

I was not alone at the graveside. Brother Infirmarer and other attendants from the infirmary stood by. Four lay brothers had acted as bearers, carrying the coffin. The Warenne twins and the Cambridge scholars came, as well as young Alfred Denny – Old Denny sending tuppence for candles. I felt badly about the whole office. As the closest friend of the deceased, I should have paid for more torches, employed mourners and given alms to the poor in Kit's name. But my purse was nigh empty and the sheriff – God rot him – yet had possession of Kit's money along with my scrip.

Reluctantly, I was reduced to borrowing coin from Tristan

to pay for bread and ale back at the inn for all who attended. I, who regard debt as a heinous sin and had ne'er owed coin to any man in my life afore, was thus forced to do so. It did not sit well with my conscience. Not one bit.

My Rose knew this and, therefore, persuaded me to delay yet one more day and we did not leave upon Sunday, as I hoped so fervently.

Instead, my dearest Rose took it upon herself to work in the kitchen on both that Saturday eve and all of Sunday, aiding the innkeeper's wife in cooking, washing pots and serving food and drink. She even patched and re-hemmed sheets for the beds. My protests went unheard. Thus, she declared, we might pay our reckoning without further debt incurred. My dearest of wives be the greatest asset any man could possess.

Sunday, the fifth day of November
Canterbury – still

Another day of rest granted my injuries more time to mend, so I suppose that was an advantage but I was restless indeed without employment of any kind to divert my thoughts. If only I yet had my scrip, I might draw a few portraits to pass the time and raise a few coins. Aye, I know 'twas the Lord's Day but needs must.

Taking Gawain for companionship and exercise, I ventured out along Mercery Lane and turned left into Burgate. Fortunately, the weather was dry, though the sky was overcast and drear with puddles aplenty underfoot after yesterday's rain. Upon this occasion, I did not get lost but found Penman's shop right readily, not far from the Rush Market. But, it being Sunday, the shutters were closed up. Nevertheless, I knocked at the door, more in hope than expectation. But I was not disappointed.

Mistress Thorn, whose likeness I had portrayed with her

goodman's upon Monday last, opened the door.

''Tis Master Foxley, isn't it?' She smiled broadly. 'Come you in. Is this a friendly visit or business?'

'God give you good day, Mistress Thorn,' I said, doffing my cap. 'Er, mayhap, 'tis a little of both, if you and Master Thorn can spare me a few minutes, if 'twould be no trouble?'

'Harry's out in the back yard, digging a turnip and worts for dinner. I'll call him. Settle yourself by the kitchen fire and I'll serve ale and wafers in a moment.'

I made myself comfortable, easing my ankle, which yet made complaint. Gawain sprawled by the hearth, quite at home in a stationer's house among the familiar scents of parchment, paper and inks.

Harry Thorn came in carrying a trug piled with muddied cabbages and a plump pale turnip.

'Welcome, Master Foxley,' he said as he washed his soil-plastered hands in a bucket of water. 'I didn't think to see you again, expecting you'd be half way back to London by now, so it's an unlooked for pleasure. Make haste, wife, a man needs his ale.'

'Aye, you be correct in supposing we would be upon our journey home by this time but matters have gone badly awry, I fear. Dame Fortune has decreed otherwise and here we be, yet in Canterbury. My thanks, Mistress Thorn,' I said, accepting a treenware cup of ale. A wooden cup as opposed to pewter to serve a guest: this made my business even more awkward, suggesting as it did that the stationer was in no way a man with coin to spare. But we were fellows in the craft, so I prayed my request would not be too great an impertinence.

'Look here, Master Foxley,' Mistress Thorn said, opening a coffer in the corner of the cramped kitchen and taking out a linen-wrapped object. 'See, we have had our portrait, which you drew so well, all set up and framed. Does it not look fine? We're waiting upon Harry...' She glanced meaningfully at her husband. '...To put up a peg so we can hang it up for all to admire.'

'Someone has made a most splendid frame,' I said, pleased to discover they set such value upon a sketch of mine.

'Aye, my brother's a carpenter by trade,' Mistress Thorn continued, 'And I insisted he used the best linden wood so it won't suffer the worm.'

'I wonder if the frame be far too good for a humble sketch. 'Tis more deserving of a piece on parchment, finely wrought, taking greater pains than the work of a few minutes. With the appropriate stuff, I could make a far better portrait for you, ensuring it fits this beautiful frame.'

'There's no need for that,' Harry said. 'This sketch is good enough for us. Besides, you haven't brought your drawing things with you.'

'Indeed,' I said, 'And thereby lie my difficulties.' I chewed my nether lip, deciding whether I dared ask this favour. I accepted the offered platter of wafers afore plunging in: 'My scrip was taken from me by… ruffians.' I settled upon the original fictitious tale, not mentioning that Sheriff Brown had appropriated it as evidence of treason.

'Stolen? What, here in Canterbury?' Mistress Thorn sounded horrified. 'Have you told the constable or even the sheriff?'

'He knows of it.' That was true enough.

'Did the rogues take everything?'

'Aye, mistress. I lost all my paper, charcoal, pen, ink, chalks and other things beside. And more…'

'Money?' Harry Thorn suggested.

'Aye, there was some coin belonging to my friend, Kit, but he will not need it now.'

'How come? It's hard to get by without it these days.'

'My friend… he was with me when we were set upon. 'Tis with utmost sorrow I must tell that… he died of the injuries he sustained. Yesterday, that was… we buried him last eve.'

'Sweet Jesus, have mercy!' Mistress Thorn gasped, clasping her hands to her heart. We all made the sign of the cross. 'But then it's murder!'

'As I said, the sheriff knows of it.' Realising I had tears upon my cheek, I wiped them away with the hem of my cloak.

'Here, let me refill your cup. You weren't hurt also, I trust?'

'Bruised but naught of consequence,' I assured them.

'You were limping when you came in, I noticed,' Harry said.

'A minor hurt is all and mending well.' This was somewhat less than truthful, I admit. 'But, as you will realise, the loss of my scrip and everything it contained be the loss of my livelihood until I return to London… unless I may replace the most necessary items, yet I have little coin remaining in order to purchase what I require. Paper, charcoal and chalks would suffice that I can do a few portraits and earn enough to pay the reckoning later.' I looked Harry Thorn in the eye. 'If you be willing and able to oblige me, good master, I should be forever beholden unto you…'

My host grinned and rose from his seat.

'Come through to the shop. Let's see what I can do.' He led the way and opened the street door to let in the light. 'As well as charcoal and stuff, you'll be needing a drawing board also. I have a writing slope of my own which you can borrow for naught, if that may serve until you can purchase one. Otherwise, choose what you will, Master Foxley.' He gestured towards the shelves. Neat reams and half reams of paper, parchment rolls and blank note books were arrayed for display on the one hand, inks, pigments, pounce and bottles of glue upon the other. He reached up to a high shelf and took down a woven basket. It held charcoal sticks of varying thicknesses. 'Choose what suits you best,' he said, giving me the basket. 'And chalk… you bought the best of my red chalk last week and I haven't yet re-stocked but I believe I had some pieces left… aye, here they are. I hope they'll do.' He set a small wooden box on the counterboard.

I recalled – as he said – that I had purchased the most suitably-shaped pieces on my previous visit. What remained were chunky lumps of the soft stone, not so easily put to use in drawing but I could re-shape them. I selected two that were most nearly of a usable size.

'Plenty of white chalk,' he said, 'And you'll need a bag to put your stuff in. I'm afraid I don't sell leather goods – I recall your scrip was of quality hide and well made – but I have linen bags that I loan to customers to carry their purchases home. Not much use if it rains hard but better than nothing. Now, paper… will half a ream suffice? I doubt you'll have time to use more.'

'A half ream will be plenty, for which I thank you right heartily.'

'And is there anything else you need?'

'Nay, Master Thorn…'

'Harry will do betwixt friends and fellows in the craft.'

'Aye then, Harry, you be kindness itself. I ask no more of you but that you tally up my reckoning so I know what I owe you. It shall be repaid afore we leave Canterbury, if only customers come who would have their portraits drawn.'

'Oh, they'll come. After the last time, to my knowledge, folk were yet clamouring to have their likenesses made. We'll spread the word to our friends and neighbours and likewise at Vespers later at St Helen's.'

'And we know folk who attend St Mary's, St Margaret's and All Saints' churches hereabouts who will do the same, if we ask,' Mistress Thorn added, wrapping my charcoal and chalks in separate linen scraps so they should not besmirch the paper afore I intended it.

'I give you both my most grateful thanks,' I said and this time I wiped not tears of sorrow but joy from my eyes. 'That puts me yet further in your debt.'

'It's our pleasure,' with which heart-lifting words they saw me from their door, sending me away with warm smiles and benedictions.

I departed Penman's stationer's shop in good heart and a better humour, a weighty linen bag 'neath my arm. The Thorns' kindness was an inspiration for which I thanked Almighty God that there were yet blessed and gentle souls in this world who bore every courtesy to a stranger in their town. Even Gawain trotted beside me with a lighter step, or so it seemed to me, and an afternoon and eve of pleasurable sketching lay ahead. Little wonder my bruises were all but forgotten.

Canterbury Cathedral
Vespers

As it was the Lord's Day and our last in Canterbury, we determined to attend Vespers in the cathedral. Besides, I thought to acquire some more holy water containing Thomas Becket's blood. I had previously purchased a small vial of it to take home for Jude, that he might anoint his injured knee – that was the point of our pilgrimage after all – but I confess I used it to treat my own injuries, to hasten their healing and thus was there little remaining for Jude's use. How effectual it was, I could not tell for certain but it did no harm to try.

The nave of the cathedral was crowded and noisy as Rose and I, with the children, pressed among the throng, accompanied by Mother Thorogood and the Warenne twins – all clad in our Sunday-best in order to honour God, aye, and mayhap to impress folk with our London fashions. For certain, Tristan and Troilus were a splendour to behold in cherry-red doublets, over-gowns of azure velvet trimmed with squirrel fur and gleaming thigh-boots of crimson Cordovan leather, all topped off by black velvet caps with white ostrich plumes.

However, I wondered at their wearing of such finery as was likely to cause them to draw all eyes, what with their devious half-brother yet at large. I went so far as to question the wisdom of the ostrich plumes, in particular, which would stand out above the crowd. But even after all the near-disastrous incidents they had suffered of late, the twins laughed off my cautionary advice. Such be the folly of youth.

Beside the font was a pricket of candles. I paused, unfastened my purse and dropped my last penny in the green box beside it, lighting a candle to Kit's memory from one already burning, offering a quiet prayer as tears threatened. One tiny flame amidst the vastness of the nave to represent one departed soul amongst tens of thousands or more. 'Twas a stark reminder of a man's insignificance in the Divine Scheme of the Creator; a wonder then that each soul mattered so much that Our Saviour gave His life, His precious blood, for our salvation.

Thus, deep in contemplation, I turned away from the candles. My sight required time to readjust to the gloom but I saw movement at the corner of my eye: the sudden darting of a darker shadow behind a column. This was no shuffling, patient member of the congregation. This was someone in haste yet furtive. I could not make out details but somehow I knew it heralded trouble. I made my way as swiftly as I might with a sore ankle to catch up with Rose and, more urgently, with the twins, forewhy I was certain the trouble was intended for them.

Hampered by the jostling and milling of folk gathering to hear Vespers, it took me too long to push my way through to where I espied those nodding white plumes in the north aisle. They served as a battle standard to signify the twins' position in the throng and if I could see them so readily, no doubt their enemy could also. I called out their names but the office began with a great chord played upon the organ echoed by the choristers. 'Twas a glorious sound indeed but made of my cry a mere whisper drowning in polyphony. None heard it, least of all those I would alert to danger.

I pressed forward, treading on toes and receiving curses in exchange but I dared not be thwarted. I tripped, stumbling over a woman's basket left on the floor and it was my turn to curse – silently, this being God's house. As I struggled to regain my feet, having to be mindful of my ribs, I saw the figure again, clearer now, his reddish hair 'neath his hat. Fenshaw Warenne, for certain. And he was ahead of me, closing on his ostrich-plumed quarry.

I reached Rose first, she being closer at hand.

'Rose, tell the twins… their brother is here. I know he intends harm.'

She nodded her understanding and, seeing the state of me, took up my errand of rescue.

'Is that the rascal? I see him,' she said, pointing. Fenshaw was almost upon his prey as she squeezed through the crowd. Everyone else was giving their attention to the office being sung, unaware of a would-be killer in their midst.

I put the children into Mother Thorogood's care and followed Rose, being far less nimble than she. And it occurred to me, belatedly, that I was sending my beloved into danger, for it appeared that she and Fenshaw would likely reach the twins at the same moment. I made greater haste, my hurts irrelevant, pushing forward.

Moments stretched out; each thud of my heart an hour as I was hindered on all sides. Fleeting glimpses of Rose's snowy linen cap amongst the crowd was all I could see of her and then the ostrich plumes turned and I realised she had reached the twins. But was she in time? Something was amiss there; a gap opened up as folk moved away. A plume disappeared from view – was a cap knocked askew or worse?

The scream was unmistakable despite the sound of the organ and the choir and folk were attempting to run. Shouts sounded and a path appeared afore me as it did for Moses at the Red Sea. One twin lay sprawled upon the tiles, tended by the other.

'Where be Rose?' I asked, realising she was not there.

The twin gave no answer but a by-stander pointed.

'The young woman went after the rascal,' she said. 'That way. My goodman and others are giving chase. That poor lad…'

I heard no more but followed on.

Chapter 19

Sunday eve
Canterbury Cathedral

'TWAS COLD in the crypt, my breath forming clouds as I made what haste I could towards the sounds of conflict. Cries, shouts and thuds emanated from the St Gabriel Chapel, the scene of little Dickon's abduction, which seemed long ago now since so much else had come to pass.

Ahead of me were a handful of the more burly congregants but of Rose there was no sign. Then, a door slammed. I could hardly believe what I saw: my dear one appeared, coming from the chapel, brushing down her skirts, dusting off her hands, such an expression of triumph upon her face as I had ne'er seen afore.

'Where is the devil?' a fellow asked her.

'Where the constables shall have him. He can do no harm now. I've trussed him up right well and barred the door to Gabriel's Chapel.' Rose came to me, triumph turning to relief. 'Ah, Seb, what a to-do that was. How are the twins? He hurt one of them, I fear.'

'What have you done, Rose?' My voice was wavering with anxiety and fear for her. 'You… you took on a villain by yourself?' I began to realise what had gone on. 'May Christ have mercy!'

She shrugged.

'I was closest. Besides, I'm quicker on my toes than most.'

'Did the wretch do you any harm, sweeting?' I held her at arm's length, looking for signs of injury. 'If he did, I shall slay him myself.'

'Well, fortunately for you then, I am whole and unmarked.' She laughed, making light of her actions whilst attempting to straighten her cap from which fair hair was escaping on all sides. 'But I have forfeited my Sunday-best apron.'

'Your apron? How come?'

'Well, I had to bind him up with something. My apron was to hand and the strings just long enough. Who is he anyway?'

'Fenshaw, the twins' half-brother. He who would have their inheritance if they were dead.'

'I thought Hugo Harper was the one trying to kill them.'

'Aye, that be so but Fenshaw was most likely his employer. I saw them talking together the other day. I suppose Fenshaw decided to do the task himself after Harper's numerous failed attempts and subsequent apprehension by the hue-and-cry – in which you also took part. Have a care, sweeting, else Canterbury will sign you up as one of its constables.' I laughed, attempting to make light of Rose's actions but, in truth, I had been much afeared for her. 'Come now, wife, we must return to the children. Let these good fellows deal with the wretch and summon the authorities. Be you certain he did you no harm?'

'Seb, I am hale and whole as ever, so cease your fussing, but we need to see what damage was done to the twins. I wasn't in time to prevent Fenshaw's assault entirely and I pray 'twas not so bad as it looked.'

Together, we returned to the nave. The Office of Vespers had continued, uninterrupted, as be proper: God's Work should not be hindered by the petty misdoings of man. We found the twins beside the tomb of Archbishop Peckham from two centuries since, a small crowd gathered around – some giving aid others gawping. At first, I could not see what devilry had been wrought upon the pair but a fine plumed cap lay discarded on the floor, looking to have been trampled in the affray.

Mother Thorogood stood by with the children – and her cat. I wondered that it dared enter so holy a place. Meanwhile,

Gawain was getting in the way. He regarded the twins as friends now and seemed to think a thorough licking would improve matters for both.

'Gawain, come away here,' I called to him and, with his exceptional ears, he heard me above the organ's thundering of the recessional anthem as Vespers ended. I drew him aside and Rose went on her knees beside the twins. Even in the dim light, I could see the ominous dark stains upon the azure gown. The next I knew, she was ripping at the hem of her shift to fashion a bandage, having no qualms about losing a second garment to the lads' cause. 'How serious are his injuries?' I asked the one who held his brother like a nursling in his arms.

'Stabbed. The bastard stabbed Tris,' Troilus choked upon the words. 'Did you get him? Did you catch Fenshaw?'

'Aye, he's shut away now,' Rose reassured him. 'He can't hurt you anymore. Now lift Tristan's arm so I can bind it tight; stop the bleeding. Tristan, can you hear me?'

To everyone's relief, the injured twin stirred and moaned.

'Oh, Tris, I thought you…' Troilus's distraught voice failed him in sobs of relief.

'You'll be fine,' Rose was saying, 'Though you'll likely need a surgeon's stitchery but it's not so deep. That bandage should slow the bleeding for now.' She stood up and addressed the bystanders, who had multiplied since the service ended. 'We need to get the lad back to The Chequers and a surgeon to attend him. Who can aid us?'

There was advice aplenty as to how these things might be achieved but naught in the way of any practical assistance until a deacon came to investigate why a section of the congregation showed no sign of departing the cathedral when it needed to be closed up for the night.

'Is there a problem here?' he enquired in a tone which suggested if we did have a problem, 'twas at our peril. And, of course, we did.

Rose took charge with a new-found confidence, explaining

to the deacon all that had come to pass.

'So this young man needs the services of a surgeon and the miscreant lies tied and locked in the St Gabriel Chapel, awaiting judgement,' she concluded. 'It's your affair now and in your hands.'

For a few moments, the deacon appeared shocked, probably taken aback at being instructed by a laywoman in his own cathedral.

'I-I'll inform the dean,' he said at last and scurried off apace, no doubt eager to hand over the responsibilities to his superior.

Meanwhile, we made Tristan as comfortable as we might, cloaks being offered to serve as pillows and blankets on the cold, hard floor.

To my surprise, as the fellows returned from the crypt to rejoin wives and families, they praised my Rose, lauding her to the roof beams and making much of her bravery. My dear one was the heroine of the hour, though she tried to shrug aside their acclaim.

'It was naught,' she insisted. 'I tripped him up, was all. He fell heavily and I got the better of him.'

'You beat him over the head with your boot,' said one.

'And swaddled him in your apron,' said another. 'It was well done... especially for a mere woman.'

'There be naught "mere" about my wife,' I told them. 'She be a wonder indeed.'

The menfolk chuckled but a few wives told them to be respectful. One fellow nudged me, meaningfully:

'I'd be careful if I was you, friend, having a wife like that. Any argument and you'll likely come off worse. I see you're limping... did she trip you as well?'

More laughter ensued. I simply smiled at their banter, quietly proud of my Rose, the best of all women.

The Chequers of Hope Inn

Although we were somewhat late returning for supper at the inn, with such a tale to tell, the innkeeper served us well with mutton stew, white loaves and a blackberry pottage. And plenty of ale also. Tristan was put to bed and upon proper cleansing of the wound in better light – the innkeeper's wife supplying extra candles – Rose and Mother Thorogood performed the surgeon's part, stitching the cut with silken thread. As Rose said, the knife had scored the lad's forearm for a length of five inches or thereabouts but had not gone deep.

Meanwhile, my wife's fame was spreading like fire in a hayrick and folk came flooding to the inn. I was fully employed drawing portraits but then I was asked to do a likeness of Rose that her heroic deeds might be bruited abroad with her image beside.

More portraits were done and another two of Rose supplied upon request. What with the Thorns advertising my talents and my wife's actions becoming the talk of Canterbury, I had more work than time to complete it. When the innkeeper began turning folk from the door and making safe the fires, I realised I could draw no more.

'Three marks and five groats,' Rose announced, counting up the coins upon the board as the last satisfied client rolled up his portrait and left. These were my evening's earnings. 'That'll see us back to London easily.'

'Remember, I have to pay Master Thorn's reckoning afore we depart. That was one shilling and three pence three farthings. And I be yet in need of a new leather scrip. I cannot bide without one.'

'Ah, my Seb,' she laughed, kissing me upon the forehead as I tidied my drawing stuff, wrapping the charcoal and chalks separately so they should not mark the few remaining sheets of paper and putting everything into the linen bag. 'Only my husband would die for want of a scrip. Come, we need a good night's sleep; we have a long walk ahead of us tomorrow. Although I was thinking, now we've money enough, it would be quicker and less of a struggle for you with the cart if we went to Fordwich and paid passage on a boat going to London.'

'A boat!' I gasped in horror. She knew well enough my deep aversion to such things, well aware that I suffered nausea simply watching the ships rocking on the Thames' swell at Paul's Wharf. How could she suggest such a thing? But then I saw her lips a-twitch with merriment and knew it for a jest at my expense. At least, I hoped it was. A boat! The very idea filled me with terror.

Monday, the sixth day of November
Departing Canterbury bound for Ospringe

First thing, I hastened to Penman's shop to pay Harry Thorn's reckoning – and sixpence beside on account of his great kindness, which had saved us from a state of penury. Both he and his goodwife had already heard of Rose's deeds in the cathedral last eve from a neighbour whose cousin's friend had heard of it from a tavern companion who had been amongst the congregation. Canterbury's web of gossip-mongering appeared to be as efficient as that of London. Thus, was I obliged to supply a more detailed description of events until the arrival of the stationer's first customers of the day put an end to my tale. I admit, despite my eagerness to depart for London, I was sorry to bid farewell to the Thorns, who had been my true friends in an hour of need. We were all damp-eyed at the thought that we should ne'er meet again but such be life, I suppose.

As I left the shop, I asked for any recommendation of a good leather seller from whom I might purchase a scrip of fine quality. Harry Thorn did not hesitate to suggest John Glover's shop in Rose Lane – Canterbury's most excellent purveyor of leather bags, girdles and such like, as well as gloves, so he said.

I thanked him for the advice without having the least intention of taking it. I would not risk another encounter with Rose's nemesis and mine, Watt Saunders, for all the gold in King Edward's treasury. Nor did I wish to put a farthing of my well-earned coin into her father's purse since he had not the common decency to so much as acknowledge my dear one's existence. May the Devil take him.

Back at The Chequers of Hope Inn, more tearful farewells were taken of the innkeeper and his goodwife, whom we had come to know well this week past – was it so short a time? So many troubles had come to pass in so few days, it hardly seemed credible. Rose and the wife embraced heartily forwhy sharing the labours of the washtub formed eternal friendships as both women agreed, promising to keep each other ever in their prayers.

Mother Thorogood, Tristan and Troilus and the Cambridge scholars were all coming with us. Young Alfred Denny was continuing to reside at East Bridge Hospital with his grandsire. Sorrowfully, far from improving the invalid's case, the pilgrimage had proved too much for the old man and he had taken a turn for the worse although, as his grandson told, he was as irascible as ever and likely to continue so until the end. I felt pity for the lad, wondering how he would fare when he was released from his burden of caring for his grandsire, having lost his father to Hugo Harper's first attempt to kill when he ate of the poisoned pottage at Dartford. Aye, 'twas that event which had set the litany of disaster in train and I was unlikely to forget it. Nor would young Alfred, I dare say.

But enough of my melancholic musings: we were going home at last.

Tristan made use of the mounting block to get into the saddle of his fine steed, sparing the strain upon his injured arm but otherwise, he was no worse for wear than I. He and Troilus had already made report to the constables regarding the crimes of their half-brother, who now resided in the Donjon of Canterbury Castle, awaiting trial for his attempt at murder alongside his inept partner in crime, Hugo Harper. Likely, they would be destined for the hangman's noose one day soon and the twins could have their inheritance without endangering their lives.

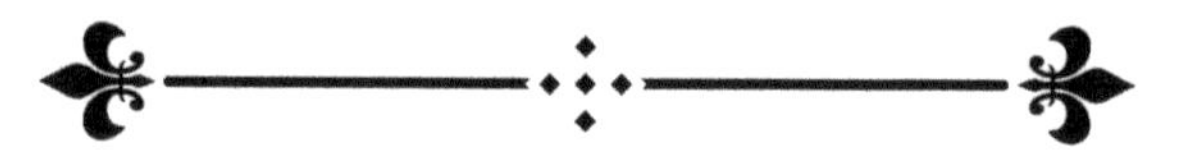

So we left Canterbury by way of the mighty twin towers of West Gate, a party much reduced in numbers, perhaps recalling those who were no longer among us. Tanner was biding here with friends, awaiting the spring and the first ship departing for Compostela. Glassman – or de Vere – gone wherever he was bound with his traitor's heart. The Dennys staying behind. And, of course, my friend, Kit, or Father Christian or whoever he truly was, now lying cold in his grave. Oh, how I missed his company already and we had barely begun our journey. As we passed the great cross beside St Dunstan's Church, I whispered a prayer for Kit's soul afore turning left upon the ancient Roman road bound for London, known as Watling Street.

'Twas a breezy day with scudding clouds, a mixing of bright sunshine and short, sharp showers – more like April than November but the underlying chill and heaps of sodden, brown leaves along the roadside were a reminder that winter was coming, not going.

Apart from a brief stop 'neath a huge oak tree to wait out a particularly heavy shower, we made good time for the most part. Upon occasion, the road was a sunken way betwixt high banks, the Roman cobbles long since buried in mire, the enclosed air tainted with the damp smell of leaf mould, tree branches dripping water down our backs. According to my *Guide for Pilgrims* – being consulted once more – this was the Great Forest of Blean.

In one such place, I was unable to pull the cart through the clinging mud, which glued its wheels and caked my boots. Even as I mourned the loss of Kit and his strong arms, I was alarmed to see Mother Thorogood's evil-eyed cat riding in amongst the sheepskin and blankets with the little ones, adding to the weight. Likely, the wretched creature had tired of muddying its paws and having its fur soaked. I tried to shoo it out but it regarded me with its disdainful yellow eyes, as though I were less than a worm, and refused to move.

But help was at hand. Seeing my struggles, the scholars came to my aid, lifting the little cart betwixt them, children and all, to drier ground where the road rose from amongst the steep banks and trees. Previously, I had thought the pair more used to lifting the weight of a volume of Aristotle rather than anything heavier but they made light work of carrying the cart, even with the additional burden of mud adhering. Their strength belied their thin, round-shouldered frames. Then Troilus lifted Dickon upon his horse – to my son's great delight – lightening the load further. Rose took a turn at pulling the cart also, relieving me when she saw how I was clutching my ribs, though I did my utmost to conceal the pain.

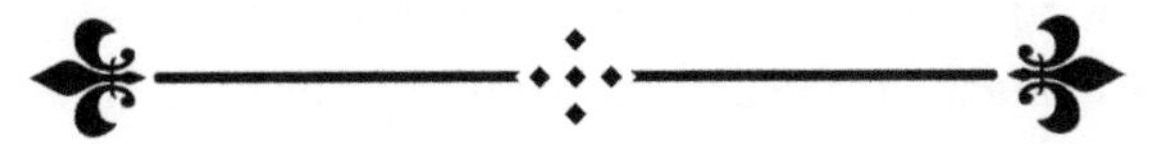

How glad was I to pause at the village of Boughton-under-Blean, where we took dinner at the appropriately named inn: The Pilgrims' Rest. My ankle was throbbing but I dared not remove my boot for fear I should not be able to put it on again. That it was swollen more than before was obvious as my hose stretched tight. I kept my foot out of sight 'neath the board so Rose should not espy it.

The food was not so good as that we had become used to at The Chequers: yesterday's dry maslin bread, a pottage – thick enough but with little flavour – and ale weak as water. But it sufficed to give us the strength to continue our journey.

After leaving the hostelry, we had not gone so far as half a mile afore I could no longer disguise the fact that I was limping severely, unable to put my weight on my sprained joint, wincing at every step. The weight of mud caked about my boot did naught to help. I was praying someone would aid me with the cart, although it was now empty of children with Dickon still up high on Troilus's horse and Julia asleep in Rose's arms. But the scholars were deep in some whispered disputation and did not notice my difficulties. I was unaware of it at the time but I was under discussion on all sides:

'Seb,' Rose said in a stern tone, which warned that her next words were not to be questioned, 'We have decided you aren't fit for this task. Don't argue!' She held up her hand to silence me afore I could speak. 'Tristan will take you up behind his saddle. He says his arm is no hindrance so long as you don't clutch at it but hold around his waist. The scholars will take it in turn with Mother Thorogood and me to manage the cart along with Julia. Now do as I say.'

Who was I to gainsay my heroic wife with her new air of confidence? At the next nearest convenient fallen tree, I made use of it as a mounting block – all ungainly and awkward, trying not to strain my ribs nor twist my ankle – and, with much assistance, succeeded in climbing onto the broad rump of Tristan's horse. 'Twas years since I had once done the same, in a dire emergency, upon Sir Robert Percy's great steed, having to cling on for dear life.

This occasion was no different and I grasped hold like a limpet on a rock to Tristan's broad leather girdle, terrified that I should slide off to one side or tumble backwards over the beast's swishing tail. That the horse disapproved of its additional, fidgeting rider was made plain as it tossed its head and snorted, side-stepping and cavorting. I closed my eyes tight, murmuring a white-knuckled prayer that I might be spared.

Eventually, Tristan's soft words gentled the beast and it behaved in more seemly wise but I did not loosen my hold one jot, though my hands cramped with the effort. Better that than a crushed skull if I fell from a great height. I recalled the fall from the scaffolding right well and it was yet fresh in my mind. Mine had been a reasonable descent, Kit's less so and the outcome could not be forgotten.

How the others were managing the cart, I could not tell. Remaining aloft took all my attention and I had none to spare to look out for Rose and her assistants. Suffice to say, Tristan pulled the horse to a stop far sooner than I expected and many hands reached out to aid my dismounting. I dared open my eyes to discover we were in a well-paved courtyard, men hastening to welcome us and tend the horses.

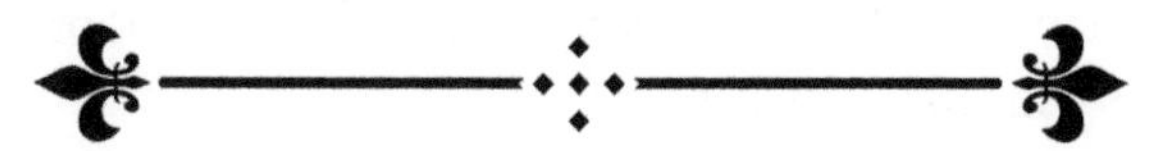

Mercifully, we had attained, without mishap, our first night's place of rest and refuge from the cold: the Maison Dieu at Ospringe just beyond Faversham. I realised I had not seen a single stick or stone of Faversham, too intent upon keeping my eyes shut, unable to look down. But this was no time for regret at missing the place, forwhy we were all of us wet and shivering, requiring of a blazing hearth and hot food.

The Maison Dieu did not disappoint, being the customary resting place of royalty on the way from London to the coast, as we were informed with pride by the lay brother attending to our needs. Hot mulled wine and warm towels were supplied within minutes of our entering the stone-built hall and being directed to cushioned benches beside the fire. I breathed a heartfelt sigh of relief even whilst forcing my fingers, frozen into a clenched position, to unbend afore I could hold my cup of spiced wine. I tasted pepper, sugar, aniseed and cinnamon – this night would come at a considerable cost to my purse but I was too weary and cold to care.

A brother entered with a purposeful air and a heavy wooden box. I was surprised when he came to me straightway.

'I'm told you have an injured ankle, master,' he said, going on his knees before me as if I were the pope and he a humble supplicant.

'Aye, well, 'tis true,' I stammered, 'But of little consequence, good brother.'

'Not what I was told. May I help you remove your boot?'

'Er, I suppose…'

'I'm the herbalist here at Maison Dieu,' he said, succeeding in untying the soaked and muddy lacings of my boot. I gritted my teeth as he eased off my footwear. Even as I watched, now unconfined by leather, I be certain I saw my ankle swelling visibly like an inflated bladder, stretching the cloth of my hose thinner than ever. How I should ever replace my boot, I knew not. 'Can you unfasten your hose or I…?'

'I can manage that much, discreetly enough,' I insisted. I must be lying witless afore I should permit a stranger to remove my clothes. 'Twas an intricate task with fingers yet somewhat benumbed with cold, unfastening laces from my nether braes which held up my hose. I rolled down the one leg, revealing a great fat ankle in all its full purpled horror.

'Oh, Seb,' Rose put her hand on mine as she sat beside me on the bench, 'No wonder you were limping. I should not have left you to pull the cart alone at any time.'

'But there be naught amiss with my arms,' I assured her – not mentioning my ribs. 'I shall be able to pull the cart on the morrow after my ankle has rested overnight.'

The herbalist mixed some thick yellow paste in a pot, adding a greenish powder and a few drops of brown liquid. A brief draught as someone opened the door wafted the most vile stink from the pot. 'Twas sufficient to make my eyes water and I nigh gagged upon it. Rose, being a woman of wisdom, moved away to tend the children, leaving me and the herbalist to inhale the stench, though he seemed oblivious to the noxious miasmas he was casting forth with his mixing of ingredients.

'Brother Mark, I have told you before about making up your potions in this chamber.' An officious monk strode over with an unmistakable air of authority. 'The smell is unbearable.'

'Forgive me, Father James, but this pilgrim cannot walk as far as the infirmary, so I brought my medicaments to him. I couldn't mix them until I saw what was needed. I'll have the poultice covered soon enough and it will stink the less.'

'Well, see that you do. And make it seemly before supper. This pilgrim may have his meal served here, rather than in the refectory, else none may eat with good heart whilst their nostrils are assaulted by such foetid airs.' Then, waving his hand before his face to disperse the smell, Father James left the chamber as suddenly as he had come, having sufficiently and publicly upbraided the unfortunate herbalist.

'I be sorry to have caused trouble for you, Brother Mark,' I said, wincing as he began smearing the yellow mess around my ankle. Dear God in Heaven, but it smelled even worse being spread upon over-heated flesh.

'Ah, never mind Father James. Like an old hound, his bark is worse than his bite but his heart is gentle.' At which statement, Gawain pricked up his ears. Sometimes, I be certain my faithful colley-dog understands God's own good English.

My ankle, poultice applied and swathed in thick bindings – which reduced the stink somewhat, or else I was becoming used to it – was propped upon a stool in full view of all eyes, advertising my infirmity. How I might put my boot on was a problem for the morrow but, I must admit, my pain was much reduced by the foul concoction.

We ate by the fire, Rose and I and the children. She refused to eat in the refectory without me, and none insisted she should. Father James even accompanied the lay brother who brought our supper on a tray, that he might say grace and bless our meal for us – an unlooked-for kindness indeed?

The food was good, too. White, wheaten bread, fresh-baked – no mixed-grained maslin here – and slices of roasted chicken in a cream sauce with sage and thyme, whole baked apples dotted with butter, sweetened with honey, topped with chopped hazelnuts and flavoured with rose water. It was delicious and I thought Rose would be making mental note of the receipt for so fine a dish. Buttered worts with halved roasted chestnuts sprinkled with crushed cubebs completed our fine supper, which we so enjoyed. Thus, I vowed, I should give no heed to the morn's reckoning but pay it right cheerfully. Likely, thinking on it, that poultice would be added to our tally also, although paying for the dubious privilege of having such a stink accompany me at every step would not be so easily accomplished with a smile.

Tuesday, the seventh day of November
Ospringe to Newington along Watling Street

The day dawned dry but frosty. The mud of yesterday crunched underfoot and puddles treacherous with ice made the way hazardous. Tristan and Troilus, not so foolhardy as they were afore, took the precaution of wrapping rough sacking about their horses' hooves to afford the beasts a better grip upon the icy way.

For this, I was right thankful since I, too, was mounted upon Troilus's horse this time. Unable to wear my boot, my bandaged ankle was likewise swathed in sacking in place of footwear and I was under strict instruction from Brother Mark – and from Rose, whose command carried even greater authority these days – that I was to refrain from walking or standing at all costs. I did not require a second telling.

And, upon the matter of costs, I had, as I vowed, paid our reckoning to Father James without demure. Maison Dieu was not a cheap place to stay but with good food, clean beds and injuries tended – Tristan had also received the herbalist's attentions, as had one of the scholars for his blistered feet – we could not claim any shortfall in the services rendered unto us.

After hearing Low Mass in the Stone Chapel beside the Maison, we were on the road once more. I shall not relate the entire journey, which was, mercifully, uneventful: no would-be assassins nor cut-throats nor outlaws hampered our dogged progress. When Mother Thorogood's cat, bell a-tinkling, decided to dash off into the brambles and thicket in pursuit of a vole, that was the sole moment of disquiet. Upon the wretched feline's return a few minutes later to present his mistress with the gift of a tiny scrap of fur, which had so recently been one of God's most harmless creatures, I could but wish the cat might encounter some much larger beast that would present it as a scrap of mangled black fur to its master. A vain hope, of course, but I could not like that animal no matter what.

A brief stop in the village of Bapchild for a cup of ale at an ale-wife's tumbledown cottage meant we pressed on for a late dinner in Sittingbourne. A pleasant place made prosperous by its weekly market, we bought pies from a street-hawker and shared them as we rested outside The Lyon, a tavern which supplied drink but, as the law stipulates for taverns, could not sell food. In the distance, the air being so clear, we could see the Swale and the Isle of Sheppey. But it was too cold to stay long and we travelled onto Newington whilst it was yet full daylight, for the ice had not melted and we needed to see our way clear in order to avoid such hazards.

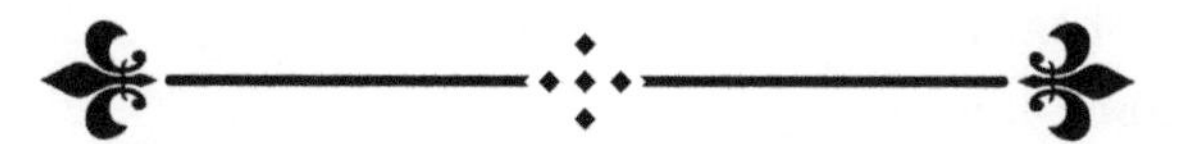

Newington was a small place but Friar Tuck's cook-shop had an inviting ring to its name – the eponymous friar being that well-fed companion of Robin Hood – but when we made enquiry, there was no place to stay the night. Apparently, we should have been advised to remain in Sittingbourne. *Mea culpa.* That was my fault for urging our party ever onwards in my haste to reach London. And my conscience pricked me even more as I watched Mother Thorogood, hardly in her prime, yet taking a turn at pulling the cart laden with two infants and the cat alongside Rose, whilst I sat high upon horseback doing naught more useful than clinging on.

But after a reasonable supper of pease pottage and onions, the proprietor said, if we did not mind sleeping with the beasts, his cattle byre had space enough for us and there was straw aplenty to make our beds. 'Twas not the best accommodation but it would be a roof over our heads and the kyne provided a degree of warmth, the steam from their flanks visible in the chill as they were herded into the byre for the night.

Even so, we were cold despite sleeping in a huddle within walls made of piled straw and thick straw strewing the earth floor under us. The cattle did not seem much inclined for sleeping, lowing, shuffling and farting, adding to the strong stink of fresh dung. Rats rummaged, squeaked and fought each other through the straw, adding their own stench. At least none could smell nor complain of the odours from thc poultice on my ankle.

Wednesday, the eighth day of November
Newington to Rainham

All in all, we did not sleep overmuch either and, frozen to the core, we were all of us right glad to leave our uncomfortable beds and begin a new day with pickled herrings for breakfast in the cook-shop.

It being Wednesday, we all attended Low Mass together in the Church of St Mary the Virgin across the way, one of the scholars remarking that we should have slept here on the church floor, in which case we would not stink as we did. I said naught for, in my opinion, without the cows for bedmates, we likely would have frozen to death but 'twas true that the few parishioners in the church kept well away from their uninvited, odoriferous visitors. It could not be helped nor denied: we smelled foul. A change of clothing would make little difference forwhy our baggage had likewise soaked up the scent of ordure. Everything required washing and airing but there was no opportunity. None of us was going to strip naked and wait around whilst items of our attire dripped and flapped in the fresh breeze.

We had no choice but to press on as we were, mile after mile along Watling Street, gradually moving closer to our objective. For us, that was London, but Mother Thorogood had come from Guildford way, the twins from Hertfordshire and the scholars, of course, from Cambridge, so all had longer journeys home than we.

This day was I determined to take my turn with the cart, to which end I cut myself a sturdy staff from the hedgerow afore we set forth. Using it as a prop to aid my injured foot, I had one hand free to help with the cart. However, after but a hundred yards, I realised that hobbling with uneven step, I was hindering Rose more than helping her. The cart's forward motion was all down to her efforts, not mine.

Having stumbled over a frozen wheel rut for the second time, Rose insisted I should forsake the effort, risking further injury as I did each time I tripped. Knowing she was correct, I left the cart to her and one of the scholars but continued my way on foot for a few miles afore being persuaded – with somewhat feigned reluctance – to mount up behind Tristan. We made better time after that without my lameness holding everyone back from a swifter pace. Pride had its place but not at a cost to all and we wanted a proper bed this night to come.

We could see the great, impressive tower of St Margaret's Church in Rainham long afore we arrived in the little town in time for Vespers. I believe, by now, the fresh air had blown away the worst of our stink. Either that or the parishioners of Rainham were of a more friendly inclination than their counterparts in Newington or, mayhap, their noses were less sensitive.

The local folk, seeing we were strangers, were eager to show us their fine church, boasting that its tower rose one hundred feet – far higher than any of its neighbours. This, I could believe, though, of course, it could not compare to our own beloved St Paul's at nigh five times that height.

They were likewise proud of their newly-painted canopy of honour above the rood screen, holding flaming torches aloft that we might observe its beauty in full, even in the gloom of a winter's eve. I felt obliged to admire it at some length, for it was spangled with King Edward's own device of the Sun in Splendour and splendid it was, too, with so much gold glinting like fire in the torchlight.

Thinking to further impress us with Rainham's assets, after Vespers was done, folk vied with each other, urging us to sample the merits of this or that hostelry, whichever was their personal favourite. Out in the churchyard, a pair of fellows nigh came to blows over the matter, one proclaiming the virtues of The Rose Inn – of which he was the owner, as we discovered – the other extolling the undoubted superiority of the food, ale and beds at The White Horse, run by his sister and her goodman.

We chose the latter simply because it happened to be the closer, The Rose Inn being back along the High Street by quite a way. We had noted it looked a welcoming place as we passed it earlier but were now wearied to the bone, the little ones griping, miserable and hungry. Besides, though I did not mention it aloud, its signboard bore a red rose, reasonably well painted, but I would rather have slept 'neath the White Rose of York – accusations of treason had rung too recently in my ears and I wanted none questioning my loyalty to the king. The White Horse of Kent must serve our needs.

Thursday, the ninth day of November, to Saturday, the eleventh day: Martinmas

I shall not relate every step of our homeward journey forwhy, once we attained Rochester, 'twas but repeating our pilgrimage in reverse. We passed through Gravesend – where we had witnessed the ducking and stayed at The Three Choughs – but upon this occasion, we hastened onwards, reaching Dartford after nightfall. On Thursday, that was, and we spent the night at The Bull as afore. No storm this time, praise be unto God, and none was poisoned by the pottage.

On Friday, having briefly renewed my acquaintance with Miles Paynter, the talented limner and admired his nigh-completed mural of St George in Holy Trinity Church – from a distance, I admit, since climbing the scaffolding for closer observation of his fine work was neither advisable nor possible in my state. Then, afore we climbed the hill to the west, we paused at the priory.

Whilst the rest of us took our dole of bread and ale in the Guest Hall, Rose and Mother Thorogood were conducted to meet once more with the prioress, Dame Anne Barnes, and Sister Beatrice Eland. The nuns required a complete recitation of our adventures upon pilgrimage, as Rose told me afterwards. This greatly delayed our departure from Dartford, even though, as she admitted, Rose avoided mentioning anything of the murderous and calamitous events that had assailed our party since last we were there.

Tristan, Troilus and the scholars were becoming restless, chafing at the delay, but, as it happened, 'twas right advantageous for me for I was called to the prioress's chamber to discuss the commission of an illuminated Gospel Book for the priory. Thus, with a new commission in hand for our workshop, we finally departed Dartford, making for Eltham.

King Edward's new Great Hall at Eltham Palace had progressed somewhat since we stood there previously, when Kit had explained to me about Archimedes, Euclid, pulleys, ropes and loads. How long ago that now seemed and my interest in such things had perished, along with my friend. If I ere observed another pulley raising stone, 'twould be too soon.

We passed the night at The Saracen's Head in Eltham, an indifferent hostelry I would not recommend to any traveller forwhy the innkeeper was a surly fellow and his wife equally disobliging. They complained about the little ones' liveliness, saying they got under customers' feet – which I refuted vehemently – the ale was upon the verge of turning sour and the food meagre in quantity and of little flavour. The price they charged for stabling the twins' horses was an outrage which led to a right heated exchange, such that I feared it might come to blows betwixt the twins and the host. Fortunately, at length, a lesser, more reasonable price was agreed without any violence being committed but I was eager to leave, as were we all.

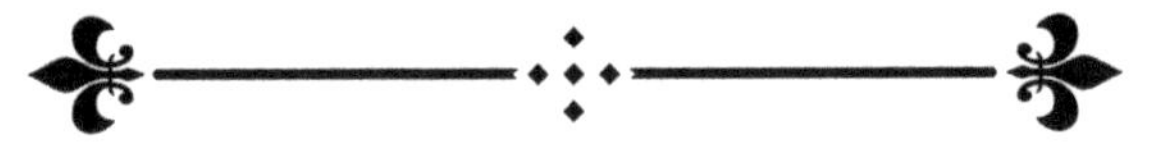

Saturday, at noontide upon the feast of Martinmas, saw us in Deptford. The others sought refreshment at The Greyhound nearby. Knowing from the previous visit that the ale was excellent and the first cup *gratis* for pilgrims, there was no question of taking dinner anywhere else, despite arriving somewhat belatedly for the meal. Whilst our fellows ate, we made for Dick and Bella Langton's house across the way.

I admit to knocking upon their door with a deal of trepidation, wondering what we might find within. We knew Bella had been close to her time of travail and had not looked to have strength enough to withstand the effort. I hoped our prayers made for her at Becket's Shrine had been efficacious in aiding her and her new babe but who could know?

Dick opened the door himself and, right away, we saw how matters stood forwhy the joy upon his face was unmistakable in meaning. All was well! And God be praised for it.

We were ushered over the threshold into a house full of women – friends and neighbours, we were informed – all eagerly supporting Bella by caring for Janey, helping with the new babe, cooking meals and cleaning and welcoming visitors such as we. A plump woman, her face full of smiles, took Dickon, Julia and Gawain to play with Janey in the yard out the back.

'Fear not, Seb, I've had the timber restacked and made safe. They'll come to no harm under Kitty's eye,' Dick reassured us. 'Bella's resting upstairs, Rose, if you want to go up and see her, you can meet my new son, Thomas. He's a fine lad with such a pair of lungs upon him… Seb, come and wet the babe's head with me. Sybilla has made us a good strong brewing of ale for the purpose.'

And thus it was that we celebrated the arrival of little Thomas Langton and drank to his good health and long life. I gave Dick the St Thomas pilgrim badge, which he said he would affix to the babe's cradle, he being the saint's namesake. Having ensured that the stopper was tight, he set aside the vial of holy water in a coffer box in case of future need.

'I lit a candle for Bella and prayed for her safe confinement at the Martyr's Shrine upon the Monday afore last, the thirtieth day of October,' I said.

Dick burst out laughing at that.

'Well, that explains all. Bella's travail began upon the same Monday morn. Progress was so swift, I hardly had time to fetch Kitty – she's the midwife – afore the babe was here, yelling lustily as you could wish. The birth took little effort and was nigh without pain, so Bella has recovered in no time. We're both greatly relieved and, clearly, your prayers served us right well. You have my deepest gratitude, Seb, you and Rose. Will you both do us the honour of standing as Thomas's godsibs, as you and Emily – God rest her soul – did for Janey?'

Of course, we readily agreed to Dick's request afore departing, in the best of spirits, to rejoin our fellow pilgrims for the last few miles to London.

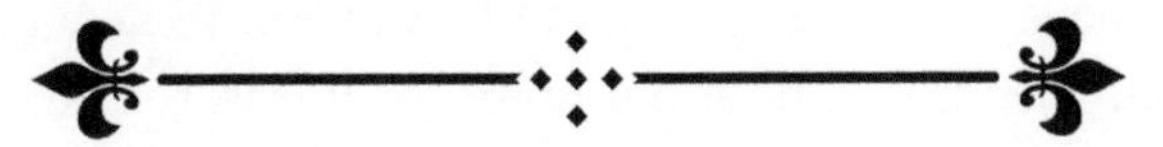

'Twas in Southwark where Rose said a tearful farewell to Mother Thorogood as she joined a merchant and his family to travel into Surrey. Aye, and that cat went also; the sight of its departing tail and the fading tinkle of its bell were a relief to me as we waved the old woman out of sight, though I know my dear one was much saddened by the parting as the two had become good friends. Rose promised the woman she would write to her but a shake of the head and a few words told that Mother Thorogood could not read.

The Warenne twins – both yet living despite all – and the scholars came with us across London Bridge, whose sights and sounds and smells were a tonic to my soul. In the deepening twilight, folk were hastening home in both directions afore the wardens closed the bridge for the night. Of a sudden, so heartened was I, my ankle no longer seemed the least impediment and I felt I could have run the length of Cheapside for the sheer joy of coming home at last.

But first, courtesy bade me direct Tristan, Troilus and the scholars, who had aided us so willingly, to the best inn on Bishopsgate Street, that they could leave first thing in the morning when the gate opened. The Bull was a good place that Thaddeus Turner and I knew well. I could vouch for the quality of the food there, although I had ne'er had reason to sleep in its beds but reports were that they were clean and comfortable.

I suggested that Tristan should visit Bess Chambers' shop hard by, if his cut arm required a salve. I also took pride in pointing out Crosby Place across the way as the Duke of Gloucester's residence – I know not why I be proud of it when 'tis none of my doing. Since the duke was not in London at present, the grand coat-of-arms I had painted was not displayed above the gateway, so I could not boast even that small contribution to the fine house, yet I felt myself a part of it somehow.

I did have one cause for regret of a sudden. I knew I should invite our friends to dine at our home, or at least to take ale and wafers with us, but I dared not extend this common courtesy. I felt anxiety in that moment, fear even, wondering in what state we would find our beloved home in Paternoster Row.

Would it be a fine house of three storeys, double-fronted,

spacious and impressive? Or would we find a heap of rubble, naked beams all awry, roofless, the haunt of vermin? I prayed God it would at least be habitable.

Chapter 20

Saturday eve, the Feast of Martinmas
Paternoster Row, London

HAVING LEFT our friends in Bishopsgate, Rose and I trundled a cartful of sleeping children along Broad Street, into Poultry and Cheapside. We neither of us spoke until we reached the Cross.

'What will it be like, Seb?' Rose said, mirroring my own disquiet thoughts. 'The house, I mean. Do you think Stephen will have finished the work? Will we be able to sleep there tonight?'

'I wish I knew, lass, but we shall see it soon enough.'

St Michael le Querne's Church was just the same as ever, as was The Panyer Inn next door to it, the latter raucous with laughter and I wondered if Jude was among the revellers though, these days, he preferred The Sunne in Splendour across the way.

And there it was! Our home.

In the nigh darkness, it looked to have a roof and walls sound enough, insofar as I could make out. And lights showed in the window. Someone was within so, although 'twas our own place, I knocked upon the street door that we might avoid startling whoever was there. No miscreant would have so bright a light to illumine their nefarious deeds. Therefore, I supposed it must be Stephen putting some final touches to the building work or Adam setting straight the workshop. But this would be unexpected diligence upon a Saturday eve.

As it came to pass, 'twas neither man but Margaret – I beg

her pardon: Meg. Upon seeing us, she spoke not a word but her broad smile of welcome said all and she, by custom not given to hearty demonstrations of feeling, embraced us each in turn, her eyes bright with tears in the candlelight.

‘’Tis a joy to be home, Meg,’ I said. ‘Be you well? And all else?’

‘We are all well, Master Seb, and the house complete, as you see. I was hoping you’d be home soon, so I’ve been staying here, putting the place in order, though I know it’ll not be quite as you’ll want it, Mistress Rose, but the beds are made ready. Nessie’s here, too. I’ll tell her to bring ale and food and hot water that you may wash.’ She glanced down at the sleepy children in our arms. ‘I’ve made up the cots in the nursery also.’

‘The nursery, Seb!’ Rose said. ‘Doesn’t that sound so grand? Oh, Meg, you’re a wonder. Thank you. I’ll go through to the kitchen and…’

‘Not that way,’ Meg said. ‘That doorway is no more.’

We all laughed. We must needs learn our way about our own house forwhy ’twas all so different now.

Home at last.

Straightway, even afore washing my face or sipping ale, I passed a slumbering Dickon into Meg’s arms and took a light into the old workshop. But so changed! The room was twice as large, expanded into the shop, as was. I spun about, looking here, espying a new desk, especially fashioned for Ralf with his bent back; looking there at another designed to make allowance for young Hugh’s left-handedness and so vast a storeroom that I be sure the king’s entire library might be kept safe inside. The shelves were neat with paper, parchment rolls, ink, pens, brushes, paste and pigments and all else required. Adam had done so fair a task. Such wonders made my heart sing.

I found Rose dancing around the new parlour, watched by Meg and Nessie, bemused. My wife’s delight was contagious and I was upon the verge of joining the dance when I recalled, belatedly, my injuries and how my ankle hurt. It seems excitement be a wondrous remedy for such ills. We both were speaking at once:

'Have you seen the new …?'

'What of this?

'What of that?'

'Is so-and-so not wondrous?'

We were as children, receiving our New Year's gifts, our enthusiasm unsparing despite a long day's walking.

Later, after a goodly supper of pease pottage, bacon and white bread – all of which proved Meg a most competent cook – we retired to our own bed chamber. No requirement now to inch past the little ones' cot with silent tread. The whole chamber was for us, alone. We could sing, laugh or dream aloud as we wished and would disturb no other. As it was, we fell asleep right readily and hardly stirred all night, so wearied were we by the day. I be certain I slept with a wide smile upon my face.

The Epilogue

Sunday, the twelfth day of November
Jude's house, Amen Corner by Ave Maria Alley

AFTER A good night's rest in our own bed, first thing, afore Low Mass in St Michael's, I penned a letter – written at my own desk in the new spacious workshop, I might add – to his Grace, the Bishop of London. I felt 'twas my duty to inform him of Father Christian's untimely death forwhy St Mary Magdalen's Church would require a new priest. Whether the bishop truly was Kit's godfather or other, I knew not and did not mention any such relationship in the letter. Nor did I so much as hint at any possible treasonous connections to his demise but I found it hard to write of the event, having to bite my lip and swallow down the lump in my throat.

After church, at which we received such a welcome from our fellow parishioners as to bring yet more tears to my eye, having delivered my missive at the Bishop's Palace, a few dozen limping steps took me to my brother's door. I hoped I was not too early, Jude being a late riser upon a Sunday after a night of quaffing ale to excess. At least, that be too often the case these days.

The window shutters were open – I took this to be a good sign that Jude was from his bed – and I knocked upon his door. Sounds of movement came from within.

'Who is it?' That was not my brother's voice.

'Seb Foxley,' I called out.

A muffled exchange came to my ears.

'Jude says you're to, er, go away.'

I heard laughter. Aye, and I doubted that he had said no worse than "Go away". An expletive or two was more likely.

'Tell him I bring a gift.' That would probably suffice to have him open the door. To Jude, the prospect of a gift was as good as that of a sweetmeat to a child: enticingly irresistible.

In due course, whilst I shivered upon the threshold, the door was opened by John Rykener, clad in woman's attire, as usual. In this case, he wore a fine gown of golden yellow velvet in the latest high-waisted fashion with flaring sleeves and slashed bodice, revealing a green silk kirtle beneath. It broke every Sumptuary Law, as did the ornate, beaded headdress with its silk gauze veil flung carelessly in the corner. But I knew 'twas all wealthy folks' cast-offs, bought from a fripperer and, upon examination, would reveal mending and moth holes and old stains. But such tawdry finery kept John – or Eleanor, as he preferred to be addressed – content.

'God give you good day, Seb,' he-she said, inviting me to enter.

'And to you, Eleanor,' I responded, earning a grin of approval. 'Is Jude at home?'

'Aye, but barely from his bed. We were late home last eve. How went your pilgrimage?'

'Er, eventful. But we be safe home now.'

'You've hurt your leg.'

'A sprain, 'Tis naught of any consequence.'

John went to the stair foot and yelled:

'Jude! Your brother's here. Are you coming down?'

'Tell him to bugger off. I've better things to do,' came the muffled reply.

'He says he's brought you a gift.'

'What is it? How much did it cost? If it's less than half a mark, I'll not bloody bother.'

John looked at me, his plucked eyebrows raised in question.

''Tis worth far more than that,' I called back.

'Wait. I'll get decent and be down.'

A few heartbeats later, Jude appeared at the stairhead,

fastening a long, fur-lined gown of dubious lineage over his nether clouts. Then, to my great surprise, he swung his good leg over the bannister and slid all the way down.

'Quicker than walking,' he said, turning to me with an expectant expression, hand held out. 'Well? Where's my gift? What is it? Must be bloody small.'

I opened my purse and took out the vial of holy water mixed with the blood of St Thomas Becket and put it in his palm, together with the latten pilgrim badge.

'What's this?' He tapped the pewter vial. 'It's not silver, I know that.' He sniffed at it, marking it with his fingernail. He did the same with the badge. 'These are bloody worthless, you lying little toad, getting me out of bed for two bits of dented metal.'

'The vial is holy water from Canterbury,' I explained, 'Along with a few drops of the martyr's precious blood. I bought it to help heal your knee and I prayed for you at St Thomas Becket's Shrine, begging a miracle that your leg might mend as it should… end your pain. Oh, Jude… I have done as I promised you I would and swore to God… '

'Holy water?' he sneered. 'I'll wager it's no more holy than what's in the piss-pot under my bed. And as for your prayers… well, they were a bloody waste of breath, weren't they, seeing my knee's the same as ever?'

'Jude, I beg you, please, try the holy water; apply it to your leg.'

Only then did my brother look me straight and frown.

'But what of you, eh? Bruises on your face?'

In truth, I had forgotten those.

'Bindings around your ankle?' he continued. 'And using a staff again, I see. Seems to me, little brother, you need what's in this bloody flask more than I do.' With which, he removed the greased stopper, flung the contents at my face and threw the empty vial and the badge upon the floor. 'Now get out of my sight.' He shoved me backwards to the door.

Unfortunately, he struck my ribs and I cried out, unable to prevent it. As I staggered back, clutching my chest, my ankle gave way and I fell over the step and into the street.

'Pilgrimage!' Jude snorted. 'What a bloody waste of time.' Then he slammed the door.

I was yet upon my knees, struggling to get up, when the door re-opened.

'I wish you didn't upset poor Jude so,' John scolded me afore throwing my staff at me and shutting the door again.

At least, with the staff's aid, I was able to stand, much disappointed and hurting anew, ignoring the small gathering of gawpers, chuckling at my expense. "Poor Jude" indeed, I thought angrily as I stumbled home. The wretch was beyond deserving of salvation. Little wonder my prayers for him went unanswered.

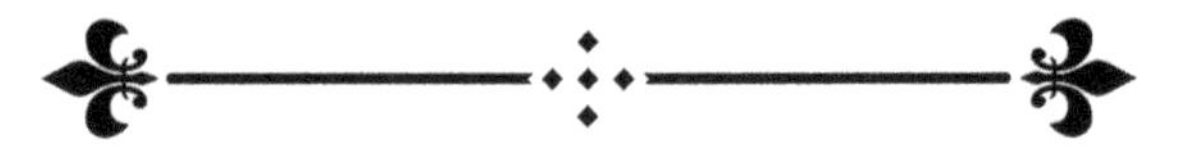

I returned home to a belated breakfast, which put me in far better heart. Adam, Simon, Nicholas and little Edmund came from Friday Street to join us for bacon collops and a herb omelette. The company was as welcome as the good food.

Rose, overjoyed with her new realm – a kitchen large enough for four women to do all that was required without tripping over each other, was singing a merry tune. She now had a double hearth and a winter hedge to be lowered and raised to dry the laundry indoors when the weather was wet.

Upon the morrow, Monday morn, Adam said, 'twas all arranged that Hugh, Kate and Ralf would return to their desks in the much-amended and extended workshop. In the meantime, he insisted on guiding me about the place as if I were a customer to be impressed. I did not spoil his obvious pride by mentioning that I had assessed the workshop last eve.

'See how much space we have for our desks.' He gestured at the whitewashed walls, the spotless paved floor, the new wooden shelves. 'And the storeroom… large enough for a bedchamber, I reckon. The paper, parchment and what-have-you we may keep in there, enough for St Martin's scriptorium.'

'You have done right well in my absence, cousin. Mayhap you no longer need me.'

'You're the one with royal patronage, Seb, and the account books say we now need plenty of new and valuable commissions to pay for all this.'

'Aye, and I can oblige there: we have a commission for a large Gospel Book from the sisters at Dartford Priory.'

'That's well, indeed. But come, you haven't yet seen the shop next door. You'll be well pleased with that, I know. It's fit for a king's visit. Stephen has done you proud.'

'Us, Adam. Us. This enterprise belongs to us all and we shall all reap the benefits.'

And thus, I prayed it would be. Having done my best to redeem my sins, of whatever colour they be, I trusted that the house, the workshop and the shop at the Sign of the Fox were ready to begin a new chapter.

Important Characters in 'The Colour of Sin'

The Foxley Household

Sebastian [Seb] Foxley – an artist, illuminator and part-time sleuth
Rose Foxley (née Glover) – Seb's wife [rescued by Seb in a previous adventure]
Dickon & Julia – Seb's children by his late wife, Emily Appleyard
Ralf Reepham – Seb's elderly journeyman scribe [acquired by Seb in a previous adventure]
Kate Verney – Seb's apprentice
Nessie – Seb's maidservant
Margaret [Meg] Russell – an ex-novice nun
Hugh Gardyner – Seb's on-loan apprentice
Gawain – Seb's 'colley' dog
Jude Foxley – Seb's elder brother, attempting to set up a printing business
John/Eleanor Rykenor – Jude's cross-dressing friend

The Armitage Household

Adam Armitage – Seb's cousin [actually his nephew] from Foxley, Norfolk, also Seb's assistant at Paternoster Row
Simon Hutchinson – Adam's stepson, a schoolboy
Nicholas & Edmund [Mundy] Hutchinson – Adam's younger step-children

Friends and Neighbours

Stephen Appleyard – Seb's one-time father-in-law, a carpenter and builder
Jack Tabor – Once Seb's apprentice, now Stephen Appleyard's
Father Christian [Kit] – Priest at St Mary Magdalen Church, Old Fish Street, Seb's friend
Peronelle [Pen] Wenham-Hepton – a silkwoman and friend
Bennett Hepton – Pen's husband, a well-to-do fishmonger and friend
Thaddeus Turner – City Bailiff and Seb's close friend
The Thatchers – Old friends
Old Symkyn – A beggar and a friend

Fellow Pilgrims

Worthy Tanner – Leader of the pilgrim band
Mother Thorogood – Elderly woman, partially sighted
Lucifer – Her guide-cat
Tristan & Troilus Warenne – Identical twins hoping for their inheritance
The Alfred Dennys – Grandfather, Father and Son
The Cambridge Scholars – Become Kit's friends
Hugo Harper – A tone-deaf minstrel
George Glassman – Fellow with his arm in a sling
The Carmelite monks

Others met whilst on pilgrimage

Dick & Bella Langton with Janey – Seb's friends in Deptford and his goddaughter
Beatrice Eland & Prioress Anne Barnes [real] – Nuns at Dartford Priory
Miles Paynter – mural painter in Holy Trinity Church, Dartford

Father John Gurnes [real] – Priest at Holy Trinity Church, Dartford
Brother Oswald – the Precentor at Boxley Abbey
Brother Luke – Monk at Harbledown with Alan, aka 'Richard the Lionheart', & Michael
Fenshaw Warenne – The twins' half-brother
Prior William Sellynge [real] – at Christ's Church Priory, Canterbury
Brother Infirmarer
Harry Thorn – Stationer in Canterbury
John & Clare Glover – Rose's parents
Watt Saunders – John Glover's assistant
Sheriff George Brown [real]
Father James & Brother Mark – Monks at Maison Dieu, Ospringe

Author's Notes

Although *The Colour of Sin* is an entirely fictitious novel, some of the people involved in the tale whom Seb meets during the journey to and from Canterbury were real and I've indicated them in the list of characters.

Likewise, most of the inns and hostelries were real and some still exist today, one example being The Three Choughs in my home town of Gravesend. It's now called The Three Daws [i.e. jackdaws] since choughs became extinct in Kent long ago but they were once common and were on St Thomas Becket's coat-of-arms. The Bull is still a hotel in Dartford, though its name changed to The Bull and Victoria after a royal visit in the nineteenth century.

The churches that Seb and his fellow pilgrims visit are still there, although some, like the Stone Chapel in Ospringe, are now no more than a few ruins. The same applies to the abbeys and priories since they were destroyed by Henry VIII during the Dissolution of the Monasteries, although St Thomas's Hospital at Eastbridge in Canterbury and the Maison Dieu in Ospringe still exist.

Holy Trinity Church in Dartford still has its splendid mural of St George and the Dragon high on the wall, as vivid as ever, although nobody knows who painted it, so Miles Paynter is my invention. A well-executed mural of Becket's martyrdom is still faintly visible at St Mary's Church in Stone.

As I was writing the chapter set in Dartford, I realised Seb was there almost on the pre-anniversary [if there is such a thing?] of Kent's infamous hurricane of October 1987 and thought that would seriously mess up their pilgrimage plans, though I didn't make the chaos so widespread as it was in 1987.

Boxley Abbey truly had the Rood of Grace and the figure of little St Rumbold, both of which were reckoned to be miraculous at the time. But both were revealed to be scams during the Reformation when such 'wonders' were taken down, their mechanisms unmasked before they were destroyed as Roman Catholic superstitious nonsense.

Becket's slipper was the miraculous relic kept at St Nicholas Hospital, Harbledown, which also disappeared at the Reformation.

In Canterbury Cathedral, although Becket's sumptuous shrine was robbed of its jewels and destroyed by Henry VIII, the murals and carvings that so entranced Seb can still be seen in St Gabriel's Chapel in the Crypt and are well worth a visit. Sadly, the infirmary and the priory are no more but we may still enjoy the heavenly colours of the Becket stained glass windows and the glorious architecture of the cathedral.

Acknowledgements

I wish to thank Julia Brown for arranging our visit to Eastbridge Hospital in Canterbury and Angel Robson for making us welcome. Her brilliant tour of the ancient building with its intriguing nooks and crannies was brimful of inspiring stories. Especially 'useful' for my novel was the revelation about the window in the pilgrims' dormitory, which they used as a loo, opening straight out into the river.

Also, my thanks go to Melodie Robson [no relation to Angel] for setting up our visit to Canterbury Cathedral and Geoff Webb, our fantastically knowledgeable guide. Thank you for pointing out that the green 'house bricks' in the Becket stained glass windows are the money boxes in which pilgrims were expected to make their donations at every opportunity.

Thank you to the dedicated volunteers at St Mary's Church in Stone, near Dartford and all the other kind people we met during our research trips who generously gave us their time and happily shared their knowledge. If any of it is incorrect in the story, that's down to either my mistake or poetic licence to suit the story – for which I apologise.

And, of course, love and thanks to my indispensable soulmate, Glenn, for chauffeuring me everywhere, taking the photos, helping with the research, sorting out IT glitches, brain-storming ideas, making the coffee, etc. etc. I couldn't do it without you.

Toni Mount

TONI MOUNT
A Sebastian Foxley Medieval Murder Mystery
THE COLOUR OF POISON

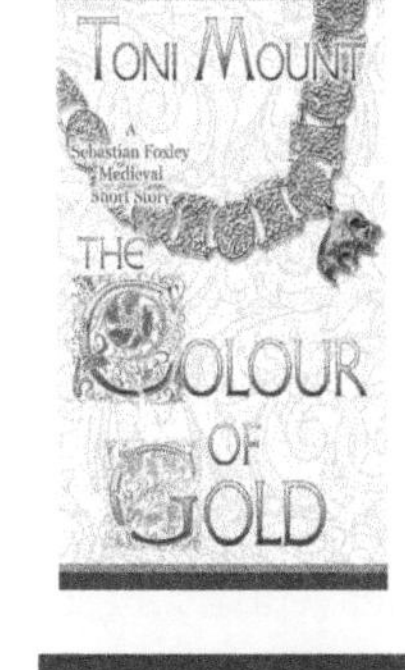
TONI MOUNT
A Sebastian Foxley Medieval Short Story
THE COLOUR OF GOLD

TONI MOUNT
The Third Sebastian Foxley Medieval Murder Mystery
THE COLOUR OF COLD BLOOD

TONI MOUNT
The Fourth Sebastian Foxley Medieval Murder Mystery
THE COLOUR OF BETRAYAL

TONI MOUNT
The Fifth Sebastian Foxley Medieval Murder Mystery
THE COLOUR OF MURDER

TONI MOUNT
The Sixth Sebastian Foxley Medieval Murder Mystery
THE COLOUR OF DEATH

TONI MOUNT
The Seventh Sebastian Foxley Medieval Murder Mystery
THE COLOUR OF LIES

TONI MOUNT
The Eighth Sebastian Foxley Medieval Murder Mystery
THE COLOUR OF SHADOWS

TONI MOUNT
The Ninth Sebastian Foxley Medieval Murder Mystery
THE COLOUR OF EVIL

TONI MOUNT
The Tenth Sebastian Foxley Medieval Murder Mystery
THE COLOUR OF RUBIES

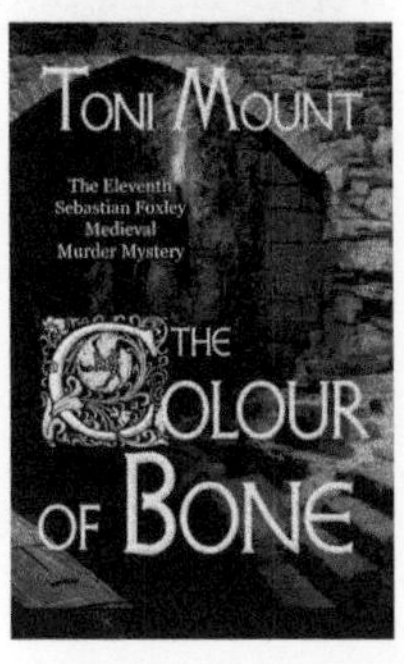
TONI MOUNT
The Eleventh Sebastian Foxley Medieval Murder Mystery
THE COLOUR OF BONE

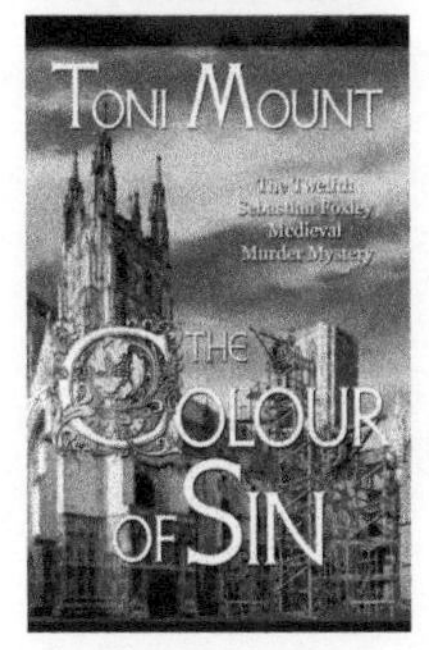
TONI MOUNT
The Twelfth Sebastian Foxley Medieval Murder Mystery
THE COLOUR OF SIN

Meet the Author

Toni Mount earned her Master's Degree as a mature student at the University of Kent by completing original research into a unique 15th-century medical manuscript.

She is the author of several successful non-fiction books including the number one bestsellers, Everyday Life in Medieval London and How to Survive in Medieval England, which reflects her detailed knowledge of the lives of ordinary people in the Middle Ages.

Toni's enthusiastic understanding of the period allows her to create accurate, atmospheric settings and realistic characters for her Sebastian Foxley medieval murder mysteries.

Toni's first career was as a scientist and this brings an extra dimension to her novels. She writes regularly for The Richard III Society's Ricardian Bulletin and a variety of history blogs and is a major contributor to MedievalCourses.com.

As well as writing, Toni teaches history to adults, is an enthusiastic member of two creative writing groups and is a popular speaker to groups and societies.

This is the twelfth novel in Toni's popular "*Sebastian Foxley*" murder mystery series.

THE COLOUR OF DARKNESS

Prologue for The Colour of Darkness

THE MAIDEN was beautiful. Where she had come from few knew. What was her purpose here? She had not said. In truth, she spoke little and answered no questions but the men of London were bewitched by such loveliness; words were unnecessary.

However, the women were suspicious of her and jealous – those who did not trust their husbands. Some thought she must be an angel come among them, to give them heart and solace in time of trouble. Others claimed she was the Devil's minion, a witch, forwhy, hot upon her arrival came the dreaded pestilence of plague into the city.

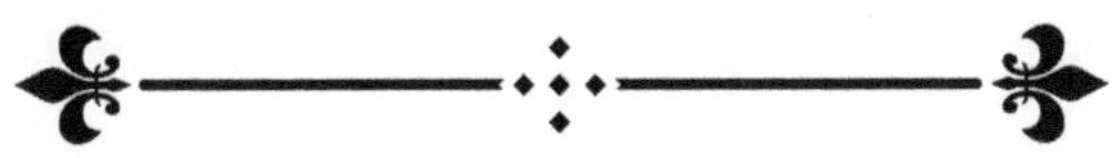

Jude Foxley of Amen Lane found his new printing enterprise to be more of a challenge than he expected. He had succeeded against the odds in assembling the mighty contraption of the press – with a deal of aid from his friends – and thought it would then be an easy matter to learn the rudiments of the craft.

Firstly, the tiny lead letters – each one back to front – had to be arranged contrary-wise, right to left, to form words and sentences in reverse in the little box. Apparently, the printer's term for the line of letters was a 'slug'. No need to ask why for the procedure was accomplished at a slug's pace. The type being so small, it was hard to make out any mistakes. How many times had he put in a 'b' instead of a 'd'? He'd lost count and the faults only made themselves known once the page was printed.

But he discovered how much ink to use by trial and error and how to handle the pristine paper without smudging it with inky finger marks; the need to let each newly printed sheet dry.

Beyond that, it wasn't unlike the stationer's craft he knew so well: correlating pages, stitching and binding. Practice. That was all it would take to have his business venture thriving: London's first printing press. It could not fail. Jude Foxley would soon be rich on the profits.

Except for one thing.

The great, fat worm in the rosy apple of his ambitions – his far more experienced rival with a press set up and running these last five years at Westminster. The name of Master William Caxton was anathema to Jude: the wretch and his workshop at the Sign of the Red Pale. Patronised by royalty and nobility, the fellow was receiving all the most valuable commissions. It was so unfair. Being the first ever printer in England, Caxton had every advantage and, thereby, was the destroyer of Jude's dreams; the ruination of all his efforts to make himself a wealthy man.

Something must be done to remedy the matter.

Jude had had thoughts upon this since autumn last; even discussed certain 'possibilities' with that ne'er-do-well apprentice, Jack Tabor. Long gone were the days when he used to have the frequent satisfaction of giving the young rascal a good beating or a clout around the head – not that it had improved the lad one peck. But now Jack was doing well enough, learning the craft of carpentry and, whatever his legion misdemeanours, was become a hard-muscled mountain of a man and beyond punishing, if you valued your safety. At times, Jude still felt tempted to strike him for his inconsiderate and irritating ways but refrained. Instead, he was coming to some kind of an understanding with Jack whose strength and size might yet be of use. A friendship it was not but it could prove of benefit to both parties.

A plan had been under consideration before Christmas but then the young scallywag had come to grief. The story ran that he – being a kindly Christian sort, ha! – was intending to aid an elderly neighbour by sawing off a branch from an ancient pear tree which grew in the garden plot behind the old man's house. The branch had grown close enough to bang against the window whenever it was windy, both a nuisance and possible danger to the roof and window glass.

On Twelfth Night it was that Jack climbed the tree at dusk to set about the task. Why then, in fading light and after a bellyful of cider and ale at dinner, was ne'er explained. And where, Jude asked afterwards, was the saw or the axe to cut the branch? Was it merely a coincidence that the neighbour's shapely daughter was within the chamber at the time, readying herself, changing her gown for the evening's festivities?

Whatever the case, Jack's great weight had proved too onerous for the aged wood. He duly removed the offending bough but not as intended: it creaked horribly and broke. Jack fell awkwardly, landing on the frost-hardened ground.

Afterwards, in the Sunne in Splendour tavern, he'd bemoaned the outcome of his virtuous act over another jug of ale or two, his broken arm splinted and his head wreathed in a blood-stained bandage. He insisted that his bleary sight and wavering step were due to the blow to his head which had quite astounded him and not to an excess of drink taken solely for medicinal purposes. Jude had heard the like before and felt no sympathy for Jack. In truth, he was much angered as the plan, so long in the devising, would now have to wait upon the wretch's recovery.

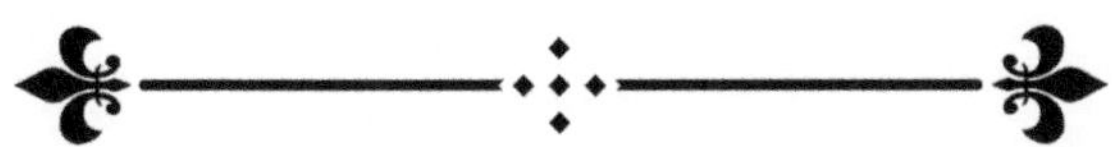

But that was months since. Summer was now come. Gone were Jack's splints and his spurious claim to continued befuddlement of his head due to the whack received. Jude didn't believe a word of it. More like an excuse for idleness, the lazy dog. Jack was never one to labour if he might avoid it. But now it was well past time to put their plan into action and save Jude's business from ruination.

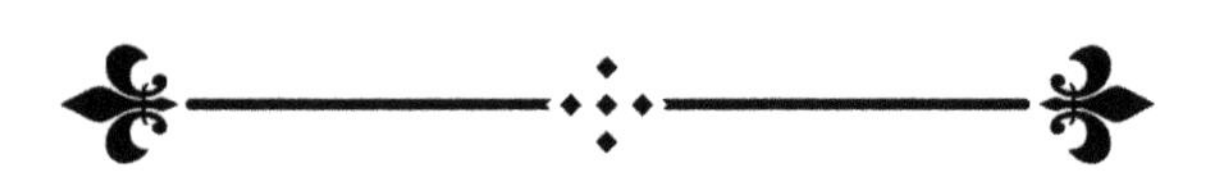

TONI MOUNT
The Sebastian Foxley Medieval Murder Mystery Series
THE FOXLEY LETTERS

Historical Fiction

The Sebastian Foxley Series - Toni Mount

The Death Collector - **Toni Mount**
The Falcon's Rise - **Natalia Richards**
The Falcon's Flight - **Natalia Richards**
The Savernake Forest Series - **Susanna M Newstead**
The Traitor's Son - **Wendy Johnson**

Historical Colouring Books

The Mary, Queen of Scots Colouring Book - **Roland Hui**
The Life of Anne Boleyn Colouring Book - **Claire Ridgway**
The Wars of the Roses Colouring Book - **Debra Bayani**
The Tudor Colouring Book - **Ainhoa Modenes**

Non Fiction History

The Turbulent Crown - **Roland Hui**
Jasper Tudor - **Debra Bayani**
Tudor Places of Great Britain - **Claire Ridgway**
Illustrated Kings and Queens of England - **Claire Ridgway**
A History of the English Monarchy - **Gareth Russell**
The Fall of Anne Boleyn - **Claire Ridgway**
George Boleyn - **Ridgway & Cherry**
The Anne Boleyn Collection I, II & III - **Claire Ridgway**
Two Gentleman Poets at the Court of Henry VIII - **Edmond Bapst**

PLEASE LEAVE A REVIEW

If you enjoyed this book, *please* leave a review at the book seller where you purchased it. There is no better way to thank the author and it really does make a huge difference!

Thank you in advance.

Milton Keynes UK
Ingram Content Group UK Ltd.
UKHW021945130324
439366UK00001B/23

9 788412 595383